HENRY OF THE HIGH ROCK

*

Juliet Dymoke was born at Enfield in
Middlesex and educated at a boarding school
in the country. During the war she worked
for the Canadian Army Medical Records and
at that time married Hugo de Schanschieff
who was then serving as an air gunner in the
Royal Air Force. They now live in Maiden-
head and have a married daughter and a
grandson.

It was while her husband was away in
the R.A.F. that Juliet Dymoke turned her
attention to writing and also to work on
scripts for various film companies. She has
published several books for children, but
counts historical novels with 'more fact than
fiction' as her particular field. She has
travelled all over the British Isles in the
course of her research, as she makes a special
point of authenticity. Among her main
interests are music, television drama and
'anything to do with the countryside'.

Also in Arrow Books by Juliet Dymoke

Of the Ring of Earls

Juliet Dymoke

Henry of the High Rock

ARROW BOOKS

ARROW BOOKS LTD
3 Fitzroy Square, London W1

AN IMPRINT OF THE HUTCHINSON GROUP

London Melbourne Sydney Auckland
Wellington Johannesburg Cape Town
and agencies throughout the world

First published by
Dobson Books Ltd 1971

Arrow edition 1973

*Made and printed in Great Britain
by The Anchor Press Ltd,
Tiptree, Essex*

ISBN 0 09 907110 X

for
Dick and Edith Stacey

Principal Characters

WILLIAM I
King of England and Duke of Normandy, about sixty years of age at the beginning of the story.

ROBERT CURTHOSE
His eldest son, a rebel against his father and in exile.

WILLIAM RUFUS
Third son to the Conqueror and most devoted to him.

HENRY BEAUCLERC
Fourth son to the Conqueror, born on English soil after his father became King.

ODO
Bishop of Bayeux and half brother to the King; also Earl of Kent in which capacity he caused his brother to arrest him.

ROBERT OF MORTAIN
Also half brother to the King.

WILLIAM OF MORTAIN
Son to the above.

LANFRANC
Archbishop of Canterbury and former Abbot of Bec, well into his eighties.

ANSELM
Abbot of Bec, renowned for his saintly life and close friend to King William.

GILBERT
Bishop of Evreux, nicknamed 'the Crane' because of his excessive height and angular figure.

HELIAS
Lord of La Flèche and later Count of Maine, close friend to Henry.

MALCOLM CANMORE
King of Scotland, married to St. Margaret, grand-daughter of Edmund Ironside.

ROGER OF MONTGOMERY
Earl of Shrewsbury, largest landowner in both England and Normandy. Lifelong friend to William the Conqueror.

ROBERT OF BELLÊME	His son, lord of Bellême which he received from his mother, the infamous Mabel.
HUGH LUPUS	Earl of Chester and lord of Avranches, powerful baron on both sides of the channel. Nicknamed 'Lupus' because of the wolf's head emblem on his shield.
STEPHEN	Lord of Aumale, half brother to Judith, Countess of Northampton, widow of Earl Waltheof.
ROBERT DE BEAUMONT	Son of old Roger de Beaumont, and Count de Meulan, counsellor of both Rufus and Henry.
HENRY DE BEAUMONT	His brother. Earl of Warwick in England, close friend to Henry.
SIMON OF SENLIS	Earl of Huntingdon, husband of Maud, daughter of Earl Waltheof.
WILLIAM OF WARENNE	Earl of Surrey, enemy of Henry.
WILLIAM OF BRETEUIL	Son of William FitzOsbern, who was friend and cousin of the Conqueror. His elder brother, Roger, is in lifelong imprisonment for rebelling against the Conqueror in 1076.
GILBERT OF CLARE	Earl of Tonbridge, wealthy landowner in East Anglia and Kent, keen supporter of Henry.
ROGER OF CLARE	His brother.
RICHARD OF REDVERS	Norman lord of moderate importance, close friend to Henry and later given much land in England.
ROBERT FITZHAMON	In the service of William Rufus, given lands that should have gone to Henry, but later faithful to Henry.
RALPH DE TOENI	Son of Ralph de Teoni, lord of Conches.
ROGER DE MARMION	Son of Robert de Marmion, holder of the honour of Scrivelsby in Lincolnshire, and Lord of Fautenoy le Marmion in Normandy.

HUGH OF GRANDMESNIL	One time Sheriff of Leicester, powerful baron, fought at Hastings.
RICHARD DE RULES	Lord of Deeping in Lincolnshire, chamberlain to both King William I and William Rufus.
ROGER THE PRIEST	Taken into Henry's service and accompanied him into exile. Later raised by Henry to become Bishop of Salisbury.
EUDO DAPIFER	Steward to both the Conqueror and Rufus, always friendly to Henry.
RICHARD HARECHER	Wealthy Merchant and citizen of Domfront in the southern part of Normandy.
MAUD	Countess of Northampton and Huntingdon, daughter of Earl Waltheof and married to Simon of Senlis.
ALICE	Her younger sister, later to marry Ralph de Toeni.
JUDITH	The dowager Countess of Northampton, widow of Earl Waltheof and niece to the Conqueror.
EADGYTH	Daughter of King Malcolm and Queen Margaret of Scotland, and great-granddaughter of Edmund Ironside.
MARY	Her younger sister.
DAVID	Their younger brother, many years later to be King of Scotland.
CHRISTINA	Prioress of Romsey Abbey near Winchester. Sister to Queen Margaret and aunt to Eadgyth.
EDGAR ATHELING	Brother to Margaret and Christina, the last Englishman of the ancient line of Cerdic, but long past any hope of the Crown. Close friend to Robert Curthose.
and	
HERLUIN LA BARRE	He is composed of three characters of whom little or nothing is known—the knight from the country, named Herluin, who paid for the care and transport of the corpse of William the Conqueror; the unknown single knight who accompanied Henry into exile; and the possible un-

known knight whom some chroniclers thought might have been responsible for the killing of Rufus.

Henry's Mistresses

ALIDE OF CAEN	Mother of Henry's eldest son, Robert, and probably a daughter. Her name is uncertain.
NEST	A Welsh girl whom he probably met on his first visit to Cardiff.
AMALDIS	A fictitious character to represent the girl who probably occupied him in Domfront.
ANSFRIDA	Widow of Anskill the Saxon, whom Henry took into his household after she had appealed to him for help over some legal quarrel. Mother of his son, Richard, later to drown in the famous White Ship.
EADGYTH	A Saxon woman living in London, possibly the daughter of Wigod of Wallingford.

Fictitious Characters

RAOUL THE DEER	Henry's marshal in charge of his horses.
HAMO	Henry's standard bearer.
GULFER	His falconer. (These three based on the three men who accompanied him into exile.)
FULCHER **WALTER** }	Henry's pages

Author's note: Although complete in itself, HENRY OF THE HIGH ROCK forms the second book of a projected trilogy which began with OF THE RING OF EARLS.

'... this witty and genial man, not
so much an emperor or king as the father
of his people.'

WALTER MAP

'He was a good man and was held in great
awe. In his days no man dared to wrong
another. He made peace for man and deer.'

ANGLO SAXON CHRONICLE

Part 1

The Rock of The Archangel
September 1087—December 1093

I

The sound of a horn erupting into the morning stillness tumbled Henry from the bed. It was no more than a rough straw pallet with a wool covering, the only bed this poor dwelling boasted, but the girl had been attractive enough to entice him here last night.

Fumbling for his shirt and tight-fitting hose he glanced down at her. She was still sleeping and he saw now that without the rushlight to lend enchantment she was rather a plain girl with irregular features; only her thick brown hair was beautiful, lying in scattered strands about their shared pillow. As he flung his tunic over his head she stirred and opened her eyes.

When she saw he was dressed she stared at him, blinking sleepily. 'Are you going, my lord? Is it dawn already?'

The shutters were still fastened, but he nodded his head. 'It must be, sweeting, for the horn has sounded from the castle. We're away to teach the French King his manners.' He bent to kiss her. She had been good to love last night and he hoped they might march back this way when the fighting was done.

She put her arm about his neck, holding him, and with one hand pushed the soft black hair from his forehead. It habitually fell forward over his eyes and she smiled a little, twisting her fingers in the thick strands. 'Will you come back, lord?'

He kissed her again, lightly this time. 'Perhaps,' and he added, 'maybe to see if I've fathered a little bastard. In the meantime here's a purse that should keep you comfortable for a while.'

She giggled, her eyes lighting greedily at the sound of the clinking coins as she tucked it beneath her pillow. 'God keep you, my lord. I shall pray to Our Lady for your safe return.'

He fastened his mantle on one shoulder, aware now that the cottage smelled of unwashed bodies, stale cooking and animal dung, for there were two goats tethered in the far corner. He nodded briefly at the man and his wife who were sitting up,

15

yawning, on the pile of straw where they had slept, yielding their bed to the girl and her royal lover.

'Your daughter has a purse,' he said and went out into the fresh morning air.

It was a bright day, the sun already up with a promise of heat. It had been a dry August and the corn was standing high and yellow in the fields as they rode south yesterday—there would be a good harvest, he thought, but not for the people of the Vexin who had dared to flout his father. Outside, his young page, Fulcher, still lay asleep, rolled in his mantle by the wall of the house and Henry kicked him gently to wake him.

'Come, boy, did you not hear the horn? We must hurry or my father will have our hides stretched out in the sun.'

Fulcher sat up, rubbing his eyes and grinning, appreciating this for a joke but one which his master would not have made in King William's hearing. After twenty years as King of England and thirty-two before that as Duke of Normandy no one made jests with impunity about the great Conqueror's antecedents, nor the fact that his maternal grandfather had been a tanner in Falaise. Only the King of France had dared to make a worse joke, a cruel and tasteless joke at William's expense, that sent the Normans marching south into the disputed territory of the Vexin. From William's sons, Henry and his elder brother Rufus, down to the lowest man-at-arms war with the French both on account of the jest and the dispute over the land was a just war.

He stood impatiently in the sun while Fulcher brought his horse, a big muscled creature with gentle eyes and a soft mouth. Henry fondled him, smoothing the silky coat. His father had loved the stag, some said inordinately, but he loved all animals and despite his haste spent a moment gentling the destrier before mounting. Then, with Fulcher behind him on his palfrey, he rode down the lane and into the main street of the little town of Andeley. There was activity everywhere now, men hurrying from the dwellings where they had found quarters for the night, the cavalry assembling before the gates on the flat ground, the horses impatient to be moving on this bright day, the foot soldiers standing about, leaning on their spears, talking, awaiting their leaders.

Henry reined in his horse, calling to his friend Ralph de Toeni, who was with a contingent of men from his father's land of Conches. Ralph had a horn of ale in his hand and was munching a piece of fresh crusty bread. He returned the Prince's greeting. 'We've a good day for our march.'

'Well enough,' Henry said, 'but it will be hot later. For the love of heaven, give me a drink. I'm as dry as an empty barrel.'

Ralph handed him the horn, laughing. 'There's nothing like a lusty night for giving a man a thirst. Here, boy,' he called to a lad hovering a few yards away. 'Fetch some food for Prince Henry, and hurry.'

The boy scampered off and Henry sat drinking, his eyes on the busy scene. 'Are they ready up there?' He jerked his head towards the castle keep.

Ralph shrugged. 'I saw your brother a while ago but your father was still at his prayers when I came down. The Bishop is inclined to be lengthy about his business.'

The boy had returned with some slices of meat and thick pieces of bread and Henry ate hungrily, realising how empty his stomach was. 'Gilbert the Crane always was a long-winded fellow as well as being long-shanked. Give me a priest who can say Mass speedily for men under arms.' He brushed the crumbs from his hands. 'Well, I'm off to find my fellows. God keep you, Ralph. I saw your father yesterday, but I trust your mother has not donned her hauberk to ride with us?'

Ralph laughed, for the lady of Conches' warlike temperament was famous. 'Thank God we left her for once at work with her needle.'

Henry waved his hand and rode on up the slope of the bailey. He liked Ralph, a lanky young man with bright blue eyes that reflected his amiable disposition. When he had something to offer, Henry thought, he would offer it to Ralph. A wave of unusual bitterness swept over him. By Christ's Cross, when would he have anything to offer? He suppressed the resentment, a resentment he revealed to no one, not even to Ralph nor to his other close friend, Richard of Redvers, and entering the inner bailey gave all his attention to the day's needs.

The place was swarming with men and horses, everyone shouting orders or calling out to their friends; accoutrements jingled and weapons sounded as men prepared their swords and spears, shields and helms for the coming fight. Already a dozen or more gonfanons fluttered in the light wind, distinguishing the great houses—Montgomery and Bellême inseparably,

17

Grandmesnil, Ivry, Giffard and Breteuil, Conches and Aumale —and Robert, eldest son of the house of Beaumont, leaned out of the saddle to greet the Prince. Robert was some twenty years his senior, a stern man, but wise and thought by most to be a just lord to his knights and vassals, and he had recently acquired from his mother's lands the title of Count de Meulan. Between him and Henry, despite the gap of years, there was considerable liking; his younger brother, another Henry and Earl of Warwick in England, was an even closer friend and Henry had spent many pleasant days at Beaumont-le-Roger where the old lord, Roger, still lived, white haired and venerable, dispensing a renowned hospitality.

'Please God today will give your father a victory,' Robert said. 'The French King's jest touched him too closely.'

'I know.' Henry stood for a moment watching the impressive gathering of Norman nobles. 'Philip is a fool and sly too, and I pity the French who must suffer him. He may be my father's suzerain but at least we don't have to swallow his insults.'

'We are only taking back what belongs to Normandy,' Robert said in his deep strong voice. His own father remembered clearly the signing of the treaty between Philip's father, old King Henry, and Duke Robert the Magnificent, by which the Vexin became Norman property, a treaty which King Henry broke when the Duke died and his son William was a mere child and a bastard at that. Now William would take the land back, conquer it as he had conquered first his duchy and its rebellious barons and then England and the English. Robert of Beaumont's house had remained loyal to William from the moment of Duke Robert's death and Robert did not now question the Conqueror's right to make war on France. 'As your father said, we will light enough candles at Mantes for the whole of France to see his churching.'

Henry's face darkened. He did not perhaps love their father as William Rufus did, but moderate filial affection and family loyalty burned in him to avenge the French King's insult. All summer William had stayed quietly at his palace at Rouen following the diet recommended by his physicians, but his corpulence, the huge stomach he had developed over the last years, did not lessen and gave rise to Philip's disgusting joke that the

King of England was lying in. Well, he would repent that remark in blood, Henry thought, for every loyal man was angry now, both Normans and the English who had followed their King overseas to fight in his army. His father might not be loved by many but he was respected by all for the stern rule that had put an end to disorder and made the name of Normandy renowned throughout Europe.

Robert's voice broke into his thoughts. 'Best get to your arms, my lord. The Mass is over.' He pointed to the inner door of the keep where men had begun to emerge and Henry crossed the courtyard to find the men of his own household. They were waiting close under the walls, his gonfanon with its device of a single leopard on a red ground fluttering in the hand of Hamo, his standard bearer. Raoul the deer held his mail tunic and as Henry dismounted and raised his arms flung it deftly over his head. It fell heavily into place and he tied the thongs at the neck while Raoul knelt to fasten on his sword. Raoul cared for the horses and had earned his nickname by being able to run at phenomenal speed and catch all but the fast runaways; he was past his first youth and had been placed in the Prince's household to add experience to the younger element.

Fulcher held Henry's reins and in a few moments, helmed and armed, he walked over to the great entrance where his brother Rufus stood awaiting their father.

Red William nodded to him. 'I thought you were still abed.' There was a mocking note as always in his hoarse, grating voice.

For once Henry felt stung to reply. 'I was about a man's pursuits.'

Rufus laughed. He was twelve years older than Henry and such a shaft from his nineteen year old brother was not likely to disturb him. 'The Cub is airing his manhood, eh?'

Henry shrugged. He disliked the nickname Rufus had for him and preferred Robert's gentle, teasing 'Beauclerc', but he took either in good part and retorted readily enough with 'Rufus' or 'Curthose'.

'But you would have been wise,' Rufus was continuing, 'to forsake your rose-bed before the sun was on it. Our father would have been better pleased to see you at Mass—and my lord of Evreux is never above counting heads.'

Henry relaxed, leaning on his sword hilt, the moment of irri-

tation gone. Red William might have odd habits and prefer a
train of pretty boys to a healthy desire for a mistress or two
but he had a ready wit that Henry appreciated. 'I thought the
Crane would not be hurried even on this morning, but he might
bear in mind that the sun's been up an hour or more.'

Rufus grinned. He had a wide mouth and a set of teeth that
appeared startlingly white in contrast to his highly-coloured
complexion. Was it their eldest brother Robert, now in exile for
rebelling against their father, or was it Richard who had first
nicknamed the young William 'Rufus'? Richard had made them
all laugh, had been gay and friendly and yet had mixed that
friendliness with his father's austerity and Henry had loved
him as he loved neither Robert nor Rufus. But Richard was
dead, killed in that forest south of Winchester that their father
had made his hunting ground. The English had bitterly resented his seizing of land that had been theirs and when Richard
was struck to the ground by a branch, breaking his neck, they
said it was God's vengeance. But whether it was Divine inter-
vention or not, Richard was dead and Henry was thrust more
into the company of Rufus, both of them dancing attendance
on their autocratic sire.

During the early part of this summer the King had been
absorbed by the great survey that was being made in England
so that he might know exactly how many hides of land, how
many sheep or pigs each man owned, but the weather had been
cold and wet and he had left the work to his barons, returning
to his duchy to rest until called from his sick-bed by Philip's
impertinence.

Rufus said now, 'We may thank the gods our uncle Odo is
clapped in prison or we'd be here half the day while he
harangued us. He's too damned officious and our father was
right to shut him up, whatever the Pope may say.'

'It's the Earl of Kent who's shut up, not the Bishop of
Bayeux. For all they are one and the same person if our uncle
acts treacherously in one capacity he can't expect the other to
protect him.'

'Odo is a fool and no match for the King,' Rufus said drily.
'Our lord knows how to deal with him and the French too.
Here he is—best pay your respects, little brother.'

William, by the grace of God King of England, Duke of
Normandy and lord of Maine, stood on the steps, tall and stiffly

erect, regarding his assembled army. His head was still bare for he had just come from his prayers and his jet black hair was only lightly streaked with grey, his face lined but with lines of strength. He held himself well despite the huge stomach that had caused the King of France to be witty, the stomach he resented so bitterly for having all his life been an abstemious man in the matter of food and drink—when so many of his barons ate to satiety it seemed an unjust thing. Yet he was still a warrior, girt with his long sword, a worthy descendent of Duke Rollo and Richard the Fearless.

By his side stood his half-brother, Robert Count of Mortain, shorter and square set, a stolid unimaginative man whose main virtue was loyalty to William, a loyalty not shared by his brother Odo, whom their nephews had just been discussing in so derogatory a manner.

Behind the King stood the eldest son of his greatest baron, Roger of Montgomery. Robert of Bellême was tall and black-haired with hard handsome features and a blue jowl, a man fast gaining a reputation for vicious cruelty and not a few who had happened to offend him disappeared into his donjon at Bellême never to be seen again. A man to be feared, Henry thought, tainted with the evil Talvas blood inherited from Montgomery's first wife, Mabille, whose savage practices had led to her murder some years ago.

Beside Bellême stood the King's chancellor, Robert Bloet, smiling and friendly, while next to him hovered Ranulf, one of the King's chaplains, nicknamed Flambard for his gay dress and overbearing manner. He stood now, his quick intelligent eyes taking in the scene, itching to be away—a man of Bishop Odo's stamp, scheming, unscrupulous, a worldly cleric. He had risen from nothing and made his way by sheer effrontery so that he even embraced his nickname with a certain pride. The giver of that name was Eudo Dapifer, steward to the King, who was a constant companion to the young princes and kept them amused with his witticisms at the expense of the members of the King's court.

Henry caught his eye now and saw Eudo glance amusedly at the Crane and raise his eyes heavenwards in an impatient grimace. But at last the Bishop was lifting his hand and Henry knelt with every man in the courtyard for the Church's blessing. When the Bishop had finished he remained on his knee looking up at his father.

'We have a fine day for our venture, sire.'

William stared down at him. 'It would have been better begun for you if you had heard Mass with us. You sport yourself too much upon the pillow and too little upon your knees, my son.'

Henry fought down the desire to laugh. His brother's attendance at church owed more to his habit of accompanying their father everywhere than to a desire to serve God. In fact, Henry knew and half the court knew that Rufus did not care a snap of his stubby fingers for the Church and that he would rather offend his Maker than his father—whereas he, Henry, did care for God, when he had time.

'Your pardon, my lord,' he said meekly and smiled up at the King. His colouring he took from the Norman line, but his smile was his mother's and because of it William bent and raised him to his feet.

'Come, boy, we must waste no more of this day. Ride with me.' He flicked his fingers at his trumpeter to sound the general call.

They moved off slowly in the growing warmth of the day, crossing the river Epte by the narrow bridge at Gasny. The advance guard kept a wary eye for any Frenchmen there might be lurking in the woodland ahead, but all was still and quiet and the few peasants who saw them ran from them, too frightened to raise any alarm. They were in the disputed land now and William sent men to either side of their path, setting torches to the corn standing high in the fields, while other groups of soldiers were detailed to spoil the vines and cut down apple trees. It hampered their progress but men should know, the King said grimly, which way their overlord has passed and not dare to defy him again.

Henry rode beside Rufus, talking little, aware of the heat in his heavy hauberk, thinking about the fight to come.

It would be his first assault and he wanted to hurry the march, to face the enemy city, to plunge into battle, to blood his sword. Last year in England Archbishop Lanfranc had presented him for knighthood and he wished now that he could have set out with the old man's blessing. It had been something of a unique privilege to have the greatest scholar in Europe responsible for his education, and in consequence he had received such schooling that Robert and Rufus treated him with an amused indulgence which hid a certain envy—neither of them could read Latin nor write and from his infuriatingly inferior position in the family it gave him a weapon they had not. Even the name of 'Beauclerc' lent him a certain prestige which counteracted, if only slightly, the fact that he had been born so much the youngest of the Conqueror's brood.

But the other side of the coin had not been neglected either and he had been taught knightly exercises by Robert de Beaumont when he was in Normandy and by Hugh Lupus, Earl of Chester and Lord of Avranches, when he was in England. Both men, old enough to have fathered him, nevertheless became his friends and with Lanfranc, still alert and keenly interested in all things despite his eighty years, brought him in due course to the great church at Winchester. There his father had set a sword at his side and he had received the Host at Mass, swearing to be God's knight and the King's.

It was all very impressive and the memory of it lingered today at the back of his mind for now he must prove his knighthood.

At last when the sun was high the great army came in ever increasing numbers over the brow of a long rise of ground above a deep valley where the city lay. Walled and gated, on the bank of the wide river, it stood seemingly strong and serene, a neat city, confident in itself, prosperous, with many church towers and a fine castle. It looked a rich prize for the invaders and as Henry and Rufus paused beside their father, staring down into the valley below, it was clear that they had caught the enemy unaware. Everywhere in the fields men were busy harvesting, piles of weapons indicating that the soldiers of the garrison had gone out to help the local people bring in the corn and the grapes from laden vines. There was an air of busy prosperity and ease and William leaned on his saddle bow, staring, the end of his whip caught between his teeth in a habit he had when he was thinking deeply.

After a moment he said, 'Wine of Christ, there will be nothing left of that place when darkness comes this night. Then the King of France will see the candles lit for my churching from the windows of his palace in Paris itself.'

Rufus' grey eyes with their curious brown flecks rested briefly on his father's huge figure and a spasm of anger crossed his face. 'What are we waiting for? Let us be at it, my lord. Look! They have seen us.'

Away below them there were startled cries now, men rushing to and fro, collecting weapons and hauberks, shouting and gesticulating, many near to panic. The castle gates were open and others were running out to see what was happening, colliding with those who were hurrying in; on the battlements more men appeared and suddenly the quiet, pleasant day disrupted into chaos.

William gave the order to his trumpeter and the Norman army crashed down on to the peaceful fields and vineyards. Those too slow to reach safety were caught and killed. Fire was set to the corn and as the smoke rose the army reached the city, the barons leading their men, gonfanons high in the light breeze, knights and vavassours behind great lords, men-at-arms jostling each other to get into the fray. At the city gates a struggling mass of Frenchmen endeavouring to gain the protection of the walls had blocked the gates so that the men inside could not close them, and William's knights fell on these unfortunates, hacking, slashing, forcing their way in over piles of bodies to the barbican itself.

Here there was fierce fighting but the garrison, hampered by the refugees from the fields, could do nothing but die where they stood. Henry and Rufus were among the first into the town. Here the Norman troops split up, pouring down the narrow streets, killing as they went. They were followed by men with torches who fired the houses, systematically. In a short while the place had become an inferno, flames and smoke shooting into the summer air, the dry wood of the houses burning quickly and the screams of those caught within mingled with the groans of dying soldiers and the shrieks of wounded horses.

Henry saw a woman running with a babe in her arms go down before Eudo's horse and a lad of perhaps ten, carrying a spear too heavy for him, endeavour to thrust it at Eudo only to be speared himself and fall beneath the plunging hooves. After half an hour of such flame-ridden, screaming horror he found himself in a narrow lane between high houses, his men behind him and with them the men of Poix and their lord, Walter Tirel. At the end of the street a small determined group of French soldiers stood spanning the narrow distance between the houses and with a triumphant yell he called his men on, standing in his stirrups and waving his sword, caught up now into a hot excitement.

From the windows above women hurled cooking pots and receptacles of all kinds down on to them and Henry saw a pot catch Eudo on the head, causing him to swear volubly. He was shaken with laughter himself even as he struck at an indefinable figure before him. The man went down and another sprang in his place, lunging with a spear. It caught the Prince's horse in the belly. The animal fell, throwing Henry violently forward into the mêlée. He fell against a mass of struggling men and found himself on the ground where he lay for a moment, stunned. Then, as the man sprang at him he rolled aside and leapt to his feet, driving his sword deep into the Frenchman's chest; the fellow collapsed with one loud cry and he swung round to fend off another attack at the same time looking about him for another mount.

A knight rode up, bearing a shield with a device he did not know, and sliding from the saddle thrust the reins into his hand. 'Here, lord, take my horse.'

He nodded his thanks and sprang up as the knight darted away. It was a somewhat sorry horse, spindle-shanked and old, but at least he was mounted again, and as the French gave way he pressed forward with the rest of his men. Young Hamo, bearing his gonfanon, caught up with him now and he heard a roar from behind him as they finally burst out of the lane into the wider street beyond. Here the fire-setters were already doing their work, women running screaming from the houses. Many were burned alive, unable to escape, some thrust back into the flames by Norman swords, others trampled by the excited horses. Pausing breathlessly to watch, Henry saw a dog, its coat aflame, running towards him, yelping and rolling over and over in an endeavour to beat out the flames, and the sight roused his pity so that seizing a spear from Hamo he put the animal out of its misery. For a woman, screeching, her hair alight, he spared less thought—she was French and part of the insult offered to Normandy.

Emerging into the main street he found William of Breteuil, his sword arm red to the elbow, fighting furiously at the head of his large following of knights while at the far end Robert of Bellême, his lips drawn apart by a smile, his dark face blazing with grim satisfaction, was bearing down on a terrified group of young men who had thrown down their weapons and were crying for quarter. They might have saved themselves the trouble, Henry thought, for they got none from the heir of Talvas. Across the street Robert de Beaumont was supervising the firing of the great church and de Toeni was shepherding some protesting priests from the vicinity of the fire. He grinned and waved to Henry and pointed down the street.

William the King, conqueror once again, was riding into the city that was now his. It was all ablaze, black smoke rising into the blue August sky, roofs crashing into the burning shells of buildings, every church flaming, a tower falling now and again with a clash of bells. Everywhere the soldiers were plundering, taking what they might, their arms filled with jugs and pots, silver cups and bolts of cloth, weapons and anything that might be carried. And through it all William rode, his face set and hard beneath the nose-piece of his helm. Smuts and sparks flew, cinders falling like black snow; one fell on Henry's gloved hand and began to smoulder until he noticed and beat it out.

He called out to his father but at that moment the King's horse trod on a burning piece of wood among the rubble. The animal reared, neighing wildly and flinging his rider hard against the iron pommel so that it was pressed deep into William's abdomen.

William let out an involuntary groan but by consummate horsemanship kept his seat and controlled the terrified warhorse. Only when the animal was calm again did he turn to his sons who were both now beside him. His face was grey and taut with the ferocity of his pain. He tried to dismount but could not get his leg over the saddle.

'G-God's Body,' Rufus stammered, his face suffused with even deeper colour. 'Quick, some of you, help the K-King down. He is hurt.'

Men sprang forward to do his bidding, Henry among them, and slowly the King was lifted from the saddle. He had not lost consciousness and his eyes were open, dilated by pain as they carried him, breathless under his great weight, to a relatively clear space beneath a stone wall that still stood. The city was utterly destroyed now, the French beaten, the castellan,

Ralph de Malvoisin, in the hands of the Normans and the insult avenged, but William the King had fallen with it.

They laid him down and someone rolled a mantle to set beneath his head.

2

Henry sat alone on a chest in the cloister and kicked savagely at the carved wooden base, scratching the surface with his spur. The sound of the monks' eternal chanting seemed to go on and on, irritating him beyond measure, and there was nowhere in this abbey where one could go to get away from it. Here in the cloister he was conscious of little else, but every day there came a point when he could stand the sick-room no longer and must needs get away to fresh air. He had ridden out briefly into the forest this morning, but had soon returned for he dared not stay far from his father's side for long. Rufus indeed had not left the King's sick-bed, sleeping on a pallet in the corner of the room rather than be out of call and he too must not be other than on the spot when the dying Conqueror decided to settle his affairs—for dying he was, none doubted that.

After the fight at Mantes they had borne him in a litter home to Rouen, but the noise of the city, the constant sound of hooves and wheels on the streets, the cries of the traders, the ringing of bells from a score of churches all caused the wounded man such sleepless tension that he ordered his attendants to carry him to the Abbey of St. Gervase in the quiet hills west of Rouen. This journey caused him excessive pain but never for one moment did he lose command of himself and now he rested more comfortably. His physical suffering was, however, intense, the internal injury to his bowels beyond the help of his physicians, Abbot Gontard of Jumèges and Gilbert Maminot, Bishop of Lisieux, but despite his agony he kept his mind alert and his senses clear, attending to whatever pressing business was brought to him.

Henry watched by the bed with his brother, uneasy, uncertain of the future without the strong hand that had always guided them. There was no man in Europe to be compared to their father for sheer might, but there were many—Philip of

France and Count Robert of Flanders among them—who would be only too eager to fall like jackals on Norman lands.

Well, the King's last act had been to take Mantes and a bloody business it had been, but thinking of the battle it seemed to Henry a wanton waste of lives and property. By God, if he ever had the chance to govern he would use war only as a last resort. He knew now that he could fight and he had seen what blood-lust could do, God knew most of the barons lived for little else, but he might have died in that fight. Without the aid of the unknown knight who had given him that sorry horse he might lie now in Vexen soil—and that, he reflected with youthful arrogance, would have been a waste too. There must be some use for the learning, the ideas that teemed in his head. Yet at the moment his own future looked wretchedly uncertain. Following the usual custom Robert, being the eldest son, would have the Norman inheritance as the King had promised and Rufus would have England—so he would have nothing at all.

In a swift mood of rebellious discontent he precipitated himself from the chest and began to pace the cloister. It must be the most damnable thing in the world, he thought, to be the youngest son of a King. What would there be for him, what could there be? Robert and Rufus would take all and he, *porphyrogenites*, the only one born in the purple, the only one born on English soil and the son of a King, an English Atheling, would have nothing.

He paused, leaning against one of the stone arches, looking across the cloister. The singing had ceased and it was quiet now, the rays of the sun slanting across the grey stones. He had no illusions about either of his brothers. Robert was gay and generous and spendthrift, but he had the slow Flemish tenacity inherited from their mother's line and he meant to be Duke—indeed it had been his very determination to have his inheritance that had caused the bitter quarrel with the King and the rift between his parents. Robert wanted the dukedom eight years ago, claiming that his father had England and enough to do there, to which William retorted scathingly that he was not accustomed to undress until he went to bed.

Henry smiled wrily—none of them could better their sire in an argument. So Robert left the court and his gaiety was sadly missed while his mother wept openly. With him went many sons of noble houses, infected with his discontent, to the annoyance of their fathers and finally it came to open warfare. Before the castle of Gerberoi, in a skirmish, Robert actually unseated the Conqueror and it was typical of him that he at once dismounted and helped his father back into the saddle. No one had won that fight. Henry had been a child of eleven at the time but he remembered the gloom that the King had brought back to court and despite a temporary reconciliation the quarrel had persisted. Robert had not been seen for the past five years, though he was not far away either in France or in Flanders with their uncle Count Robert the Frisian.

Had he heard in the mysterious way that news travelled of their father's mortal sickness, Henry wondered, or had Rufus sent a messenger? He would have to ask him, but his brother seldom left the sick-bed and no one mentioned Robert in the King's hearing. If Robert had been their mother's favourite Rufus was their father's, he thought bitterly. Yesterday when the dying man's pain had been excessive, Rufus had wept, tears coursing down his red face making dark, ugly blotches. And at the thought of that pain and the disruption of life that must come, Henry felt his own eyes smart. But only for a moment. Then he straightened and walked on round the corner of the cloisters where, coming towards him, he saw his brother.

'Your page told me I would find you here,' Rufus said abruptly. 'Our father wishes to speak with us.'

Henry said, 'Why did you not send Fulcher to find me?' But he was thinking, it has come, the moment when I shall know what the future holds for me. He walked slowly, eager yet uncertain. He was nineteen and the youngest but he wanted—something! He glanced sideways at Rufus. His brother was dressed in a long green tunic girt with a jewelled belt and embroidered in the English manner, his square figure strong and well-made, lacking their father's inches but with his air of authority and there was a confidence in his very walk that Henry envied.

'I wanted to speak to you myself,' Rufus said, 'to tell you I have sent word to Curthose.' He seemed to enjoy using the name the King had given to his eldest son whose legs were so painfully short.

'I wondered if you would. Will the King see him?'

'No, he has said he will not, but I thought our brother should know.' Rufus gave his short harsh laugh. 'I'll wager ten marks he is already at the border waiting for news. He'll not be slow to take what is his. Our father knows that and for all their quarrel he will keep his word to Robert because that is his way.'

Henry wanted to ask what more their lord had said but his brother's lips were closed hard in a manner he had when he thought he had said enough. They walked in silence along the cloister and it was Henry who broke it first.

'I think Lanfranc would say it would be wrong for him to go to God with the quarrel still unmended.'

Rufus shrugged. 'Maybe, but Lanfranc is in England—and anyway I doubt if God cares. He must be used to men fighting, we do little else.'

'Unless we are monks.' Henry glanced through the arches to where, on the far side, he could see black-robed figures passing silently.

'They have a private arrangement with Him—and they're welcome to it,' his brother retorted. 'Don't tell me you want to join them?'

'Not I,' Henry answered goodhumouredly, 'but the priests are right when they urge a man to make peace on his death bed. Who would go to God laden with more sins than he need?'

A cynical smile lifted the corners of the younger William's mouth. 'Our holy Archbishop has taught you well, my little brother. But as far as I am concerned I am as I am and God, and everyone else too, must take me so. As for Curthose, he chose to defy our father and must stew in his own pot. But what sort of Duke do you think he will make?'

Henry was surprised at the sudden question. 'How should I know?' He added as an afterthought, 'But the barons need a strong hand and I doubt if has that.'

'Exactly, and if I see the need it is I who shall be that strong hand.'

'You? You would fight Robert?' For a moment an indefinable fear seized him, a moment of prescience when he seemed to see strife between the three of them, a warring that would bring no good. 'You would turn against Robert?' he repeated.

Rufus laughed again. 'Only if it is for the good of us all. Well, we shall see how things go.'

Henry put his hand on the latch of the door that led into the church through which they must pass to reach the guest house. It occurred to him that Rufus' laugh was incongruous at this moment, and further that there was no mirth in it. 'Yet I could wish him here,' he said. 'Once we were close. Do you remember,' a sudden recollection came to him and he paused, savouring it, 'do you remember when we were at L'Aigle, years ago, and Robert had a new mantle and strutted like a peacock? He was playing at dice with Ivo and Alberic of Grandmesnil and some others—Ralph's father was one, I think—and he called us children and sent us away. and we went up to the gallery and threw water from the chamber pots all over them.' His smile widened. 'What a scrap it was until our father heard the din and came to separate us. He was very angry and had me beaten because I laughed so much.'

Rufus' mouth had tightened. 'This is not the time for thinking of old jests. He is to tell us of his will.'

Sobered, Henry opened the door and went into the church where he genuflected and crossed himself. Rufus did not trouble himself to do either and Henry followed him out with only one prayer in his head—God, let me have something, something to make my life my own.

In the largest room in the guest house King William lay in his own great bed that had been brought from Rouen. His face was drawn and grey above the red mantle wrapped about his shoulders, but his dark eyes were alert still and as the princes entered he was listening to an impassioned plea from his brother of Mortain.

It seemed to Henry that the room was filled with barons and prelates. The Bishop of Lisieux was carefully watching his patient while on the other side of the bed the Abbot was superintending the mixing of a potion in an effort to ease his lord's pain. Hugh of Grandmesnil was by the window, and Walter Giffard, the Duke's old friend, William of Breteuil, Robert de Beaumont, the elder Ralph de Toeni and his son, were all gathered about the bed.

As Henry entered his cousin Stephen of Aumale, son of William's sister Adeliza, the Countess of Champagne, caught him by the arm, his thin dark face grave. 'The King has said that all prisoners are to be released in a general amnesty except Bishop Odo, and to my mind he should be left to rot. I'm not enamoured of our uncle.'

'Neither am I,' Henry agreed in a low voice, 'but our other uncle of Mortain may get his way.'

'I implore you, sire,' Robert of Mortain was saying urgently, 'as you must make your peace with our Lord Christ let your forgiveness extend to our brother.'

William stirred uneasily, his great bulk shifting under the fur coverlet, his square hands restless, fingers deep in the fur. 'You are a fool, Robert. Do you think God will commend me for leaving my realm in danger? I tell you, Odo, if he is free, will make trouble for you all.'

'But if he returns to Bayeux, to his diocese . . .'

The corners of the King's mouth lifted grimly. 'If you think he can keep from meddling in state affairs, then you are an even bigger fool. It will be difficult enough for Robert to rule the duchy which is his by right—for all he's been a traitor to me and no true son I'll not deny him that—but if he has Odo to contend with and give him bad counsel, then by Christ's wounds I fear for you all.'

'Odo has learned his lesson,' Mortain pleaded. He was some years younger than William and despite his grey head strong still and stubborn without a great deal of sense. 'William, we three have done so much together. All the years when we strove to make Normandy a place fit to live in, when you brought justice here, when we fought for England and won it, are these to count for nothing? Odo and I were ever at your side.'

William's glance rested for a moment on his half-brother's stolid countenance and a faint smile crossed his face. 'Of your loyalty I was never in doubt.'

'Then for my sake, brother, forgive Odo. Let your last act of charity be to release him.'

There was silence now in the room, no other man daring to put forward an opinion on this issue. Grandmesnil, nearing sixty himself, who had served William for forty years, shifted uneasily for he would rather Odo stayed where he was. His own sons had rebelled with Robert and been pardoned and consequently he had no desire to see the Bishop putting his wily counsel into Robert's ears. De Beaumont also looked wary but his house was powerful enough to be less concerned. William of Breteuil did not care either way, having enough faith in his own right arm to snap his fingers even at Odo. Henry glanced at Rufus but his brother's face reflected nothing of his feelings. Stephen leaned against the door and studied an old scar on the back of his hand.

Mortain repeated, 'William, I beg of you . . .'

The King sighed. He seemed weary now and accepting the potion Abbot Gontard handed him swallowed it obediently, grimacing with distaste.

'You are tired, sire,' the Abbot said gently. His black robes, his quiet manner contrasted with the rich dress and the almost tangible tensions of the other men in the room. 'Rest now and give your mind to this matter tomorrow.'

'Tomorrow!' Mortain exclaimed. 'Tomorrow may be too . . .' he stopped abruptly. 'It is too urgent to wait. Brother . . .'

William lifted his hand. 'If you must have your way I will pardon him. But you will all rue it.'

Mortain's face was alight with relief. 'I thank you, William. It is an act of mercy that will commend your soul to Our Lady and . . .'

'See to it,' William interrupted him as if he had had enough of the subject and Mortain went out.

The King stared past Grandmesnil's upright figure to the window. 'Release the English Earl Morcar and give Harold's brother, Wulnoth the Saxon, leave to return to England if he wishes.' His eyes clouded for a moment and silence fell again, a silence no one liked to break.

Wulnoth was the youngest brother of the dead King Harold, the last of the house of Godwine and his name carried those old enough to remember back to the day when they had won England for Normandy. The King's eyes were fixed beyond them all on the window, the shutters open to the mild September air, the sun still warm. His thoughts too had returned to that evening more than twenty years before when he had stood in gathering darkness on the summit of Telham ridge, victor of the field of Senlac, and they had brought him the body of Harold. He had liked Harold and if the English Earl had kept faith with him they might have been friends. He had not wanted to see him, hacked and bloodied by Norman swords, lying thus at his feet. So long ago, and yet so clear in his head as if it were but a few days past. It was a small act of reparation to release Wulnoth now. He thought too of that other English Earl whom he had sent to his death, Waltheof Siwardson whom he had married to his niece Judith; he had liked Waltheof too but Waltheof had become implicated in deep treachery and though many thought him innocent Judith herself had spoken against him and at last William had permitted his execution. It was the only time in all his life when he had sent a man to death other than in war and now, remembering, he faced within himself the knowledge that he had almost certainly condemned an innocent man. For that there was no reparation.

He said, 'Is Abbot Anselm come from Bec?'

Gilbert of Lisieux shook his head. 'No, my lord. A messenger came an hour since to say that he started out as you bade him but he fell sick on the way and lies abed himself, waiting for his fever to subside. He will come as soon as he can travel.'

Another deep sigh escaped the King. 'I wished to confess myself to that good man but it seems it is not God's will. I cannot wait.' He surveyed the crowded room. 'Leave me, all of you, but you, Bishop, my Chancellor and my sons—and I conjure you, remember your oaths to me and my house.'

Gradually the room emptied. As he went to the door Stephen whispered to Henry, 'God send he makes your fortune too, cousin.'

At last only the Bishop remained by the bed, Henry and Rufus stood together at the end of it, and Robert Bloet, his pleasant face grave, stood by the door. For a while no one spoke.

The King's eyes had closed but presently he opened them again. 'Bloet, my friend, send gifts from my treasury to that city I have ruined. See that every church in Mantes is rebuilt, that the citizens are housed, and make reparation in my name. In my anger I destroyed too much.'

'It will be done,' Bloet said quietly and began to write the order on a parchment so that the King might make his mark and seal it.

William went on, 'And write to Lanfranc. Tell him the crown of England is not mine to bestow . . .'

Henry felt Rufus stiffen beside him, saw his brother's face darken and his fists clench.

The King was struggling to rise in the bed and the Bishop lifted him a little to set another cushion behind his head. A spasm of pain crossed his face but after a moment he seemed more comfortable. 'I took England,' he said clearly, 'when I had no right. All my life I had been forced to live by blood and the sword and I know my sin was great for that people had not offended me,' he saw the surprise on the faces of his listeners but he went on without a pause, 'therefore now I

35

have no right in its bestowal. It is for the people to give the crown as has always been their custom—but write to the Archbishop that I believe my son, William, to be the best man to wear that crown, to be the only man who has claim, and that he is my choice. Pray God he is the people's choice also.'

Henry had a wild desire to laugh. For all the noble phrasing his father meant Rufus to have England and Lanfranc would know what to do. It was so obvious and yet he saw his father clearly in that moment as a man who had somehow kept an integrity that neither Robert nor Rufus would ever have. He felt rather than heard Rufus' sigh of relief and the tension leaving his stocky body.

Nobody spoke and the silence was broken only by the scratching of Robert Bloet's quill. Presently it was done and he brought the letter to William who made his mark with a surprisingly steady hand and then sealed the red wax with the seal bearing the impress of his own seated royal figure.

'Go with Bloet, my son,' he said. 'I know that I have little time left and you must be on your way to England when I go to my fathers.' He held out his and and Rufus knelt to kiss it. Red William was in tears now and held his father's hand in his own, weeping unrestrainedly.

'I cannot go—not while you live.'

William raised his other hand to touch his son's tow-coloured head briefly. He seemed deeply affected. 'You have my blessing, but you must go. We are not burghers who can afford to indulge more tender feelings. You have a high duty, my son, and not even the love you bear me must keep you from it. Make haste, I beg you.'

Rufus rose and wiped his face. Then he bent to kiss his father's forehead. He could not speak and left the room without a word or a backward look, followed by the chancellor.

The King had turned his head away and lay so still with eyes closed that for one awful moment Henry thought he was dead, gone without a word for him, but William breathed deeply and opened his eyes again.

'I would confess myself. If Anselm cannot come, beg Abbot Gontard to hear me . . .'

At that his youngest son came round the bed and knelt beside him. 'My lord, what of me? Am I to have nothing?'

A faint smile crossed the drawn features. 'Well, my son, and what do you think you should have?'

'What you will, my lord. I know I am the youngest but I was born the son of a King which Curthose and Rufus were not, yet they are to have everything while I . . .'

'Tush!' William broke in, 'will the three of you fight like dogs over a bone? There is meat enough for all.' After a pause he added, 'write an order and I will seal it, that you are to have five thousand pounds in silver from my treasury.'

Henry was startled. It was a great deal of money, more than he could have expected, but his instinctive reaction for once got the better of native caution. 'My lord and father, I thank you for this generous gift, but am I to have no land? What good is money without land?' It sounded churlish but he could not help it.

William regarded him gravely. 'You are right, my child. All men must hold land but I have none to give you for I cannot go back on my word to Robert. And if I send you into England, what do you think your brother William would give you? If your birth makes you an English Atheling, he still has the claim of years. Trust in God and let your elders go before you.'

Henry was silent for there was only one answer to this, but nevertheless he felt his cheeks colour with a wave of frustration. He could not meet his father's eyes and kept his gaze on the fur at the edge of the bed, studying the ridges in the pelt, the shades of brown.

'My mother's lands . . .' he said at last.

The King nodded. 'Yes, those you should have, the manors of Wessex and in the southern part of Wales, but you will have to make issue with your brother for those. I do not think he will deny you. Child, don't fret. I see further than you think.' For a moment the old William re-appeared, strong, dominating, reading men's minds, winning his battles because he could out-think his enemies. 'Take your money and guard it well for I tell you this—a time will come when Robert will have thrown his inheritance away, when William's excesses will have made him too many enemies and then—then you will have it all. I conquered because I knew when to trust and when not to trust. Robert trusts too many and Rufus none at all. I see it clearly . . .' his breath was coming in laboured gasps now, his eyes dilated, and the Bishop laid a hand on his arm.

'Rest, sire, I beg you.'

But William did not heed him, his stern gazed fixed on his son. 'It is you, the last of my children who will hold in your hands everything that my mother dreamed I would hold before I was born.'

Henry still knelt, folding his father's hand in his own. 'My lord, how can I hope for that?'

'Wait. Watch and learn. Be just and use the good sense God has given you and you will find I am right. I remember when you were born your mother said . . .' He closed his mouth hard as if the memory were too precious to reveal. 'Thirty years we lived together and these last four without her have been the most wretched of my life.' His fingers tightened on his son's. 'See that masses are said for her soul and for mine. Now write that order.'

Henry rose. He found to his surprise that his legs were unsteady and there was a sick sensation in his stomach. This end, this parting asunder of a period of his life, of his boyhood perhaps, was more painful than he had expected, and from now on all things would be different. He wrote awkwardly and made a blot on the parchment. Then he handed it to his father for the King to make his mark. He remembered he had once said in his father's hearing that an unlettered King was a crowned ass and how his sides had smarted for that piece of impertinence. His father had risen high above such strictures and the shame, if any, was his own.

'Take it,' William said, 'and put your money in a safe place. Then come back to me.' He seemed exhausted now, lying back against the cushions, but there was a faint smile on his drawn face. ' "*How are the mighty fallen in the midst of battle, and the weapons of war perished.*" Well, God's will be done.'

Henry knelt again. 'I will not be long, sire.'

'Not long may be too long,' William said half to himself. His eyelids fell and he slept.

'I will stay with him,' the Bishop said softly and Henry, the parchment in his hand, went to the door. There he paused, looking back at the still figure in the bed. There was no man greater than his father, he thought, and for a moment felt a vicarious pride in him, a grief that he lay broken at last. But broken or not he was still to be obeyed and his son left the room. Ten minutes later he was on the road to Rouen.

The great Abbey of Bec lay in a pleasant valley where two streams met, flanked by wooded hills. The founder, Herluin, had chosen his site well for there were fish in the clear waters, game in plenty in the woods and the land was rich for cultivation. The Abbey buildings covered a large area now for the schools had become famous and students flocked here from every part of Europe. Lanfranc had come more than sixty years ago from Italy and Anselm, the present Abbot, from Aosta, and still the cleverest young men travelled to the place where they would find the best teaching. The guest house and school were being enlarged and the sound of builders' hammers reached the sick Abbot's lodging, making his head ache though he voiced no complaint.

He sat in his chair by the fire, shivering for all it was a warm day and, despite the Prior's pleading, insisted on attending to what business was in hand. When a lay brother came in to announce a visitor he held up his hand to silence the Prior's protest.

'Bid Prince Henry come to me.' And when the young man knelt by his chair for his blessing Anselm gave it, regarding him affectionately. It seemed to him such a little time since this young man had been a stripling boy and now he saw him developing a strength and personality, the soft almost black eyes masking a growing sense of purpose combined with a tenacity which reminded Anselm of the old King. From under the falling thatch of thick dark hair the Prince returned his look gravely and Anselm liked what he saw.

'My son, how is your father? I trust you are not come with ill news?' He indicated a chair and Henry took it to sit facing him, accepting the wine the Prior poured before excusing himself and leaving them alone.

'There is no change, my lord, but he is dying. I fear it cannot be long now.'

Anselm sighed and crossed himself. 'I prayed that I might go to him, but God did not will it for my legs would not bear me. Our country will be sadly lost without him. He has kept order for many years.'

'I know.' Henry's gaze wandered round the familiar room. He had been here many times, had read here with the Abbot and with Lanfranc on the latter's occasional visits to Normandy. Here he had sat once and studied St. Augustine and some words

39

came back to him now. *'For no sooner do we begin to live in this dying body than we begin to move towards death.'*

An involuntary shiver ran through him. His body was young and strong and he did not want to think that he too would lie one day as his father lay now, death as inevitable as the next dawn. He straightened his legs, flexed his arms, feeling their supple power—death was as remote as the mysterious lands beyond the eastern trade routes and eternal life no less nebulous. His father might be on the edge of that leap into the unknown but he did not want to contemplate it when life was only now opening up before him.

The Abbot's voice broke into his thoughts. 'How may we serve you? Do you wish masses said for your father? We are already doing so.'

Henry brought his gaze back to Anselm, noting the occasional tremor that shook the thin body, all spare flesh long since driven away by devout fasting. Anselm was near enough a saint, Henry thought, and remembering that his uncle Odo might even now be stepping into freedom wondered that the same Church could foster two such contrasting priests. 'It is a personal matter,' he said at last. 'My father has given me a grant of money and I must house it somewhere. I can think of no safer place than your treasury. Will you hold it for me?'

Anselm seemed surprised, not so much at the request but at the gift itself. 'Your father is generous.'

Henry kept his eyes on his feet in their brown leather shoes. 'Robert has Normandy and Red William has already left for England with a letter for the Archbishop, while I—I have a grant of money,' He paused and when Anselm did not speak, he came out with what he must say. 'What I am to do with it? Where shall I go? Does Robert want me here? Will Rufus welcome me in England? All my life my father has kept me close and now—it is as if I had been cast adrift on the sea.'

Anselm folded his hands together, his gaze on the Prince's face. Despite his aching head, he put his own discomfort aside to attend to the needs of a spiritual son. 'This is hard to say, my child. I cannot advise you other than bid you keep peace with your brothers. God has a destiny for you, I am sure of that.'

'My father says . . .' he broke off and rising went to stand by the window. In the courtyard below where he had entered through the gatehouse his small retinue was waiting—Hamo

leaning against the wall where he had propped his lord's standard; Raoul the deer using the spare moment to inspect a horse's
hoof; Gulfer standing with arms folded—he had left his birds
at Rouen and when not tending them could stand as still as a
hawk on the pole, his hands gnarled and hardened by constant
handling; and young Fulcher whose father had once been page
to the King and who conceived of no higher honour than that
his family should serve the royal household. There were some
twenty men-at-arms, earning their bread in the manner of
soldiers, guarding the four mules who bore the chests of silver,
the animals standing quietly in the sunshine, used to burdens
upon their backs, shaking their heads against the flies, patient
and obedient.

Henry came back from the window. It seemed stifling to him
in this little room and he swung off his woollen mantle, letting
it lie on a stool. 'A destiny, my lord Abbot?' he repeated. 'Where
should I seek that?'

'You will not need to seek it. When it is God's will it will
come to you.' Anselm leaned forward earnestly. 'I know a little
of your father's mind. He believed he was right in educating
you above the rest of your house. One day you will be able
to use that knowledge for good. In the meantime . . .'

'In the meantime I cannot live on dreams of the future. I have
not even a castle to call my own—every baron in Normandy has
more than I have!'

Before Anselm could reply there was a sudden commotion in
the courtyard below and a sound of hooves. Henry crossed
swiftly to the window but by the time he looked out all he
saw was a lathered horse. There were urgent steps on the stair
and then a knocking at the door. A man almost fell in and threw
himself on his knees before the Prince.

'My lord, I have been to Rouen and they told me you were
here.'

'You have found me,' Henry said. 'What news, fellow?' Yet
even as he asked he knew the answer.

'Your father, lord . . .'

Somehow he had known, known he would not get back to St.
Gervais in time, known it when he had left his father's bedside. Yet there was still grief that he had not been there. 'He is
dead?'

The messenger was struggling to get his breath back 'Aye, my lord. Yesterday morning.'

Anselm clasped his hands together and bowed his head, the ready tears in his eyes. '*Requiescat in pace....*'

Henry crossed himself. Then he looked down at the kneeling messenger. 'Tell me ...'

'It was early and he had slept well, they said. He heard a bell ringing and asked what it was, and when they told him it was the bell of Rouen Cathedral ringing for Prime he commended his soul to God and Our Lady and died quietly and in peace—so suddenly that, one of the brethren told me of it, he said ...' he broke off abruptly. 'It was a scandal, a sacrilege ...' He stopped again and dared not look up.

Henry stood rigid. 'Go on.' And when the man seemed to have lost his tongue, added sharply, 'God's wounds, don't hide the truth from me. Tell me what happened.'

'It—it seemed as if with his going men lost their senses. Every lord and knight who was there fled to his own place to secure what he had. They were afraid that with the King dead no one would be safe.'

'And then?'

'Even the servants,' the messenger hesitated again, hardly able to speak the words to the dead King's own son, but encountering a look forced himself to go on. 'They robbed the King, even in death, taking everything from the chamber—his clothes, his plate, his linen and furs. It was if no one had wits left.'

'Christ's cross!' Henry swore. 'I'll have their thieving hands lopped off for this. Has nothing been done for my father? Was there no one to prepare his burial? He wished to lie in his own abbey at Caen.'

There were tears in the messenger's eyes now. 'I know, my lord. Ten years I've served him and a good master he was to me. I did not know what to do.'

Henry raised him to his feet. 'You did right to come to me. I will go back to St. Gervais at once.'

'There is no need now, my lord. A man came—I did not know him—a knight from some part of the Côtentin, I think. He said he had come to pray for the King and when he saw how all the high-born men had fled and none would stay to see honour done to the King's corpse, he undertook to arrange for it to be cared for and carried down the river to Caen.'

Henry turned away and stood by the window, staring out into the sunlit courtyard yet seeing nothing. It appalled him, outraged something deep within that his father should have been deserted in helpless death by those whom he had ruled and who owed him all they had, and it offended him that only an obscure knight should come forward to perform the last services for one who had been the greatest statesman in Europe. A wave of hot colour rose to his cheeks.

'By God, that knight shall be my friend.' He turned back to the messenger. 'Do you know his name?'

'Herluin, my lord, but I do not know his fief nor his badge. His clothes and arms were not those of a man of wealth yet he paid men to do what had to be done.'

'He shall have it back and more beside.' He turned to Anselm and knelt. 'Give me your blessing, father, for I must go at once to Caen.'

Anselm gave it, the tears still lying on his cheeks. 'Go with God, my son. I will follow you to Caen if I can ride tomorrow. Your treasure you may safely leave with me.'

Henry kissed his ring and then rose, and bidding the messenger to come with him went down to superintend the unloading of his silver. An hour later he and his men rode out of the gates and took the road to the north-west.

Throughout that warm day he sat in the saddle, silent for the most part. The men behind him were his and his immediate attendants such as Hamo, Raoul and Gulfer closer than most, but they were not men of rank and he could not confide to them the grief, the doubts, the anxieties that alternately tore at his mind. He wished Ralph were here, or Eudo, or his other close friend Richard of Redvers, even his cousin Stephen. He could have talked openly to any of them but now, sitting in the saddle under the warm September sky with the sun beating down on his back, he felt alone as he had never done before. It was as if his father's death had removed a shield and he must go on without it, out to his own future, his destiny, as Anselm had called it. Only at nineteen he was sure of nothing—nothing but an intolerable loneliness.

He rode into Caen to find it teeming with nobles and knights, prelates and abbots and humble folk all come to do the last honours to their sovereign, many with shame at their previous panic. The dead King's brother was there, Henry's uncle Robert of Mortain, with his son William, a sulky lad in his early teens who glared at Henry without bothering to hide his jealousy of the deference paid to the Prince—they had grown up together and the dislike was mutual. He saw William of Breteuil across the square, swarthy face expressionless—his father, William FitzOsbern, had been the King's cousin and close friend; and among the great barons were Hugh of Grand-mesnil, the de Toenis, Robert de Beaumont and Robert of Bellême, and with them a very tall dark man who disengaged himself from among them and came at once to Henry. He was handsome and slender, his hair neatly cut, his face smoothly shaved, and his grey eyes fearless and direct. He was Helias de Beaugencie, lord of La Flèche, and a grandson on his mother's side of Herbert Wake-dog, Count of Maine. Herbert's daughter had been betrothed to Robert Curthose but had died before the marriage could take place. Through her King William had claimed Maine for his son but Helias, Henry thought, had as good a claim. At the moment, however, Maine was Normandy's and here was Helias coming to him with both hands held out; they had hunted often together and of all this great gathering Helias was perhaps the man he most liked and trusted.

'My lord Henry! I am glad to see you though it is upon so sad an occasion. Are your brothers not come?'

'Rufus has gone to England,' Henry said briefly, 'as for Robert, I think he must be on his way to Rouen but I have not heard.'

'Then you must lead us.' Helias glanced round at the gathering, representatives from every great house there in the square, awaiting the funeral Mass. 'One wonders how many mourn.' His glance fell on one particular face. 'Did you hear that the lord of Bellême was on his way to St. Gervais when he heard of your father's death and at once turned round and expelled all the ducal garrisons from his castles before he came here?'

Henry's face darkened. 'There will always be trouble from that devil. I doubt Robert will be able to hold him in check.'

'He is no Christian,' Helias said and for him that was the worst that could be said of a man. 'Your uncle Odo came yesterday from his prison and is gone with the Bishops of Lisieux and Evreux to attend the procession here for the Mass.'

In all his life afterwards Henry never forgot that burial. The sight of his father lying still on the bier, that strong face at peace at last beneath its golden coronet, the square hands clasped on the swordhilt, the rich purple pall, all were engraved on his mind. He was hardly conscious of the men about him, hardly heard the expressions of grief, but walked silently behind the bier, aware of death as he had not been at the height of the fighting at Mantes. He saw his uncle Odo, dressed in the richest of vestments, his black eyes alert, his keen glance missing nothing, the soldierly Bishop Geoffrey of Coutances, Abbot Gontard who had attended his father, and Abbot Anselm who still looked very sick, and leading them all the Archbishop of Rouen, the procession stretching out all the way from the river, the poorest folk bringing up the rear.

And suddenly there was a cry of 'Fire! Fire!' and a house seemed to burst into flames right in their path. Within a few minutes the wooden dwellings on either side of the narrow street had caught and the flames began to spread rapidly. The procession disintegrated in disorder, the citizens fled to protect their own property and every man who could lent a hand to fight the fire.

Henry told the monks in charge of the bier to hurry on to the Abbey church which was outside the walls and he with Helias of La Flèche and a number of others formed a long line, passing buckets of water to stop the fire spreading. Hot and grimy he took a leather bucket from Grandmesnil and said, 'That house won't catch now. We'd better soak the next to be on the safe side.'

Grandmesnil, his lined faced streaked with sweat, brushed a hand across his forehead and stood still, staring at the smoking ruin in front of them. 'It is an omen. God and His saints have mercy!'

Henry paused, the bucket in his hand. 'What do you mean?'

'I remember, years ago, at his coronation some houses caught fire and there was a panic among the English so that we ran from the church to see what had happened. He was crowned King with hardly any of us there to see it. And now—it is the same at his burial.'

'No,' Henry said sharply. 'God's death, Grandmesnil, are you so infected by the English that you read omens into everything as they do? The men here can deal with the last of the

45

fire. Come,' he called out to those around him, 'Come to the Abbey, my lords. My father will not be laid to rest without his liegemen around him.'

He led them out of the smoking streets, over the fallen rubble beyond the walls to the great church of St. Stephen that his father had built as a marriage offering. Outwardly calm, Grand-mesnil's words stayed in his head as he visualised his father's crowning—fire then, fire at Mantes and fire now. What did it signify? Surely not God's anger, for his father had loved the Church, had given her great gifts, yet a dread lingered and not even the monk's singing, the Mass, the candles, could drive it away.

At last the bier was brought forward and laid by the coffin near the opening in the floor where the King was to be laid and the Bishop of Evreux mounted the pulpit to deliver the funeral oration. He spoke of William's achievements, of his victories, of his harsh but just rule until Henry, for once usurping the role of Rufus, felt that it was no mean thing to be the son of such a man.

'Fearless he was,' the Crane was ending, 'and brave and stark but no man can live without sin and I beseech you for the love of Christ that you will all forgive him if he ever offended you. I would ask you . . .'

At that moment there was a stir among the lesser folk at the rear of the church and a man pushed forward, gesticulating. 'You shall not bury him there,' he shouted. 'My name is Ascelin and this land is mine. He took it from my father and never paid for it. I have proof!' And he waved a parchment.

There was a stunned silence and then an outbreak of angry murmurings. Men-at-arms sprang forward to seize him but he shouted his claim again so that every head was turned towards him, Odo from the altar, his face dark with anger, and the other Bishops shocked at this rude interruption, while the Crane stared over other men's heads to see what was happening.

'God's wounds,' Henry said under his breath and stepped from his place. In a loud voice he asked the fellow what he wanted.

'The price of the land, my lord.'

'This is intolerable,' Odo called out angrily. 'You shall be paid later if your claim is good, but step aside now and do not interrupt these holy obsequies. You defile God's house.'

'No,' Ascelin retorted and set his legs firmly astride. 'I'll not go without justice.'

There was another silence in the crowded church, incense rising, the white-robed figures still while men looked first at Henry, then at Odo or his brother Robert. Henry seized the moment for authority, some instinct barely realised suggesting that he might not have another for a long time.

He strode down the church. 'You shall have justice. What is the six feet of ground my father requires now worth to you? You shall have a fair settlement of the rest later.'

Ascelin shuffled uncertainly. He had lost a little of his truculence. Then he said, 'Five marks, my lord.'

Henry took the purse from his belt and handed it to Robert de Beaumont who was nearest to him. 'Pay him,' he said briefly and went back to his place. The disturbance subsided and Odo, a look of thorough disapproval on his face, turned back to the altar. He would have preferred to see the fellow whipped from the church.

But there was worse to come. The monks who were lifting the body of the King carefully and reverently from the bier laid it in the coffin only to find that the stone had been cut too small. In fear and rather than cause further upset by calling for a new coffin, which could not be found without delay, they tried to force the body into the narrow space. An indescribable sound struck the mourners as the bowels burst and a revolting stench rose, filling all the church.

In an appalled few seconds of stillness no one moved. Then the bishops backed away and the monks stood trembling, staring down in fixed terror. One stumbled away and another dropped the tall candle he bore so that it rolled across the floor until caught by a lay brother. There was a retching sound as yet another fled out by the sacristy door. Many of the barons and their attendants retreated to the rear of the church and some even pushed open the doors and hurried out into the fesh air.

Grandmesnil stayed where he was but his face was white. William of Breteuil stayed too, his lips pressed tightly together, but the elder Ralph de Toeni hurried away followed by old Walter Giffard; Robert of Bellême folded his arms and stared with arrogant scorn at those who could not stay and Robert de Beaumont remained staunchly in his place.

Henry stood his ground, aware of horror and shame that the

burial of his father should be so desecrated. The stench was nauseating and he felt his stomach heaving. Beside him Helias of La Flèche said, 'Holy Jesu!' He was pale and shaken but he did not move from his place beside the Prince. Mortain's tears had turned to outright sobbing but he too remained, his legs refusing to bear him away.

Henry bunched his mantle against his face and cried out to the paralysed monks, 'For God's sake, get on with it,' and turned his eyes to the ground while they did the obscene things that had to be done, stuffing the body somehow into the coffin, forcing down the lid, all of them sweating and sick. Incense was piled into thurifers but it could not sweeten the air and Odo gabbled through the last of the rites as the coffin was lowered into its place. Then every man fled the building.

Outside Henry leaned against a wall, his stomach rebelling, and how he kept himself from vomiting he never knew—only that he must not disgrace himself by being sick in front of the gathered nobility of Normandy.

Helias held out a small horn. 'Here, my lord, drink this.'

He took it and drank, feeling the wine go down into his stomach and somehow quell the awful nausea. 'The saints bless you for that, Helias.' He drew deep shuddering breaths, filling his lungs again and again with clean air.

'It is over,' Helias said. 'It is over, my lord.' He took Henry by the arm and led him away.

3

That night the Prince supped at the house of Thurstin, a wine merchant and leading burgher of Caen. He had been bidden to the Abbey guest house but the company of his uncle Odo and the grief-stricken Mortain was more than he felt he could bear and accepted instead Thurstin's hospitality. It was a simple house consisting of one room on the ground floor, two above and two more high in the eaves, a thin house in a narrow street but with more freedom, he thought, than the spacious refectory in the Abbey.

Helias was with him and Richard of Redvers who had arrived late for the burial and was now secretly thanking God for his lame horse. Ralph de Toeni had gone, unwillingly, with his father to attend Mortain and de Redvers said, a faint smile on his broad-featured face, 'Poor Ralph will have to wallow in grief tonight but you, my lord, you will put it behind you—as you must.'

'Yes,' Henry had said, 'yes, by God.'

So now he sat at Thurstin's table and ate the spiced meat and drank the good wine the merchant offered and tried to drive from his mind the horror of that scene in the church this afternoon and from his nostrils the stench he could still smell. Only food and drink and the company of such friends as Helias and de Redvers could keep him from thinking tonight and he turned to his host to congratulate him on the excellence of the wine.

Thurstin beamed with pleasure. 'Ah, my lord, you have not yet tasted the latest I have brought from Sicily. See my daughter is bringing you the greeting cup.'

Henry turned and saw a girl approaching, her long red gown trailing on the rushes, her hair almost hidden beneath her white veil, her eyes fixed on his face. She was carrying a silver cup and as she approached the table she bent the knee to him.

'Pray, my lord, drink of the best wine in my father's house.'

She had a low and pleasant voice and now that she was close he saw that she was no young girl, but a woman of perhaps twenty-three or four. He took the cup and drank and then moved along the bench, begging her to sit beside him.

'What is your name, lady?'

'Alide, lord.'

He glanced down at her hand. 'I see that you are wed. Is your husband among our company here?'

She shook her head. 'He is dead. He died of the sweating sickness last summer. My mother too is dead so I have returned to my father's house where I can be useful.'

She had dark grey eyes, thoughtful eyes and quiet so that a man might rest in her company and her figure was soft and rounded, falling away to a small waist above more generous hips. She was beautiful, he thought, and knew then that he needed love tonight. He thought of that room above where he must sleep in an empty bed when he needed warmth and tenderness and the oblivion of loving. He looked at her again and wanted her, wanted to lay his head between those rounded breasts and hold her in his arms. Yet how could he? For all she was no virgin he did not think he could abuse his host's hospitality to that extent for Thurstin was no peasant to be bought.

He joined in the talk, laughing and capping Richard's stories with witticisms, overdoing it all in an endeavour to hide the turmoil she had raised in him. He tore a capon apart with his fingers and ate, washing the meat down with the good wine and wishing he had a few more years behind him. Presently when Helias was discussing with Thurstin the wine harvest at La Flèche and de Redvers was listening to some chatter further down the table, Alide turned to their royal guest, speaking so that no one else could hear.

'Lord, I grieve for what you have had to suffer today. I can see that you need to put it from your thoughts tonight.'

He was taken aback by her perception and putting up a hand pushed the falling hair from his forehead. 'Yes,' he said at last. He had never liked to take too much wine, a lesson learned from his father, but tonight was a rare exception and he wondered if his voice sounded slurred. 'I would not be alone.'

He had not intended to say it and wished he had not used

those exact words. 'I meant . . .' he began and then stopped, not knowing how to explain.

She said nothing and he reached out impulsively and took her hand where it lay in her lap. 'Alide,' he said and repeated her name, 'Alide.' For a moment his gaze caught and held hers. Then her father spoke, bidding her send a servant for more wine and there was no chance of further speech between them. But he felt a tension, a current of feeling so that when accidentally she brushed his shoulder as he leaned forward to answer a question from Helias he knew that she was as aware of it as he.

When the meal ended Alide made as if to rise but for one moment he detained her. 'You are no green girl,' he said in a low voice, 'but I did not think you an easy woman. Forget what I said.'

She smiled and he felt his stomach turn but in a more pleasurable manner than it had this afternoon.

'I did not misunderstand you,' she answered. 'My husband was a clerk and taught me much of the Scriptures, and it is rightly said *"how can one be warm alone"*.'

He looked silently at her, astounded that he could feel thus about a woman he had known scarce above an hour and equally astonished at her acute words. 'I am a prince of Normandy,' he said at last, 'yet I would command no woman against her will. If I say to a peasant, send me your daughter tonight, he will do it because I am who I am—but still I would not press an unwilling girl, whatever her station.'

'I did not think,' she answered slowly, 'that you would.' She rose and her eyes were veiled as she bent the knee and bade him goodnight.

He said, 'I could have de Redvers with me tonight, but I will not ask him.'

No one else had heard the low words, nor did she answer. She asked her father's leave to retire and disappeared up the narrow stair.

Serving men cleared the trestles now and laid out pallets on the floor while Henry's host conducted him to the guest chamber, setting a rush dip in the sconce on the wall. Helias had gone to the house next door where he had been promised a bed and had made his farewells for he was to return to La Flèche early on the morrow, and it was Richard alone who lingered.

51

'Shall I stay?' he queried. 'There's space enough for two.'

Henry sat down on the edge of the bed. His head was throbbing. 'Not tonight.' He glanced up at his friend. De Redvers was utterly dependable, one of the few whom he could really trust. De Redvers was a descendant of a bastard line from Duke Richard the Fearless and was thus a connection by blood as well as friendship. At twenty-four Richard was his own master but there was not an ounce of arrogance in him and he took no offence, merely helping Henry out of his clothes.

'There, my lord. Rest well. Tomorrow . . .'

'Tomorrow!' Henry broke in and laughed ruefully. 'What am I to do tomorrow?'

'Come to Vernon,' Richard said at once. He had a wide mouth and a rather flat nose that made his face seem one large smile. 'We'll hunt and amuse ourselves while we see which way the wind blows.'

'Perhaps,' Henry said. He liked Vernon on the upper reaches of the Seine, some twenty miles on the Norman side of Mantes, yet he sensed this was not the time to be away from the heart of the duchy. 'I think I must go to Rouen.' He would not hurry, he thought, he would let Robert get there first and take his inheritance and then he would see what sort of a reception he would get.

When Richard had gone, closing the door behind him, he began to pace up and down the little room. Since he was sixteen he had been aware of his body and its needs and knew that the austerities of his father were not for him. But neither was the lust of men like Bellême and William of Breteuil. He scorned to take for mere lust or revenge which seemed to him to make one less than a man.

Had he been a fool to speak as he had done to Alide? He had asked her to be wanton—no, not wanton but compassionate. Yet would she come? He did not know. Women could be capricious and she might stay away to make him see that even a Prince of Normandy could not have all he commanded, though he had commanded nothing of her. He felt hot at the thought. He did not want to go out and seek his pleasure in one of the houses which did exist despite his father's ban—a cheap whore would not comfort him after today's ordeal. He did not want any woman, only this particular one.

And then, as he paced, there was a tap at the door and she

stood there, her face a pale blur in the darkness, a long mantle covering her white chemise.

He drew her in and stood, his hands on her shoulders, looking at her. Then he said, 'I think I am abusing your father's hospitality.'

She smiled, her lips curving in a manner that enchanted him. 'As to that I am a widow and no virgin awaiting marriage. My father knows I go my own way, and—I need not have come if I had not wished it.'

'That is true,' he said and in that moment felt the burden, the horror of the day receding. He took her hands in his. Her hair was unbound now and lying in a dark chestnut mass on her shoulders. He unfastened her mantle and let it fall, setting his fingers in her hair.

'You are beautiful, Alide,' he said unsteadily. 'Your husband was fortunate to have enjoyed such beauty.'

'I think he was more interested in his books,' she said briefly. 'I bore him a child but it was a girl and it died and then he died and I feel as if none of it had happened.'

He held her head between his hands, looking into her face, into the calm eyes, and with a leap of the heart he thought— the man never touched her, never awakened her into love, despite the years of marriage he gave her nothing. It mattered, suddenly, that it was he who should do this for her. He kissed her slowly and then with gathering intensity until he felt her mouth respond to his. Then he drew off her chemise, and carried her to the bed.

When he lay beside her he saw that her body was as beautiful as her face, and as he touched her breasts, her thighs, her legs in homage to that beauty, he wondered at the strangeness of circumstances that had brought them to this shared bed on this night. He began to make love to her, drawing from her an ardour that he sensed was wholly new to her, so that her ecstasy matched his own; and when it was over and they lay quiet, close in each other's arms, it was she who soothed him, who whispered endearments and drove out the fear of evil dreams.

Lying on his back, his arm under her shoulders, he said, 'I do not think I shall want our ways to part tomorrow.'

Quietly she asked, 'Yet how should they go together?'

'How does not matter. Do not tell me you do not feel what I felt the moment you came down the hall to me?'

She laid her hand on his chest where the dark hair grew thick. She thought he seemed older, more mature than his years—at first she had deemed him a boy, but not now. 'If I denied it you would not believe me. I was never a good liar.'

'Your eyes are too honest,' he said smiling and leaned over her to kiss first one and then the other, and when at last he fell asleep it was as he had wished, with his head between her breasts.

It was not until the following morning that he remembered the unknown knight, Herluin, and he sent Hamo to make enquiries. While the lad was gone, he went to Thurstin and told him he wished to take Alide for his mistress.

'I want her with me,' he said without dissembling, 'I want her to come to Rouen with me now and I promise you she shall need for nothing.'

Thurstin, a phlegmatic man, considered this for a moment. 'What does the wench say?'

'She wishes it too, but she hesitates to leave you.'

'As to that there are serving women enough to see to my needs.' The merchant scratched his chin. 'You don't waste time, my lord Henry. Well, I suppose she will do what she wants. It's many a year since she heeded me for all I'm her father.'

He did not seem unduly put out but more flattered by the honour paid his daughter. To be mistress of a Prince of Normandy and England and not just for a passing night was something many women would envy and few would sneer at. He sat talking amiably to his royal guest while Alide packed her belongings—to him the young man seemed cheerful and sensible with a lusty body and a strong arm and he had no doubt that his daughter would emerge well enough from the relationship however long or short a time it lasted. In the meantime he had his business to run and more on his mind than the whim of a woman, and he would find no shame in boasting to his neighbours of his connection with Prince Henry.

Presently Hamo returned with a stranger and as Henry turned to greet him he gave a start of astonishment.

'I know you,' he exclaimed. 'You are the knight who gave me a horse at Mantes.'

The knight bowed. He had a long, grave face and thoughtful grey eyes. 'I had that honour, lord.'

'And it was you who acted so charitably to my father?'

54

'It seemed no more than the Christian thing to do. I could not see him want for the decencies accorded to the meanest serf.'

'A Christian act most others forgot that day,' Henry said cryptically. 'Well, I thank you for it. They told me you paid for embalmers and for the boat to bring my father's body down the river? You shall be repaid in full for your goodness. Your name is Herluin, I think?'

'Herluin La Barre, my lord, of Barre le Heron near Avranches. My father holds a small fief of the lord Hugh.'

Henry nodded. 'Hugh the Wolf—he has been both friend and tutor to me. You are welcome, Herluin. And I owe you a horse too, for after the fight I had no idea whose mount I had taken.'

'A gift I made willingly,' Herluin said. He had a melancholy smile. Henry indicated that he should sit beside him. 'Do you serve one of our great lords?'

Herluin shook his head. 'I have been in the service of Count Roger of Sicily for five years. I am a younger son, my lord, and must make my own way. But this last summer I had a desire to come home and in Rouen I asked for a place in your father's army when he went to fight the French. He was generous to me and that was why when he was hurt I came to St. Gervais to pray for him, and why I was there when no one else would . . .' he broke off, a faint colour tinging his cheeks. 'It was as if they had all, monks and barons alike, feared the Devil would take possession of Normandy. Perhaps it was because your father had ruled for so long, but I would not leave a bondsman thus, let alone a king. And I dare not lose a chance to . . .' he broke off abruptly and when Henry looked at him enquiringly, not understanding his words, he lowered his eyes and did not speak.

'Well, I am grateful to you,' Henry said, 'as my brother William will be when he hears of it. Where are you going now?'

Herluin shrugged. 'I do not know, my lord, but I've a fancy to stay in my own country. I would like to take service with your family.'

Henry was silent for a moment, staring thoughtfully at the stranger. Herluin was in his late twenties, thin and wiry with long legs and slender fingers that nevertheless knew how to hold the reins hard and wield a sword, and he had the weathered skin that came from years of living in the southern sunlight. Henry liked what he saw and presently said, 'You could go to Robert, my brother the Duke, who is a spendthrift and may lavish gifts on you and a give you rich entertainment, or do you fancy Red William for a lord? He is generous too when the mood is on him but he might . . .' he paused, glancing amusedly at Herluin, 'no, you are too much a man for his fondling, but he treats his fighting men well. Or will you link your fortunes to mine? I too am a younger son so they are, to say the least, uncertain.'

Herluin seemed surprised now and was silent, considering the matter in a manner that was particularly his own and which Henry would come to know. Then his odd smile came, twisting his face. 'If you will give me the horse you owe me, my lord, I will ride with you.'

Henry slapped his knee cheerfully. 'I have only a small retinue, as you will see, but I pick my men with care and you, I think, will do very well among us. Now, let us be on the road. I want to see if my brother has claimed his inheritance.'

When the Prince's men were assembled and Herluin was strapping his modest saddle bags on the horse found for him by Raoul the deer, he said to the latter, 'The Prince is generous to give me so good an animal. Is he always thus—so friendly to strangers?'

Raoul leaned against the saddle, smoothing the horse's coat, proud of its silkiness, his rugged face expressionless. 'Aye, he's seldom put out. For all he's young he knows what men need in a lord. If he likes a man he does not care how low his birth may be.'

Herluin turned to look at the doorway of the house where Henry stood pulling on his gloves. Alide was beside him, wrapped in a long blue cloak and when a man-at-arms led up a horse he lifted her into the saddle.

Herluin said in surprise, 'I did not know the Prince had a lady?'

'No more did any of us.' Raoul cocked an eyebrow and grinned at Hamo who had joined them, his honest face unable to hide his surprise. 'He has had many a wench for a night but this is something new. God knows what chase we shall be on now.'

'Is it marriage?' Hamo asked.

Raoul shook his head, glancing at his lord, his eyes narrowed. 'I doubt it.' Gulfer had joined them, carrying in one hand a pole with cross-bars on which were tied his lord's peregrine and two hawks. Overhearing the last words he said laconically, 'Raoul is right. Our Henry won't be swept away by a pretty face for all he's still a lad.'

'I don't see how you can know,' Hamo objected. 'She is very beautiful.'

'Oh aye,' the deer agreed, 'but a man who may be King one day must look for more than beauty in his bride.'

'A King?' Herluin queried, smiling a little.

'So his father prophesied,' Raoul said and closed his mouth on further conversation.

The great hall at Rouen was crowded at the dinner hour, the trestles packed close together, men on the lower benches jostling each other for room. Servants hurried back and forth bearing great silver dishes of meats and fish, trying to dodge the dogs that scurried under the tables chasing the scraps men threw away.

On the dais Robert of Normandy sat sprawled in the ducal chair, his round face flushed, smiling and gay, as he called out greetings and jests and drank from the golden cup he held in his hand. He could scarcely suppress his joy that at thirty-four his days of exile were over and his inheritance fallen into his hands at last.

He was magnificently dressed in rich blue cendal embroidered with silver, his mantle of crimson cloth edged with ermine and he wore thick gold bracelets on his solid arms. Already he was inclining to fat and the fair hair on the crown of his head was thinning but his face was handsome enough and his smile always ready to attract. The barons of Normandy who crowded to his table saw in him a lord who would be easy-going and lavish, who would entertain them richly and indulge their demands, releasing them from the iron rule of the past reign.

Already Bishop Odo was making the most of his opportunities, sitting beside his nephew and dropping words into his ear.

'It is sad, nephew,' Odo said smoothly, 'that one who promises to be so great a ruler should have only half my brother's realm.'

Robert paused with his cup half way to his lips, uncertain exactly what his silken-tongued uncle was insinuating. 'You surely do not mean . . .'

'Rufus?' Odo snorted. 'Most certainly not. It is you who are the eldest and to my mind you should have had the crown as well as the coronet.'

The Duke put down the cup and tilted his head proudly. 'Why, so I think, but brother William made haste to take it before I'd set foot on my own soil.'

'Kings can be unmade.'

Robert slewed round in his chair so that he startled the hooded falcon on the stand beside him. With one finger he soothed the ruffled feathers while keeping his eyes on his uncle's face. 'What is on your mind?'

'Only that there are many of us here, and in England too, who do not like to see England and Normandy split under two rulers. Your father held both and I told him it would be a mistake to divide the realm. We would see it continue as before.'

Robert's fair face was flushed now. 'You—you think I could oust Red William?'

Odo inclined his head, his black eyes snapping with eagerness as they always did when he had his own interests at heart. He saw himself as the adviser of this easily cozened young man, the virtual ruler of two great countries and he moistened his thin lips in anticipation of this prospect.

'Who would stand for me?' the Duke asked.

'My brother Mortain, he has already left for England to sound out some of the barons—Grandmesnil, De Toeni, I think, and Montgomery certainly and his son, our Count of Bellême here.'

Robert glanced along the table. He did not like any member of the Talvas family, his namesake least of all, but Roger Montgomery, Earl of Shrewsbury, was the largest landowner in both countries and a powerful baron whose help he would need.

'De Warenne,' Odo was continuing, 'Gilbert de L'Aigle perhaps, William of Breteuil, and many others.'

'You tempt me, uncle.'

Odo leaned forward. 'The wealth of England is almost without end—you would be the richest man in Europe. Why, the gold and silver in the treasury at Winchester is beyond counting, though I've no doubt my miserly brother knew exactly how many pieces each chest contained.'

Robert licked his lips, his fingers playing with the jesses on his hawk's fierce talons. He drank deeply. 'And what of my suzerain, Philip? Would he aid me?'

'It is hardly the King of France's affair,' the Bishop answered loftily, 'but we need his agreement that he will safeguard your borders while you are in England.'

Robert hesitated. 'You think I should lead an army there as my father did? Would it not be better if the barons rose and proclaimed me so that I had the right before setting foot on English soil?'

'Your presence would be vital.'

'I must think about it.' The Duke glanced round, aware that they had talked too long in low voices. 'We will discuss it again later.' But his flushed cheeks, the light in his pale eyes, the twitching fingers told Odo all he needed to know and he leaned back in his chair, a smile of satisfaction on his dark face.

It was shortly after this that the doors at the far end of the hall opened and one of the Duke's ushers called in a ringing tone, 'Prince Henry craves audience of his brother, the Duke of Normandy.'

Robert sprang up. 'Bid him enter,' and he left his place and went down the hall, both hands held out.

Henry found himself clasped in a great hug, kissed soundly on both cheeks and then held at arm's length.

'Well,' Robert said, smiling, 'my little brother Henry Beauclerc that I left behind has gone! Here indeed is a man.'

Henry laughed. 'It is five years and more, Robert. Holy Face, you are broader than I remember.'

The Duke patted his stomach ruefully. 'God knows why, for I hunt every day.' He flung an arm about his young brother. 'It is good to have you here. We'll go hawking in Roumaire tomorrow and do the things we planned together so long ago. Now I am Duke you shall be at my side and we will live rich, you and I.' He swept Henry down the hall to a seat by the ducal chair and plied him with food and drink.

'Have you news from England?' Henry asked, his mouth full of roasted swan's meat. He saw his sister Adeliza smiling at him and waved his hand to her.

'A messenger came yesterday. Our brother was crowned a week since, Lanfranc saw to that. It seems the people have accepted him as their lord and the country is quiet.'

Henry shrugged. 'What rival did he have? There's no Saxon left but Edgar Atheling, and for all he's old Edmund Ironside's grandson his arrow was shot long ago.'

'True, though there are some who think . . .' Robert encountered a sharp glance from his uncle and broke off immediately. 'Well, we'll leave Rufus to deal with that part of our father's legacy and enjoy ourselves here, eh?'

He poured more wine for Henry and watched the tumblers performing in the open space between his high table and the great log fire in the centre of the hall. They somersaulted, walked on their hands, climbed on each other's shoulders, fell in heaps on the floor to spring up again and send the hall into shouts of laughter at their antics until, exhausted, they bowed before the Duke and he threw them a shower of coins. Then a minstrel sang a plaintive love song and he too received more than his due.

Rollo, the court jester, leapt before the Duke, shaking his bauble and giving a comical grimace when it made no sound.

'By Our Lady, it is empty—as empty as your grace's treasury will be if you throw so much money to us poor fools. Will you give me the price of a few dried peas for my bauble, lord of Normandy, or . . .' his wicked eye glanced at the dignified figure of the bishop, 'or will your noble uncle reprove you? "Fie, nephew," he will say, "I've not yet set my own fingers dabbling in your treasure." '

There was a roar of laughter at this, though the Bishop's face was dark with anger and he aimed a blow at the jester who ducked and crossed to Henry's side.

'Why, here's our little clerk who's too clever for most of us. Will your wit protect me, brother Henry, for I've none myself.'

'You are rightly called fool,' Henry said good-humouredly, and from his own purse took a coin for the impudent fellow. It struck him at once how the atmosphere of the court had changed even in this short time from the decorous formality of the Conqueror's table. At one point there was a quarrel, a scuffle and some blood-letting at one of the lower trestles which William would never have tolerated. He said as much to his sister when she sat by the fire afterwards with Robert de Beaumont and her ladies.

'Perhaps,' Adeliza said. 'When Robert ceases to give away his patrimony with such speed it will be better for everyone.' She glanced across at her eldest brother who was surrounded now by a crowd of eager young men. 'To give too much too quickly is to set men at odds with each other.'

Henry saw a swift frown cross Count de Meulan's face. 'Does that apply to you, Robert? I hear that the Duke has given your holding of Ivry to William of Breteuil. Are you at odds then with him?'

De Beaumont shrugged, an unwilling smile crossing his face. 'Your brother has given me Brionne in exchange, so I am at odds with naught tonight except a venison pasty that sits too heavily on my stomach.'

Henry laughed, but after a moment he pursued his first thought. 'Our father would never have suffered such disorder in the hall.'

'I think,' Adeliza said, 'it was because he was husband and father and had a greater sense of his responsibilities.'

Her brother sat down astride a stool and bent down to caress the head of a great dog who slept at her feet, nose to the warmth of the fire. 'We're a strange family,' he said. 'Eight of us our lord begat and yet we've done little about the next generation. I suppose Robert has been in no position to attract a high-born wife and Rufus has no desire to—as for me I've time yet, but there's Constance in Brittany, childless, Agatha dead because she would wed none but Earl Harold and he spurned her. Cecily has taken holy vows and only Adela in Blois has borne children to her lord.' He glanced at Adeliza. She was the most beautiful of his sisters, her complexion without flaw, her figure perfect, her movements graceful. 'What of you?' he asked. 'Robert will be looking for a noble husband for you.'

She shook her head, smiling. 'I do not want to marry, but neither do I want to be a nun like Cecily, so I am going to live as a guest at the convent at St. Leger de Preaux.'

He raised his eyebrows. 'What does Robert say to that? You could make an advantageous match for him.'

'He has given his permission.'

He can refuse no one anything, Henry thought with sudden scorn, and wondered at his brother's lack of foresight.

'What will you do then?' he asked.

'Oh, I shall care for the poor and the sick. Did you hear that Earl Harold's sister Gunhilde died a few weeks ago in Bruges? She had lived thus for many years, caring for others.'

Henry put up a hand to touch her cheek. She had long plaits, their fairness inherited from her mother, and he let his hand slide down one.

'What a pity to waste so much beauty.'

De Beaumont said, 'She will gain a greater beauty in the eyes of God for what she is doing.'

'I shall be under the guardianship of the Count here,' Adeliza explained, 'and I promise you, brother, I shall be safe and happy. Come and see me sometimes.'

He promised readily and the next day saw her ride away. If he had been Duke, he thought, he would have found her a man who would have turned her thoughts another way, to pleasures she had not dreamed of, and filled her lap with a brood of beautiful children.

He found a small house in the town for Alide to lodge in and stayed a month with Robert at the court. They hunted together in the royal forest of Roumaire, and in the saddle Robert was a different man from the plump, lazy, easy-going head of the royal table. He was a brilliant horseman, swift and energetic, and he could hold the wildest horse in the stables; even Henry, fifteen years his junior, found it hard to keep up with him. But once the hunt was over it was Bishop Odo who claimed Robert's attention. They were often closeted together, now and again calling important barons to them, and Henry grew certain that they plotted something. He had one or two clashes with his uncle and at length, tired of Odo's interference, begged Robert's permission to accept Richard de Redvers' invitation to visit Vernon.

With Alide, Herluin and the rest of his men in attendance, he left the court and spent the whole of November in the homely wooden castle on the banks of the Seine. He and Richard hawked and hunted each day; he found a palfrey for Alide and a gentle merlin to sit on her wrist instead of the fierce falcon that clung to his own gloved hand. After the long days out in the woods they lay together at night, their joy in each other growing with the knowledge of what gave pleasure to the other.

Men who sought a night's hospitality or a chapman travelling with his wares brought desultory news to Vernon. Odo, they said, had been reinstated as Earl of Kent and had gone to England with Robert of Bellême—to try to get Rufus under his sway, Henry thought—and the new Duke continued to dispense lavish hospitality and to give to any baron whatever he chose to ask.

Then, a few weeks before Christmas, a young knight of Eu came with a message from the Duke for his brother. Henry listened with growing amusement for Robert it seemed had temporarily exhausted his father's vast hoard and asked his brother for a loan from the silver that had been his inheritance.

With a grim smile on his face he surveyed the envoy. 'Am I a Jew to lend money? My brother offers no security—tell him my answer is no.'

The young man looked acutely embarrassed and departed, but a week later he was back.

'My lord, his grace bids me say he will offer you land in exchange for the money.' He saw the sudden gleam in the Prince's eye and went on, 'If you will come to Rouen an agreement can be drawn up—he suggests a part of the Côtentin.'

Henry listened to this speech in silence, without any outward sign of the sudden intense attention it raised. Presently he sent the envoy back to Robert and ran up the spiral stair to the tower room he shared with Alide.

She was seated by the fire, a piece of embroidery in her hand and he knelt beside her, freeing her fingers from the silks and holding them in his own.

'At last,' he said and was surprised to find his voice less steady than usual, 'at last I am to have something of my own.'

'My love,' she touched his cheek, looking down into his eager face, 'you have always had something that is your own.'

'Why, what have I had?' he asked in surprise.

'What it was that made me leave my father's house, that made Herluin give you his sword, and Richard his friendship.'

'You are talking in riddles.' He kissed her fleetingly. 'I cannot stop to play at guessing now, so pack your chests, my heart. We go back to Rouen.'

'You drive a close bargain,' Robert Curthose said ruefully the next evening. 'It seems my little brother has a hard head on his shoulders.'

They stood facing each other in the Duke's solar, alone except for a clerk who waited, quill in hand, to set down the arrangement on the blank parchment before him. Henry had a sudden memory of this room as it had been in his father's day and he had been summoned here to answer for some misdemeanour.

'Three thousand pounds is a great deal of money,' he said

plainly, 'and if you want it you must give me what I want—all the Côtentin, the castles of Avranches and Coutances and Mont St. Michel.' It was almost a third of the duchy but he saw it as a chance not to be missed and watched his brother pacing up and down, uncertain, torn between possessiveness and the need caused by his extravagances.

At last after a few more grumbles the Duke said, 'So be it,' and told the clerk to write.

So Henry set his hands between his brother's, paying him homage for the land, and then took his little company westward; de Redvers came with them and Ralph de Toeni whose father was in England, and they spent the Christmas feast at Avranches in the fine stone castle built by Hugh the Wolf, Earl of Chester, in whose lordship it was.

And for the first time, as Count of the Côtentin, the Prince sat in the high seat at the centre of his own board, dispensing his own hospitality to his friends. In the weeks that followed he rode from one end to the other of his new property, holding courts and listening patiently to men's complaints giving justice as impartially as he could and favouring none. He began to love this western part of Normandy, from the thick northern forests of Valognes where bears and wild boars flourished, to the wild sea coast, the sand dunes and pines, and the rocky island of Mont St. Michel, the rock of the Archangel, crowned by its great church and monastery. He rode over the causeway and stayed two nights there making sure it was in a defensible state.

Wherever he rode now Herluin La Barre rode beside him, seeing that everything was prepared for him, acting as his lord's steward, and their friendship grew, an odd friendship for in many ways Herluin was the reverse of his master—reserved, inclined to gravity, more devout than most in that he lingered in church after Mass, when Henry was on his feet and away to hunt or ride to some part of his county before the last blessing was pronounced. Imperceptibly Herluin became the first among Henry's knights and was seldom far from his side.

The elder Herluin, a busy little man, came from Barre le Heron to pay his respects to the new Count and was delighted at the favour shown his son—he had a large family to provide for and Herluin, he thought, might help one or other to progress in the world, but he soon learned that Herluin would ask no *douceur* from the Prince, and he returned home, grumbling to his second wife, Herluin's stepmother, that his son's head had been thoroughly turned, even though he knew it was not true.

One afternoon in April, listening to the Prince dealing with a vavassour who had a complaint against his neighbour, De Redvers said to Ralph, 'Already he is getting a name for fair dealing. Did you think six months ago when the old King died that we would be sitting here thus?'

'Not I,' Ralph agreed. He was astride a bench at the far end of the hall where they were out of earshot of the little court. 'But will the Duke stick to his bargain? I hear he regrets already the revenue he has lost, for he has nearly spent the money Henry paid him.'

'Holy Cross, what does he do with it? He is shiftless we all know, but I did not think him dishonest.'

'He will do what Odo says,' Ralph remarked, 'so I suppose we should thank God the Bishop is in England.'

Richard laughed. 'I doubt if King William shares your view. The latest news is that many of the great Norman lords, Montgomery and his sons, Grandmesnil, and Odo himself, refused to attend the King's Easter feast.'

Ralph sat up straight. 'Oh? That is near treason.'

'I know. It seems that rebellion is brewing in England.'

'God's teeth, what are they after?'

'How should I know?' Richard was frowning now. 'But I thought, didn't you, that Odo was planning something with the Duke in the autumn before he left. Perhaps they want to unseat Rufus and give the crown to Robert.'

Ralph stirred uneasily. 'My father is in England. If it is a question of taking sides which one will he take? But I don't like it—brother against brother. It is not right.'

'Maybe not, but did you not see it was inevitable from the moment the old King died?'

'No,' Ralph answered honestly. 'Perhaps I've a dull wit but . . .'

'Of course you have,' Richard told him drily. 'Rufus wants Normandy as well, and Robert wants England. Neither will be satisfied with things as they are.'

'And Henry?'

De Redvers glanced down the hall to where, in his high seat beneath an arras of crimson cloth, the Prince sat talking earnestly to the two men whose quarrel he must settle. 'Henry, if he is wise, will bide his time.'

But the kind of wisdom Richard of Redvers wanted for him was not the wisdom of nineteen.

After Easter news came that rebellion had broken out, that half the great lords in England had come out openly in favour of Robert Curthose and awaited impatiently his arrival on English soil. He did indeed send troops to Odo's town of Dover but continued to lounge in his hall at Rouen, promising to come when his uncles had done their work.

'What a fool he is,' Henry said derisively. 'At least if I had put my hand to such an enterprise I'd not have left it to others to carry through.'

To everyone's surprise the English rallied round their King. For all he was a Norman he was their anointed King and when he called them to his banner, proclaiming that any man who did not come would go by the odious name of 'nithing', men flocked to fight for him, seeing in him one who would support them against the Norman overlords they hated. In an astonishingly short time he had reduced the rebellion to two small outposts. The saintly old Bishop Wulfstan of Worcester had quelled the rising in the west and in the east Odo was forced to surrender Rochester. Taken to Robert of Mortain's stronghold at Pevensey he had begged to be allowed to go into the castle in order to persuade his brother to surrender, but once there broke his word, rejoined the rebels and refused to come out. And there he and they were still, besieged by Rufus and his English soldiers, with no hope of victory.

'I am for England,' Henry said gleefully when he heard this news. 'I would see Odo brought low, the lying treacherous dog. By God, my father had his measure after all!'

He left his garrisons secure, said farewell to Richard and to Ralph at Falaise and turned north to Caen with Alide. She was pregnant now and he thought she would be better in her father's house during his absence. That night he lay with her in the little guest chamber where they had first become lovers. She was calm outwardly but he sensed an underlying tenseness.

'You need not fear for me,' he said softly. 'I am not going to embroil myself in this quarrel. Let my brothers fight it out between them—only Robert is too lazy to raise his own standard. But I want Rufus to see I have not taken sides—and as I want my mother's lands in England this seems a good time to ask for them. Then I shall begin to have a fair inheritance.'

'You are ambitious, my lord.' It was dark in the bed with the curtains drawn and she wished she could see his face. 'And I think your ambition will take you from me.'

He kissed her hair lightly. 'Now why should it do so when,' he laid his hand on her swollen body, 'when you are to bear me a son, please God? We knew, did we not, from the beginning how it would be with us?'

'Yes,' she said very low. 'I had no designs to be other than your mistress. I know that one day you must marry—a politic marriage—but I shall not mind if my womanhood has been crowned by bearing you a son.'

He folded her in his arms. 'I am not thinking of marriage yet. And all I want is to lie by your side at night and find peace in your arms.'

'Then that is what I want,' she said.

But when she slept, he lay awake and pondered on the truth of her words. He knew he had become the heart and centre of her life, but for himself his horizons were growing daily wider like those of the sea he would cross tomorrow if the wind was favourable.

4

Bishop Odo hated indignity as he hated little else and to be made to sit thus on his own travelling chest on the shingle at Dover was to him the culmination of a week of shame and insults. From the moment when he and Mortain had surrendered at Pevensey and his nephew Rufus had refused to accord him the honours of war so that he might emerge with banners flying and trumpets sounding, he had lived every moment in shame and fury. They had been forced to leave Pevensey without trumpets, with their standards lowered and gonfanons pointing to the ground and the common English soldiers, whom he loathed, shouting and jeering at him.

'Bring halters,' they had cried, 'hang the traitor Bishop!' so that he had thought to die.

And there was his nephew Rufus, a great grin on his red face, enjoying every moment of his uncle's discomfiture. Now he was deprived of his earldom once again and banished from England, though Mortain and the rest were busy making their peace with the King. They had even taken away his renowned mace, 'the skull-smasher', which he had always carried into battle because no priest might shed blood.

He sat, deep in his rage, humiliated beyond bearing, staring at the ship drawing ever nearer, a ship from Normandy that was to bear him back to his native land, and as the tide brought it in, the shingle drawing noisily under the hull, he was glad he would soon be away from these mocking guards, to shake the dust of England from his feet.

But the fates that make sport of men had not done with him yet, for after the sailors had made the ship fast, the first man ashore and walking up the little wooden wharf was his nephew Henry, followed by some half dozen attendants.

The Prince stopped dead in his tracks when he saw his uncle. His eyes swept over the disconsolate Bishop sitting with his robes drawn about his knees, the piled up baggage, the lack of retinue.

'What is this? My uncle, you look like a poor pedlar waiting to take his wares outremer.'

The knight in charge of the guard, one Roger de Marmion, said stiffly, 'His grace of Bayeux is banished the country, my lord Henry. He is to leave aboard the ship that brought you here.'

And suddenly the sight of Odo, the proud and haughty uncle brought so low as to be sitting on a travelling chest on the beach, waiting to be shipped off like useless baggage, was too much for Henry. He began to laugh, hands on hips, and he laughed until the tears came.

Odo's face went a dusky red and his mouth trembled with fury so that he could scarcely speak. 'By the living God, nephew, such behaviour becomes you ill. Be silent, I command you.'

'You can command nothing here, it seems,' Henry was endeavouring to control his mirth, 'certainly not me. If you could but see yourself . . .'

All the men about him were smiling now, and to Odo that laughter was the last and final straw. He shook with rage, hands clenched, and swore to be avenged, his thin body wracked with the intensity of his emotion.

De Marmion said stiffly, 'My lord, I beg you—I must take the Bishop aboard.'

Henry wiped his sleeve across his eyes and nodded to the knight. 'You are going aboard now? The wind is south-westerly.'

'I know, lord, but I have orders that his grace is to be conveyed to the ship at once and to be kept there until the wind changes.'

'So my brother wants you off English soil with all haste,' Henry turned to glance again at his uncle. 'You have used him ill, my lord.' He looked up at the clear, warm June sky. 'I fear you may have many uncomfortable days before the wind changes. The weather is set fair, I think.'

Odo rose with all the dignity he could muster. 'I can well do without your comments, nephew.' He turned his back on the Prince and stalked away along the wharf followed by his guards.

'I have little liking for this task,' de Marmion said in a low

voice. 'I pray the wind will soon change and he will be gone.'
He was a tall young man, son of Robert de Marmion who had
been one of the Conqueror's companions at the time of Senlac.
He held the honour of Scrivelsby in the county of Lincolnshire and his son was already high in Rufus' favour.

'God speed you in your task,' Henry said amusedly, and as
the young man walked away after his prisoner, Herluin watched
him go through narrowed eyes.

Then he said, 'My lord, I fear you have offended your uncle
deeply. He will not forget.'

'I care not. He will not raise his head again.'

'Not here perhaps, but in Normandy he is still Bishop of
Bayeux, and deep in the Duke's confidence. You are Count of
the Côtentin and must be much in Normandy, therefore it
seems to me you have made not one enemy but two.'

'May be,' Henry said non-committally, 'but . . .' he turned to
look at the blue sparkling sea, the brilliant sunshine on the
water, the sailors busy on the ship, 'I doubt my uncle can turn
Robert against me.' He laughed and set his hand on Herluin's
shoulder. 'And I am too much my father's cub to care for any
man's spite. Come, let us go and see what kind of a king Rufus
is making of himself.'

He recounted the scene on the beach three days later at Winchester where the court was in residence.

The King sat in his chair listening a sardonic gleam of
humour on his ruddy face. 'He will not set foot in England
again. By the Mass, was there ever a worse traitor? As for his
brother bishop, William of Durham, I will bring him to trial
for his treachery.'

'What of the rest?' Henry glanced round the crowded hall.
'I see Montgomery and the Count of Bellême, and our uncle of
Mortain.'

'They have made their peace with me.' Rufus gave a quick
harsh laugh. 'They have learned, little brother, that I've enough
of our father in me to be a match for all of them together.'

Henry was silent for a moment, recalling his own words to
Herluin, using almost the same phrase. Had they all too much
of their father's blood for there to be peace between them?

'My subjects are of a mind with me,' Rufus was continuing,
'and that took the wind out of Odo's sails.'

'So I heard. Well, Ralph will be glad his father is not in one of your donjons.'

'The rebels have paid for their freedom.' Ranulf Flambard spoke from his place by the King's chair. He was even more lavishly dressed, his manner more arrogant, and as usual his mother was seated not far from him. She was small and bent and had lost one eye, so that men said she was on nodding terms with the devil. Henry thought she was evil and was surprised at Rufus tolerating her at his table, but Rufus it seemed was well-served by his chaplain, who was pointing out that his master gained more from the rebels' money than he would by their absence.

Walter Tirel, lord of Poix, and a close companion of the King, nodded, 'My good lord will have no more trouble in that direction. What is the news from Normandy, Count Henry?'

He told them of Robert's extravagance, of the squabbling of the barons, the feuds and sieges that disturbed the country, and while he spoke, the King's frown grew. But at the end of the tale he merely compressed his lips tightly and spoke of something else.

Their cousin Judith's daughter, Maud, was to be married to Simon of Senlis in two days' time and though Bishop Walkelin of Winchester was to perform the ceremony the Archbishop of Canterbury would preach the nuptial sermon. He was expected to arrive on the morrow, and if there was one man in England Henry wanted to see it was Lanfranc.

In the meantime he relaxed, enjoying Rufus' table; the food was richer than in his father's time and he ate well of the different sorts of meats, finishing the meal with a pasty of spices and honey and almonds and some sweetmeats of marchpane that were always to his taste—but like his father he drank sparingly, despising drunkenness and considering wine something to be savoured in small quantities. He sat beside the chancellor, Robert Bloet, whom he had not seen since the latter left the old King's sickbed with Rufus and he told him of the strange burial that had followed, and the fire and the man Ascelin, and he saw that Bloet was troubled.

But on his other side sat his old companion Eudo Dapifer who kept him entertained with stories of the court and it was from Eudo that he began to form a picture of his brother as a King.

Presently he went to greet his cousin Judith, daughter of the old King's sister and half-sister to Stephen of Aumale. She was a dark slender woman, still with that beauty which had long ago turned the English Earl Waltheof's head, but her expression was melancholy, her conversation inclined to be bitter, and Henry had heard that her remorse after her husband's death had been so great that she had built and endowed a convent for nuns at Elstow near Bedford, spending much of her time there in acts of penance. The Conqueror had wanted her to marry Simon herself but she had disdainfully refused him and in annoyance William had given Waltheof's earldom of Northampton to Simon and Maud for his bride into the bargain.

Henry wondered how Judith felt about this. 'I am glad to be here for Maud's nuptials,' he began. 'Does the match please you?' But if he had expected to get any sort of illuminating answer from Judith he was mistaken.

'It was your father's command,' she said coolly.

'And Maud? Is she content with her bridegroom?'

Judith shrugged. 'She has not complained, and seeing Simon has her inheritance already, that is just as well.'

Henry sat looking at his cousin. Dinner was over, few people were left in the hall now, and none to overhear. 'You wed for love, I believe. Is that so bad a thing?'

Her dark eyes flashed suddenly, as if he had trodden on dangerous ground, but were almost immediately veiled and he thought she was not going to answer. However after a moment she turned to look at him.

'You must know what happened or you would not have asked such a question—and knowing, you should not have asked it.'

'I beg your pardon, cousin,' he said awkwardly. She made him feel a beardless boy. 'But I hope Maud will find joy in her marriage bed.'

Judith inclined her head and stared down at her hands folded in her lap. 'That I had once.' She seemed to be speaking to herself, and not knowing what to say he asked if he might greet his cousin Maud.

He found her walking with her young sister Alice and two of Judith's ladies on the grass below the great hall of the castle, and at once she ran to him, her hands held out, despite the admonition of one of the women.

'Cousin Henry! Oh, I am so glad to see you and so glad you have come for my bridal.'

She had laughing blue eyes, pale blonde hair and a bloom of heal:h in her cheeks. He kissed her soundly on the mouth and then stood for a moment, holding her at arms' length.

'You grow more lovely every time I see you—and Alice too. You will soon be a woman, little cousin.'

Alice was slighter and darker than her sister, favouring their mother's looks, and she bobbed a curtsey to the Prince. 'I am betrothed too,' she told him proudly. 'Did you not know?'

'No,' he said in surprise. 'Who is to be your bridegroom?'

'Your friend, Ralph de Toeni,' Maud put in. 'It was arranged between the King and the lord of Conches this week.'

'Well, it was part of the King's peace-making, no doubt. Ralph knows naught of it yet, but,' he glanced again at Alice, 'he is a good fellow and I wish you joy, child. You will do well enough with him.'

'I hope so,' Alice answered gravely, 'but of course we will not be wed until I am of marriageable age. I am but thirteen at the moment.'

Maud and Henry laughed, and Maud added, 'Off with you, sister. Play at ball for a while—I want to talk to our cousin.'

Despite the reproving glances of her women, she sent them off with Alice and walked aside with Henry.

'Is there something amiss?' he asked. 'Are you not happy in this marriage?'

'Simon is a good man—a little dull, but good.' Maud sat down upon a bench and he sat beside her. 'He will not ill-treat me, nor is he cruel and lustful like the Lord of Bellême or Ivo of Taillebois, so I suppose I should be grateful. No, I am not unhappy, but I wanted to tell someone, and perhaps you will understand, that I am sad because my father is not here to give me in marriage. The King will do that office on Thursday, but I wish . . .' she broke off.

'I did not know you remembered your father.' He took her hand and held it in his. She was wearing a blue gown and he thought how well it became her.

'I loved him too well to forget him,' she said sadly. 'They tried to hide the truth from me, but for all I was not six years old I knew what had happened. Did you know that at home they call him a saint? His old friend, the Chamberlain Richard de Rules

—you remember him—built a shrine for his burial place and men come from all parts to Croyland to pray at his tomb.'

'So I heard,' he nodded. He remembered too hearing that relations between Maud and her mother had never been good and it seemed to him that marriage would release her from a daily contact that was irksome. 'You must be happy on your marriage day, your father would wish it. And,' he began to swing her hand to and fro, 'I swear that if we were not cousins I would ask for you myself, for, by all the saints, your beauty would turn any man's head.'

She laughed delightedly, her sadness banished. 'If you were not my cousin, I would accept. But what of yourself? You must certainly marry a princess.'

'I? Where can you find me one? The King of France has a daughter, but she's a mere child and who would want Philip for a father-in-law? I've no fancy for a girl from the north countries, they're barely civilised. There are the Spaniards, of course, but they say the Princess Uracca lives too close to her own brother . . .'

Maud was pondering the matter. 'The King of Scots has two daughters and they are Edmund Ironside's great-grandchildren, for their mother is Edgar Atheling's sister; either of them would be very acceptable.'

He was still laughing. 'I suppose so. Will you arrange it for me? Unless they are both so plain that I would not enjoy my marriage bed.'

She shook her free hand at him. 'Now you are teasing me. Well, we shall see.' She leaned forward and kissed his cheek. 'I am so glad you are here. To tell you the truth, I am a little afraid of your brother.'

'Some may need to fear him,' he said drily, 'but not you.' And as they began to walk back towards the castle, he added, 'When you are bedded, you can forget all the rest of us.'

'Except you. You will come and see me at Northampton, won't you?'

Which promise he gave and led her back to her companions.

The next day he was by the window of a turret stair when he saw a cavalcade ride in from the east, a procession of hooded monks and men-at-arms, priests and servants, and at once he ran down to the courtyard to greet its leader.

The Archbishop was in his eighties now, thin and wrinkled,

his high domed forehead creased, his head bald, but his blue eyes, bloodshot from overwork though they were, still looked keenly down at the Prince kneeling meekly before him.

'My son,' he raised his hand in blessing. 'This is a pleasure I had not looked for. Come and talk with me this evening.'

And when he did, in Lanfranc's bedchamber, it seemed to Henry that he was a boy again, learning his lessons from the cleverest man in Europe. He thought of the hours they had spent together, the serious study of the early fathers, lightened by occasional readings from Nennius' tales of King Arthur, his boyish imagination lit more by hero-worship of that chivalrous king, than by the blood-curdling stories of the early martyrs in the circus at Rome. He talked now of his own hopes, of his lands in Normandy and how he meant men to know him by his fair dealing.

'And I would have lands here in England. Do you think Rufus will yield me my mother's holdings?'

Lanfranc considered, fingertips together in his customary manner, for he still kept the affairs of England under his watchful eye. And Henry, who in the last twenty-four hours had been surprised at the decorum of Rufus' court, realised that it must be due to the influence of this one man.

'I can see no reason why he should not,' the Archbishop said at last. 'But choose your moment to put your request, my son. Your brother's temper can be uncertain and he is loth to give up anything he holds.'

'I know,' Henry answered, 'but neither he nor Robert can think to keep for themselves all our father left behind.'

Lanfranc pursed his lips. 'Can they not? I fear when I am gone there will be much quarrelling among you.'

Henry flung away to the window and looked out into the darkness 'By the death of Our Lord, they have enough. Would either of them care to be in my shoes?'

His old tutor looked at his back severely. 'Child, you have no cause for bitterness. You have much silver and a third part of Normandy. Now perhaps you will have lands in England—is that not enough?'

The Prince came back and sat down beside the old man. In the soft candlelight he saw how aged and tired he was. A faint smile crossed his face. 'My lord, what was ever enough for the Conqueror's brood? And for all I'm the youngest, my ambi-

75

tion matches that of my brothers. We're a sore trial to you.'

Lanfranc gave one of his rare laughs. 'You have spoken truly, my son. But you must learn to be content with what you have.'

Henry grimaced. 'I'll be content if I can keep it, but my father said,' he hesitated and then certain that his sire had had no secrets from this man he went on, 'he said more than once that I should one day have all that my brothers now hold.'

Lanfranc compressed his thin lips. 'Dangerous talk, my child. I beg you to say no such words to any but myself. Do you think to oust your brothers?'

'No—only to be sure that they will not squander my inheritance.'

'Be careful,' Lanfranc warned. 'I think your time will come but you may imperil everything if you act hastily. Wait for God's will to be done.'

Henry said nothing. It was easy, he thought, for a monk and a priest to wait upon the slow movements of Almighty God, but a fighting man and a King's son at that, must needs push forward his own designs at greater speed. But Lanfranc was right at least in bidding him pick his moment wisely and this he was prepared to do.

Rufus bade him go hawking the next morning and as they walked to the stables, their birds on their wrists, the King said suddenly, 'I've a fine collection of horses. Choose one for yourself, brother.'

Henry glanced at him in surprise. William the Red's acts of generosity were always unexpected. He thanked him and walked round the stalls looking at the large percherons, the swift coursers, the gentle mares and smaller palfreys, but stopped by a destrier that caught his fancy. The animal was reddish chestnut in colour, with fine legs and a strong body. Henry fondled the soft nose, looked at the teeth and smoothed the muscled neck.

'I like this one,' he said at last, 'and in honour of your gift and because of his colour, I shall call him Rougeroy.'

Rufus laughed, appreciating the joke, and nodded to a groom to saddle the animal. 'Very well, brother. He is yours.'

They rode together into the new forest south of the city, followed by their falconers and numerous train of knights and attendants. Gulfer brought three birds for his master, and as they rode into the wild woodland Henry saw occasional traces of broken stones where once villages had stood. Now wild willowherb and ragwort grew among them and on one occasion his peregrine brought down a pigeon in what had once been a church.

He called the peregrine back to him with his lure and fastened the bird to his wrist. 'A good quarry,' he said and gazed up into the blue sky. 'Give me the long-wings every time.'

Rufus grunted, stroking his hawk. It had evil yellow eyes and talons that dug into his wrist but he did not seem to heed. 'Sparrowhawks and goshawks are well enough for a priest or a serving fellow,' he said contemptuously. 'I would hunt with naught but the true hawk, eh, my beauty?' He spotted a bird high in the sky and sent off the hawk. She rose, seemed to hover interminably, and then swooped, bringing down her quarry in a distant patch of bushes.

Today, however, Henry was more absorbed by his new mount than by the hunt, and he tested the animal, riding him hard, demanding much. To his intense satisfaction he found the destrier responsive and obedient to his touch, but strong and swift and when he caught up with the King, he said enthusiastically, 'I've never ridden a better horse.'

'You sit him well,' Rufus said. 'Ha! What's that—there in the bushes.' He signalled to two of his men and running forward they plunged into the undergrowth. There was a scuffle and a yell and a few moments later they emerged, red-faced, and dragging behind them a serf. He was a poor creature, dressed in a rough tunic with no more than strips of cloth binding his legs, and he was trembling with terror.

'There's a dead stag in there, sire,' one of the men said. 'This fellow slew it.'

The King's face darkened with anger. He sat still, looking down at the shaking peasant. 'So you would kill the royal deer, eh?' And as the man did not answer, he shouted, 'You! Fellow! I'm speaking to you. Do you not know the law?'

The man grovelled, scared out of what wits he had, so that though he opened and shut his mouth no sound came.

Rufus regarded him with contempt. 'B-by the face of Lucca, men shall learn whose forest this is.' He beckoned to a man-at-arms. 'You have a rope on your saddle. Hang him.'

It was clear the fellow did not understand one word and

Henry repeated his brother's command in the English tongue —which Rufus had not bothered himself to learn.

The man on the ground gave one agonised cry. 'Lord—have mercy. I have a wife, children . . .'

'That oak will d-do,' the King said and watched as the soldier slung the rope over a branch.

The little group about him was silent. After a moment Tirel said, 'My lord, your father would have had the man's hand lopped off and then sent him back to his family. Surely that would be enough?'

'Ha!' Rufus swung round. 'And thus the thieving goes on. I say this man shall be an example to others who have the same idea.'

The Count of Bellême nodded, clearly relishing the business. 'But I, my lord King, would hang him by his heels with his bowels slit open that he might die more slowly. Perhaps then these savages will know who is master.' Hugh of Avranches, Earl of Chester, who had joined them, gave a bellowing laugh, 'By God, Bellême, I'm glad I'm not one of your vassals.'

Henry had sat silent through these interchanges, but now he edged his horse nearer to his brother. 'Hang him if you must,' he said in a low voice, 'But for God's sake without Bellême's devilish refinements.' He looked down at the man whose head was lolling, his eyes half out of their sockets in an extremity of fear. 'Make your peace with God, fool, for you must pay for your crime.'

The fellow reached up and clung to Henry's stirrup. 'Lord, for the love of Jesus, save me—save me . . .' He was weeping, tears running down his grimy face. 'We have always hunted here —my father and grandfather before me, and my children need food.'

'Pay no heed to the fellow, Henry,' Hugh called with the familiarity of one who had been both instructor and friend. 'Would you foster thieves and robbers at your brother's expense?' He heaved his great bulk round in the saddle, grinning cheerfully.

'Take him,' Rufus broke in, and at once two men dragged the serf away while his young brother sat stiffly, watching as they set the man on a horse and fastened the rope.

Then one of them ran the horse off and he fell. There was a choking sound as he struggled and swung to and fro, clawing wildly at the rope about his throat. Presently his hands fell and after a while the twitching stopped. He hung limp, his face distorted, his tongue protruding. At the King's command the men-at-arms decapitated the stag and tied the antlers to his legs.

Rufus turned away. 'Now others will see I will n-not brook robbery in my hunting grounds.'

Bellême laughed. 'These scum must have it beaten into them, my lord. Will you hunt some more?'

They rode away together with the Earl of Chester and Henry, with one last glance at the swinging figure, moved off more slowly with Herluin, Walter Tirel, and Eudo Dapifer.

Tirel said, 'Your father was never a hanging man except in war.' His tone was noncommittal.

Herluin was pale, his expression more melancholy than usual. 'What in God's name is justice? Will it ever be something for poor folk as well as rich.'

Henry was frowning, his whiplash between his teeth, a habit he had inherited from his sire. 'The man was guilty.'

'Aye, guilty,' Herluin agreed, 'but of no more than trying to feed his children as he had always done.'

'Treason, my friend,' Eudo answered lightly, 'if men were allowed to plunder the King's forests at will, it would be the court that would not only go hungry but lose its sport into the bargain.'

'I love the hunt as much as any man,' Herluin said with his usual candour, 'but I think it is the baser part of my nature that enjoys it when it means a serf is hanged to preserve my sport.'

Tirel was shaking his head. 'You go too deep for me. I am a plain fighting man who likes to hunt and be damned to that bondsman for his insolence.'

Henry was silent, preoccupied with the thought of justice coupled with the preservation of the rights and prerogatives of princes. It seemed to him that the two should not be incompatible. He thought of the man they had left hanging in the forest, the antlers tied to his feet to tell all men of his crime. A woman would weep tonight and children go hungry because of what had been done. This was inevitable, for surely a man must pay for what he did against the law—as they must all pay for their sins one day before God's judgement seat—but his compassion was aroused, not for this particular man above his fellows, but for the poor and the hungry and the down-trodden. God, he thought, would surely commend a man for what he could do for such as these. On an impulse he called Hamo aside and gave him a silver piece.

'Find that man's widow and give her this,' he said abruptly, and turned away from the devotion in Hamo's eyes, which he did not feel one small act of charity in any way merited.

The next day saw Maud wedded to Simon of Senlis in Winchester church with pomp and ceremony and after a day of feasting Henry was among those who escorted the bridegroom to his bridal chamber. Simon was a quiet, sensible man, no longer in his first youth and with a limp from an old wound, but he was still young enough and prepossessing enough, Henry thought, to give Maud happiness. When the two were bedded and blessed by the Archbishop he leaned over to kiss Maud and whispered, 'God send you joy this night, and a son to show for it.'

She laughed, blushing and shy, and drew up the white bearskin that covered her. 'My father was conceived beneath this skin,' she whispered, 'and so was I. Perhaps it will bring the same good fortune to me.'

Rufus took his brother by the arm. 'Come, Henry Beauclerc, there's not room for three in a bridal bed and Simon's impatient to be about his business.' He was in high good humour and led Henry out, followed by a laughing crowd of men and women.

As the company dispersed for the night it seemed as good a moment as any to speak to the King without the usual hangers-on, and Henry followed him to his chamber. Two sleepy pages awaited the King but he sent them off with a flick of his fingers and poured wine into two silver cups. Then he sat down on the bed and stretched his legs. It was a large bed, spread with a rich coverlet and hung with embroidered curtains that slid smoothly along wooden poles, and it seemed strange to Henry that his brother had no desire to share that bed with either wife or mistress.

'God's body,' Rufus said, 'but I'm weary tonight. Nothing but tedious state business all morning, attending to my lord Lanfranc who has lost none of his preoccupation with work for all his hoary years. I shall sleep sound, and swifter than our little Maud, I dare say.'

Henry drank his wine and set down the cup. 'Well I don't

suppose Simon is wasting his time and I'll not waste yours. Brother, will you give me my mother's lands?'

Red William sat up, alert again, his flecked eyes narrowing. 'Oho, so that's what you came for?'

'Not entirely. I came to see how the crown sat on your head, but our mother's English holdings were always due to me as the only one of us born here in this country.'

The King rose and began to pace up and down the chamber. It was only part bedroom for his treasure was kept here, locked in large chests that occupied half the room. His finery seemed to irk him and he threw off mantle and tunic, gold chains and arm bracelets. Then he sat down again in shirt and braces. 'I suppose it is your right. Do you intend to stay in England?'

'Only for a month or two.' An odd expression in the King's eyes and some deeper instinct warned Henry to be careful what he said, but as he was not sure why he needed to be careful he could do no other than say what was uppermost in his mind. 'I would know where I stand before I return to the Côtentin.'

Rufus got up and put a friendly arm about his shoulder. 'You stand close to me, as a brother should. Ride west tomorrow and take seizin of the land, with my goodwill.' He spoke cheerfully, candidly, and Henry took himself to task for his suspicions.

Later, in the small turret chamber allotted to him he found Herluin already asleep on a pallet at the foot of his bed and Fulcher curled up on a chest near the door. He forbore to wake them and went to stand by the narrow window, looking out at the stars in the clear night sky. It was warm and he had no desire for sleep—he was in too exultant a mood. Now he was Count of the Côtentin, and lord of all the holdings that had once belonged to Brihtric the Saxon and others, lands in Gloucester and Cornwall and in south Wales—Cardiff castle was his and other strongholds, though he held them as a vassal of the King, and it was as if he had seized and grasped that destiny of which Abbot Anselm had spoken. He was no longer the landless cub, the Prince with nothing but a hawk and a horse, and he felt power seeping through him to his very fingertips, a sense of ability, of desire for the next step and the next, a reaching out for what must follow. Life seemed to throb in him tonight, and the consciousness of power grew, yet he sensed it was a power from without rather than within, a power that seemed to envelope him and the night together in pulsating harmony. He leaned against the stone embrasure, his eyes on the immensity of the night sky.

'Lord,' he said aloud, 'if You have set Your hand on me for some great purpose it shall be done that men may see it is so.'

Herluin stirred and opened his eyes. 'Is that, you my lord?'

Henry came back into the centre of the room. 'Who else?' he asked, lightly. 'Go back to sleep, my friend.'

Undressing, he lay down on his bed. He had forgotten the man, swinging from his tree, cold in the warm night, but the thoughts that had sprung indirectly from a bondsman's death remained with him for a long while.

Count Robert of Bellême was a man of many facets. Strong and self-possessed, with a cruel lift to his mouth, he had boarded the *Lilias* with a parchment in his hand and a concentrated frown on his face. Already he had left behind him in England an impression of evil, a reputation even among unscrupulous barons for lust and cruelty above the average, but when he wanted he could exert himself to be a witty and entertaining companion, and he had chosen to do this two months previously when he had accompanied Prince Henry to the West Saxon country while on his way to his father's Welsh marches.

Now they stood together aboard the *Lilias* bound for St. Valery. A breeze blew Henry's dark hair about his face and the spray rose and fell, but he cared nothing for the heaving sea that had sent several of his men to lie where they might until they reached the solidity of land again. He held to a piece of rigging and pondered on the success of his visit to England.

Rufus had treated him handsomely, giving him gifts of clothes, a set of silver cups and two kestrel-hawks as well as Rougeroy who was held amidships now with several other horses under the soothing hands of Raoul the deer. In the west he had taken possession of his mother's lands, fair rolling country near to Gloucester, with fine manors and many hides yielding well. He had stayed two weeks in Cardiff castle, a homely wooden structure that he had ordered to be rebuilt in stone, and a smile curved his mouth as he remembered Nest, the Welsh girl he had taken to his bed while he was there. He had grown tired of his solitary nights and she had attracted him, little and dark, so small that when he held her in his arms it was like embracing a child. But there was nothing childish about her loving. Her father farmed a few virgates of land and owed boon service to him, and he had first seen her driving geese up from the river when he was inspecting every tenant's holding. He had left a purse with her father to see they did not want, for they had little enough, and he had promised her he would return. She had give him pleasure with her pert, pretty face and dainty body, but now with his face set towards Normandy and a fair wind behind him he was thinking of Alide, Alide who was warmth and comfort and peace after joy, and who might by now have borne him a son. His impatience grew to see this child of his flesh—the first of which he was, at any rate, aware.

He could have done without Bellême's company today, but the Count was holding out the parchment for him to see.

'There, my lord, that is how I would do it.'

Henry looked down at the drawing. 'It is a mangonel I see, but what is that shaft of wood there?'

'That is to change the balance and give the arm extra throwing power. I will have my men build one and if my plan is right this will give it greater lift.'

'It would be a useful siege weapon if it would pitch the stones higher. I would like to see it when it is done.'

'Come to Bellême soon, my lord, and I will give you a practical demonstration.' The Count put a hand to his eyes. 'There is our coastline. I wonder how the Duke your brother fares? He has had three months of your uncle Odo which would be enough to sour any man.'

Recent messengers from Normandy had talked of Odo as Robert's most influential counsellor now, but Henry, watching the sailors about their work, found the idea more amusing than alarming, especially when he recalled the last time he had seen his uncle.

The ship was drawing in towards the harbour in the deep water of high tide and he could see the usual number of people about, men to make the ship fast, merchants awaiting goods, others ready to embark, and at the end of the wharf a large group of men-at-arms, leaning on their spears, talking in the mild October sunshine.

He was the first ashore, followed by the Count, while their attendants prepared to land their animals and goods and they walked together, talking amiably. Immediately the captain of the men-at-arms called his troop to order and marched towards the new arrivals.

'What's this?' Henry queried amusedly, 'has Robert set a port-watch for my return?'

'I do not think this is a friendly escort.' Bellême's eyes were narrowed as he saw the bristling spears, the unsmiling face of the captain. He clapped his hand to his sword hilt but before he or the startled Henry could do anything further they were surrounded and a dozen men stood by the ship's side to prevent their attendants coming to their assistance.

'What in God's name are you about?' Henry demanded. 'I am Prince Henry—call off your men.'

The captain was a wooden-faced man in his forties. 'Your pardon, my lord, I know you well, but I am acting at the command of your brother the Duke and of Bishop Odo. I am to take you and the Count of Bellême into custody.'

Robert of Bellême was struggling furiously with several soldiers who were endeavouring to hold him, and so strong was he that it took three of them to overpower him. 'Blood of Christ, let me go!' he exploded. 'On what charge do you dare to seize us?'

'On a charge of plotting treason, my lord Count.'

Henry stared at the captain, dumbfounded, too surprised and certainly too sensible to struggle against overwhelming numbers. 'Treason? Good God, what treason? I have been in England, fool!'

'As to that I cannot say, my lord.' The captain signalled to his men. Several came forward and before Henry realised what they were about they had manacled his wrists. A wave of angry colour flooded his face, and he swung out wildly with his hands, catching one man a blow in the face with the chain. Blood spurted from the cut cheek, there was a moment's breathless struggle and then he found himself so firmly held that, sweating and furious, he was forced to be still. He saw Bellême in the same position, dark face mottled with rage, he saw the curious faces of the crowd and behind him Herluin, Raoul, and the rest of his men held at bay, their hands on their swords yet impotent, on the gang plank.

'In God's name,' the Count was shouting furiously, 'where are you taking us?'

'You to the donjon at Neuilly,' the captain said. 'Prince Henry to Bayeux.'

For a moment the ground heaved under Henry's feet. The joy of his landing, the anticipation of his meeting with Alide, his confidence in his newly acquired state, all these were as water seeping into the ground and leaving no trace. Suddenly he was a prisoner, soon to lose the freedom of the earth to walk on, the sky above his head, to be shut in a narrow prison. He stared down at his manacled wrists and then he understood.

It was Odo who had set these chains on him, Odo who had persuaded Robert to issue the orders, Odo who was seeking revenge for his laughter on that other beach across the channel. Christ, he thought, was he now to pay dearly for that mirth?

5

Snow came before Christmas, the flakes falling thick and silent about the castle at Bayeux, settling in great drifts against the walls so that men had to dig out the stored logs in the courtyard and clear a path to the barbican.

From his prison high in one of the towers Henry watched them, seeing them about their normal work, the men riding out to hunt, the women drawing water from the well, breaking the icicles on the buckets, and hurrying back to the warmth of the kitchen; but mostly he sat huddled by his fire, a mantle about his shoulders against the draught that came in even when the shutters were closed.

He had been allowed some books and he read Boethius again, some of the sermons of St. Jerome which he found tedious, and the writings of Augustine which he liked, but it was irksome and the lack of acitivity chafed him daily. He wanted to feel a horse between his knees, his hawk on his wrist, and for himself the freedom even his birds had. But here he was with chains on his ankles far stronger than the jesses that bound his hawks, and with only Fulcher for company.

The boy was growing tall, past thirteen now and at the gangling stage, all arms and legs. He had been distraught at his lord's captivity but his grief had been somewhat assuaged when he found that he and only he was to be allowed to serve the Prince in prison. The fact that it meant a barred door and a loss of freedom to himself was as nothing beside the joy of being allowed to stay with his master. The Prince was teaching him to read, for he had an alert and enquiring mind, and the walls were gradually becoming covered with his scratchings as he endeavoured to trace his letters with the point of his eating knife. He was sitting now, curled up by the fire, a book on his lap, a book laboriously written by some unknown monk, the capitals elaborately coloured and decorated, and there was a frown of concentration on his face as he endeavoured to make out the words.

Henry sat silent, watching him, a faint smile on his face. These lessons gave them something to do, but he was growing desperately weary of prison. No word came from outside. He saw no one but his guards, and this morning as it was Christmas Day he had been allowed to leave this room for the first time in nearly three months, to be taken to the chapel for the Mass of the Nativity. Yesterday at his request a priest had come to shrive him and he had said plainly that he was not guilty of the crimes of which he had been accused; the chaplain had somewhat sententiously commended him to trust in God and await deliverance. Well, he did trust he supposed, but, by Heaven, he was tired of waiting.

He had seen Bishop Odo once, a month after he had been brought here. His uncle had sat in his great chair on the dais in his hall, dressed in all his episcopal splendour and surrounded by his household, and he had surveyed his nephew with a most unpriestly expression of triumph on his face—he might almost have been said to gloat over the reversal of their fortunes.

'Well, nephew,' he had remarked, 'and who is laughing now?'

Herluin had been right, Henry thought, when he had warned him on the beach of the Bishop's vengeance. It had been small use to protest his innocence, to swear he and Bellême had been nothing but companions, to declare that he knew nothing of any intention Rufus might have to try to wrest Normandy from Robert. The Bishop did not even attempt to listen. Instead he treated his nephew to a long lecture which boiled down to the fact that he, Odo, was virtual master of Normandy and his nephews had all better attend to him.

'Robert may do so, but Rufus has your measure,' Henry had retorted with spirit, 'and so, by the Mass, have I. If you do not release me, the King will take steps on my behalf.'

'Do you think so?' Odo queried. 'I doubt it.'

'He and I are on the best of terms. I hold lands in England, lands he himself gave me.'

'And which he has now given to Robert Fitzhamon.'

There has been a silence in the hall then, the men about his uncle staring at him, some amused, and their smiles flicked him on the raw. He did not believe it and said so.

'It is true,' the Bishop retorted smoothly. 'Fitzhamon now holds all Queen Matilda's land and sits in Cardiff castle which he invests for the King.'

He had to believe it then, for he could not conceive that Odo would tell such a lie in front of his whole court.

'If my brother knew the truth,' he began.

'Oh, he knows,' his uncle broke in, his thin fingers tapping an impatient rhythm on the arms of his chair. 'He is aware that you lie in prison with but one page to attend you.'

Someone behind Odo's chair sniggered. 'Aye, and the King said, "that should serve him well enough".'

There was a ripple of laughter through the hall, and an angry flood of colour suffused Henry's face.

With what dignity he could muster he had said, 'I call God to witness that I am guilty neither of plotting nor treachery, nor bloody heathen practices.'

But the laughter was there, and the indignity and the manacles, and Odo, he thought, was well revenged.

He went back to his prison filled with loathing for his uncle, and as for Rufus, he would not easily forget his brother's jibe— which he could not have believed for one moment—nor his two-faced behaviour in taking back what he had so recently given. And he remembered how some instinct had warned him not to trust the Red King.

Since that scene in the hall, he had been left to kick his heels in the tower, and he sat in his cell with no very amicable feelings towards either King or Duke, nor to his companion in distress —Bellême, he thought, sowed trouble wherever he went. As for his brothers it seemed that they, despite all they had inherited, were envious even of what little he had and would wrest it from him. As far as Robert was concerned it was all Odo's doing and he thought with scorn of Curthose's fatal weakness. But how long would he and Odo keep him in this dreary place of which he was so heartily sick?

Fulcher's voice interrupted his thoughts. 'My lord, I cannot understand this. What does *lumbis* mean?'

He looked up in surprise. 'It means loins—what in heaven's name are you reading, boy?'

'It is this book of St. Jerome's writings, but it is very difficult.'

88

Fulcher read out the Latin words slowly. ' *"Diabol virtus in lumbis est":* The virtue of the devil—that's easy enough—is in the loins, I suppose, but I don't understand. What did the blessed Father mean?'

Henry had collapsed into laughter, glad to have something to laugh at. 'Sweet Mary, boy, why did you have to pick that piece? It means—it means the devil gets at us in our weakest place, as I should know, and yet . . .' he saw the lad staring at him in some bewilderment which only made him laugh the more until Fulcher began to look offended.

'If I am so stupid, my lord . . .'

'No, no . . .' he controlled himself. 'You are not stupid, indeed you are doing better than I ever hoped. In short, St. Jerome is saying that our natural instincts are base and used by the devil to make us sin, whereas God calls to our higher selves.'

'I understand now,' Fulcher nodded profoundly, 'but is holy marriage not blessed by God? Or,' his colour deepened, 'does it only mean other sorts of loving?'

Henry was laughing again. 'The priests would have us think so, but I can't believe God meant it to be thus or why did He choose that we should procreate our race in so pleasurable a manner?' He saw Fulcher looking puzzled again and suggested hastily that they should read something else. But the laughter had done him good, for all the cause of it made him think longingly of Alide.

They were presently interrupted by the guard who brought their dinner and as he set it down on the table they saw that at least their fare was better than normal and in keeping with the day. Only Henry was not as hungry as if he had been out hunting all morning.

From somewhere far below came the sound of music and of merriment and he guessed that the Christmas feast must be in full swing. Odo was in Rouen attending the Duke, but his household here were obviously enjoying themselves.

After he had eaten he lay on his bed, dozing, while the short winter daylight died and Fulcher scratched ceaselessly on the wall. The sound had begun to irritate him when the boy said suddenly, 'My lord! There are riders coming through the gate and—yes, it is! Lord, it is Richard of Redvers and Herluin Le Barre.'

He leapt off the bed and ran to the window. Through the

narrow slit he could see the horses, the sound of their hooves muffled by the snow, and the grooms running to hold them as the riders dismounted. He saw Herluin's unmistakeably lanky figure and de Redvers' more stocky shape. Richard had thrown off his hood and was already running up the steps to the hall, while his attendants dismounted and began to lift packs from their horses' backs. Then Herluin too was gone into the hall and he leaned against the wall.

Why had they come? For a few moments his natural stability deserted him and he was shaken with emotion. If only it was to bring him freedom, if only the guard would strike off his chains that he might ride away with them, out of this cold, lonely place. Sweet Jesu, he prayed, let it be freedom! But even if it were not, let them come! It was so long since he had talked with friends, since he had had any company other than a child's.

The minutes passed with intolerable slowness. He thought half an hour, an hour, must have passed, but it was barely fifteen minutes before the bolts were drawn and then they were in the room.

Richard came first, both hands extended. 'My dear lord, are you well? Have you been ill-used? Do they care for your needs? By God, when we heard . . .'

Henry went to them, his chains rattling, to grasp the outstretched hands. 'I am well and no one dares to beat me or starve me.' He turned to greet Herluin and saw his eyes go to the chains. 'Do not heed them, my friend. One soon gets used to them.' He looked from one to the other and could not keep the painful anxiety from his face.

'Jesu,' Herluin said softly, his long face taut. 'We should have sent a man to warn you, to say . . .'

'A Christmas visit,' De Redvers broke in swiftly, 'to bring you gifts . . .'

The disappointment was worse than he could have imagined, but he recovered himself almost at once. 'Then let us make the most of it. By Our Lady, I'm glad to see you both.'

Herluin let out a sigh. He should have known, he thought, that neither chains nor prison, nor Odo's spite, could make any inroads on his lord's inherent resilience.

De Redvers said in a distressed voice, 'I wish we could have brought you better news, but we have had to work mightily on the Duke to gain permission to visit you at all, for Odo has been always at his elbow. However last week the Bishop went to Séez to see the Bishop there and we seized our opportunity. The Duke did not need too much persuading without your uncle to drop poison in his ear.'

Henry sat down on his pallet bed and indicated that they should take the stools. He did not look at Fulcher, who was busying himself laying out their packs, but he sensed that the boy was weeping tears of frustration. 'Does my brother really believe the lies they tell about me?'

Richard shook his head. 'No, I swear it. He has sent you a thick mantle of fur to warm you in this bitter weather as well as wine from his own cellar.'

He could see it so clearly—Robert, warm-hearted and weak, grieving for his imprisonment yet yielding to Odo's commands.

'By God,' he said, 'I swear if I were Duke no man should tell me what I must do.' He glanced at his friends. He saw that they were watching him, assessing how imprisonment had affected him, how he was reacting to the bitter disappointment that neither of them had anticipated, and he saw that he must not fail them, must show himself a Prince of Normandy. 'Well, let us forget Odo for the moment,' he said cheerfully, 'I have heard something about gifts, but as yet I've seen none and it is Christmas day.'

Richard rose, laughing, his relief obvious, and bade Fulcher help him undo the packs, which the boy did, scrubbing hastily at his eyes. Herluin shook out the Duke's gift, the velvet mantle lined with fur, and set it about Henry's shoulders, while Richard poured wine into cups; there were sweetmeats and raisins and a cold capon; some fine leather gloves for the Prince and a new tunic of bright scarlet wool for Fulcher which set him capering with delight.

'It was good of you to remember the boy,' Henry said and drank the wine slowly, savouring it. 'Now tell me—there is so much I want to know. What happened after Bellême and I were taken? What of my men?'

'Messire de Redvers came to our rescue,' Herluin said in his brief manner. 'They are at Vernon.'

'Yes, but it was Herluin here who kept them together when none knew what was best to do,' Richard put in warmly. 'We expected your release daily, but as the weeks went by I saw that they must have employment, so I sent them to Vernon with your hawks and horses and other gear.'

'I am grateful.' Henry laid his hand on his friend's arm. 'Perhaps one day I shall have a chance to repay you, but at the moment . . .' he gave a wry smile. 'Tell me how things are at court. I cannot believe Montgomery took his son's arrest lightly.'

'No, he did not. He came hell-bent back to Normandy as soon as a ship could bring him and put all his castles in a state of defence. He still defies the Duke and demands Bellême's release.' Richard laughed. 'He has been rampaging about the duchy like a grey-bearded lion and has stirred up a deal of discontent against the Duke, but Ballon and St. Cerneri have yielded to the ducal troops. The Earl of Chester and other lords of the Côtentin are with him in demanding release for both of you.'

'Then why, in heaven's name, does Curthose not yield? What does he think we have done?'

'He knows you have done nothing,' Herluin said.

And de Redvers added, 'That is true, but last month a monk of St. Gervais dreamed he saw Normandy running with three rivers of blood and your uncle claimed that it meant you and your brothers would divide the land with your strife, so the Duke dare not free you.'

'Odo! It is always Odo!' Contempt rose in Henry, and he slammed one fist into the other. 'What ails Robert? Is he afraid of dreams and portents as well as of Odo? Has he none of our father in him?'

'He fears your uncle more than he fears God, I think,' Richard said. 'But there is more than that. The Bishop has been mighty busy since he returned. He urges the Duke to seize what he may, he exacts money for the impoverished treasury, and he builds churches, encouraging gold and silver smiths, masons and weavers to make fine goods, so that your brother thinks to be known as a great patron of the arts. Have you not seen the tapestry Odo commissioned showing your father's taking of England?'

'Once.' Henry got up and began to pace restlessly. His uncle's complex character at the moment interested him less than the prospects of freedom. 'Is there no chance Montgomery and the others will prevail on the Duke to free us in spite of Odo?'

'Every chance. Grandmesnil will be for you when he returns

from England—his eldest son is dead and he comes to make a tomb for him at St. Evroul—and your cousin Stephen has spoken for you, as well as De Beaumont.'

'And the lord of Conches?'

'He and Ralph have gone to England to see Ralph contracted to the lady Alice, but they are sure to return soon. Helias de Beaugencie rode in from La Flèche to spend Christmas with the Duke and added his name to ours—he sent you his greeting, and so does Gilbert de L'Aigle and Walter Giffard. I'm sure the pressure will soon be such that the Duke must yield.'

'Please God,' Henry stopped his pacing. He turned to look at them. 'As for you, my friends, I do not know how to express my thanks for your loyalty.'

Richard laughed and poured more wine. 'As you call us, so we are—your friends. Come, let us have some more wine to warm us. And we have a piece of good news for you.'

'Oh?' He paused, the cup half way to his lips. Then he said suddenly, 'Alide?'

Herluin smiled. 'You have a fine son, my lord.'

'A son? God be praised. Have you seen him?'

'Aye,' Richard put in, 'and a lusty babe he is, very like you, my lord, with a head of dark hair.'

'And Alide?'

'Well, and proud of her child. She has named him Robert.'

Henry sat down on the bed, his pleasure like a tide that warmed him more than the Duke's fur mantle about his shoulders. 'That has always been a good name in our family. Let us drink to my son—Robert of Caen.'

When at last they had to leave he turned his back on Fulcher and went to stand by the window, immersed in the teeming thoughts their visit had engendered. Despite the initial disappointment hope was alive again, and he felt sure of deliverance. Soon he would go back into the world and when he did he would take with him the things that prison had taught him. He remembered that night when he had stood by another window in Winchester, looking out at the same stars, when he had been so confident of his destiny, aware of a power that he could command, certain too that God would be with him. At first, cast into this place and miserably chained, that certainty had been shaken, but now he saw that he had not been mistaken—only prison had taught him that his strength must lie in himself, so that he would never be at the mercy of shifting conditions, and that from now on he must be master of events, not mastered by them. Which would, he thought, be the difference between himself and Robert. Poor Robert, so swayed and cozened that he was master of nothing, least of all his dukedom!

Now, with so much clear in his mind, he wanted to be away out of this tower, to get on with the business of living, to go back to his lands and rule his people as he had sworn to do the day they hanged the bondman. He wanted to see his son, the child of his flesh, and looking out of the narrow slit at the snow-covered bailey, the moon-light casting great dark shadows across the whiteness, and listening to the sound of gaiety below, he found the longing for Alide almost unbearable.

Leaving the window he went to the door and banged on it, calling for the guard.

'Lord?' Fulcher queried hesitantly, 'is something amiss?'

'No, boy, but it's a dull enough feast day for you here. Would you not like to see what merriment they make in the hall?'

'I do not mind,' Fulcher said stoutly, 'and now Messire de Redvers has brought us wine and gifts it is more like Christmas.'

Henry set a hand on his shoulder. 'I'll not forget how you have shared my imprisonment with me.'

When the guard came he said, 'Let the boy go below and share the feasting. There's no one here to blame you for an act of kindness.'

The man hesitated for a moment but then sent Fulcher off and the latter, once he was sure his master meant him to go, ran down the stairs in eagerness to see the tumblers and minstrels and whatever other delights there might be.

'And you, my lord Count?' the guard asked warily, but moved by compassion on this Christmas night. 'I can't let you past this door but if there is aught I can do . . .'

'Yes,' Henry leaned against the wall, 'find me a willing kitchen maid or serving wench. I've had enough of my solitary bed.'

A broad grin crossed the amiable features. 'Well, I was told to look after your needs.'

'You're a good fellow,' Henry said and that night at least there was warmth in the darkness.

But it was three more weary months before release came. By

then he was heartily sick of his own company and more than once indulged his irritation on his page mainly because there was no one else to vent it on. Fulcher bore it patiently knowing it would not be long before his lord regained his normal cheerfulness, and somehow the dreary hours passed. The spring came, the days grew longer and a little warmer, and Henry woke each morning thinking, will it be today? At last a few days after Easter he was awakened by the rays of the sun slanting across his pillow, and rose to watch the dawn as the new light touched the roofs and towers of the town, dispelling the pale mist on the distant trees. He was still gazing at the brilliant sky, his body tense with the longing for freedom, when the door opened.

Richard de Redvers stood there, his mantle powdered with dust, his broad face one large smile. 'You are free,' he said.

He had ridden from Rouen without pause. The Duke, overwhelmed at last by the opinion of practically every great lord in Normandy, had prevailed on Odo to yield and the command was given to free both captives. The Bishop had looked down his thin nose in a supercilious manner and did not condescend to come to Bayeux himself to release his royal prisoner, but Richard was glad of it and rode part of the way with Earl Roger of Montgomery who went to Neuilly to set his son loose.

'You are free,' he repeated as the prisoner still stood there, half in disbelief.

Henry strode across the room, hands extended. 'Then for the love of heaven let us get these damned chains off,' he said and began to laugh. Freedom! By God, did any man value it who had not once lost it?

'I have sent Herluin to Vernon to bring the men to meet us in Caen,' Richard went on. 'I thought you would want to go there first.'

Henry stood, while the guard removed the chains and two castle servants brought his sword and other gear that had been taken from him on his capture. 'To Caen,' he said, as Fulcher, almost weeping with joy, knelt to fasten on his sword, 'and then to my own lands. I suppose Robert has not shorn me of those?'

Richard sat on the table, swinging one leg. 'No, my lord. You will not go to Rouen?'

'Not I—I've no desire to see him at the moment, unless—did he ask that I should?'

'He said nothing. By the way, Edgar Atheling is returned from Italy and with your brother; I think it was his pleading that finally persuaded the Duke.'

'Edgar was always kind to me,' Henry said. There had been a bond between himself and the Saxon Prince from the very first for they were both Athelings. Edgar had been nominated King once, when he was a mere lad, but that was more than twenty years ago when the Conqueror came to take England and Edgar, gentle and quiet, was no match for the lion of Normandy. Since then he had been at court either in England or Normandy, or travelled about Europe. Despite the fact that their father had taken his birthright, he treated the Norman princes as brothers and had had no hesitation in begging the Duke to release his prisoner.

At the door Henry paused, glancing around the tower room. Six months in this tiny space—how, he wondered, had he endured it?

By evening they were in Caen and riding down the narrow streets. He watched the bustle of the place, carts rumbling by empty after the day's market, men walking home in the twilight, women gossiping at their doors, children playing, and it seemed to him to be inexpressibly good to be plunged again into the world of men. Dismounting at the merchant's door and hardly hearing his greeting, Henry ran up the stair that led to the rooms above the place of business, and there, seated by a cradle, he found Alide.

She gave a low cry when she saw him and then she was in his arms, swept off her feet by his embrace.

It was a long while before he released her. Presently he said, 'Now let me see this son of ours.' and when she laid the babe in his arms found himself looking into his own dark eyes. The boy, sturdy and healthy, lay contentedly in his hold and reached out for the chain he wore about his neck.

He glanced at Alide, his pride undisguised. 'He is a fine boy, and for all he's a "mantle" child, he'll not find me lacking in care for him.'

She leaned over the babe, her eyes alight, crooning softly. 'There is no knowing what he may become. Your father was a bastard, yet he was Duke and then King, and if you should . . .'

'No,' he broke in sharply and with one arm about his son

held her wrist in a hard grasp. 'He is mine and I will acknowledge him before all men, but as a love child only.'

'He is your true son,' she said stiffly.

'Aye, but not my heir nor will he ever be. We'll not again have the taunt of bastardy flung at us—my father bore that long enough.' He paused, hesitant to be cruel, yet so certain of what he felt that he must speak. 'Alide, I would not hurt you, but this you must understand. Some day I must marry and beget legitimate heirs. Curthose has nought but bastards.'

'I know,' she said in a low voice, 'and his woman suffered the ordeal by hot iron to prove them his.'

'You would not need to do that to prove my paternity,' he answered sternly, 'that is not in question. The point is that clearly Rufus will have none, and our line must continue.'

The child, sensing that he no longer had his father's attention, set up a wail and Alide took him, setting him in his cradle and rocking it with her foot. She was very pale.

'You knew,' he said, 'you knew from the very beginning . . .'

'Yes,' she whispered, 'I knew, but I thought . . .' The baby's crying had ceased now and he slept. She straightened her back. 'Perhaps it would be better for him if you left us and he grew up here in my father's house. What else is there for him?'

He had never heard her speak so coldly and he was surprised for a moment, for he had thought her intelligent above the average, a woman of perception, and he could not understand why she could not see what was so clear to him. And then he saw her, not as Alide, but as any woman protecting, defending her young. He had seen a wild cat once, crouched before her litter, teeth bared, ready to die in their defence, and it was an instinct, he thought, as deep-rooted as any.

He bent down and took her hands, drawing her to her feet. 'He will have everything it is in my power to give him when the time comes—knighthood, land, a suitable bride—but that is all. And that is how it must be.'

She stood reluctantly, her hands imprisoned. 'I did not know you cared so much about your father's bastardy.'

He looked at her, startled and then relieved. He had been right at first for she had perceived now the heart of the matter. He let her hands go and folded his arms about her. 'Dear heart, what are we about, quarrelling the moment I am returned to you? Are you not glad to see me?'

She gave a little sigh and the rigidity left her body. 'I think I do not live when you are not with me. Forgive me, beloved.'

He held her close. 'There is nothing to forgive. We are together again and we have our son. I am going to Avranches in a few days and I want to take you both with me. Will you come?'

'Of course,' she answered. How could she not do what he wished? Yet that night and the next day as they awaited the arrival of Herluin and the men from Vernon, she saw that he had changed, that six months of captivity had dismissed the boy in him, that now he was stronger, more decided, a little harder perhaps and—who could blame him—less likely to trust his fellows. And she knew beyond doubt that he would not alter his attitude towards their son.

Three days later they set out soon after sunrise, a company of some twenty men, herself, the babe and her serving woman. De Redvers had perforce to return to the court to inform the Duke that his orders had been carried out, though he left them promising to ride to Avranches in the summer. But Herluin rode beside his lord, and Raoul the deer, Gulfer with his falcons, Hamo once again carrying the Prince's gonfanon, and young Fulcher, proud that it was he who had been the Prince's companion, was bright as a peacock in his scarlet tunic.

Raoul was grumbling at the lack of any provision made for his lord, considering the Duke might have sent provender for their journey.

'Why, what we have is a feast compared to the fare in Bayeux tower,' Fulcher said, 'some days we had nothing but soup and bread, and I can tell you . . .'

'Spare us,' Hamo said, laughing. 'We heard it all last night twice over.'

'And will do so again, I suspect,' Gulfer put in laconically. 'Anyone would think none of us had served our master but you, young Fulcher. You grow too puffed up in your own conceit.'

'Oh, did you not know?' Hamo said wickedly, 'master page here has learned to read in Latin and thinks to challenge Odo himself when he is grown. What is it to be, Fulcher, a bishopric for you, or perhaps a barony in England?'

The others laughed and Fulcher stuck his chin in the air. 'I do not care for your teasing,' he said with dignity.

98

'Maybe not,' Raoul retorted, 'but you'd better remember you're still a green lad and not above being put across my knee.'

The others laughed. Fulcher flushed but a rueful grin crossed his face. 'Well, you can say what you like, but I wanted to be with him, and not for gain either.'

'We know that,' Hamo said consolingly, 'and if you did but know it, we all envied you.'

It was a fine day, the sky a clear blue, the woods bearing the pale green leaves of spring, fresh growth everywhere and the ground strewn with anemones and violets. Once more astride Rougeroy Henry felt his own spirits in tune with the bright day; with his hawk on his wrist and his own company with him, the constriction of the last months slid away.

As they breasted a rise he heard a bell ringing and saw a small chapel below, a solitary place serving a village of scattered dwellings.

On an impulse he said, 'Come, we'll go to Mass,' and led them all down the hillside.

The chapel was dim, little of the bright morning penetrating the one small splayed window. Candles burned on the altar but their yellow light seemed pale after the brilliance outside, and the place smelled of stale incense and candle grease.

There were a few worshippers there already, and they glanced round in surprise as Henry and his company filled the church. The priest, young and slight and thin, was also startled by the advent of this unexpected congregation. He could see they were travellers, knights of high degree and men-at-arms, and being a sensible man got on with his business with some speed.

Kneeling with Herluin Henry kept his eyes upon the altar and his thoughts upon God and the words of Isiah ran in his head. '*I have given you a covenant . . . to bring out the prisoners from the dungeon, from the prison those who sat in darkness.*' And the fact that he had freedom again, freedom to go where he might, to enter this church on this particular morning was cause enough for gratitude. He glanced at Herluin and saw him kneeling, hands clasped, a look of intense devotion on his face —sometimes he thought Herluin should have been a priest or a monk for his mind turned in that direction, absorbed by the things of the spirit. Yet the knight from Barre le Heron was a fighting man too and good at his trade, and the tenacity of his loyalty was another thing for which Henry felt disposed to give thanks.

Having paid God His due, a thought came to him and when they left the church he sent Hamo to bid the priest speak with him.

Raoul the deer said, 'Master priest was as swift with his words as I am with my feet. That was the shortest Mass I ever heard.'

Henry laughed. 'So I thought. It would horrify our good Anselm, but this fellow is a soldier's priest, eh?'

'I do not like to hear the Mass gabbled,' Herluin said gravely, 'but for all his speed I think he truly served God.'

The priest came, hastily smoothing his black gown. 'My lord, your man has told me who you are. How may I serve you?'

Henry was silent, studying him. He saw a young man of about twenty-six or seven, with a thin intelligent face and lively brown eyes; he saw that he was well washed and shaved and that his hands were clean.

'Are you lettered?' he asked abruptly. 'Could you deal with a household's business, with deeds and accounts, as well as the things of the chapel?'

The priest's eyelids flickered but he merely answered that he could.

Henry glanced round the poor village, the tiny chapel, the priest's house which was no more than a hut. 'Would you leave this for a castle, or is it to your taste to minister to the poor?'

There was no hesitation in the smooth answer, yet the man's tone was sincere enough. 'I, like most men, my lord, would better myself. If I might serve a great lord I would be well content, for surely the poor are as easily to be found at the rich man's gate.'

'And you would not wish to suffer Dives' fate?'

'Not I, my lord,' he smiled faintly, 'but neither would I wish to sit as Lazarus sat if I might be within the palace in comfort.'

Henry burst out laughing. 'That's honest! And you can say a speedy Mass for the soldier, and act the clerk. Well, will you be my clerk, my chaplain, for I've none to attend me and must set up my household afresh.'

They looked directly at each other. Then the priest's mouth curved into a smile. 'Aye, my lord Henry, I will.'

'Your name?'

'Roger, my lord.'

'Then, Roger, arrange your business and join me at my castle at Avranches as soon as possible.'

And it was typical of him, Henry discovered, that he was in Avranches no more than three days after his new lord. It was the beginning of a friendship that was to last a lifetime.

6

Some weeks later towards the end of May an old man lay dying. He was Archbishop, Primate of all England, but for all that he lay at the end as one should who was first and foremost a monk and a priest, in a simple cell surrounded by his brethren. He was eighty-three years old and having been long at the heart of affairs in England he was much troubled.

His monks, clustered about his bed, saw his anxiety and begged him to rest, to put the business of the world from his mind.

'I would that I could,' he answered them wearily, 'but I see signs of evil to come. I have dreamed strange dreams and I fear that you, my children, may have much suffering before you.'

They knelt about his bed, assuring him that they would bear any trial God might send.

Lanfranc sighed. 'I have lived so long and seen so much. In the days of my old master, we had order and authority—you must urge King William to be as his father was, but I fear—I fear for you all.'

'The King will surely remember your words to him,' the Prior said tentatively, 'and does he not honour his father's memory?'

'Aye—but it is not enough.' Lanfranc bent his tired gaze on the angular face of the Prior. 'And who shall succeed me? It is a great office and the burdens of it are enough to break a man, but they must be borne and borne with courage—Maurice of London, perhaps might be the man, or the Abbot Baldwin of St. Edmunds at Bury. There is Gundulf of Rochester, or Bishop Walkelin, or my successor at Bec—Anselm is a good man but I doubt he'd wish for my shoes. Beseech God, my children, that the King will choose wisely.'

They answered him that they would and watched the old man as he sank into a doze from which he stirred only to talk of days long past when he had been Abbot of Bec and both adviser and friend to Duke William the Bastard, long before the latter had become both Conqueror and King. They annointed him and gave him Viaticum, but still he lingered, old and emaciated, the skin drawn taut across his fine-boned features, until at last on the morning of the twenty-fourth of May his eyes opened for the last time. He raised a hand to bless them, and so faint was his breathing that they barely noticed its ceasing.

He was laid to rest in his own church at Canterbury and the funeral procession wound through the streets seemingly unending, a great concourse of people both rich and poor following the coffin, for he was the most respected man in the kingdom and even those who had suffered from his stern adherence to law, came to honour him at the end. The poor who had received his bounty wept for his passing.

The Prior awaited a summons from the King to discuss the succession, for the Archbishop must also be Abbot of the monks at Canterbury, but no summons came. It seemed that the King was in no hurry to choose at all.

Eventually the Prior journeyed to London where the King was for the Whitsun feast and spoke to him in the hall of the palace of Westminster. It was crowded with men all eager to present their requests to William and he was plainly impatient to be done with business that he might ride out to hunt.

The Prior found himself jostled to and fro in a most undignified manner and when at last he reached the King's chair he felt hot and ruffled and Rufus' 'Well, master Prior, what is it? Make haste about your business,' was hardly conducive to quiet discussion.

'It concerns the abbacy, the archbishopric, sire,' he said with as much dignity as he could.

'And what business is that of yours?' Rufus demanded. He emphasised the last word, and looked the Prior's plain figure up and down in a manner little short of insulting.

'Sire, as Prior of the Abbey, surely . . .'

'The appointment is in my hands and by Lucca's face, it will be done in my own time.'

The Prior's face was pale. 'I thought, my lord, you would care to know that Archbishop Lanfranc suggested various names and . . .'

Rufus interrupted again, clearly relishing the discomfiture of the unfortunate monk, and there were smiles on the faces of the men clustered about the royal chair. 'I honoured Lanfranc for my father's sake, but they are both dead now, and it is I who shall say which man I will have for my archbishop though frankly I could do as well without one.'

The Prior decided tact was the only thing left to him but inadvertently said the wrong thing. 'I will pray that God will guide you, sire, for His Church needs a man of high character to rule over it.'

'No one rules here but myself,' Rufus said bluntly. 'And God has nothing to do with my choice. In fact the less He interferes with me the better. The next world may be His but this kingdom is mine.'

'Sire!' The Prior's voice rose, shrill with shock, 'That is near to blasphemy.'

Red William was slouched in his chair, one leg over the carved arm. 'And if it is, what then? I tell you, master Prior, I'll not be dictated to by any churchman. Go home and pray, if that is what your Abbot told you to do, but it will do you precious little good. Now a large gift to me from your treasure might!'

He roared with laughter and his attendant knights joined in the amusement, mocking the unhappy priest.

The Prior was utterly taken aback for he had not expected this kind of treatment. He saw Ranulf Flambard, Roger de Marmion, Ivo Taillebois—men hardly known for their care of the church—regarding him with humorous contempt, but remembering his dead Abbot he summoned up his courage and spoke severely to the King. 'My lord, it ill becomes you to mock me or Holy Church whom I represent, and I must say that the King of England should not . . .'

'Be silent!' Rufus shouted and got to his feet. 'Get back to your cell and leave the King of England to his own affairs.'

Ranulf Flambard, resplendent in flowing red mantle and tunic, leaned forward, whispering in his ear. Rufus laughed again, banging his fists together.

'Ha! A rare jest. As for the archbishopric, fellow, you can wait upon my decision, but in the meantime all the revenues from Canterbury shall revert to the Crown. See how you like that, my friend.'

The Prior backed away, too frightened now even to take offence at being called 'fellow'. 'My lord, you cannot mean it.'

'Can I not?' the King queried grimly. 'I tell you the Church shall not consider itself above me. If Bishops and Abbots grow fat on the land they own then they shall pay me gold, and send knights to my service like any other baron.'

'And the King's men shall collect the moneys and lodge freely as well,' Flambard added and Rufus laughed again.

'You shall be my Treasurer from this day, friend Ranulf, I can see that I shall grow rich with you at my elbow!'

Flambard flushed, his head lifted and he stared arrogantly at the Prior. 'You at least, my lord King, shall be richer than churchmen who've no right to be.'

'Sire,' the Prior began hotly, throwing caution to the wind, 'I must protest. Messire Flambard is dabbling in matters beyond him. Holy Church cannot be robbed. Why, the Pope himself . . .'

'Is in Rome and like to stay there and therefore no bother to me.' Rufus gave another burst of laughter. 'Let him have Peter and Paul for company but not the King of England. I've had enough of tiresome priests. Perhaps when you have to tighten your belts and live for a while as monks should, you will learn who is master here. Where are my boots?' And when a page brought them he kicked them from the lad's hands, shouting for his Chamberlain.

Richard de Rules came, a neat punctilious man nearing forty, lord of Deeping in Lincolnshire.

'These boots are not fit for a K-King,' Rufus said, stammering in his annoyance. 'Fetch me a better pair.'

De Rules went out with the page and presently came back, the lad bearing another pair which King William set on his feet and strutting, went off to hunt followed by his barons and knights and a crowd of mercenary soldiers and younger sons who hoped to make their way in his service.

De Rules and the Prior were left facing each other in the empty hall, while serving men began to clear away the debris of the dinner.

The Prior was trembling now. 'My lord de Rules, can he really mean it? Surely he must know that to take from Holy Church is a grave sin. His father would never . . .'

'He is not his father,' de Rules answered gravely. He had been in the Conqueror's service since he had been a lad of eighteen and comparison between the two Williams was inevitable. 'I fear we have seen the beginning of a new way of doing things,

Prior. My advice to you is to go back to Canterbury and stay quiet for a while. Do not arouse his anger further by refusing him the revenues. It cannot be for long.'

'I will do as you say,' the Prior said humbly, 'but God have mercy on us all if a creature like Flambard is to advise the King.'

'I agree with you.' de Rules nodded. A wry smile crossed his face. 'It may amuse you to learn that for all his pride the King does not know a good pair of boots when he sees them. I could not find any better so the second pair I brought him were of a cheaper leather!'

Which was small comfort to the Prior as he rode back along the dusty roads to Canterbury.

As the months went by Lanfranc's prophetic words began to come true. Changes came thick and fast. Any abbacy or bishopric that fell vacant was kept vacant, the revenues held by the Crown, unless some creature entirely the King's could be found for the post; wild mercenaries roamed the land at will seizing what they wanted, and the King condoned their conduct.

At Flambard's instigation he levied geld far heavier than the people had been used to bear. Any man who brought a grievance to the court had to pay heavily in money for redress, and men who had groaned under the Conqueror's stern rule now looked back to his time with longing for at least then there had been a reasonable justice for those who kept the law.

In the summer there was a great earthquake which shook the strongest of buildings, tumbling lesser ones to the rumbling earth, and men saw it as a portent of evil. The harvest was bad and the corn not reaped until Martinmas, and fortune tellers and wise women predicted that there would be worse to come.

The King laughed and hunted and blustered his way through the day's business; his favourites were not women but pretty youths, and churchmen began to look with horror upon the vices of the court—such vices, said those of Saxon birth, as were unknown in Saxon lands. Men began to grow their hair long, their moustaches flowing; clothes became more effeminate and the older generation sighed for Norman neatness and Norman austerity.

'Soon we shall not be able to tell men from women,' Gilbert of Clare said to Robert Bloet. Gilbert was the son of Richard de Bieufaite, a baron of high degree with vast holdings in Suffolk and in Kent and, being a lean, hard-living man, he looked with disgust on this new set of young hangers on. Bloet was of the same opinion, but he felt that men of honest character must hold to their offices to preserve a leaven.

'They will have a hard task,' Gilbert answered pithily, 'seeing they will be outnumbered ten to one.'

In Normandy affairs were even worse. In England William was at least King and brooked no opposition, but in the duchy the land was torn with internal strife, baron fighting baron, brigands riding loose while the indolent Duke lounged in his hall at Rouen, smiling at every man and yielding to every request. Robert de Beaumont demanded Ivry back and defied the Duke, William of Breteuil once more attacked Ralp of Conches; Robert of Bellême raided the lands of Helias of La Flèche and there was peace nowhere but in the Côtentin. Sensible men looked longingly to the west where Count Henry kept order and gave justice.

Henry let it be known that no man was too poor to seek his help and that no crime would go unpunished. He went from Avranches to Coutances, from St. Sauveur to Cherbourg and back to St. Michael-in-peril-of-the-sea, listening to grievances, curbing great lords, and encouraging simple knights in his service. He hanged a few thieves and murderers and castrated two men who were guilty of rape.

'My father may not have hanged men,' he said, 'but I will; have it known that I will not tolerate disorder in my county.'

Helias de Beaugencie came to Coutances at Easter, bringing his wife, Matilda of Château-du-Loir; she was a graceful, quiet lady who obviously adored her husband, and they stayed several weeks at Henry's small court, but the news that Robert of Bellême was harrying the lands around La Flèche, burning and seizing prisoners, sent her lord hurrying home.

'Robert the devil is about his work again,' Helias said grimly to his host. 'With no strong hand to curb him he does what he may, but not to my people, by God.'

'One day one of us will have to deal with Bellême,' Henry said to Herluin, who remarked that it was unlikely to be Duke Robert. It was plain Duke Robert feared his most powerful vassal for despite Helias's protests, he did nothing to restrain

Bellême and it was reported that none of the captives from La Flèche ever saw their homes again.

As the new year came in Rufus began to look to Normandy and saw there something approaching anarchy. At least in England he was ruler; for all he allowed his men freedom to oppress he did not allow the barons to feud against each other nor to disobey him and he set his mind to holding Normandy also under his hand. He sent messengers with smooth words and money bags of gold and won first his cousin Stephen of Aumale to his cause, then the Count of Eu, Gerard of Gourney and several other lords on the eastern limits of the duchy. With these castles invested with his garrisons he began to extend his influence without as yet setting foot on Norman soil.

Duke Robert, stirred from his sloth into sudden activity, sent urgent messages to his suzerain, King Philip of France, and Philip, fat and gluttonous, was forced to bestir himself for his vassal, leaving his well-spread table to belch his way to war.

In England Rufus gave a great snort of laughter and sent a gift of money from the treasury at Winchester so large that Philip allowed himself to be bought off. Wheeling his army about he went back to Paris and rich living, leaving Duke Robert to clear up the mess in his own stable.

When Walter Tirel came to Normandy for his wedding to Adeliza, the daughter of Richard be Bienfaite, Lord of Clare, her brother Gilbert took advantage of the nuptial banquet to tell Prince Henry of affairs in England.

'We miss the Archbishop,' he said, 'at least he restrained men from the worst excesses, but now it is only money that talks.'

Grieving for his old tutor's passing, Henry said, 'No one had greater influence for good. Has my brother named his successor?'

'No, nor does he seem likely to do so. When the Prior of Canterbury came asking for a new abbot to be elected he sent him packing in no uncertain terms. We all do Flambard's bidding now.'

'That cheap trickster? God knows how such a fellow wormed his way into high office.'

'He achieves what your brother wants,' Gilbert told him drily, 'and I know that it is he who pours more soldiers and money into the eastern part of the duchy. My grandfather has a bet with Robert de Marmion that the Red King will be the Red Duke as well before five years are out.'

Henry glanced briefly at Walter Giffard, sitting beside his grand-daughter on her wedding day; the old man had served the Conqueror all his life and was renowned for his far-sightedness. Could he be right? After his brother's two-faced action over his mother's lands Henry did not relish the prospect of a Rufus all-powerful in Normandy, and he remembered what Rufus had said to him once in the cloister at St. Gervais when their father lay dying, that if he had to fight Robert he would.

'The Duke can hardly be said to keep order in the duchy,' Gilbert was continuing. 'No man dares ride alone for fear of the ruffians that rob and plunder unchecked—indeed,' he glanced at Henry, 'I have heard it said more than once that there is justice nowhere but in the Côtentin.'

'I'd not tolerate the state of things Robert endures,' Henry said and was conscious of a moment's pleasure in Gilbert's compliment.

'We could do with your methods in England,' the latter added, feelingly, and it seemed briefly as if there was an undercurrent of meaning in what he said. But then he went on to talk of the Countess Maud and the fine son she had borne to her husband, Earl Simon.

Henry was glad for her, knowing what happiness he gained from his own son. Alide was pregnant again and he hoped this time for a daughter, finding to his surprise that his own children delighted him, and he rode back to Avranches from the nuptials glad to be returning to his own city and domestic harmony.

His southern borders were safe enough now for Helias had become Count of Maine, ousting a cousin who had proved so useless that the Manceaux drove him out, cast off Normandy's overlordship and invited Helias to rule them. He entered his city to overwhelming acclamation and the women of Le Mans lost their hearts to the tall handsome count as he came riding through the streets.

Peace might reign now in Maine and in the Côtentin, but in the autumn of 1090 unrest flared into open rebellion in the very heart of the duchy, in Rouen itself. The citizens of that city, tired of Robert's misrule, or more correctly no rule at all, rose in protest. Under their leader, Conan, a wealthy merchant, the citizens rebelled against their Duke, declared for King William, dreaming perhaps of making their city into an independent commune, merely acknowledging the King as their overlord.

Robert, shut in his castle, cast about desperately for help. Personally brave, he would have dashed out with a few men at his back and attacked his enemies, but his advisers restrained him, warning him of the possible disastrous results of an attack without sufficient troops, thus throwing him back upon the need for moral courage which he sadly lacked.

It was useless to approach Philip of France who preferred Rufus' gold to martial glory, and instead the Duke sent south to Bellême, to William of Breteuil, and west to the Count of the Côtentin.

'Will my brother come?' he queried doubtfully. 'Has he forgiven those months in Bayeux tower? It seems to me, uncle, that if you have made me an enemy out of young Beauclerc you have rendered me poor service.'

Bishop Odo bristled. 'Nonsense. We merely taught him who was master here. He owes his freedom to you—of course he will come.'

Henry did come, but not from any sense of gratitude.

'We will go,' he said grimly to his men, 'because rebellion against a Duke must be punished. God's wounds, my father would have made mincemeat of such traitors as Conan and his fellows. This is Normandy, by heaven, and they must learn whose house they serve.' He did not add that if the citizens of Rouen successfully seized power, the men of other cities might choose to follow their example.

Leaving Alide in Avranches, watched over by Roger the priest and a small garrison, he collected troops from all parts of his county and took them across the duchy with a speed that put at least one of his barons, Earl Hugh of Chester, who was on a brief visit to his native city, in mind of the old Duke.

Approaching the outskirts of Rouen, they paused briefly at Hermentrudeville, by the half finished monastery of Our Lady of Good News. It had been begun by the Duchess Matilda and Henry went in briefly to pray for the soul of his mother. A further half mile and they were on the west bank of the Seine where they found the bridge open and, crossing without hindrance, entered the city by the south gate.

The streets presented an unusual aspect. No one was about their normal business; companies of men were moving towards the castle, stalls were deserted and women stood about talking together, their tasks neglected, while children ran wild, excited by the turmoil. Henry and his followers were cheered the moment they appeared through the gates, and when he asked how things stood one man told him that Conan and his forces were gathering in the northern and western parts of the city and had occupied all the streets in that area.

Henry immediately turned into the castle fortifications and found Robert, who had seen his approach from the tower, hurrying to greet him in the bailey as he dismounted. There was a broad smile on the Duke's face and his words of welcome were given in his usual open manner.

'You would think he had never set fetters on our lord nor sent him to Bayeux tower for six months,' Hamo remarked to Raoul the deer.

Raoul grunted. 'We've come on a fool's errand if you ask me. Let the Duke fend for himself, I say. We were well enough where we were and our master owes him nothing.'

'I suppose Bishop Odo is here?' Fulcher put in tentatively. 'I wonder what he and the Prince will have to say to each other.'

Gulfer spat expressively. He had left his birds behind and carried a spear in hands gnarled and hardened by years of handling fierce hawks. 'The Bishop can choke on his own spleen, for all Henry cares now.'

The Duke swept his brother into the castle, arm in arm. 'I knew you would come,' he said gaily. 'That business eighteen months ago was none of my doing, you know. It was our uncle who said you had engaged to help Red William seize my duchy. I never believed it.'

If he had not, Henry thought, why then had he left him to kick his heels in prison for so long? But he did not say so, merely asking what had been done for the defence of the castle.

'I've all my own men here,' Robert said, 'and some from Bayeux, Ivo and Alberic of Grandmesnil came in a day or two ago with theirs, and messengers have gone to Gilbert of L'Aigle and Bellême, Breteuil and others to come with all speed.' He squeezed Henry's arm. 'It is good of you, little brother, to hurry to my side.'

'Rebellion is not to be countenanced,' Henry said briefly and entering the hall saw his uncle standing by a table spread with parchments.

Odo's eyes narrowed when he saw the Prince. 'Well, nephew, I see you have come about your duty this time.'

'I never did otherwise, as you well know,' Henry retorted. He neither bent the knee nor kissed the Bishop's ring, an omission not lost upon Odo. 'And I may as well tell you, uncle, that I hold you responsible for the rift between my brother and myself.'

Odo opened his mouth to return a sharp answer, but Robert stepped hastily between them. 'Well, there is no rift now and we are grateful to Beauclerc for coming to our aid. Here is Edgar, brother, returned from Italy to join us.'

Henry turned to meet the Saxon Prince who had long been Robert's boon companion. Edgar was tall and slender with a gentle face and fair hair beginning to grey a little. He held manors in England and lands in Normandy and was no longer considered a menace to the Norman royal house. He spoke in a low pleasant voice and embraced Henry, calling him cousin, though their relationship was somewhat distant, and accompanied him and the Duke on a tour of the castle to see what troops and arms were gathered. Most of the soldiers were assembled in the inner courtyard, sorting arms, sharpening swords and spears, everyone talking and shouting orders at once. Ivo of Grandmesnil, Hugh's son, called a greeting to Henry; he had his father's powerful frame, a fighting man who, with his brother, had adhered to Curthose all through the latter's exile. The troops seemed in good heart and cheered their Duke so that he walked among them, smiling and gay.

During the afternoon, on Henry's advice, he sent one last message to the rebel Conan, commanding him to yield to his liege lord, offering him reasonable terms if he did so. 'Better a treaty than a battle,' Henry said, but by dusk the man had returned, bringing Conan's refusal in insolent terms.

'What folly,' the Prince remarked angrily to his brother, 'he will bring fire and death on our city, and for naught.' And with vigour he set about preparations for the morrow's inevitable fight. At this point Odo, deeming a street brawl unworthy of his personal attention, departed to watch affairs from nearby Hermentrudeville.

Fighting broke out soon after dawn, the citizens who were for Robert surprised while barely from their beds, and Conan and his men won through to the south gate. Henry stood with the Duke and Edgar on the roof of the tower, watching.

'Come,' Robert said eagerly, 'we must attack. We cannot stay mewed up here while our friends in the town die.' He had his sword out, and his face was flushed with excitement.

Henry laid a restraining hand on his arm. 'Not yet. Look!' In the distance where the hills sloped gently towards the river he could see the pale November light reflected on steel, and again to the south beyond the bridge a cloud of dust indicating many riders.

'Aid has come,' Robert exclaimed exultantly, 'I knew they would not fail me. God be praised. Now we shall send the rebels packing.'

'Give them time,' Henry urged. 'For the most effect we must attack when they reach the gates.'

They waited, Robert fuming and impatient, Henry well aware that a cool head was needed at this moment, and Edgar whole-heartedly supporting his assessment of the situation.

He watched his brother in some exasperation as the Duke hurried about the castle, asking superfluous questions, disturbing the armourers at their work, seizing the archers' arrows and feeling their balance, and generally getting in everyone's way.

'I know one thing,' Henry said amusedly to the Saxon prince, 'Robert may be a gallant captain, but by God he'll never make a general!'

The men too were straining at the leash, eager to be out in the fight, which at the moment was little more than desultory, though a few houses had been fired, but still Henry, who had taken complete command, held them back, calmly confident that he was right to do so.

Then Gilbert de L'Aigle attacked the west gate. At the same time Bellême and William of Breteuil thundered with their troops over the bridge and launched themselves at the south entrance with battering ram and fire and mangonels, while archers aimed at the men on the walls.

'Now,' Henry said grimly. The castle gates were opened and the ducal troops poured out.

There was utter confusion in the streets, disorganised fighting in lanes that were too narrow for anything but wild hand to hand scraps, and the fires spread, timbers crashed and sparks flew, catching in thatch and straw. Henry led his men in an attack down the main street towards the open space before the cathedral church, hacking and thrusting at citizens who were ill-armed and untrained, and anger at this utter waste of life and property lent a strength to his arm.

Robert galloped out and flung himself into the fray, wielding his sword with considerable skill, but without bothering to see if any supported him. Henry tried to keep some sort of order, but as soon as the loyal townsmen saw their Duke and began shouting for him Robert was away, laughing with excitement. His superb horsemanship was such as to draw admiration, but he appeared to have no sense of what was needed in a Duke and behaved as if he were a simple knight and his life as expendable.

'He will be slain if he exposes himself like that,' the younger Grandmesnil said to Henry. 'My lord, what point to this fight if he is killed?'

Wiping the sweat from his face Henry, with his own men solidly behind him, rode down the street where the fighting was hardest and making his way through the mêlée, seized Robert's rein. His men forced a passage and he dragged his brother clear.

'You fool,' he said in a low voice. 'Will you throw your life away with those whose duty it is to die for you? Come away.'

'No—no . . .' Curthose struggled to free his rein. 'I will be a fighting Duke as my father was.'

'He was never foolhardy,' Henry retorted tartly. He ducked to avoid a missile thrown from a window and Rougeroy reared wildly so that he was hard put to it to hold his seat. The Grandmesnil brothers came up on either side of the Duke and swept him back.

'Come, my lord Duke,' Ivo said. 'You cannot stay here.'

'Get him away,' Henry shouted to to them. 'Out of the city, if you can—try the east gate.'

The last he saw of Robert then was the Duke, red-faced and protesting, being forcibly led off by the Grandmesnils and several other lords.

Now he could get on with the serious business without the hindrance of Robert's ill-timed heroics, and he sent a detachment of men to the south gate which was burning fiercely. It fell in with a crash and the attackers from outside, the men of Breteuil and Bellême, regardless of the flames, poured in over it, their lords in their midst. They rushed through the streets yelling their battle cry, 'Talvas! Talvas!' and not long afterwards the soldiers of L'Aigle with Richard of Redvers and his followers broke in at the western side of the city so that the forces of Conan were forced back and contained in an ever decreasing area. Only the east gate remained free, and this was mainly because it opened on to a strip of marshy ground, almost under water on this damp November day and useless to troops, and it was out of this that the still protesting Duke was led, to be put into a boat and ferried across the river to await the outcome in his mother's monastery.

In the city the streets were one mass of struggling men-at-arms. Those from Bellême and Breteuil were slaughtering indiscriminately, fleshing their swords on the town, killing men, women and children, seizing prisoners for ransom, so that the air was filled with terrified shrieks. Rufus' hired soldiers who had come to assist Conan, now saw no point in continuing the fight and fled towards the north gate.

Standing on the steps of the cathedral church which had caught the flames Henry directed his men as they endeavoured to dowse them. The clergy had come scurrying out, protesting volubly and only too eager now to make their peace with the victorious brothers. Henry promised them life and limb—they were men of God, holy priests, and he would not risk his own condemnation by harming them, in spite of their support of Conan and Rufus.

Edgar Atheling came up, his fair face pink with exertion. For all his gentleness he had spent half his life fighting and had a professional attitude towards war. 'There's not much defiance left in the rebels now,' he said cheerfully and went off down a lane where a pocket of them was being rooted out.

The market was a shambles, pigs squealing wildly, and all kinds of fowl, ducks and geese, waddling and flapping their wings and tripping up the men under whose feet they scampered; stalls were overturned, buckets of milk spilling so that more than one man met his death by skidding in a white pool of liquid to fall at the mercy of an enemy.

Henry had his sword in his left hand for he had been slightly wounded in the right one, his gauntlet stained with blood, and his helmet was dented by a missile, but otherwise he was whole. Herluin stood beside him, his long face more melancholy than usual as he gazed at the carnage in what yesterday had been a fair city.

Bellême and Breteuil, their swords arms bloodied to the elbow, were riding from one street to the next, killing as they went; Bellême was laughing, his lips drawn back from his teeth, his head lifted as if the scent of blood was life to him. At one point he seized a woman by the hair and slit her throat so that she fell, a red-stained horror to be trampled under his hooves.

'God in heaven!' Herluin said. 'These are our own people. What harm had she done?'

His mouth shut hard, Henry ran down the steps and remounted, taking the reins from Hamo, but before he could move off Ivo of Grandmesnil came up, dragging with him the dishevelled figure of Conan.

The rebel leader was blackened by smuts, his clothes rent, a cut on his cheek, his head bare. They had set a halter about his neck and dragged him by it so that he was choking and half throttled.

'See, my lord,' Ivo said, 'we have taken their leader. They have all yielded now—those that still live.'

Henry glanced swiftly across the street where Robert of Bellême and his companions had gone to slay and burn, to seize men for ransom, women for their pleasure. He said to Hamo, 'Send trumpeters. Bid every captain call off his men. The fight is over.' But he knew well enough that there was little chance that the Devil of Bellême would heed.

He looked about him, at the gutted buildings, the burning church, the trampled bodies. And then he looked at Conan.

A cold, slow emotion seized him. 'Bring him,' he said between closed teeth and strode through the castle gates and up to the top of the tower. There he took the wretched man by the scruff of the neck and forced him to look out.

'Look,' he said in a voice taut with gathering rage. 'Look on your city. This you would have seized from the Princes of Normandy and made your own. Look beyond, look at that fine park the forest where your dukes have hunted. Look at the river, rich in trade. Look, by God! Was this yours to take?'

He forced up Conan's shaking head, holding him by the hair. 'Look your fill. See the fire, the dead, the women lying in their blood, the children spitted. All this is your doing. You'd best prepare for hell for God will punish you for your presumption.'

Conan was trembling with terror, all the resistance gone from him. 'Have mercy, lord Count. Have mercy.'

'Mercy! What mercy have you earned?'

Conan groaned and wept. 'None, lord, none. But take all my wealth, all my treasure, everything I have as a ransom for my life.'

Henry's fingers tightened about the rebel's throat. 'There can be no ransom for an arch traitor—only the death you have earned.'

Conan looked once more across the burning city, the pall of smoke lying heavily over the wreckage of once pleasant houses, cries and yells still rending the air. He fell at the Prince's feet. 'I own it—I own my guilt. I deserve to die, only permit me a confessor first. Let me confess my sins before I face my Judge.'

'Do you think we've time to accommodate a lousy rebel?' Henry flung the words at him. 'Hell is waiting for you, damned traitor that you are.' The rage had him now so that he was aware of nothing but its thick suffocating alien tide. He was shaking with it, suffused with it, his face flaming, his stomach a hard pit, iron strength in his hands.

He did not even hear Herluin's request to be allowed to fetch a priest. He seized Conan, the author of the day's black doings, and thrust him backwards over the stone ledge. Conan's arms clawed wildly, his legs kicked, but to no avail. He fell with one wild shriek, his body twisting and turning as it spiralled down to fall with a horrifying crash on to the stones below.

There was a stunned silence on the tower, but several soldiers ran to look over the parapet.

Henry leaned against the wall, his breath coming in great gasps.

Herluin, white-faced, crossed himself. 'Holy God,' he said and stared at his lord.

Raoul the deer was also staring in some astonishment, but Gulfer and the men-at-arms looked grimly satisfied.

Slowly—very slowly—Henry felt the red tide recede, the fog leave his brain. He saw the staring faces, Herluin's constricted grief and knew it was not for the dead traitor.

'Well?' he said sharply, 'well? I am as I am, Herluin of La Barre, and if you do not like it, you are at liberty to leave me.' He pushed through them all and away down the narrow stair.

A few hours later the Duke rode triumphantly back into his capital, cheered by his men as if he had acted the part of their leader instead of that of an undisciplined boy whose folly might have threatened the outcome. His barons gathered about him as he greeted them all and embraced his brother Henry whom he congratulated on the speedy end he had meted out to the rebel leader. Conan's body had been tied to the tail of a cart and dragged through the streets, and Robert thought it well calculated to strike terror into any man who still thought of raising his sword against his betters.

Henry listened to the talk with little to say and when night came and he went to the tower room that had always been his, he slammed the door in the surprised faces of Herluin and Fulcher, shooting the heavy bolt into place.

There he paced, his mind torn by the knowledge of the thing he had done. He was furious with himself, for his judgement had been swept away and rage, a rage he did not know he could produce, had betrayed him into a wild act of revenge, of cruelty such as he would condemn in others. Was he to be as the Devil of Bellême, or William of Breteuil? God forbid.

He found he was trembling. Yet the truth was that he had sent Conan plummetting to hell without the chance to be shriven. He could as always find reasons for the things he did, and for Conan's death he felt no guilt for the man had to die, but Lanfranc had taught him to fear hell and the pains of hell, and for the injustice of sending Conan to that death unshriven there was no mitigation.

He was aghast to find that he could be seized and possessed by one of those fits of rage, rare but terrifying, that had been a part of his father's nature. What had happened to his reason, his commonsense? They had been swept away by a physical tide of fury such as he had never known before and it tormented him that he, who wanted to be known as Henry the Just, had so far lost control of himself. It was as if he had looked into the depths of his own nature and seen a horrifying stranger sharing his mind and body.

During the next few days he went about the business of assisting Robert to restore order, though he could not persuade him to command Bellême and Breteuil to release their captives. On the third morning after the fight a man rode in with a grim tale of the lord of Bellême's doings, how he had driven his prisoners to his nearest stronghold and there was occupying himself with torturing for his pleasure those who could not ransom themselves. The man said he had heard the screams of the victims, and it was even rumoured that Robert the devil had impaled not only men but women too, leaving them to writhe in agony until they died.

'Blood of Christ,' Henry swore. 'You must stop him, Robert. These are bloody pagan ways, Moorish practices that have no place in a Christian country.'

Robert said, weeping, 'God have pity on those poor wretches, but I can do nothing. He is too powerful and I need his aid.'

'What are the lives of a few lousy rebels?' Odo demanded impatiently. 'You are overnice, nephew.'

'I'd rather be overnice,' Henry flashed back, 'than condone what Bellême does. But it's all of a piece to you,' and he stalked out of the hall.

He was sharp with his friends, ate little, and spent his time in the town doing what needed to be done.

Richard of Redvers said to Herluin, 'What ails him? I've never seen him like this.'

They were in the bailey preparing to ride out to hunt with the Duke. The Prince had declined to come and had gone up to the tower to stand there as he had done several times since the fight, and Herluin glanced up at the battlements. 'He is troubled. I think it is the business of Conan's death.'

'God save us,' Richard exclaimed in surprise. 'That traitor got no more than he deserved. It's not like Henry to be bothered over the death of such a man. He might as easily have slain him in battle.'

'It would have been better if he had,' Herluin commented and said no more, but he had fairly assessed the state of his lord's mind. Ignoring Henry's remark to him on the tower, only once when they were briefly alone had he referred to the affair. 'None of us can fail to see you are troubled, my lord,' he had said carefully. 'When we do violence to our true selves there is only one way to peace.'

A faint smile had crossed Henry's face. 'I'm glad you did not choose to leave me.'

'Never,' Herluin spoke with unaccustomed vehemence, and nothing more was said between them of the affair of Conan.

But it was not ended in Henry's mind. The doubts remained and Herluin's words, until he knew he must seek that very remedy which he had denied to Conan, and from the one man whose judgement he could trust. Tormented and restless, on the fourth day after the fight, about one o'clock in the morning he flung himself from his sleepless bed and rousing a drowsy groom ordered him to saddle Rougeroy. Then, with only that one attendant, he took the road to Beaumont-le-Roger and to Bec.

It was a brilliant moonlight night, the sleeping countryside bathed in white light against the dark shadows of the woods and as he rode past peasants' huts and small villages it seemed that no one in the world was awake and that he must bear his wretchedness in an empty void. But at last he came to Bec and there the monks were awake, as he knew they would be, singing the office of Lauds. As they left the church in procession to return to their beds he stepped from the shadows and spoke to Anselm.

'Father, confess me. I cannot sleep until you hear me.'

Anselm, good priest that he was, showed no surprise, as if it was the most normal thing in the world for a prince of the royal house to arrive at two o'clock in the morning asking to be shriven.

7

The stag was startled, tilting his head to listen, scenting something in the wind, aware of the stealthy approach of hunters. For a brief moment he paused and then the great antlers lifted and he came forward across the clearing.

At the same moment the hunters moved among the trees some way off, treading carefully that their feet might break no twigs nor make any warning sound. The leader, sliding behind a great beech tree, nocked an arrow and after careful aim loosed the shaft. The arrow struck the stag in the shoulder. He seemed to pause, then lifting his head brayed loudly and crashed through the nearest clump of bushes.

'Quick,' Henry shouted, 'slip the hound. We don't want to lose him.'

The lymer did as he was bid, and the dog leapt forward, sniffing, following the scent of blood, the hunters running after. The lymehound disappeared into the thicket but within two minutes came to a halt for the stag already lay dead, the arrow sticking from its shoulder.

Gulfer called, 'A good kill, my lord.' He took hold of the fine antlers, 'This is the biggest buck we've had yet. Shall I blow the prize?'

'Aye,' Henry said, wiping the sweat from his face and surveying the stag with satisfaction. He handed his bow to Herluin. 'By Our Lady, I'll have those antlers in my hall at Avranches.'

He waited, his favourite hound Lyfa at his feet, as the horn sounded through the forest, and presently the rest of his men came up, Raoul the deer leading Rougeroy and his own shaggy mount. The huntsmen set about dismembering the stag, giving the neck and the offal to the scrambling hounds who were all about the fallen animal now, while the rest of the body was tied by the legs to a pole and borne by two men.

'Well, I'm for my supper,' the Prince said, and mounting, turned Rougeroy's head towards the ducal hunting lodge, with Herluin beside him.

Already the bright February day was waning, the pale sun well down in the west. The air was crisp and there would be a frost tonight, he thought. Fallen twigs crackled under the horses' hooves and there was ice on the marshy pools where the ground was treacherous. Henry guided Rougeroy carefully away from a patch of bog; there was now a rapport between them that made the big destrier sensitive to the slightest touch of his hand and he had a love for Rougeroy more intense than he had as yet experienced. He thought there was no forest in Normandy to compare with this of Valognes in the north western tip of the Côtentin, and now intended to stay a week at least hunting here. The freedom, the sheer physical joy of the chase never changed for him and his happiest moments were spent thus when he could forget the complexities of life and care for nothing but a good horse and a day in the forest. He called to Herluin, 'Is there any sport to compare with this?'

'I have snapped my new bow,' Herluin said laconically.

'You should have good English ash, there's nothing finer.' They had emerged into clearer land now, and entered a rough track, the horses' breath and their own vaporising in the frosty air. 'I would like to journey to England for a while—but I doubt it's the time to go.' He gave Herluin a wry smile. 'With Robert and Rufus spending Christmas together. I think I do better to stay in my own country. God knows what they may be hatching.' He glanced across at Herluin, but the latter remained grave.

'I think so too, my lord. Surely you do not trust your brothers now?'

'Trust them? No, by God, but they can fight as they will over the rest of Normandy. I'm content enough here and they'll not encroach on my preserves.'

Herluin said no more but he was uneasy, had been since they heard that two months after the business at Rouen the King and the Duke were meeting to settle affairs in Normandy. Rufus was not likely to give up the castles he now held, and with Robert in possession of less than half his duchy it was possible that their eyes might turn west. Yet could they stoop to attack and rob a younger brother? Herluin rode silently, pondering; his own sense of what was right told him they could not but some instinct, born of a well sharpened perception, told him that they could. He cast a swift sideways glance at his lord. Henry seemed to be his normal self again, cheerful and energetic, with the affair of Conan if not forgotten, at least thrust far beneath the surface. Herluin did not know what Anselm had said to the Prince on that nocturnal visit, but the latter had returned in a very different state of mind and Herluin was profoundly thankful. He saw so much of potential good in the Prince he had chosen to serve, so much that was worth the King and the Duke put together, that he had been doubly distressed by the violent, unworthy fury that had sent Conan to his death. But because he combined sense with his principles he saw that which was best in his lord far out-weighing what the darker forces might throw up and at the thought of those forces his body grew tense, aware of how they threatened himself, in a manner he had as yet revealed to no man.

He looked at Henry seeing the thick hair falling forward as always over the broad forehead, the dark eyes alert and smiling. Please God no danger for him, not now!

The winter twilight was falling when they reached the hunting lodge and inside found the table ready, a smell of roasting meat tantalising to men with empty stomachs and in a short while they were eating hungrily of venison and partridges, hashed duck and crane dressed in a rich spicy sauce, while their dogs roamed freely waiting for scraps.

'Enjoy this, my lord,' Herluin said. 'It is Lent next week.'

Henry groaned. 'By my soul, so it is. Once a year the Church condemns us to fish and what satisfaction is that to a hungry man's belly? I wonder if God created the fish to make us do penance?' He grinned across at his friend. 'But I've had my fill.' Stretching and yawning, he added, 'We'll hunt again tomorrow and go back to Avranches for the holy season.'

In his chamber, the only other room in the lodge, it was bitterly cold despite the shutters closed to the night air and he told Fulcher to go to the kitchen hut and tell one of the serving maids to bring him some hot spiced wine.

Presently she came, a big full-breasted girl with tawny hair and laughing hazel eyes. He drank the wine as she stood there, holding her by the hand though she showed no disposition to leave, her eyes appraising his strong body.

Finding her to his liking he smacked her rounded buttocks whereat she gave a giggle, her eyes inviting him so that he chased her across the room, laughing and demanding payment from her rosy mouth, finally chasing her into his bed. There they spent a joyous tumbling night and when he woke in the morning it was with a pleasurable sense of physical well-being.

The girl was long gone about her work so he rose and went to stand by the window. It was another fine day, the sun well up for he had slept later than usual and outside his men were making preparations for the day's hunt. In a little chapel he guessed Roger would be saying his Mass and Herluin would no doubt be there, but Raoul was below, grooming Rougeroy, brushing his fine coat and long mane; Gulfer was sitting on a log mending some torn jesses while Hamo lounged against the edge of the well, eating some bread and cheese. Goodnatured Hamo was the lazy one, Henry thought, never at work if he could take his ease.

The air was still crisp after the night frost, the sky a pale blue. It would be a good day to hunt, to ride through the forest feeling the strength of Rougeroy bearing him, the strength of his own arm using bow and spear, and the chase raising an appetite for good food. And tonight he might send for that obliging wench again.

He flexed his arms, at one with the bright day, and rubbing his chin decided it was several days since he had been shaved. Crossing to the door he shouted to Fulcher for water and a barber.

The operation was almost finished when he heard the sound of a horse galloping fast and then drawing to a sharp halt below. He sent Fulcher to find out who had arrived so precipitously and a few minutes later the lad returned with a young man of perhaps eighteen, travel-stained and weary. He bent the knee at once.

'My lord, I've ridden since yesterday . . .'

'What is it?' Henry pushed the barber aside, sending the fellow away, and wiping his face with a towel. That it was urgent and bad news he did not need telling, and already the pleasure of the morning was dispelled.

The traveller remained on his knees. 'Lord, I am Simon of La Barre, youngest brother to Herluin. My father sent me to seek service with the Duke when we heard of his triumph at Rouen

'. . .' he saw Henry smile a little but he went on, 'only when I got there I found the court gone to Caen, so I followed.'

'Well? What happened to send you scurrying here?' Henry studied the lad as he spoke. Simon had the same colouring and the same angular figure as his brother though he was not so tall, but his eyes were blue not grey, widely alert, without Herluin's heavy lids, and his features were more regular, smooth and boyish, the mouth curved like a woman's. He looked up at the Prince with unabashed curiosity.

'Lord Count, most of the great men of Normandy are gathered there, some for the Duke and some for the King. I was surprised not to find my brother there with you, but . . .' he broke off briefly. 'Lord they have made a treaty.'

Henry stood very still, stiff with a premonition of evil. 'My brothers?'

'Yes, lord, and with many barons to witness it—Count Stephen of Aumale and the Count of Eu, I know. And Gerard of Gournay, Robert de Beaumont, the lords of Auberville and Freville . . .'

'What of the Lord of Conches?'

'He was with the King too, and his son, Ralph.'

So they had all gone over to Rufus, even after Robert's victory, he thought angrily. He pulled his mantle more closely about his shoulders for the room seemed chill. 'And who stands for the Duke?'

Simon's brows were drawn close together in a frown. 'The Count of Bellême, my lord, and William of Breteuil, Hugh of Grandmesnil and his sons, and some others, but I cannot remember all the names.'

Henry swung away to the window. They were alone in the room but for Fulcher who was standing silently by the door, watching his master in acute anxiety. Outside the men had gathered in groups, talking together, wondering at the reason for this urgent visit.

'And the treaty?' he asked at last, indicating that Simon should rise from his knees. 'What do you know of that?'

'Mostly what was common talk afterwards, for everyone was speaking of it. It was sworn to by twelve men for the Duke and twelve for the King.'

'Tell me,' he said sharply. That his brothers should agree a treaty without him was indefensible—was he not Count of the Côtentin, owning a third part of the duchy?

Simon paused, as if hesitating now that he had come so far to be the bearer of bad news, but he was about to speak when there was a tap on the door. Annoyed at the interruption Henry opened it himself in a spurt of irritation, however seeing Herluin with Roger the priest, he bade them enter and shut the door behind them.

Herluin looked at the visitor in astonishment. 'Simon! What in heaven's name are you doing here.'

Henry gave a harsh laugh. 'He has come to shatter the pleasure of our hunting, my friend. It seems my brothers plot my ruin.'

Roger folded his arms in his sleeves. 'That was to be expected, my lord.'

'Was it, by God! I did not think so. But Simon was about to tell me of this treaty they have agreed behind my back which bodes no good to me, I'm sure of that. Speak, boy.'

Simon cast a quick glance at his tall, frowning brother, and then came out baldly with the truth.

'My lord, it was agreed that the King will continue to hold those castles he has already invested, the Duke to keep his and . . .' he looked from one to the other, 'and the King is to have Cherbourg and Mont St. Michel while Duke Robert will take the rest of your county.'

'What!' Henry was almost speechless with astonishment. What right had Curthose and Red William to parcel out his lands as if he were a chattel, a nithing—as if he were not also their father's son? He beat one fist into the other in impotent fury. By God, had he not paid three thousand marks of silver for this very land on which he stood?

Herluin had seized Simon by the shoulder. 'Think, boy! Are you sure? It cannot be true.'

Henry said drily, 'I think it can. I am beginning to know my brothers too well, though even I did not believe they could do this to me.'

Simon was silent, staring at this unknown Prince who meant little to him other than his brother's chosen lord; the fact that de Redvers had sent him here to Valognes gave him a sense of importance, fed his desire to be at the centre of things.

Henry began to pace rapidly, as if the small room could not

contain his growing rage. 'Do they think I am a child to have sweetmeats taken from me?' Robert's perfidy astounded him most, for had he not gone to Robert's aid less than three months ago? 'And the barons?' he burst out. 'Did none speak for me?'

'One or two, my lord, at the beginning. Earl Hugh was one— Messire de Redvers too, but the Duke and the King together were too powerful. They have agreed each to be the other's heirs and none of the barons dared dispute after that.'

'And Prince Edgar? Was he there?'

'Aye, he was, but he fared no better than yourself, my lord Count. He is banished, his lands in Normandy and England confiscated.'

'Edgar banished?' Henry stared at Simon in disbelief. 'In God's name, why?'

'Well, it seemed the King's will, though the Duke did not want it at first. Only he yielded in the end.'

'He would!' Henry thought of his gentle Saxon cousin. 'Poor Edgar, what does Rufus think he will do?'

Roger the priest had been standing quietly, listening to the talk. Now he said, 'The King has made a grave error. Prince Edgar at court and with lands of his own would be less potential danger than Edgar banished. I would guess, my lord, that he will go, as he has done before, to his brother-in-law the King of the Scots, and then the Red King will have enemies at his back door. Likewise he has made a needless enemy of yourself.'

'You are right, by God and His Mother!' He stood by the window, trying to assimilate this appalling news. It meant, and he knew it, that the combined forces of his two brothers would be marching against him to implement their infamous treaty. Despite their former double dealing, their treachery towards him, he had not wanted to think them capable of this. Did they want his life too?

He had been so sure of his future, his destiny that Abbot Anselm had predicted for him, but now, on this bright morning, a slow trickle of fear crept into his bones. If they were against him, had weaned all his friends from his side, what chance had he in a fight against them? Unsentimental though he was the loss of those friends—Earl Hugh, de Redvers, Ralph de Toeni, hurt damnably. He felt utterly alone. Not half an hour since he had stood by this same window rejoicing in the prospect of the day's hunting—now the morning held a menace, a hint of death. If they caught him, would his brothers kill him? Imprison him, perhaps for life? Once he would have repudiated the thought. Now he did not know. Only he wondered what he had done to make them think him their enemy.

'My lord,' Herluin's voice broke into his furious thoughts. 'What will you do?'

He turned back to face them and saw them looking at him expectantly. He did not answer the question immediately, but instead said, 'Simon La Barre, it was good of you to come to warn us. What now? Will you stay with me?'

There was a pause. Simon opened his mouth and shut it again.

Henry smiled wrily. 'Or am I so poor a case that you will go hurrying back to my perfidious brothers?'

Simon glanced at Herluin and then said easily, 'My lord, if I had entered the Duke's service I should have been at the lowest end of the knights' table—if I serve you as my brother has done, I think his good offices will secure me a better place.'

Henry burst out laughing. 'By St. Peter, you are honest. And you are right. You shall be among my own household. Will that suffice?'

Herluin sent his brother an annoyed look, but the irony was lost on Simon, 'Thank you, my lord,' he answered coolly. 'Messire de Redvers thought when he sent me to you that you would be glad of another sword. He told me to tell you that he would aid you if he could, but the King has garrisoned Vernon with English troops.'

Somehow the news cheered him beyond measure for it meant at least that Richard would aid if he could, was still his friend.

'What will we do?' he said, at last answering Herluin's question. 'We will make a fight of it, by God. I will show them I am not a weakling to be driven off my lands by their plots. If they want the Côtentin, they will have to seize it by force.'

He saw the satisfaction in their faces and when they rode out half an hour later they made a small but brave company, his gonfanon fluttering on the pole borne by Hamo, his hawks in their gay hoods carried as usual by Gulfer, his leashed hounds and alaunts in the capable hands of Walter the lymer, the pack horses following laden with his household gear.

They rode first to Coutances but there found the gates barred to them by Bishop Geoffrey, always Duke Robert's man. Henry did not waste time attempting anything there, merely commenting that his brothers had hastened to spread the news that he was deprived of his lands.

Riding on southwards towards Avranches Simon La Barre drew his horse close to his brother and said in a low voice, 'It may be you have given your sword to the wrong prince.'

Herluin retorted sharply, '*I* have? Are you not his man too?'

'Oh aye, at the moment. But would you wreck our fortunes by setting them on one target?'

Herluin looked at him in surprise. 'What ails you boy? Can you not see he is the best man to serve?'

Simon shrugged, staring between his horse's ears. 'Our father was maybe not so foolish in wanting me to enter the Duke's service.'

Herluin snorted. 'That was probably because he thought it expedient to have a son in each camp. I'm surprised he didn't send Milo to the King.'

'He did suggest it, but Milo has gone to Mont St. Michel to be a monk.'

'As he always wished,' Herluin sighed. 'Who shall say he has not chosen the better part?' He was silent for a while, but then roused himself to say vigorously, 'Well, I'm glad for him. But I hope you see that you will do better with us than elsewhere.'

Simon glanced at his brother in open astonishment. 'You can say that now—when, if the King and the Duke have their way, the Prince will be banished with naught but his sword?'

'I can say it. If he must be exiled, why I will go too—but I tell you this, a day will come when he will be greater than either of his brothers. I have always believed it.'

Simon laughed derisively. 'You dream, Herluin. Our father says you were always the dreamer. I see things as they are, and the Duke and the King have more to offer at the moment.'

'I know my master,' Herluin said confidently, and smiled at the sulky young man beside him. 'And I tell you he'll hold his own. You'll not regret this, Simon.'

He cantered on to join the Prince, certain that a few weeks in Henry's service would dispel the lad's doubts. Even defeat, he thought, would do no more than deflect his master's course for a while.

At Avranches Earl Hugh, who had ridden to his native city at the express command of William Rufus, saw the company approaching and ordering the gates to be shut fast heaved his great bulk up the narrow spiral stair to the roof of the gate-house. Below him the Prince, riding his magnificent red destrier, drew rein and called for the gates to be opened. The Earl did not like what he had to do but he leaned over the parapet and shouted down, 'My lord, I cannot let them open to you.'

Henry started at the familiar voice and soothed Rougeroy's restless prancing. He looked up in silence for several moments before he spoke.

'Hugh! I did not think this of you.'

The Earl shrugged. There were dark clouds scudding up from the west and it was beginning to rain, adding to the irritation of his mood. 'I am sorry for it, but I tell you frankly that the King and the Duke combined are too strong a force for me. And I've no mind to lose my earldom in England.'

Henry leaned on the saddle, frowning. The loss of Avranches and Hugh's defection were blows he had not expected. 'Will no friend stand by me? Not even my old tutor?'

The Earl seemed honestly regretful. 'I wish I could—you were ever a good pupil, Henry—but I've too much now to risk losing all in a rash act of folly, for folly it would be to set yourself against the might of Normandy and England. You would be well advised to ride on, over the border to Brittany, or where you will, until the times are better for you. You cannot pay an army to defy the Duke.'

It was too far to see the expression on Hugh's face, but with a cold fear in him Henry asked, 'He has taken my silver?'

'Aye.'

He chewed his whip, trembling with rage and frustration. He wanted to hit out, to meet them face to face, challenge them, throw their perfidy back at them.

As if sensing this, Hugh called, 'Go, boy, anywhere. You cannot think to hold your brothers at bay.'

'Nevertheless I will try,' Henry shouted back vigorously. 'They have robbed me unjustly and I appeal my cause to Almighty God.'

'Then may He aid you,' Hugh answered, 'I cannot.'

There seemed no more to be said.

Herluin edged his horse up to the Prince's. 'Let us go to Mont St. Michel. I doubt if they can have seized that yet and some of our Breton friends will surely ride to help us.'

'Aye,' Roger agreed, 'we could hold out on the Mount as long as maybe with the sand and the sea to aid us—long enough to give your brothers time to reconsider.'

Henry was silent. This was his city, his castle—inside was his hall, filled with his possessions and to be robbed and cheated thus, before his staring men, was an indignity he would not easily forget.

Roger said, 'come, my lord.'

But he had not yet finished with the Earl. 'Hugh Lupus,' he shouted up at the burly figure on the roof of the gatehouse, 'I trust you're not so much the Wolf that you'll keep my mistress in your lair. Is Alide of Caen in the castle with my children?'

'She's here and unharmed.'

'Then bid her join me.'

There was a slight pause and it seemed as if the Earl was about to deny him but then he gave a laugh that shook his great belly. 'I'll not deny you your pleasure, my lord,' he called back, leaning over the parapet, his shield in his hand, the wolf's head clearly visible painted in black on a scarlet ground, as if he expected one of Henry's archers to loose a shaft at him.

'And my garrison?'

The Earl nodded. 'Those that wish to ride out may do so.'

He disappeared and the small cavalcade waited outside for what seemed a long time, the horses pawing the ground, tails switching, some of the dogs growling and snapping at each other, several stretching out on the ground, closing their eyes against the rain. At last the gates were opened and some twenty men rode out with Alide in the centre. She was mounted on a small palfrey, with a maidservant behind her carrying her youngest child, a babe of barely three months, while young Robert was held in the arms of one of the soldiers, chuckling with delight at the unaccustomed pleasure of being on horseback.

They rode down the slope and Gerard of St. Lo, the knight Henry had left in command, raised his hand in greeting.

'The first we heard of the treaty, my lord, was when Earl Hugh came himself. I could do naught but submit. Your lady is safe.'

She was wearing a long blue mantle, the hood about her face for the rain was heavy now. She seemed calm, refusing to show to the world the desperate anxiety she had suffered since she had learned that all Normandy had turned against her lover.

He rode forward to meet her and reaching across set his hand on hers. 'Well, my heart, it seems our fortunes are low, but please God only for the moment.'

She smiled at him, caring for nothing but the fact that he was beside her again, his hand warm on hers, and she was free of the confining castle and even more constricting fear.

They turned their backs on Avranches and its barred gates, and he sent Herluin ahead with a scouting party to the island of Mont St. Michel. Presently Herluin returned to say the rock of the Archangel still held for him, but the tide was now up and would prevent their crossing before morning, and he suggested that the night should be spent at Barre le Heron. Their arrival threw their host into a paroxysm of activity in his endeavour to feed and entertain his guests, but it was clear the old man was uneasy. He could scarcely veil his annoyance at seeing his younger offspring joining Herluin in the service of one whose star seemed, at the moment, in the decline. His eldest son, Gilbert, ponderously gave it as his opinion that the Duke and the King would be in the Avranchin within the week and they had all best make peace as soon as they might, to which Herluin replied sharply that when it was a question of might against right, too many men took the expedient way. Simon sat listening sulkily to the arguments of his elders and the youngest boy, a lad of fourteen, begged to be allowed to ride with the Prince, to which his father replied with some asperity that he thought two sons in the Prince's service was enough.

In the morning when the tide withdrew Henry led his small force across the causeway and in at the castle gateway. Above him the path rose steeply to where the claustral buildings covered the highest point in the island and the monks came hastening down to assure him of their loyalty. His own garrison cheered him in, but nevertheless his solder's instinct told him that despite the solid walls and the protection of the sea he was entering a false security, that he was cornered in this last resort, for there was no escape except by water and he had no ships.

They were trapped and he knew it.

The mount was in itself no more than a small rocky island set in the midst of great sand banks, the causeway providing access to the mainland only at low tide. Here were castle and monastery and little else but wild sea birds' nests, gulls crying mournfully overhead, and the sea grey and turbulent under a leaden March sky.

It was more than a week now since Henry's small force had arrived here and this morning he paced along the sands by the causeway, the smell of the sea in his nostrils, the keen air fanning out his red mantle like a sail behind him, his hound, Lyfa, following his footsteps. He was glad to be alone for a while, though Roger and Herluin walked by the causeway, talking together and watching him. They were his friends, but he needed solitude occasionally and it was singularly hard to come by.

Beneath his feet small rocks jutted from the sand, encrusted with mussels and other shells and now and then he saw tiny crabs in the pools left by the receding tide, while Lyfa slithered about in the water, snapping vainly at the crabs. He liked this wild coast, the sense of freedom the sea gave, a freedom that might, now, have all too short a duration. For, looking across the short distance that separated him from the mainland he could see movements of men and horses and a few days ago one of his scouts had brought in the news that the Duke with his forces had arrived at Arderon, blockading the southern side of the sand banks, while further away to the north-east English soldiers and mercenaries in Rufus' pay had entrenched themselves at Genets on the northern coast. The King himself it seemed was at Avranches, royally entertained by Earl Hugh in the castle that until ten days ago had been Henry's.

So, cut off on three sides by his brothers and with the sea at his back, it was small wonder that he paced now with no pleasant feelings towards his closest kin, for he who had been Count of the Côtentin was now, by their will, Count of no more than a rock set in a wilderness of sand and sea. Robert, indeed, had defrauded him in so flagrant a manner that he still found it hard to comprehend, especially when he remembered last November in Rouen. Were they his brothers, Rufus and Curthose, born of the same mother from the same noble seed, or were they the devil's spawn?

He, who was rarely bitter, turned now into the biting March wind, and found it hard to maintain his usual sanguine outlook. Not only did he have the lives of his followers in his hands, but Alide and his children were within the walls and even when he lay with her at night, thankful for the comfort of her presence, he wished he had sent her to safety before his brothers blocked the way.

He would not let either her or his men see his anxiety, which was why he walked alone, nor would he return to them until he had fought and beaten this mood of desperation and doubt —miserable doubt, for deep below the surface he had begun to wonder if this reversal of fortune was not a punishment for his treatment of Conan. Was God so angry with him that He had sent this lonely reversal, driving him to the last windswept corner of his county, that he might be chastened and brought low? He knew more of his own nature now, that he was capable of violent rage, that it could seize and dominate him, yet he had repented and Anselm had absolved him. What was it Anselm had said? Penances indeed he had laid on him, coupled with some words which came back to him now—'if misfortune should come, take it not as a blow from the Hand of God, but as His path to strength'. He had not thought a great deal of those words at the time, but now began to understand what the Abbot had meant. If this present change of fortune was sent to prove him, then it was imperative that he summon up every resource to meet it with courage.

He turned so that the wind was behind him and began to walk back, bracing his shoulders against its buffeting, as if it were a physical expression of the forces he must resist.

When he reached them, Herluin said, 'My lord, we are short of water. Let me take a party across the sands to fill our casks.'

Henry stared out towards the mainland, brown and dull grey-green, awaiting the new clothing of spring. 'Do you think my brothers will stand by and let you ride where you will? There have been enough skirmishes these last few days to show us that.'

Herluin smiled. 'You forget this is my own land. I know every track, every stream, every wood hereabouts, and I can find my way in the dark with no need of a lantern. Six men will suffice.'

'We need the water,' Roger put in. 'There is only one cask left in the castle and less in the Abbey.'

Henry agreed reluctantly, though he knew they were right. Together they walked back through the gates. The castle was a simple affair of hall and gatehouse, walls and a single tower, which Henry had at once put in a state of defence, setting Gerard of St. Lo in command of the garrison. Abbot Roger's monks eagerly offered their services, appearing with cudgels in their hands prepared to support the Prince whose rule had brought order to the Côtentin, and with them came Milo La Barre to greet his brothers. He was a lean serious young man and said gravely that no one in the Abbey wanted anyone but Henry for their overlord. Still smarting from the lack of support at Avranches, the enthusiasm of his pitifully small band of supporters here on the mount was some comfort. The Bretons among the garrison were eager for the fight; border warfare with the Dukes of Normandy was bred in them and the fact that Henry was of the same house bothered them not at all.

In the castle his men were gathered in the hall for dinner. Provisions they had in plenty for a long siege, and but for the water problem, he thought, they could last out here for months. He was somewhat reluctant to let Herluin go on a foray—he was too valuable a leader—but there was no other man so well qualified, and they were laying their plans after the meal when the cry went up from the guards, 'Raiders on the sands!'

Every man scrambled to his feet, stools were overset and benches tipped up as there was a concerted rush for the courtyard where arms were stacked and horses stabled. Men ran for hauberks and helms, thrusting their arms into stiff chain mail, cursing as they struggled to fasten swords and find shields. Gerard the captain joined the stampede and outside marshalled the men, selecting some twenty or so to drive the enemy off, not risking all their small force in one skirmish.

Henry himself, growing used to these raids, went calmly to the top of the gatehouse and there saw a party of horsemen galloping over the sands seemingly chasing two riders who were making for the causeway.

He called down to Gerard to take out his troop and chase off the enemy. 'It seems we have two friends left. It would be churlish not to escort them in, eh?'

Gerard grinned appreciatively and led the way out. Within a few minutes they had reached the two riders who turned and rode with them straight for the ducal forces. There was a short sharp scrap, which seemed to Henry more like a tourney than a serious fight, and then their opponents disengaged and rode off for the mainland. A cheer went up from the watching men on the mount and Gerard led his soldiers back with the addition of two knights from Brittany who came to offer their swords to the Prince.

He greeted them warmly. Even two swords were welcome in his present predicament, but it was his own cheerful and optimistic presence that kept spirits high and to Herluin it was a source of intense annoyance that the only glum countenance was that of his own brother.

'If you knew Henry as well as I do,' he said as they watched the riders returning, 'you would not fear that he will survive this and any other adversity that may come.'

'You are besotted by him,' Simon scowled. 'Just because he smiles and make jokes you think he has lost nothing. I tell you, you will find yourself without a roof over your head or a silver piece in your pocket if you stay with him.'

Herluin looked down at him. 'I was earning my bread by my sword before you were breeched and I can do it again if I have to. Better fall on bad times with a Christian prince than serve a blasphemer or a goodnatured weakling. And who is to say Henry will come out of this the worst?'

'You delude yourself if you think otherwise,' Simon retorted.

Herluin fought down the desire to slap his brother's handsome, insolent face. 'And you forget yourself.'

Simon glared at him. After a moment he burst out, 'And I've not even had the chance to fight yet. There have been half a dozen skirmishes but that captain has not once chosen me to go.'

Herluin smiled faintly. 'If that is all, I'll ask him to send you on the next foray.' He did not mention his own proposed raid planned for tonight; he did not want a fiery young hothead with him, but chose quietly and without causing attention only men who were seasoned fighters, Raoul the deer among them.

They went in the darkest hour soon after midnight, slipping unobtrusively out of the castle and over the causeway when the tide was at its lowest, thankful that there was no moon to light their going. Their horses' hooves were wrapped in cloths, the mules bearing the casks led by ropes instead of harness.

Henry rose from his bed and went to stand in the highest room of the gatehouse, peering out into the darkness and waiting anxiously for his friend's return. An hour passed and then another. He wrapped his mantle about him and went up the narrow stair and out into the clear cold air.

The sentry turned smartly as he came through the narrow arch. 'If they don't return soon, my lord, the tide will catch them.'

'I know,' the Prince said. When the tide turned it seemed to come in very fast, sweeping over the sands, cutting off all access to the mainland, and there was still no sign of Herluin and his men.

But at last when he could both see and hear the return of the waters he caught sight of darker shadows in the darkness and then the faint sound of muffled hooves far below. He ran down the stair and was in the bailey as Herluin led his foraging party under the gateway.

'Thank God,' he said and clapped his friend on the shoulder as he dismounted. 'I was beginning to be anxious.'

Herluin looked grave as he eased the helm from his head. He was sweating inside the heavy chain mail and his hair clung damply to his head. 'We succeeded this time, my lord, but your brothers' men are everywhere and a pedlar fellow we disturbed from his sleep in a wood told me that more arrive all the time.'

A week later the need for water was again acute. It had been a week of small raids. A few men had been lost, two killed and several wounded or captured, but otherwise the time dragged by wearily. Henry walked the shore or the castle walls, chewing the end of his whip, cheering the men, inspecting arms, organising practice at the butts and knightly exercises to keep them alert. But it was heavy work and he wondered how long his brothers would sit on his doorstep before making their intentions plain.

He sent Herluin to the mainland again for water, but this time the royal forces were waiting for them and they came back empty-handed. The water on the mount was low now, and even though he rationed it strictly the casks were almost empty.

Alide came to him, her face anxious. 'I must have water for the children, my lord, Robert cries from thirst.' A spark of anger lit her eyes, 'Are your brothers so turned against you that they would deny us what we need to live?'

'I wish I knew,' he answered grimly. 'Do not ask me what activates them, for I do not know.' He paused, laying his hand on her plait where it lay over her bosom. 'Don't fret, my love, I'll get water somehow. Robert shall not cry any more.'

He called a knight to him, a Breton suitable for a go-between, and bade him ride under a flag of truce to Duke Robert's camp at Arderon.

'Tell my brothers,' he said, 'that if they wish to make war on me that is one thing, but they need not press the powers of nature into their service by depriving us of our bodily needs. Ask them to allow my men to fetch fresh water and let the valour of our soldiers decide the outcome.'

He hoped his messenger would find Duke Robert alone, for his eldest brother was more likely to yield to his request than the harder headed Rufus. In due course the knight returned, his white flag fluttering from his spear, not only with the request granted, but bearing with him a tun of the Duke's best wine.

Henry set his hands on his hips and laughed as he had not done for some days. 'God's death, but Robert is predictable! I'm very sure Rufus would not have parted with wine nor allowed Robert to do so had he been in the camp. He'll roast Curthose for that.'

His men went out at once and returned with laden casks for the Duke kept his promise, despite, as Henry had suspected, some hard words from his fellow commander.

'Holy Face,' Rufus exploded when he rode into Robert's camp the next day. 'What are we doing here? Making war or fighting a tourney? You are a fool, Robert.'

For once the Duke did not allow himself to be swayed by his brother's bluster. 'I may be a fool,' he retorted with spirit, 'but I'll not be inhuman. Beauclerc was thirsty and I gave him to drink, that's all.'

'We are m-making war,' Rufus repeated, stammering in his annoyance, 'And in war sentiment has no place. We mean to b-beat Henry, do we not?'

'Beat him in fair fight, yes, but I'll not stand by and see him die of thirst. If we lose him where shall we find another brother? Heaven would frown upon us if we caused a brother's death.'

Rufus gave a great burst of raucous laughter. 'What has heaven to do with it? To hell with heaven, I say,' and he slapped his thigh in amusement at his own joke. 'What is the difference? We are out to put Henry in his place and if he resists us and suffers in consequence, who is to blame but himself?'

'I suppose so,' The Duke looked reluctant. 'At least—I would have his lands, but I would not harm him.'

'Oh, rest you,' Rufus cast him a scathing glance, 'he'll come out of this in one piece as long as he yields to us. If that is not why we are here, then by Lucca's face, I'll take my men home again.'

Afterwards Robert de Beaumont said to Grandmesnil, 'I swear there were never two stranger bedfellows than the King and the Duke. This alliance will not last overlong.'

'How can you have peace when three dogs fight over one bone?' Grandmesnil queried caustically and sighed for the days of his old master.

William of Breteuil laughed. 'And who wants peace, for God's sake? What would a fighting man do all day if we had peace?'

For the next few days the skirmishes continued and one morning Henry and Herluin stood by the gate and watched as Gerard led out a party, one of whom was Simon La Barre.

'The boy is developing some skill in the art of fighting,' Herluin said with satisfaction. 'He handles his horse well and his sword.'

'Thanks to your teaching. I've watched you show him how to bear himself. Look—see that troop coming over the sands? I know that emblem, that's de Beaumont, and there is de Toeni's banner too.' Was Ralph there, Henry wondered, and how many more of his friends come against him? It seemed that when the King and the Duke commanded together no man dared to disobey the call.

It was fine today, the persistent rain of the last few weeks had cleared away and a pale watery sun had broken through the clouds, lighting the pools in the wide stretches of sand. To the watching men the sand seemed to stretch out endlessly as the two groups of horsemen converged.

There was a short exchange of blows, a clash of weapons. One of the Prince's men fell, a spear in his chest and his maddened horse galloped for the mainland. Henry swore under his breath.

Herluin kept his eyes on Simon. 'Oh, well done, boy. That blow was hardly dealt. See, my lord, Simon has unhorsed a man.'

Henry put up a hand to shade his eyes for the sun was directly before them. It was difficult to see exactly what was happening in the fight, men splitting into groups or fighting singly hand to hand but in the mêlée he had picked out young Simon

139

striking out at an opponent. The enemy broke his spear on the pommel of Simon's saddle and at once Simon swung round and caught the man a blow on the back with the flat of his sword, sending him to the ground. The horse reared and thrust its way from the group, dragging the unfortunate rider flat on his back along the sand, for his spur had caught in the stirrup. Simon, yelling 'La Barre! La Barre!' at the top of his voice rode after the animal and catching the reins sprang down from the saddle. Shortening the sword he stood over his gasping enemy, ready to deliver the death stroke.

And then to the surprise of the watchers he stood transfixed, the blow undealt.

'What's the matter with him?' Herluin asked sharply 'He'll not make a soldier if he hesitates to kill.'

Henry said, as if he could scarcely credit it, 'Do you not see? Look, the fallen man has lost his helm.'

Herluin stared and was silent. There was no mistaking that tow coloured hair nor the ruddy face beneath it.

Neither spoke. They saw Simon lower his sword and hold out a hand to assist the King to his feet. They saw though they could not hear Rufus' bellowing laugh, saw him slap Simon on the back. Words passed between them and then he held out his hand. Simon knelt and kissed it. They mounted and rode off together to join the rest of the royal forces who had disengaged and were hurrying towards where their King had fallen.

Herluin stood rigid. Then a slow flush rose in his cheeks. 'God's cross,' he said hoarsely. He turned to look at Henry. 'My lord . . .'

Henry forced a smile. His men were riding back now, outnumbered and lessened by two men and two horses and somehow the perfidy of Simon La Barre had become the final stroke to break his resistance. But he would not let Herluin see it. 'We are not responsible for our brothers' actions,' he said with dry humour, 'or I should not be here at this moment. You need not blame yourself.'

He took Herluin's arm and walked him back into the hall. 'No doubt Rufus seduced him with fair words. My brother's one virtue is that he appreciates a good fighter and will keep his word to a knight when he breaks it everywhere else. I have lost two more men, it is true, but you have lost a brother, and for that I am sorry.' He added wrily, 'We are not fortunate in our brothers, you and I.'

Herluin said, 'He has brought shame on my house,' and shut his mouth on further speech. The fact that every man was discussing it at supper that night did not make it any easier to bear, for he felt every eye turned towards him as if Simon's treachery had laid its taint on him too and men looked to see if he also would desert their lord. He carried himself with dignity and met curious glances with a cool hard stare.

Henry ate without knowing or caring what he ate, and drank nothing at all. The noise and chatter in the hall, the clatter of dishes, the snapping and occasional barking of the dogs, and the sad cries of his hawks, all came and went like waves on a shore and he heard nothing of it. He was aware only of bitter resentment at the injustice of the attack on him, coupled with anxiety for his men, for Alide and the children, for himself—and a fury against his brothers who had brought him to this moment, for he had no doubt now that to hold out much longer would bring nothing but gradual diminishment, more incidents like this morning's, the paring away of his resources. Surely they would be satisfied with all his possessions without forcing him to his knees?

He must make terms, terms of some sort. It was worse, he thought, than the time in Bayeux tower, for here he must surrender himself of his own free will and his pride revolted at the prospect. At the same time, commonsense and his care for those dependent on him ordered his decision as always.

After the meal he called a council of war which included Herluin, Gerard, his Breton messenger, Roger the priest and Abbot Roger of the abbey. They met in the Abbot's lodging, more privily than in the hall full of soldiers spreading their pallets for the night, and he said in plain words that he could no longer see any point in prolonging the situation.

'My brothers mean to take what I have,' he said and kept his voice firm, 'and they will keep us penned in here until I yield. What point in risking lives to no purpose?'

'We can hold out as long as you will, my lord,' Gerard said stoutly. He was a big fair man with immense skill in sword play and he regarded fighting as the only occupation suitable for a man who was a man. 'We cannot be properly besieged because the sea fights for us twice a day.'

'That is true,' the Breton agreed, 'but my lord is right. If the Duke and the King will not go away without that for which they came our food will run out before theirs.'

'But Count Alain of Brittany, or the Count of Maine may come to our aid,' Gerard was beginning when Roger interrupted.

'Count Alain does not want to go to war with Normandy any more than the Count of Maine.' He had a smooth, precise voice and always saw clearly to the heart of any problem. Despite the fact that he was the least either by birth or rank he was listened to with attention. 'They are both friends to you, my lord Henry, but neither I think will jeopardise his land by taking sides against your brothers when they are allied together.'

Henry leaned back in his chair. He glanced at Herluin who shook his head—after this morning's affair he shrank from putting forward his views in council. Henry turned to Abbot Roger.

The Abbot had his hands folded before him. He had not been here long and harboured plans for rebuilding the church and many of the conventual buidings and was not overjoyed at the prospect of falling foul of the reigning Duke for all he would have preferred Henry for his liege-lord.

'I regret that I cannot see that you have any choice,' he said at last, choosing his words with care. 'No one grieves more than I at this sad reversal and I will beseech God to restore you to your rightful place as Count, but in the meantime . . .'

Henry straightened. 'In the meantime I must sue for peace and take what terms I am offered.'

In the morning he sent Gerard to his brothers under a flag of truce, asking only that he and his garrison might march out with full honours of war, trumpets sounding and banners raised. If they refused, if he had to ride out with shame, gonfanons pointing to the ground as Odo had done at Pevensey, his uncle would laugh a second time, and if he prayed at all at this moment of desperate uncertainty it was that God would hear this one request.

While Gerard was gone there was an air of tension over the whole island. In the abbey the monks prayed, as it was their business to do, and even the Abbot who was generally concerned with his plans for the builders, spent more time in church than was usual. Perhaps he had heard that the Red King had no scruples about relieving monastic houses of much of their wealth, nor in deposing Abbots and taking their revenues into his own hands.

The men in the castle sat about waiting. It was a bright spring day, the sun having some warmth in it at last after the long winter, and Raoul led out the Prince's horses, grooming them in the bailey while Gulfer sat crooning to his birds. Hamo lounged on an empty water cask and lifted his face to the sun, his eyes closed though he was far from sleep. Walter, good-natured and phlegmatic, had his lyme-hound on a leash and was fondling the great head—the only man who dared to do so without fear of losing a finger to those sharp teeth.

Fulcher sat cross-legged on the ground beside him. 'What do you think the King and the Duke will do?' he asked not for the first time.

Raoul grunted. 'How do we know the minds of princes?'

'We know the mind of ours,' Gulfer said laconically. He smoothed the feathers of a merlin, whistling a little tune to her.

'Gerard says they will banish him,' Fulcher went on, his young face creased with anxiety. 'And what will he do then? Where will he go?'

'For God's sake, boy,' Hamo opened his eyes and yawned. 'You've asked us that question a dozen times. How should we know—except that we'll go with him, we four anyway, and Herluin too.'

'And the priest,' Raoul said.

'Roger? He's a sly one and too quick with his answers for me,' Gulfer shook his head ponderously and Hamo laughed.

'That's because you are a dull-wit,' he said cheerfully, 'Master Roger suits our lord because he too has a brain, but whether his loyalty will stretch as far as exile, God knows—at least I suppose He does as Roger is one of his elect.'

Raoul made a sound that might be construed as a laugh. 'Maybe, but he's not above amusing himself. I saw him pinch the rump of a serving wench as quick as you please in the passage last night.'

'Well, I suppose most of us need our pleasurable moments—though we'll maybe find ourselves short of them if we go into exile.'

'We'll earn our bread somehow,' Hamo predicted with lazy

confidence, 'even if we have to sell our swords to the Emperor or the Pope himself.'

'God forbid,' Gulfer said hastily. 'Wed a year I've been and I don't fancy leaving my woman in Avranches to the mercy of the Red King's men—not but what she couldn't give a good account of herself with a frying pan if they so much as laid a hand on her. I've felt it on my backside before now.'

'I'd have thought you'd relish some respite then,' Walter grinned. 'I've a mind to see Paris. Do you think fat Philip would welcome us?' He whistled between his teeth and the hound pricked his ears.

Fulcher who had been staring from one to the other, burst out, 'I don't see how you can make such a joke of it when maybe even his life is threatened.'

Hamo gave him a friendly blow on the shoulder, tumbling him backwards. 'We joke, child, because we dare not do otherwise.'

The others were silent and Fulcher picked himself up, dusting off his tunic. 'I—I am afraid for him.'

Raoul stood smoothing Rougeroy's coat. 'So are we all, boy.'

In the hall Herluin sat with Roger the priest. They talked in low voices, agreed that if banishment was to be the order Gerard brought back, then they too would go.

'I am used to wandering,' Herluin said, 'it makes small odds to me where I am. But you . . .'

'I have developed a taste for being in the centre of things,' Roger said drily, 'and would not return to being a country priest again. And if we are to go, you'll need a priest to say mass for you.'

Herluin was silent for a while, staring down at his feet, his expression more melancholy than usual.

Roger went on in a low voice so that no one else might hear. 'There is something further on your mind, something other than your brother's defection? I have sensed it more than once.' He thought at first his companion was not going to answer, but after a moment Herluin raised to him a face haunted by inner grief.

'I will tell you a thing I have told no one.' He glanced around the hall, at the men settling for the night, the dogs sleeping by the fire, the servants dowsing the lights, leaving only one or two dips burning in their sconces. One group of men-at-arms were still playing at dice, a few talking quietly together. It was familiar enough and yet tomorrow night none of them might be here. He turned back to the chaplain. Roger, he thought, might not be the best nor the most holy priest in Normandy, but he had a quick understanding which was, perhaps what he most needed at the moment.

He said, 'I think a curse lies on me.' He saw Roger's startled glance but went on, 'When I was born one of my mother's serving girls brought in a woman who could read the stars and all manner of portents. She could tell what omens there were and she—she foretold a shadow lying over my life. She spoke of a downfall, a desolation . . .'

He sensed rather than saw Roger's startled attention but kept his gaze lowered. 'She did not say what it was to be—only some evil, some moment that would bring a black shadow over me.'

'Death?' The word lay between them like an omen itself but Herluin shook his head.

'No, that is the odd thing. She prophesied not my death but an end to living. I do not know what she meant.'

'Did your mother tell you of it?'

'Aye, before she died, one night when we were alone together. She was afraid, she thought she must warn me—and I a lad of no more than seventeen. You can imagine . . .' he broke off momentarily. 'That was why I went away, to sell my sword where I might, so that whatever evil there was should not fall on my family. Perhaps it is superstitious nonsense—now that I am of sober years I tell myself so, yet I know the shadow is there. I know it.' He raised his head at last and looked at the priest. 'I have never spoken of it since my mother died, not even to my father.'

'How can you be sure?'

'I feel it,' Herluin said. 'Sometimes I forget for a while, but then I am aware of it again. One day it will come upon me, destroy me and perhaps those I love. I meant to be solitary, never to give more than my sword to any man, nor my love to a woman. And yet,' he broke off, looking towards the door of the Prince's chamber, 'before I realised it I had given him my love and cannot keep from serving him. Only I fear, I fear what I may bring upon him.'

'It was a strange prophecy,' Roger said, 'but you have lived

145

these many years without it coming true. Perhaps the dread of it in your mind is more real than an old woman's vision—if vision it was.'

'Perhaps. I wish I could believe it. But—I am as certain of it as I am that I live. Yet how it should be an end to living though not death, I cannot see. If it must come then I pray only that God will let it fall on me and not on any other.'

'My dear friend,' Roger laid his hand momentarily on Herluin's where it lay slack on the table, 'if the devil is at work here, you are equipped to fight him. I know that.'

Slowly Herluin straightened. The tension went and the dread receded—if only for the moment. 'That is why . . .' he said and knew he need say no more.

'I know,' the priest nodded. 'I have seen you keep vigil, I have seen your acts of charity. I remember what you did for the old King. Now—I will watch with you.'

'I don't care for myself—only for him. Perhaps I should go away, but I cannot bring myself to leave him, and especially not now. If they want to send him back to Bayeux tower . . .'

Roger was silent for a moment, staring at the closed door of the Prince's chamber. 'He'll not let them cage him again.'

Inside that chamber Henry paced as though he were caged already while Alide sat on a stool with the baby Matilda on her knee. Robert was walking on his solid little legs behind his father, his dark eyes fixed on that purposeful figure, trying to catch the long jewelled belt that swung out whenever he turned.

Presently Henry halted and stood looking down at her. 'You are so calm.'

'Calm!' she echoed. 'When tomorrow hangs in the balance, when only God knows whether we will have a tomorrow.'

He laughed suddenly. 'Do you think my brothers mean to have my head? I am very sure it is not so much their ill-will that I have to fear but their over-abundance of greed. Robert may bring himself to steal my treasure, but I doubt he would take my life.'

'No, I did not think that.' She did not meet his gaze but sat with her eyes fixed on the flickering flames of the fire burning in the brazier. 'Only that it may be . . .' she broke off and held the babe close to her, her face troubled.

He knelt beside her, his arm about her, his other smoothing the child's head. Robert came and leant against him and he felt a moment's rush of emotion, of protectiveness for these three who depended utterly upon him. To what had he brought them on this rock of the Archangel?

In due course Gerard returned. The King and the Duke granted their brother's request. If he would yield up all his possessions he should have life and limb for all his men and march out with full honours of war.

'And for myself?' Henry asked.

Gerard met his straight stare. 'A day to depart out of Normandy, my lord.'

Henry gave a bark of laughter. 'Wine of Christ, my brothers are generous—a whole day!'

With head high and a cheerful face he addressed his men, bidding them ride out with every piece of harness shining, their banners high, their swords and helms bright.

'After that,' he said, 'I would beg your escort as far as the border with Brittany and then you must go where you will, for I can no longer give you the pay you earn so well.'

They surged about him, begging him not to leave them, and when they found him adamant, entreated him to keep at least a small troop with him.

Their loyalty touched him. 'Ten only,' he said at last. 'My falconer, Raoul the deer, my standard and my lymer, and six others. Draw lots if you will, I cannot take more and those that come can expect little profit.'

There was a flood of talk, of protest, cries of loyalty that broke over him like a tide. He shouldered his way through them, speaking to each man, thanking each for his service. There was a bond between them all now, the few who had fought together and lost the fight on this tiny island.

'I will come back,' he said over and over again. 'I swear that I will come back.'

He left them at last and went to his chamber for the night. The children were asleep, the baby in a wooden cradle, Robert on a pallet at the foot of his parents' bed, his dark hair rumpled, one arm flung out in abandoned sleep. His father bent and tucked the arm beneath the bed clothes.

Alide sat on her stool by the fire, a mantle about her shoulders, her feet bare below her white shift. He could not read the expression on her face.

Standing opposite her he leaned against the wall, his arms

folded. 'I am tired,' he said. It was as if, now that the decision was made, the terms agreed, he could afford to rest—he had not slept at all last night.

But the future was bleak before him and he knew now how deep was his love for Normandy—it was rooted in the very marrow of his bones, passed down by the seed of men from the days of Rolf the Ganger. And he could see nothing before him but exile, loneliness, and the charity of foreigners.

Abruptly he began to undress and in equal silence Alide follow him to bed. For a while he lay still, not attempting to touch her, staring at the flickering light of the dying fire. She watched his face, an ache within her for the struggle she saw there, the struggle between despair and courage—but because he was the man he was she knew that courage would win. At barely twenty-three he had learned to stand alone and to depend on none but himself. Her eyes filled with tears but she controlled the desire to cry, turning her head aside to let them trickle unobtrusively into the pillow.

At last he spoke. 'I will give you half a dozen men to see you safe home to Caen.'

She said, 'I will stay with you.'

He sensed, though he had not touched her, the rigidity in her body. 'No. I do not know where I will go or what I will do, or even how long my exile will be. I cannot take you or the children into further danger.'

'My serving woman can take them home. I will come wherever you choose to go.'

'No,' he said again. 'God knows how hard my life may be.'

'I do not care.' She caught her breath on a sob, 'Only take me with you.'

'I cannot,' he said. 'Go back to Caen with young Robert and the babe and wait for me there.'

'Wait!' she whispered, 'but for how long?' She sat up, hugging her knees, her long hair falling to her waist, her eyes shadowed in the firelight. 'I always knew that I could not hold you. Is it now that I must let you go? Oh,' as he began to deny it, 'I know that circumstances force us apart, but I think you will be swept from me by other circumstances, that you will go forward to other things I cannot share with you. Only—take the boy, my lord, when he is old enough. Let him be your son if he can be nothing else.'

'Why, what is this?' he asked. 'Robert shall always be my son, and I will come back to Caen.' He looked up at her, at the curve of her bare shoulder, the line of neck and cheek that he knew so well. She had been a part of his life, though he sensed now how small that part was in truth. But because he did not want to hurt her, he said lightly, 'How could I keep from you?'

'There will be others,' she answered in a low voice as if she did not want him to hear, 'and where you are going I cannot come.'

Quite suddenly all her calm deserted her and she cast herself down beside him, her arms about him, shaken with crying. 'I know that I must go, but if only it were not tomorrow.'

He held her close to him, soothing her with gentle words, until these turned into more passionate loving that for a while at least shut out the thought of the inevitable parting. She clung to him as if she would make this night's joy so intense that it would suffice for all the lonely nights that must come. Three years ago at Caen it had been she who had been strong and comforting, who had taken a bewildered nineteen-year-old boy to her bed, but now it was she who was broken and grieving and he a man to comfort her. But there was no comfort, only aching loneliness and the certain knowledge that they would be divided tomorrow by more than divergent roads.

In the morning the company rode out as Henry wished—every man armed, every blade bright, the gonfanons high on their shafts. The Abbot blessed them as they went, out on to the wet windswept sands and back to the inhospitable mainland.

There the royal and ducal troops lined the way. Henry rode straight between their ranks, his eyes fixed on his horse's head. His brothers sat their mounts, surrounded by barons and knights, triumphant and satisfied, but he did not look at them, he did not want to see their faces. He would have liked to ask them why—why they had done this to him, but he knew the answer, knew their jealousy and greed and he did not think he could have borne to have spoken with them just now.

Out of the corner of his eye he caught sight of the emblems of Bellême and Breteuil, de Toeni and Grandmesnil, Beaumont and Aumale, all there to see his humbling and he rode past them all, his gaze straight, his face unsmiling for once. By God, one day they should all bend their proud knees to him and blot out the memory of this dark morning. The only crumb of comfort lay in the fact that Rufus would not tolerate Odo's presence and therefore his uncle was not there to witness his humiliation.

Out on the highway at last he watched Alide, her face pale and taut, ride away with their children and a small escort of men-at-arms, and he set his own face to the south. At the border he left Gerard of St. Lo and the rest of his men, except for the few who were to accompany him.

Then he crossed over into Brittany, for the first time in his life an exile on foreign soil.

'Where shall we go, lord?' Hamo queried. He sat his horse well, never indolent in the saddle, the Prince's standard firm in his grasp.

'Where shall we go?' Henry echoed. 'Jesu! Does it matter?' He saw their anxious faces, their concern for him, and quite suddenly he threw back his head and laughed. 'Why, we will go where the wind takes us until it changes, as change it must, to blow us back to Normandy again.'

Scottish Interlude

Autumn 1091

Scottish Interlude

The Countess Maud of Northampton considered herself a fortunate woman. She was singularly happy in her marriage, with a good husband, a healthy son on her knee and another child already within her strong young body. She had inherited a naturally happy nature from her father and on this bright September morning sat by the window of her chamber watching for her lord's return from the town whither he had been to transact some business.

Her mother Judith had returned after a two month stay to her foundation of nuns at Elstow and Maud was not sorry to see her go—even with young Simon to unite them they never seemed to agree—and now she was looking forward to the visit of her sister Alice, soon to wed to Ralph de Toeni. Alice was inclined to be nervous and a little prickly in her conversation, taking after their mother, but Maud was fond of her and anticipated some happy hours discussing bridals.

It was peaceful sitting in her bower, watching Simon playing on the floor with a little wooden horse, the sun making patterns on the wall beside her. There had been peace in England for some time and still was here in the south, but in May King Malcolm of Scotland had broken the border and marched into Northumberland, burning and plundering. No one quite knew why he had chosen this particular moment to invade. He had, it was true, refused to do homage to the King of England but he had taken no part in the barons' rebellion against the Red King three years ago, and his grievance was one to be fought out with words than with deeds. Earl Simon thought, and his wife with him, that Edgar Atheling's banishment from Normandy was more likely to have stirred up the trouble, for Edgar was with the Scots King and might conceivably be making one more bid for the Crown.

Maud had always liked Edgar who had been friend and companion-in-arms to her father, but she was sure he had long given up all hope of his inheritance and was content enough to be on the edge of affairs rather than in the heart of them. It seemed probable that King Malcolm's raid was designed to persuade the English King and the Norman Duke to restore Edgar to the lands he had lost through the treaty of Caen. Whatever the reason Malcolm had chosen his moment well, for the Red King was across the sea in Normandy, and he ravaged and plundered to his heart's content until met and held by the forces of the Earl of Northumberland, nephew to Bishop Geoffrey of Coutances.

But sitting here in the sunshine, watching her son at play and dreaming of the new babe in her womb, danger seemed very far away. Presently the sound of hooves broke into her quiet thoughts and she looked up in happy anticipation to see her husband riding in through the open gate.

Earl Simon had gained in strength of character since his marriage and though he was nearing forty and his hair was greying, he carried himself like a man ten years younger and with a self-confidence that came from his new contentment. With him rode his marshal, Hakon Osbertson, who had once been the most devoted of Earl Waltheof's men and now served with equal loyalty the daughter of his old master and her lord. Hakon's two sons, lads in their teens, were eager to prove themselves in Simon's service and rode with the men-at-arms; there was a bustling air in the courtyard as they dismounted, passing what was obviously some momentous news among the household gathered there.

Maud went down into the hall to greet her husband. He came with his limping walk and embraced her. Then he said, 'The King is returned. We found messengers in the town on their way to summon me to join him with all the men of the shire. We are to send the Scots tumbling back over their border.'

She held his arm tightly. 'My dear lord. This will be the first time you have left me to fight.'

He set a hand under her chin, smiling. 'I doubt if it will be much of a fight. We shall outnumber the Scots three to one. Don't fear, dear heart, I shall come home safe again. In the meantime, prepare for guests—the King will spend a night here on his march north.'

'Here?' She exclaimed. 'How soon? I doubt if we've enough wine and ale for all the King's household. I must send to our other manors for supplies—there's plenty of mutton at Ryhall and fruit at Connington, and of course the ale must come from Huntingdon. We need fresh rushes too.'

He laughed and left her to her plans, sending for Hakon to prepare a list of men who owed service. Haken went about his work remembering when Waltheof, last of the Saxon earls, had sent out the summons to fight the Norman invaders and he himself had been a green youth. Yet he would ride with Earl Simon cheerfully enough for a man must live in the world as it was, and the old days were gone.

The royal armies arrived, the men camping where they might in the town and the surrounding villages while the King and his company rode into the courtyard of Earl Simon's demesne. They streamed in, barons and knights with their attendants, servants bearing the King's baggage, men-at-arms bringing hauberks and helms, arms and shields, until the bailey was filled with a mass of men all endeavouring to find a place for themselves and their goods.

Maud and Simon were in the hall together to greet their royal guest and she saw to her astonishment not only the Red King but also the plump figure of the Duke of Normandy and beside him her cousin Henry whom she had thought far away in exile. She bent the knee to Rufus, received a boisterous embrace from Robert and then turned to Henry, both hands held out.

'I did not think to see you. We had heard . . .'

'Later,' he said in a low voice, 'we will talk later,' and aloud, 'dear cousin, greeting. It is noble of you to receive this great gathering under your roof.'

There was no chance to ask how he came to be here, for she must attend to her guests and it seemed that all the great names of Normandy and England were here. She sent a servant for the greeting cup and bore it to the King herself.

At supper she sat on his left while her husband occupied his right hand with the Duke of Normandy next to him, and she was glad to have Henry on her other side.

He kept up a light conversation with her, making witticisms at the expense of many noble barons, and keeping her laughing throughout the meal.

Nevertheless she thought him changed, older and more reserved for all he appeared his familiar smiling self. She sensed a wariness that must come, she thought, from the change in his fortunes, a change that had grieved her deeply and she could not imagine how he came to be here with his brothers. But she did not ask, merely laughing at his sallies and biding her time.

'What a company,' he said lazily, 'even our grey-bearded uncle of Mortain has bestirred himself to ride with us and I've not seen him for many months. I could wish he had left my cousin William at home—how he sired so ill-tempered a youth, I cannot imagine. Our dislike is mutual.'

'And did I hear someone say the Bishop of Durham is with you?'

'Aye, but he sleeps tonight at Peterborough with the holy monks. He is to be restored when we reach his city. At least Red William is acting rightly by the Church for once—and he made Flambard leave his familiar at home.'

'His familiar?'

'That mother of his, the one-eyed bitch, or witch, or both! I've heard her moaning incantations that would send a chill down your spine, little cousin. It's a wonder the devil hasn't carried her off to his dark regions.'

'I'm glad she is not under my roof,' Maud said with a shiver. 'Who is that handsome youth who waits on the King?'

Henry frowned. 'That is Simon of La Barre, brother to Herluin, the tall knight who serves me. The less said about Simon the better. By St. Peter, look at Walter Tirel, I swear he's had enough of your wine to fill a barrel.'

'You have hardly touched yours,' she pointed out and saw that wary look again behind the smile.

'I prefer to keep a clear head,' he said lightly, 'which is more than you can say for your future brother-in-law. He's joined Tirel on the rushes.' He pointed to where Ralph had slithered from his bench and lay with his head on Tirel's chest, happily asleep. 'Simon's men will spend half the night getting Rufus' courtiers to bed.'

She laughed and touched his hand fleetingly. 'It is so good to have you here again.'

The King's voice broke in on their talk. 'You seem in good spirits tonight, cousin Maud. I can see you do not fear the Scots will march this far south.'

'Not I,' she retorted, smiling, 'when you have such an army

to beat them back. King Malcolm must be a fool if he thinks himself a match for England and Normandy.'

'Well said,' Robert leaned across and raised his horn to her. He was past his youth now and losing his hair at the same time as gaining a stomach, but his affability remained unchanged and she wondered why he had come to England.

The house was crowded and the only guest room was naturally occupied by the King and the Duke, the barons and knights making what shift they could with pallets laid out in the hall. Even the most senior, the Count de Meulan, was forced to lie by his brother, Henry of Warwick, on a pallet behind the high seat. Henry however, found his set at the foot of Maud and Simon's curtained bed in their chamber, and there the three of them sat talking far into the night.

He told them of his months of exile, of days spent riding about France and Brittany, seeking what hospitality he might. He had gone first to his widowed brother-in-law, Count Alain of Brittany, and then spent some time with Helias at Le Mans but he knew that his presence there heightened the tension between Maine and her overlord of Normandy and he did not wish to involve Helias, who had enough to do consolidating his position as count. He moved to the Vexin and then on into France.

He had been at Chartres with his sister Adela, the Countess of Blois, enjoying playing the uncle to his little nephew, Theobald, when a messenger found him and told him that the King was returning to England to deal with the invading Scots and required his presence. He thought the matter over carefully. Clearly Robert and Rufus wanted him with them if they were both to be away, and Rufus equally clearly did not want to leave Robert behind in the newly partitioned duchy. Or was it that having taken his possessions they wanted him back where they could see him? Could he be their brother as long as he took nothing from them, nor held a place of his own? He did not know but because he was curious and because he wanted to see England again, he went.

They had greeted him affably, calling him their brother Beauclerc, clapping him on the shoulder and giving him gifts of clothes and hawks and hunting dogs, but no word was said of any return of his lands, nothing of reinstatement. He was no longer deceived. The fall of the rock of the Archangel and his resulting exile had taught him to dissemble so that he smiled and talked cheerfully, but kept his own counsel and let neither know what he thought.

Of the boredom of exile, the sense of loss he felt, the indignity of being a prince without as much as a hall to call his own, he spoke little, but Maud, knowing him well, had no need of telling.

Simon said, 'Please God exile is behind you.' He glanced curiously at his guest. 'You do not fear any evil intent towards you?'

Henry shrugged. 'It is a possibility—as I knew before I came, but somehow I doubt it. Anyway I was getting tired of exile.'

'Better be bored in freedom than shut within four walls.'

'Maybe, but they will learn I am not as easily cozened now, nor am I prepared to be a lap dog either at court here or in Normandy.'

Maud was sitting on her great bed, wrapped in Simon's thick mantle, listening to the men talking. Her long hair was unbound, her blue eyes resting on them both with affection, and Henry thought Simon was a fortunate man. That the Earl too knew this was apparent in his face whenever he turned to look at his wife.

She was smiling now at Henry. 'Perhaps you will meet the Scottish princesses and then your fortunes will change. Do you remember I told you to marry one of them?'

He laughed. 'Will King Malcolm consent to give his daughter to a landless man? And Rufus give me back Coutances and Avranches and the rock of the Archangel? I have nothing to bargain with, cousin. Besides the girl may squint.'

'I do not see that it matters,' Simon said, taking the idea seriously, 'if she may mend your fortunes.'

Maud gave a peal of laughter. 'It is an old joke, my lord, and my choice of a bride for cousin Henry, that is all.'

'And you, Simon,' Henry put in, 'stole the prettiest girl in England, so what are the rest of us to do?'

But long after their quiet breathing told him that they slept behind their curtains, he lay awake absorbed in thoughts that would not let him rest.

Here in England he counted his friends—Henry de Beaumont brother to the Count de Meulan, Richard Bienfaite of Clare and his sons Gilbert and Roger, Roger de Marmion and his father, all came to him separately and assured him of their friendship; even Earl Hugh, explaining privily that he had not wanted to bar the gates at Avranches, told him that he still stood his friend. Robert Fitzhamon came, saying that though Rufus had given him Queen Matilda's lands, he considered himself no more than a custodian of them for the rightful owner. Gilbert of Clare said even more plainly that he wished England saw more of Prince Henry.

It gained him nothing but it was cheering and though at least half the baronage of Normandy weighed treachery by its chance of success, nevertheless he felt he knew how far he could trust them. And the next day when they left the Countess Maud at the doorway of her hall and rode north with the added numbers of Earl Simon's company, he relaxed in the saddle, prepared to enjoy the sunshine and the English countryside. If he loved Normandy deeply, he also cared for this green land that had borne and nurtured him. The air was sweet with the last of the harvest, the fields shorn of corn, nuts and blackberries ripe on the bushes. If a man ruled England, he thought, he need envy no other.

But as they went north the weather turned colder, blustery rain beat in their faces and turned the roads to quagmires and the food ran short. They took what they could from the countryside, but men seemed more hostile here than in the south; the barons who held these northern lands deemed themselves far enough from the seat of authority to extort all they could from the wretched people and with so large an army to feed there was insufficient forage left for men or beasts.

At last they reached Durham where there were supplies and spirits were restored by the magnificent ceremony in the church when the Bishop was returned to his episcopal throne. In a generous mood, Rufus handed over gifts of gold and silver and fine vestments.

'For all he scoffs at religion,' Herluin said caustically, 'he would buy his way into the next world.'

Henry, with Roger de Marmion, Eudo Dapifer and Ralph de Toeni went out afterwards to wench and to drink in the town, and returning to the Bishop's palace arm in arm at dawn scandalised the monks on their way to sing the office of prime. He felt the tedium and responsibilities of the last months slide away, relaxing in the company of three other equally young men.

'It's good to have you back,' Ralph said frankly, 'my father has tied our fortunes in with Red William, but I don't wish to share his lighter moments.'

'Just as well,' de Marmion said. His face was pallid in the morning light, for he had drunk too much last night, 'or I'd feel sorry for the Lady Alice. Where's the well in this godforsaken place? I must stick my head in a bucket of water before it splits in two.'

In the courtyard of the castle Ralph and Eudo boisterously hauled up a bucketful and dowsed not only his head but the rest of him so that his clothes were soaked and he was dripping from head to foot and yelling furiously at them to stop.

Henry leaned against the wall, watching them, his hands on his hips. It was good to laugh, to act the boy again with other boys and forget he was a man fighting for the right to be what he was born to be.

Some two weeks later they reached the shores of Scots Water on the borders of Lothian, that country which King Malcolm claimed as his own. The cold had grown more intense, the country wilder, some men died of fever or sickness, including one of Henry's faithful six, and not a few of Rufus' army slipped away in the night to go back to their homes, but it was still a considerable force that encamped on the inhospitable shore.

The Scots were gathered on the farther side and in the evening Rufus, Robert and Henry stood together on the bank looking across as the last rays of the October sunshine turned the water to pink and silver. The evening star had already risen in a translucent sky and over the slow moving water an occasional bird dived and rose again.

Behind them men were busy making camp, preparing supper, setting up tents and lighting fires. Already they could see the fires in the enemy camp.

'Do we fight?' Henry asked, 'or do we talk first?'

'We talk,' the King answered, 'at least Robert does. That is why you are here, is it not, brother?'

Robert, who stood between them, took each by the arm. 'I will get the terms you want, William, never fear. United we cannot fail in anything.' He squeezed Henry's elbow. 'This is better than exile, eh? You are one of us again, Beauclerc, and restored to your place.'

Henry inclined his head, but he said nothing, his eyes on the blue distance. The cool effrontery of it astounded him. They could, it seemed, rob and cheat him and then calmly call him back and pretend they were bestowing a favour. Self-deception, he thought, could be limitless.

He sat with them at supper in William's tent, talking effortlessly, but in effect saying nothing and afterwards in his own small tent flung himself down on his pallet in a mood of impatience. Fulcher was polishing his sword. Herluin sat on his own pallet inspecting the Prince's mail tunic.

'By God,' Henry said, 'I never knew until now how hard a virtue patience is to come by.'

Herluin glanced across at him. 'It will stand you in good stead one day, my lord.'

Henry linked his hands behind his head. 'I have lived too long for "one day". That will do, boy, seek your bed now.' And when Fulcher had gone, he went on, 'So we are here at last and Robert negotiates, perhaps we'll fight, perhaps not, but afterwards—what do they want of me? They have said nothing yet.'

Herluin laid down the tunic, satisfied that it was in good order, and got up to adjust the smoking wick of the small lantern that hung from the tent pole. 'They want you with them to show the world that they can bring you to heel.'

Henry laughed, but without much mirth. 'Why did I come, I wonder? Curiosity, I suppose. Perhaps I hoped, and still hope, they may restore part of my lands. It is inconvenient to say the least to have all one's worldly possessions on a pair of pack mules.'

The corners of Herluin's grave mouth lifted. 'And a considerable task the men have to get everything on to two mules. At least your brothers might give you another pair.'

'I wonder where they get their parsimony from? My father, I imagine. My mother was always generous, in fact the only time I can recall her quarrelling with my father was when Robert was in exile and she sent him money. Well, there's no one to send me a pouch or two, more's the pity, and my cousin of Mortain loses no opportunity to harp on my poverty.' He yawned. 'What a sober fellow Walter Giffard is. He told me today he thought I had better enter the Church for I would find no profit elsewhere.'

Herluin laughed outright. 'Now that I cannot envisage.'

'Nor I,' Henry agreed cheerfully and settled himself to sleep, signing himself nonetheless, without which act he would not have thought to close his eyes for the night.

In the morning Robert rode away and for three days they waited. The barons hunted in the nearby forests, some of the men foraged in the surrounding countryside, seeking food and drink and women, while others sat huddled by the camp fires. Henry played chess with Red William and had the satisfaction of beating him. At length Robert returned bringing with him Edgar Atheling, both in high good humour and apparently on the best of terms themselves having negotiated equally well on behalf of the two kings. Malcolm agreed to renew the homage he had paid to the late King and in return to continue to hold the earldom of Lothian and twelve manors in England where he might lodge on his way to and from the English court. Edgar was also to be restored to his lands. So there was after all to be no battle and the men grumbled, disappearing in small groups to plunder where they could that they might not return home empty-handed.

Rufus did nothing to hinder them, even though it was their own countrymen they were robbing. He was satisfied with the outcome of the march north, for he could consider himself lord of England, Wales and Scotland.

'I think he'd try and seize the Holy Roman Empire if he thought he had a chance,' Henry said rather caustically to Herluin.

Malcolm crossed the water with his elder sons and in the open before William's tent did simple homage. Rufus sat on a stool with his brothers standing on either side of him, flanked by the chief of the barons headed by Earl Roger of Montgomery, Robert de Beaumont, the chancellor Robert Bloet and the treasurer Ranulf Flambard.

Henry stood with the point of his sword resting upon the ground, his hands folded on the hilt. He was wearing chain mail and a long scarlet mantle which became him well, and his helm and shield were carried by Fulcher who stood behind him. He looked curiously at the Scottish King, a great solid man with thick legs, a head of flaming hair, a red beard, and eyes as fierce as a hawk's. Slung over his shoulders was a huge bearskin that made him seem even broader, a man to strike terror into his enemies, but he was smiling and affable today as he paid homage, setting his hands between William's as if it were a mere polite ceremony, which was perhaps all that he meant it to be.

They dined together in the King's tent and it occurred to Henry how well Robert and Edgar could manage when they were about other men's affairs and how ill when they were about their own. Malcolm said that he and his Queen, Edgar's sister Margaret, so gentle and holy that already people called her saint, wished their two daughters to be brought up in the convent where Margaret's sister, Christina, was prioress. This was in Romsey near Winchester and he proposed to send the girls south under the King's escort. Rufus agreed willingly and it seemed that after all Maud's wish would be granted and her cousin Henry would meet the Scottish princesses.

It was a week before they arrived from Edinburgh, two shy girls as like as two peas in a pod; a pair of young fauns they seemed to Henry with their fair plaits, their soft blue eyes and gentle movements. Eadgyth, the elder, was also the prettier for Mary had slightly protruding teeth which marred her otherwise attractive features. They were attended by a Scottish lady, several serving women and some men-at-arms, and as they ate and slept in their own tent, he saw little of them, but once or twice he rode near their litter, or spoke to Eadgyth during the pause for a meal at mid-day. She answered his overtures gravely and was obviously very much in awe of him; as often as not her guardian stepped in and spoke up for them all.

Generally he watched her from a distance, thinking of Maud's words. She was very young still, barely in her teens, and though she was not perhaps a great beauty, nor likely to be, nevertheless she had a certain charm of her own and a smile that, though it had not yet been directed at him, was indicative of a warm and gentle nature. He did not suspect at first that she was capable of temper and though he thought she might well make a suitable wife, he was not disposed to consider the matter seriously until a few days before they reached Winchester.

They had taken a different road back and had not passed through Northampton to his regret, and it was a somewhat weary company that was anticipating the comparative comfort to be enjoyed at Winchester. The road was badly potholed, and the long line of march was strung out over more than a mile, the King and the Duke at the head, Henry towards the rear and a little behind the litter bearing the two princesses. He was riding at an easy pace, his eyes on the November woods, watching for game in the thick undergrowth, delighting in the sight of a startled hart leaping away into cover, when one of the horses plunged his hoof into a hole. He fell awkwardly, there was a snapping sound and the litter toppled forward, so that the girls, screaming with sudden fright, tumbled through the curtains in a jumble of rugs and cushions.

Henry flung himself down from his horse and ran to them. He reached Eadgyth first and lifted her; she was crying, but more from shock, and a few quick touches assured him that she was no more than bruised. Edgar, who had also seen the accident, had extricated Mary; apart from a cut on her cheek from a stone and a grazed arm she too though sobbing was unhurt and by this time several men at arms were trying to raise the horse while the women who had been riding pillion surrounded the scene of the accident, all clucking anxiously.

The horse's leg, however, was broken and Raoul the deer, who had been kneeling by him while the men pulled the shafts of the litter clear, said laconically that the animal would have to be slaughtered.

Eadgyth raised a tear-stained face from Henry's shoulder. 'Oh, poor thing. Must he be killed?'

'I'm afraid so. We cannot mend his leg.' He nodded to Raoul and walked off a little way with the girl still in his arms that she might not see.

'I liked that horse,' she confided to him, and drew a sobbing breath. 'He was so slow and gentle. I gave him some corn last night.'

'You are fond of animals?' He saw a fallen log and set her down there, sitting beside her and taking her hands in his to warm them.

'Oh yes,' the tears were drying now on her pale cheeks. 'I had a coney at home that came everywhere with me. My uncle Edgar brought him from Normandy as we have none in Scotland and he followed me everywhere but they would not let me bring him with me. Perhaps my aunt would not have wanted him at the abbey.'

'Perhaps not,' he agreed smiling, 'but I expect there will be ducks and chickens for your tending. There, the horse is out of his pain. They will put another in the shafts and you will ride safe.'

But one of the long poles was snapped and as another was not forthcoming it was decided that the girls should ride; Henry spoke briefly to the Scottish attendants and then remounted with Eadgyth up before him, while Edgar carried Mary. Both girls were calmer now and after a while Eadgyth began to talk, to ask him questions about Normandy and his life there.

'My uncle says Normandy is a beautiful country with fine towns and many castles. Is it very different from Scotland?'

'I do not not know,' he said, 'for I've never been further north than where we met, but perhaps you will see it one day. You have not seen England either, have you?'

'Nothing but the road we have travelled these last weeks. Only . . .' her face clouded, 'if I am in a convent I am not likely to see any more, am I?'

'Do you not want to go to your aunt?'

'Not very much.' A frown puckered her forehead and she twisted round so that she might look up at him. 'Would you want to be shut in one place all the time with only women for company?'

He threw back his head, laughing. 'Well, it would be a different position for me!' Then he glanced down at her serious face. 'No, child, indeed if I were you I would not. You have no vocation to be a nun?'

'No—never! She spoke so fiercely that he was surprised. 'I'll not have them set those horrid clothes on me, nor shut me up away from horses and the fields and woods and any company I choose. I would hate it.'

'I have one sister a nun and another who lives most happily in a convent, but I doubt it is the life for you.' He was still smiling. 'And I have a feeling that if they try to force you to it they will not be successful.'

The frown disappeared and she gave a giggle. 'I would make my aunt regret she ever tried. But,' she became grave again, 'do not think that is because I do not respect Holy Church. Indeed, my lord, my mother has taught me to love

God and Our Lady and all the Saints, but I do not think He wants everyone to be a nun, do you?'

'Not I,' he agreed amusedly, 'or where would we men be with no wives to love us?'

She laughed again and settled herself more comfortably against his chest. 'I wish I were coming to court so that I could see you again. I hate people who are too solemn.'

He was silent for a moment, looking over the top of her head to the long line of riders, the grey November sky above. 'I will ask my cousin Maud, who is a Countess, to invite you to stay with her and then I will come to visit you if—if I am in England, and if your aunt will allow you to go.'

'If' seemed to be the paramount word for him just now and when she asked what he meant he found himself almost involuntarily telling her of his exact positon. For all her youth she grasped the situation at once, asking intelligent questions that surprised him as much as the giving of his own confidence.

Presently she said, 'It seems that when one is born of a royal house one has less freedom than a bound man.'

'You are right,' he agreed soberly. 'Neither of us can choose what we would do. But if you wish it, I will arrange somehow that we meet again.'

'I do wish it.' She clasped her hands together over the pommel of the saddle, ceasing in that moment to be a child and taking a step into womanhood.

And at the same moment he knew that Maud, for all her teasing, had been right. This girl had reached and touched him in a strange way, as if it was predestined that he, the English Atheling yet a Norman, should marry a descendant of Edmund Ironside, one of the line of Cerdic that every Englishman revered, yet one who was also a Scottish princess. It was a marriage that would fix his destiny without doubt.

Yet doubts there were. She was over-young to wed but her father must be thinking of espousals and he would also have to gain Red William's consent to the proposition. If he waited it might be too late and he was not at all sure how he stood with Rufus.

Abruptly he asked, 'Has your father spoken to you of any betrothal?'

She cast him a quick look and then lowered her gaze, her colour deepening. 'No, my lord, not yet, but I am certain he would rather see me wed than become a bride of Holy Church.'

'Well, thank God for that,' he said. 'You are very young, child, but don't let anyone force you to a life you do not want.' It was a queer thing to say. His own sisters had had no choice in the disposal of their lives, but he did not want to see this girl beside him unhappy, muffled in nun's clothing when she needed a man to love her.

She had lifted her head a little, her chin thrust out. 'If anyone tries, I will think of you.'

A silence fell, disturbed only by the rhythm of the horse's hooves and the jingle of the harness. He pondered on her last words and the odd sense of understanding that had arisen between them. But when he spoke again it was to distract her with talk of horses and dogs.

They reached Winchester in the evening and he saw no more of her until two days later when she and her sister were to go on to the abbey at Romsey. He and Robert rode the short distance with them, meaning to hunt in the forest on their return, and as the girls were on horseback he was able to ride beside her. They talked of unimportant things until on the top of a rise they looked down to see the abbey church and the conventual buildings sprawled below them.

He glanced at her and seeing the expression on her face he said quickly, 'It is not a prison, lady. You are only there to learn.'

She shivered a little in the cold morning air and drew her mantle close. His use of the adult form of address had not escaped her. 'I will feel like a captive. And—I do not like my aunt.'

'I am sorry,' he said, 'but you are not entering as a novice. You will only be there until you reach womanhood.'

Her mare shook its head, breath vaporising, and she quietened the animal with a gentle but firm hand. 'I felt a child when I left Scotland, but not now.'

'I know. ' He reached out to touch her hand lightly where it lay holding the reins. The other riders were moving down the hill now and for a brief moment he and she were alone. He saw tears well into her eyes.

'You will not forget me?'

'Forget you?' He smiled and gave her hand a quick warm squeeze. 'No, Eadgyth, I will not forget you. I have had to learn patience and so must you. Wait a little while and things may be very different for us.'

'For us?'

'Aye, for us. But you are cold. Come, we must catch up with the others.' He saw her heightened colour giving her a rosy, glowing look that he thought enchanting. He said no more, but in the silence that followed he found himself wishing his mother were still alive for she, with her quick intuition, would have taken this girl to her heart and forwarded his cause—of that he was sure. But Queen Matilda lay in her tomb in her own abbey of Caen and he must fend for himself.

At the abbey the Prioress was waiting for her nieces. She was a tall, thin woman with a stern face and lips folded in a forbidding line. She offered wine to the royal brothers, looked her new charges up and down and told Eadgyth to tuck her hair beneath her hood. Both girls looked at once young and defenceless. After the freedom of the long weeks of journeying south the narrow walls of this guest parlour did indeed seem like the cage Eadgyth had dreaded and Henry had a swift desire to seize her by the hand and take her out of this place and back into the free air they had left. He looked across at her where she stood beside the Prioress and saw her eyes fixed on him, her fingers gripped together. Even if they would have spoken there was no need of words.

The lady Christina was a woman of sharp intelligence and she both saw and interpreted that look.

'My lord Duke,' she turned to Robert, 'my nieces must be weary after their long journey from Scotland. You will forgive me if I see about settling them into their quarters. Pray take some more wine if you wish before leaving.'

Nothing could have been more pointed. Robert set down his cup and rose. 'We had best be on our way. Your brother, madam, bid me say he will visit you tomorrow.' He smiled at the girls and bade them goodbye, kissing them both soundly in his usual manner. Henry took Eadgyth's chilled fingers in his and they clung to his own warm hand. He too bent to kiss her formally and found her mouth trembling.

He left her there, standing by her little sister, forlorn and lonely, and when the great gate of the abbey closed behind him determined to speak to Rufus immediately, to ask not only for Eadgyth but for the return of his mother's lands to give him at least some place to be his own. But riding silently beside Robert, chewing the end of his whip, he viewed his prospects clearly and coolly and found little to encourage him.

'What ails you, brother?' Robert's voice broke in on his thoughts. 'You have not spoken since we left Romsey. Are you cast down by the loss of our two little birds?'

His words hit too near the mark and Henry turned the conversation aside with a joking remark about the manner of the Prioress Christina and her lack of similarity to her brother Edgar.

In the hall at supper he missed the wise and calming presence of Lanfranc. Although the old man had been dead for eighteen months Rufus had not yet appointed a successor to the see of Canterbury and was cheerfully collecting the revenues of the archbishopric himself. Bishop Walkelin was at the high table but Henry did not find him easy to talk to and Wulfstan, the aged Bishop of Worcester, was now near ninety years old and seldom left his own city. There was no one whose advice or support he could seek and looking round he found Rufus' court very little to his taste. There were too many foppish young men with hair nearly down to their shoulders, a fashion he thought unmanly, and the newest fad seemed to be pointed shoes, the toes extended and turning upwards, an idea begun, he had heard, by the Count of Anjou.

'Though why anyone should follow the eccentricities of a fellow with deformed feet, I do not know,' he remarked to Ralph de Toeni.

Ralph laughed, scooping meat from his dish with his fingers and licking them noisily. 'I don't like them myself but I think I shall buy a pair for my marriage day. You will stay to see me to my bridal bed at the Christmas feast?'

'I expect so,' Henry said absently. He glanced across at the lady Alice, Ralph's bride. She had obviously fallen in love with her future husband for she was looking at him now, her cheeks warm, her thin sallow face almost pretty for the love that lay there.

Would Eadgyth one day look at him like that? It mattered first and foremost that he should make a good marriage, but if love came with it, how much better. He looked along the table at Rufus, noisy, arrogant, unpredictable, greedy. How would

Red William take his request? He felt a chill settle on him and turned to see if some careless serving man had left a door open to the winter night.

Herluin, coming later along the gallery above the new hall at Winchester where the King's apartments lay, heard the sound of angry quarrelling and raised voices even through the closed doors of the solar. Seeing his brother seated astride a bench he paused beside him. 'What in God's name is going on in there?'

Simon shrugged. 'I suppose they are at each other's throats again.'

'Who?'

'Our three royal lions. Did you think they would agree for long? I did not.'

Herluin sat down on the bench beside him. 'What is it this time? There is nothing more they can take from my lord.'

'Perhaps he asks for something they do not want to give. But I don't know, I'm not in the King's confidence.'

Herluin gave him a caustic look. 'Are you not?'

His brother laughed, swaggering a little. 'Not altogether. Some things he shares with me, but not all.'

'Some things!' Herluin got up as if he could not bear to sit on the bench any longer. 'Simon, I make one last appeal to you. Come back to Normandy—or if you do not want to go home, at least take service with the Duke, or Count Helias, or Robert of Flanders. Don't stay here where . . .'

'Yes?' Simon queried provocatively. 'Where what?'

Herluin looked down at him. Simon was a good fighting man, that he knew, he was strong and light on his feet, with good hands and well set legs, but there was now something about him that had not been there before, something in the way he lounged on the bench, long hair curling about his face, his body relaxed in an oddly sensual manner that turned Herluin sick. It did not seem possible that they had been reared together, that this was the brother he had left behind, a mere child, when he had gone to Italy nearly ten years before.

'I must go,' he said abruptly. 'Your way is not my way. I only beg you not to bring grief or disgrace upon our parents.'

He walked away down the passage. In Henry's small chamber he busied himself in tidying away the Prince's hunting gear, a task that should have been done by Fulcher, but the boy was nowhere to be seen and anyway it gave him something to do. He was still scraping mud from a pair of hunting boots when the door opened and he saw his lord standing in the entrance, white faced, dark eyes blazing with that rage he had not seen since Conan's death.

'What is it?' he asked urgently. 'What is it?'

Henry slammed the door and set his back to it. He was shaking so that he could scarcely speak. 'He is a devil—a devil, not fit to be a King. He will give me nothing, *nothing*! I think,' he drew a deep shuddering breath, 'I think he would have me sweeping out the stables if he could do it. And Robert too . . .' tears of fury and frustration came into his eyes but he shook them aside, 'Robert upholds him. I am banished again—not to set foot in England or Normandy. They deny me even my birthright. By the living God, my father cannot be resting in his grave when they do this to me.'

Herluin was standing still, an arrow in his hand. 'I don't understand. Why are you banished? What has happened? Yesterday . . .'

'Yesterday is gone,' Henry said between his teeth. 'I asked—I asked for the Princess Eadgyth and for my mother's lands again, and you'd have thought I'd asked for the kingdom and the dukedom as well. They said—I'll not speak the things they said. Blasphemy, lies! But I am to be nothing, to have nothing, to go from them—I, their brother!'

Herluin was looking at the arrow, balanced across his index finger. 'Don't you see my lord, it is because they fear you will one day have everything?'

Henry leaned against the door. He gave a sudden harsh laugh but there was no trace of amusement in the sound. 'So my father said when he lay dying—an old man's dream! But how should they fear me? They have left me no weapon to fight with, and that is the reality.'

'Now, yes,' Herluin said, 'but a time will come . . .' he paused, his eyes on the arrow and some half defined thought, some instinct stirred at the back of his mind. 'A time will come as certain as an arrow reaching its mark.' He did not know why he said it, nor why the arrow should seem important. He dropped it suddenly as if it burned him and looked at Henry. 'My lord . . .'

Henry had both hands clenched hard. 'Damn them to hell— a devil and a fool. My God! That two such men should rule.'

He flung himself down on the stool and with a wild gesture swept everything off the table, cups and horns and oddments all clattering to the floor. He set his head in his hands, his fingers in his hair. 'Damn them, damn them, damn them!'

In the morning he rode out of Winchester, outwardly calm, his last few loyal men at his back. And this time not one one of them asked him where they should go.

Part II

The Rock of Domfront
December 1093—November 1100

I

In the first cold grey days of Lent, 1093, the King of England
fell sick, so sick that he thought himself to be dying. Fiery
pains seized his chest and back, fever deepened the habitual
ruddiness of his face, and he breathed with difficulty. Taken ill
at his hunting lodge at Alverstone, his attendants bore him
back to Gloucester where he might be more comfortable, and
he lay now in his great bed in the castle there, surrounded by his
friends and great men, by bishops and abbots.

They too thought him to be dying. 'It is the wasting sickness,'
Robert Bloet said and Bishop John of Bath, a man learned in the
art of medicine, agreed.

'His lungs are affected with ill humours. I doubt if any of
my remedies can heal him.'

Bishop Wulfstan, despite his ninety years, came slowly from
Worcester, and at the King's bedside, with John of Bath,
Bishops Gundulf of Rochester and Geoffrey of Coutances, be-
sought the King to make his peace with God. One matter
weighed heavily upon them all. Since the death of Lanfranc
nearly four years ago the see of Canterbury had been vacant,
the Church in England without a leader. The King was receiving the moneys and dues of the archbishopric, robbing Holy
Church, and more than one of them hinted that his mortal
sickness was probably a direct divine punishment for that sin.

Rufus lay on his bed and groaned. 'Are the priests praying for
me? Do I not give gifts to abbeys and churches so that they
should pray for my welfare? Tell them their prayers have done
me no good . . .' He felt ill and weak, and angry that he should
be so—he who was never still for long, who could outride most
of his court, who could be on the move from dawn until sunset
and not tire. He remembered his father's last illness, the painful
dying, the necessity for repentance, for making at least good

gestures on one's deathbed. He had mocked at God and His priests, it was true, and now suddenly he was confronted with the prospect of meeting Him face to face. It terrified him. All he knew of death and hell and the last judgement came before him until he was trembling with terror and eager for once to listen to his ministers.

Pressing his face into the pillow he said, 'Send for Anselm of Bec.'

The men about him exchanged significant glances.

Last summer Anselm had come to England at the request of Hugh the Wolf who had endowed a foundation at Chester and wished not only for the Abbot's advice but for monks from Bec. Anselm crossed the channel and spent a night at Canterbury where the monks received him with joy, making no secret of their desire to see him their abbot as well as archbishop. He shook his head, smiled and blessed them, and journeyed on to Chester where the work of the monastery was set in hand, and then paid a visit to the King.

William had received him kindly and they had talked long together. Anselm, however, took it upon himself to reprove the King for his behaviour and for the standard of morals at his court. Rufus took this remarkably well—perhaps because his father had so highly honoured the Abbot of Bec—and turned the conversation with a laugh.

'They tell stories about me,' he had said. 'I beg you, my lord, only to believe half of them.' To which Anselm replied gravely that half would be enough to make him anxious for the state of the King's soul.

Rufus remembered this anxiety now, lying sweating and shivering alternately on his bed. He drank the foul concoctions they gave him, submitted to being bled, but he felt no better and now thought only of Anselm's coming.

The Abbot was still in England for the simple reason that William had refused him permission to return to Normandy. Having the uneasy feeling he might be driven by public pressure to appoint a new archbishop, Rufus had to admit that no other man was so suitable, and he began to believe that Anselm's presence at the time of his sickness could be no other than the jealous Hand of God pointing to what must be done.

'May the devil protect me from holy men,' he had once said to Flambard, but that defence had crumbled in the face of death, and he lay waiting for Anselm to come, restless, his sleep disturbed by unhappy dreams, his body aching with undefined pain.

Old Wulfstan knelt by the bed, his bearded face buried in his hands in prayer; John of Bath knelt beside him while Abbot Serlo of Gloucester sat by the other side of the bed, his lips moving constantly in silent prayer. Some of the barons stood near the door—Grandmesnil, FitzHamon, Earl Hugh, Roger of Montgomery, Robert de Marmion and others, while Flambard, arms stiffly folded, stood firmly at the end of the bed looking down at his master, one thought only in his head—that if this man died he could expect little preferment from anyone else.

At last Anselm came, attended by his companions, the monks Baldwin and Eadmer. The room was cleared. Abbot and King remained alone for half an hour. Then Anselm summoned the barons and clegy back to the King's bedside. Rufus lay calm and quiet, his hands folded, an expression on his face that no man had ever seen there before.

'Our lord has made his peace with God,' Anselm said, 'he sorrows for all his sins and will make amends.' He turned back to the bed and smiled encouragingly at the sick man.

Rufus opened his eyes and looked round the room, crowded now with his great men. 'It is true,' he said and saw the curiosity, the surprise on their faces. 'It seems I must soon go to God and should therefore right any wrong I have done. I will have a proclamation drawn up—all the old laws will be kept, all the vacant sees and abbacies shall be filled and you, my friend,' he glanced across at Robert Bloet, 'you shall be Bishop of Lincoln from this day. I will make gifts to all the abbeys my father endowed, all prisoners are to be freed and debts to me forgotten.'

This speech tired him. His voice trailed off and he closed his eyes again, the general burst of approval, the words of thanks from Bloet, seeming to flow over him unheeded.

Earl Hugh, taking advantage of the moment, said, 'My lord King, there is one whom you have forgotten in your generosity —your brother Henry. He finds exile bitter.'

The King stirred uncomfortably, twisting his solid body under the covers. 'Beauclerc—I wish him no harm.'

'Then call him back, sire,' Anselm added his plea to that of his friend. 'Grant him some part of your lands again.'

'It is not his day—not yet.' He was lost in a muddle of

thoughts, remembering his father's deathbed and the three of them, waiting for the crumbs to fall. Even though Robert had not been there in body he had been as present as if he had stood by the Conqueror's bed. Remembering the grim inevitability of those days, Rufus felt a wave of fear break over him. Sweet Jesu, the awful inevitability of dying!

Wulfstan's voice, close to him, said, 'My lord, there is another, greater, matter. I beg you to tell us your choice for the archbishopric. Your Church must have a shepherd.'

He roused himself. He must make one more effort, crush down his will, give up what had been his for so long. Gasping for breath, feeling the heat of fever in his face, he heaved himself up a little in bed, supported by the strong arms of Abbot Serlo, and he pointed to the Abbot of Bec. 'Then I name this holy man, Anselm,' he said and fell back on the pillow.

There was an immediate outcry, all the barons voicing their joy at this choice, Wulfstan's bloodshot old eyes filled with tears of satisfaction; the Bishops unanimously nodded in approval and Bloet held out both hands, smiling, to Anselm.

But the Abbot shrank back. Thinking to refuse this demand, he shook his head and said half humorously, 'Would you yoke an old sheep to an un-tamed bull, my lord King? What good could come of that but the poor sheep would be torn apart?'

Rufus hardly seemed to hear this. He repeated in a stronger voice, 'I choose Anselm for my Archbishop.'

And at that Anselm saw that he could not turn this aside with a light refusal, that his wishes were not going to count at all. The reality of it, starkly before him, turned him pale and he began to tremble. 'No,' he said, 'no, I beg you, my lord . . .'

'The King has chosen,' Bloet said, 'you must accept, Anselm, my friend. It is his will and ours too.'

Anselm looked piteously from one to the other. 'No,' he repeated, 'no, I cannot. It is too great a burden. Lord,' he turned to the bed and fell on his knees, 'I beseech you, let me go back to Bec. The affairs of the world are not for me. I desire only the peace of my abbey, time to pray, to give spiritual advice to those in need. That is my only function.'

Rufus was tired. 'I have chosen,' he said.

'You must accept.' Geoffrey of Coutances came forward, leaning on his staff, his face pallid for he had pains in his stomach and could take no food these days but milk. 'It is clearly God's will.'

They pressed about him, raising him to his feet, not only the clergy but the great lords, all eager, thrusting their approval on him, bearing him away on their desire until he felt himself to be suffocating, oppressed by the weight of wills against his own.

He thought of the great house of Bec in its peaceful valley, the gentle woods about it, the stream that watered the place. He saw the cloisters where he walked, the high stone church with its beautiful rounded arches and columns where he worshipped God, he saw his own cell where there was silence and peace and simplicity and he remembered his qualms when he had left it.

Had he known, when he landed in England, that it would come to this? Had he known but thrust the dread beneath active consciousness, hoping that if he did it would no longer be there? He looked at the faces about him and saw no man who understood his fear.

'My lord,' Abbot Serlo said and there was a new deference in his voice, 'it was God's providence that you should be here and at this time. What could be more fitting?'

Anselm was weeping now, unable to restrain the tears of despair. 'Jesu, have pity, it is too much. I cannot . . .'

'You can,' they all said. 'You are our new Archbishop.'

But he still had strength enough to resist. 'I am not willing. You cannot elect a man who is so unwilling. It cannot be right. I am old, unused to worldly affairs . . .'

'That is no argument.' Wulfstand laid his hoary hands on Anselm's shoulders. 'Dear friend, if all good men who shrink from the world's burdens, who wish to serve God in the quiet of a holy house, were to have their way what would the poor world do? Would God have us hide away and let his people starve for guidance? No, my friend, hard though it is, that is not the way. Once long ago I begged not to be appointed Bishop, but God ordained that I should be—and you can find peace in the midst of business if you do His will.'

Anselm, speechless, shook his head, burying his face in his hands. Then suddenly he lifted his head to look directly at the King.

'I am the subject of another realm,' he said through his tears

179

and clutched at this straw. 'I am Duke Robert's servant. I cannot accept without his agreement, nor without the approval of my own monks at Bec.'

But this argument availed him nothing for the Bishops assured him that there was not a man at Bec who would disagree and as for the Duke, despite the fact that he and the King were hardly on good terms, his approval could easily be gained.

'Is there no way for me to persuade you to leave me in peace?' Anselm whispered. 'Ah, my lords, if you but knew to what you condemn me.'

Rufus stirred, a heavy frown on his sweating forehead, 'Anselm,' his voice was hoarse, 'Anselm, would you send me to hell? I beseech you, by the love you had for my father and my mother, do not torment me so. If I die with the archbishopric still in my unholy hands, I shall be damned—I know it.'

Wulfstan said, 'My lord Abbot, you cannot refuse. You will kill the King by your obstinacy.'

Even Baldwin, Anselm's own monk, added his plea. 'Dear father in God, it is His will. Do you not see?'

There was a brief silence in the stuffy crowded room. The King lay still, pulling at the covers with restless fingers. The barons moved uneasily, glancing at one another, and Bishop Geoffrey whispered something to Gundulf of Rochester who slipped out of the room.

Anselm looked from one to the other, as if he read his doom in their faces. His legs were threatening to give way and he clutched at the bed post. 'I am not fit for such a place.' Slowly he sank to his knees. 'I kneel before you, your servant. Once more I beg you . . .' and yet he knew it was useless.

They raised him and pulled him to the bed. Gundulf returned bringing a pastoral staff with him and thrust it into the King's hands. Rufus held it out unsteadily and pressed it into Anselm's unwilling grasp.

They all knelt to him, asking his blessing, and there by the King's bed, they sang a *Te Deum*. But even as they sang their joy, the new Archbishop-elect could feel none—only that his peace was shattered, and from his wretchedness there arose no *Te Deum* but a *Miserere*.

From the time of his repentance the King began to recover. The fever subsided, the pain in his chest eased and he breathed more easily. As the season of Lent drew to a close he was able to leave his bed and by Easter he was on his feet again.

The nation, rejoicing in the reforms begun when he lay ill, rejoiced even more at his recovery. He was to be their benefactor now, to rule wisely in a new manner.

But their optimism was short-lived. As Rufus' health and vigour returned he began to think of all the revenue he had lost by his generosity; abbots would grow rich on the dues he had yielded and the debts he had foregone meant a half empty treasury. With Flambard at his elbow he began to retrench, putting a stop to the reforms begun in his name. Fresh taxes were laid on the people, his rapacious barons returned to their normal occupations. Rufus continued to be lavish to his particular friends, to the knights who were closest to him, but for the rest of the country the weight of oppression returned and grew heavier.

'Someone must pay for my good impulses,' the King said wittily.

Only as far as Anselm was concerned did he keep his word. Flambard said, 'Send the holy man back to Bec, my lord. It is what he wants.'

'No,' Rufus answered obstinately. 'I gave my word on his appointment and I'll not break it. If I did, I'd make more enemies than even I could stomach.'

It was true, but Rufus, to his surprise, soon found that the new Archbishop—for all he was holy and gentle and called himself an old sheep—had a streak of obstinacy as strong as his own, for Anselm immediately made certain conditions without which, he said, he would shut himself up at Canterbury and refuse to act the part of Archbishop. in astonishment Rufus heard him demand that he should return to Canterbury all the lands in its possession at the time of Lanfranc's death, that he should cancel all leases made since, and that he should allow Anselm's allegiance to Pope Urban to stand.

Rufus haggled and argued, gave half promises, made jokes and blustered, but after much grumbling he yielded, mainly because he had no alternative. All he could do was to treat his new Primate to the edge of his mocking tongue in the process.

Gilbert of Clare said cynically to Ralph de Toerni, 'I thought the King's change of heart would not last.'

'We are back where we were,' Ralph agreed. 'Did you hear

that when Anselm asked him to appoint abbots to the vacant positions he told the Archbishop to mind his own business?'

Gilbert frowned. He was watching a groom inspect his horse's hoof, while on the other side of the courtyard two huntsmen stood by the King's courser awaiting their royal master. 'And what did Anselm say to that?'

'What you would expect—that the Church was God's and not the King's.'

'Don't tell me Red William agreed to that?'

Ralph gave a dry laugh. 'Not he. And when the Archbishop bade him remember his sickness and his sorrow for his sins, Rufus told him no man could keep all his promises and that God would never see him a good man for he had suffered too much at His hands.'

Gilbert was shocked. He was a man of hard life, strong, vigorous, loyal to his friends, stern to his enemies; he was also devout and aware of what was due to God and His Church. 'How can he not see he ought to be grateful that that he is well again?'

Ralph said slowly and thoughtfully, 'Perhaps he does and that is what he hates. You know Red William—he would owe nothing to any one and be master of all. I sometimes think he challenges God Himself.'

Satisfied with his horse, Gilbert took the reins and mounted. 'That is one fight he cannot win,' he said heavily and rode out of the courtyard.

In the hall at that moment Rufus was once more supremely confident that he could. Anselm had asked leave to go to Rome for his pallium.

'No, my lord,' Rufus said plainly. 'You may not go. You are needed here. There is plenty for you to do.'

'I am no true Archbishop until I have received my pallium,' Anselm pointed out obstinately.

'As to that, if that is how you see it, it is your misfortune. The Pope can send it, since you prize it so much.'

Anselm stood stiffly before the King's chair, his hands gripped on his staff. 'I must have it from his hands.'

'Then you won't have it until I say you can go. By Lucca's face, I never thought I was choosing so self-willed a man for Lanfranc's place.'

'My lord,' Anselm said desperately, 'release me then. I never wanted the archbishopric, and if I am so ill a servant to you . . .'

Rufus banged his fist on the arm of his chair. 'We will do well enough of you will yield a little—but no, you who were as mild as milk now stand at bay as a stubborn dog who will not be turned from his quarry.'

The Archbishop was pale and near to tears but he stood firm. 'Sire, I hold Christ's honour in my hands. I must do what seems to me to be right for His Holy Church. But you are King and I will serve you—after God.'

Rufus grinned at him and there was more amusement than anger in his face now. 'I see—you would have me fight with God over a matter of precedence. Well, we shall see. In the meantime, go to Canterbury and prepare for your enthronement with prayers and fasting and whatever you deem needful. I am going hunting.'

And he strode away down the hall, unruffled, laughing and shouting for FitzHamon to come with him.

Anselm stood alone by the dais. He was trembling. What had he done, to what had he condemned himself? Why had he not fled, back to Bec where peace awaited him?

In utter misery he walked to the great new church Abbot Serlo was raising to the glory of God and there fell prostrate before the altar. But it was consistent with his character that he did not plead for release from his task. Having accepted it he prayed only for strength to do it well, to uphold that honour he treasured, to protect Christ's servants.

The two monks, Baldwin the Norman and Eadmer the Englishman, stood together at the back of the church, watching him.

Baldwin said, 'It was a sad day for him and for Bec when he left that blessed place.'

Eadmer answered, 'Do not be afraid, my brother. It was a good day for England.'

2

' "*Adhaesit anima mea post te, quia caro mea igne cremata est pro te, Deus meus . . .*" ' sang the nuns at Vespers on the feast of St. Lawrence the martyr, their voices swallowed up in the high arches of the abbey of Romsey. The Prioress, who was leading the singing that day, had a thin tuneless voice and Eadgyth, standing among the novices with her sister Mary, felt a swift desire to kick the bench in front of her and shout her defiance at her aunt.

She was no novice, neither was her sister, yet Christina insisted on them wearing the long black robes she hated so much. She wanted to tear them off to hurl them at the rigid figure of her aunt—how, she wondered could that aunt be so different from her gentle, loving mother? Mary was more submissive, but even she, child though she was, shared her hatred of the round of singing and prayer, of study and tedious sewing that filled their day. Sometimes she escaped to feed the ducks, or to help Sister Gudrun with the bees, and when it was time to make the bread she liked to knead the dough with Sister Aldyth in the great warm kitchen, but for the most part it was a confining tedium. She thought of appealing to the Abbess but the old woman was sick and bed-ridden and left all things in the capable hands of her Prioress.

'It is all right if you have a vocation, I suppose,' she said to Mary, 'but I have not and neither have you.'

'But what can we do?' her sister asked.

'Do?' Eadgyth repeated, 'Why, we can refuse to take the vows, that is what we can do. Our aunt would like nothing better than to tell our father when he comes that we have taken the veil.'

'Why should she want that?'

'To spite him. She does not care that we should be nuns only that she should hurt him, for she always hated him. She thought our mother should have been a nun too.'

Mary considered this carefully. Then she said, 'I think our mother is holy enough to be a saint, yet if she had not married our father she would not be what she is to the people at home and to us. Our aunt is jealous.'

Mary sometimes said surprisingly penetrating things, Eadgyth thought now, as if in her quiet way her sister observed more than the average person. A wave of homesickness swept over her and she shivered for despite the fact that it was very hot outside it was cold in this high gaunt building. It was cold at home in Edinburgh often, but there was comfort there—great fires and rich hangings, spiced wine and warm beds. She felt the tears sting her eyes and looked imploringly at the little carved Virgin set at the side of the pillar and lit by the candles of pilgrims who came to this church dedicated to Her name. If only the Blessed Queen of Heaven would hear her prayers and send her home again—or send release of some sort.

A richer colour tinged her cheeks. How could she still be thinking of him after so long? Two years since she had seen him, two years since he had pulled her from the broken litter and tumbled cushions, two years since he had said 'wait and things may be different for us.' Well, she had waited and nothing was different. She rose in the morning and prayed and ate and sewed and listened to her aunt lecturing her and went to bed at night and it was all dreary and everlastingly the same. So he had been wrong and had probably no more than a vague memory of her now.

Forgetting to sing she looked downwards at her own figure, breasts small still but rounded, waist narrow, hips wide and a good shape for child bearing, but all too concealed by these shapeless black garments. She longed to wear new dresses—perhaps a blue gown edged with silver embroidery, and a jewelled belt that would fall to her feet; shoes of red leather and a red fillet in her hair. Would he like that?

She felt the colour burn her face. Why could she not stop thinking of him? How could she ever hope to see him again? One day her father would come back, would take her home to Scotland, give her in marriage to some rough border lord and that would be the end of her dreams.

Sometimes at night, lying wakeful in her narrow pallet bed and listening to Sister Gudrun snoring—Sister Gundrun always snored—she imagined him riding up to the Abbey gates. She could see him so clearly, in the red mantle and tunic he had worn the day he and the Duke brought her here, his dark head bare, the familiar lock of hair over his forehead, his brown eyes smiling at her, his mouth wide—a mouth for kissing, she thought, and felt herself blush even deeper. He had kissed her once, in formal farewell, but there had been more warmth in it than convention demanded. His lips had been set apart on hers, holding hers for a moment that sent shivers of bliss running through her. How could she forget that or cease to hope that he would come back?

Little news reached her of his doings, but she did hear that he was now in Flanders, now in France, sometimes in Brittany. One visitor told the nuns who served in the guest house that Prince Henry was wandering about with only a knight and a priest and three men-at-arms to attend him, and the sisters regaled their companions with this titbit of news at recreation time.

Eadgyth tried to imagine him thus but she could not. She had seen him wealthy and confident, the brother of a King, and she could not bear to think of him as an exile, with nothing but his title to show that he was a Prince of Normandy and England. Surely she thought, now that the King was well again and Anselm of Bec was become Archbishop he would soon be recalled? Anselm was his friend and must surely plead for him. Then he would come back, stronger and more handsome than ever and he would not, could not have forgotten her.

But the gates never opened to him and she had not seen him riding in astride that reddish horse he favoured above all others. It all remained a dream. Yet it had seemed so right. Her uncle Edgar, whom she adored, was an Atheling, and to have wed another Atheling, the first of the new reigning house, would have been good, surely not only for herself but for Scotland and for England too? The tears spilled over her cheeks and she rubbed them away hastily. She felt utterly alone and longed for the comfort of her mother's arms.

Vespers ended and the nuns filed out of the church into the cloister. There the sun slanted across the stones, the heat seeming to rise and smite the moving figures after the chill within.

Eadgyth, thinking she would go to the herb garden where Sister Gudrun kept the bees, tried to loosen the fastenings of her habit about the neck and then, seeing the Prioress watching her, dropped her hands.

'You were not singing,' Christina said.

Eadgyth did not meet the stern gaze, nor did she answer.

'Well,' said the Prioress, 'see that you sing properly at Compline and do not let your thoughts wander. Now take your sister and go to the guest house. The Countess Matilda of Northampton wishes to see you.'

Eadgyth looked up, startled. 'The Countess of Northampton? But I do not know her.'

'Nevertheless she has asked to speak with you and I have given permission. Her father had cousins in Scotland, perhaps she feels a friendship for our family on that account. Go, child.'

Eadgyth went, seizing Mary by the hand and controlling a desire to run for that would have brought down a further reproof on her head. She remembered now—Henry had spoken of his cousin Maud, almost as if she might be an ally to them, and she could not help wondering, as she hurried her sister along, if he had asked the Countess to come.

The lady Maud was in one of the guest chambers with her husband and a little boy of about four who was climbing about his father's knees. She had a child, a plump little girl, sitting solidly on her lap and there was a certain roundness to her figure which told Eadgyth that she was expecting another baby. Eadgyth curtseyed to Earl Simon who greeted her kindly, and then she turned to the Countess and thought her beautiful.

Maud reached out her free hand. 'Come and sit by me. You are Eadgyth?' For a moment she looked the girl up and down in surprise. 'You wear the robes of a novice, yet I did not hear you wished to take the vows.'

'I do not,' Eadgyth said honestly, 'but our aunt, the Prioress, makes us. She says it is to protect us from marauding Normans,' and then, recollecting that Earl Simon was a Norman, she hung her head in confusion.

Maud laughed. 'Not all Normans are to be so feared, I assure you.' She turned to the younger sister. 'And you must be Mary. Would you like to hold this babe of mine? She is heavy, so take care.'

Mary, laughing delightedly, took the little girl in her arms and cradled her, sitting beside the Earl on the stone embrasure of the window. She was soon talking animatedly to him and Maud gave her attention to Eadgyth.

'Well, my child, I expect you are surprised that I asked to see you.'

'A little, my lady,' Eadgyth said shyly, 'but my aunt said that perhaps it was because your father had kin in my country and . . .'

'Yes, he had,' Maud nodded. 'Perhaps you know my cousin, Gospatric, whose father fought with mine and with your uncle Edgar?'

For a while they talked of people and families and the girl found herself warming to the Countess as she had done to no one since she left home.

Presently Maud said, 'Do you hear much news of the outside world within these walls?'

'Sometimes, when there are guests here. We heard,' Eadgyth felt herself to be greatly daring, but went on, 'we heard of your cousin Henry's exile.' She saw the Countess looking intently at her and added, 'I met him when we rode south. The litter broke and he took me up on his horse.'

'So I was told.' Maud took her hand. 'You liked him, Eadgyth?'

She found herself blushing again, the hot colour in her cheeks though she wished it elsewhere. She nodded but found no words to answer.

Maud smiled. 'He asked me to visit you.' And when the girl looked up, astonished, her sudden joy showing in her face, Maud began to see why Henry had found her so likeable. She said, 'A man came to Huntingdon, a chapman with silks and sendal and fine wool, and he brought me a message from my cousin. He had seen Henry in Paris, I think.'

'Oh?' Eadgyth knew her disappointment must be obvious. 'He has not come himself?'

'Not yet, but his exile cannot last forever. He wants me to assure him that you have not taken the veil. Well, I can send him word on that score. And he wished you to know that he has not forgotten. He bids you be patient and not to yield.' She saw the girl's rosy colour, the gleam of understanding. 'You know what he meant?'

'Yes, I know. My lady . . .'

'What is it, child?'

Eadgyth paused, her fingers twisting together, longing to confide in this gracious woman who seemed to combine gentleness with vigour, tact with honesty and who, clearly, was in Henry's confidence. For a moment longer she hesitated, but the need was too strong for her and she was sure she could trust Henry's cousin even as he did.

'My lady—oh, is it wrong of me to think of him? Is it foolish to hope?'

'It is never foolish to hope.' Maud glanced across to where her husband, knowing she wished to speak to the elder sister, was amusing the younger one of his own children. Young Simon was riding on his father's cocked leg while Mary laughed and bounced the baby. 'Only it depends on what you hope for. What do you dream of, Eadgyth?'

Her blush deepened even further. 'I dare not say it. Yet I am sure he . . .' she broke off, not knowing how to frame the words, for what had he said? Little enough, surely? 'He spoke not of himself, nor of me, but of us. He told me to keep from the vows, to wait until—but I do not know what was in his thoughts.'

'A bridal, perhaps?' Maud suggested, smiling. 'Did you know that when you came here nearly two years ago he asked the King for you?'

Eadgyth's eyes flew wide in astonishment. 'He asked for me? No, my lady, I did not know. Oh!' She put a hand to her mouth, her eyes dancing, and then slowly the light went from them. 'But I see—the King must have refused.'

'He did refuse then, but that is not to say he would not change his mind. Would your father approve such a match, I wonder? Or has he other plans for you?'

'I do not know,' the girl answered uneasily. She thought of her father's unpredictability and then added, 'If my mother thought it for my good, she would help me. But the Prince is so far away and with nothing to commend him, without land or money.'

'Of course,' Maud agreed, 'it cannot be considered just now. I wanted only to find out how matters stood with you. But I know my cousin. He is . . .' she paused, 'he is thorough and careful in whatever he does and he knows how to wait for the right moment. When that comes you will see how things will change for him. I promise you, I look to see him back from his exile before too long.'

Her optimism conveyed itself to Eadgyth and she brightened. 'If it were possible . . .' She looked at the Countess, scarcely able to put such a thought into words and at that moment the great bell of the abbey began to sound, heavy resonant chimes that fell sombrely on the moment's joy in this sunlit room. She shivered. 'We must go back. It was kind of you to come. I can be patient now, I can wait.'

Maud bent to kiss her. 'I am glad of it. I will get word to my cousin that he need have no anxiety concerning you. But you are a King's daughter and he is a King's brother. You cannot wed at will. Your father is journeying south, did you know that?'

Eadgyth clasped her hands together. 'No, I did not but I am so glad. Perhaps he will take me from here and then . . .'

'We shall see,' Maud said. She touched the girl's cheek. 'Run along now, and do not be afraid to dream.'

She watched them go, Eadgyth bright with happiness, and turned to her husband. 'I have given her hope again, but was I right? I am afraid Henry is further from a change in fortune than I let her think.'

The Earl set his son down and put the small girl in her cradle. Then he limped across and took his wife into his arms. 'My love, of course you were right and anyway, it was what Henry wanted, though myself I can see no good outcome at the moment And I fear King Malcolm may well have plans for his daughter now she is of marriageable age.'

'But if Rufus thought the alliance to his advantage?'

'I think you are over sanguine, my heart. Much as I wish it for Henry, at the moment it would be to no one's advantage but his own, and I see no sign of the King changing his mind about his younger brother's state. I think he is glad to be rid of a third contestant for Normandy.'

'Why can they not agree?' Maud queried sadly. 'I think Eadgyth's happiness may well be sacrificed to their quarrels—unless King Malcolm has thought of the match himself.'

Simon frowned over her head. 'I doubt it. He is a strange tempered man, as hot as Red William. Well, he is to visit the court, so we shall soon know how he and our King agree. As for Eadgyth, that matter may have to wait until Henry returns.'

Maud leaned against his shoulder. Simon might not be handsome, he might be slow and lame and no longer young, but she thought him the most comforting man she knew. 'I hope he comes soon,' she said, 'I would see Eadgyth as happy as I am.'

Eadgyth herself returned to the confines of the nun's enclosure hardly able to believe she was the same girl who had walked out of it only an hour ago. The knowledge that he had not forgotten, that he had sent her such a message, gave her so much joy that she scarcely knew how to contain it. Young and inexperienced as she was, she did not yet know enough to hide that joy from her aunt, and when they all filed into the church for the last office of the day, she sang with such bubbling eagerness, her eyes so bright with her secret knowledge that Christina pursed her lips and wondered what had been said in the guest parlour. She tried to find out from Mary but the child only talked of the kindness of the Earl and Countess and the charm of their children. She also asked Eadgyth herself but the girl merely smiled happily and answered, 'Naught of any consequence, aunt,' so that Christina was forced to suppress her curiosity.

A few weeks later a storm, in the person of King Malcolm himself, descended on the quiet of the abbey.

He had ridden to see the Red King on a matter of some disputed land, some taxes he did not think he ought to yield and a few other minor affairs over which he considered he had a grudge. Rufus, however, annoyed at his high-handed demands, merely deputed the Count de Meulan to say that he had no time to see the Scottish King and considered all matters determined between them two years ago on the borders of Scots Water.

Malcolm lost his temper, shouted abuse at the Count and demanded an apology for the affront to his royal estate. Robert de Beaumont heard him out and then said calmly that his master did not attend to his vassals when they abused him. At the word 'vassal' Malcolm's face turned purple with fury. For a moment those present in the great hall at Gloucester thought that he would draw his sword on the Count and several men edged nearer. De Beaumont himself, for all his calm, was keeping a wary eye on the enraged Scot, but in the end Malcolm throttled his rage and stamped out. He was no fool and too far from home to risk a fight with only a small retinue at his back.

Consequently it was in no very pleasant mood that he arrived at Romsey, bellowing at the doorkeeper to take him to his daughters. Before the terrified nun, who was not permitted to leave her place, could summon another to conduct him more correctly to the Prioress he strode past her and into the cloisters where no man but a priest might enter. There the nuns were walking to the refectory for their dinner and in the midst of them he saw Eadgyth in habit and veil.

He seemed to explode with rage and leapt forward, pushing the startled nuns aside until he stood before his daughter.

'Why are you wearing that hellish thing? You have not taken the vows? By God, if you have . . .'

Eadgyth, panic-stricken by this sudden appearance of her sire and in such a rage, stood speechless, staring at him in utter astonishment.

He took her by the shoulders and shook her. 'Answer me, girl. Answer me, I say.'

'No—no.' She gasped, his roughness precipitating her into speech. 'No, my lord, I have not taken the vows. I would never . . .'

At this moment the Prioress, summoned by the sudden commotion, came hurrying up and tried to step between the King and the terrified girl. 'Brother-in-law, I beg you to remember where you—where indeed you should not be. This is holy ground on which you stand.'

He gave a caustic laugh. 'It would be a deal holier if you did not tread it.' He pointed to his daughter. 'Was it your doing that she should wear these clothes? She says she has not taken the vows but if I find that you have forced her . . .'

'She has not,' Christina answered stiffly. She was white with a still tense anger in contrast to Malcolm's hot-blooded fury. 'And I made the girls dress as my nuns to protect them from the Normans who, as we all know, do not respect any woman's virginity.'

'Oh!' Eadgyth gasped, 'how can you say so? Many men have come to the guest house who would never . . .'

'Be quiet girl,' Christina snapped. 'Speak when you are spoken to.' And turning to Malcolm, she added, 'I did it for their good.'

'You are a scheming bitch,' Malcolm said. He heard the indrawn breath, the recoil of some of the gentler sisters at hearing their Prioress thus described, and looking them all up and down he gave a great guffaw of laughter. 'Holy Jesu, you have these timid coneys well trained. But you'll not number my daughters among them.'

He put up a hand and tore the veil from Eadgyth's head so that her fair hair, released from its confines, fell about her shoulders, and calling Mary, flung hers also to the ground trampling the white clothes until they were torn and muddied by his feet.

'That is what I think of your veils, sister-in-law. Now have the girls' possessions packed. I am taking them back to Scotland in the morning.'

Eadgyth, hardly knowing why she did so, burst into tears and her father put an arm about her shoulders. 'Tush girl, there's no need for tears. You will soon be home. Now hurry, we ride at dawn.'

He took not the slightest notice of Christina's angry protest and stalked out of the cloister to the guest house where he and his attendants, served with trembling hands by lay sisters, promptly ate and drank their way through a week's supplies.

On the journey to Scotland Eadgyth scarcely knew whether she were the most happy or miserable. She was thankful to be out of the abbey, away from her aunt's perpetual nagging, but she was also going further from Henry, further from any contact with the Countess Maud. Yet she could not be wholly cast down. Henry, she thought sensibly, would reach her wherever she was when he thought the time was right, and in the meantime she was free, riding in the fresh summer air, the fields rich with corn, the woods shaded with thick foliage, the streams sparkling and gay with yellow flowers, the birds singing so that every day her spirits rose. She was young and she was free and life had become, once more, bright with hope. It was as well, just then, that she did not know how long and how wearily she would have to tend that hope.

On the third day of the journey, her father broke some news to her that shattered her joy.

He waited for her palfrey to catch up with his great destrier and then said, bluntly and without preamble. 'I've a mind to wed you to Count Alan of Richmond. He's a powerful man and wealthy and he owns much land not far from our borders. An alliance with him would keep the Earl of Northumbria in check.'

She did not know what to say. The events of the last few days had crowded so upon one another that she was not prepared for this proposal. She hardly knew Count Alan, but either good or bad, he was not for her. She simply did not believe there could be any man for her but one. However she dared not say this to her father, nor threaten to disobey him. Glancing at his strong face, seeing the set of his jaw, the thrust of his red beard, his great square hands on the reins, she knew he could break her and her heart sank. If it came to a battle of wills she could not fight him. All she could do was to use guile and pray for time. She smiled, surprised how easily she could dissemble, and merely begged him not to arrange a betrothal yet as she was over young.

'Young?' Malcolm gave his great bellowing laugh. 'God's blood, girl you're near fifteen. You should be betrothed by now.'

'Only wait then, my lord, until we are home, until I see my mother.'

His anger with Rufus, with Chrstina, gone now that he was on the road to Scotland and had thumbed his nose at them by removing his daughters, he answered amiably enough that it would be proper to do so.

Eadgyth gave a great sigh of relief.

'Do you not like Count Alan?' Mary whispered curiously. 'Do you recall, we met him when we stayed at Richmond on the way down?'

'He was well enough,' Eadgyth whispered back, 'But I do not want him.'

'You will have to do what our father says,' Mary told her prosaically, 'and had best forget the Norman prince.'

Eadgyth lifted her whip and gave Mary a stinging blow across the knuckles. 'Be quiet, stupid. I told you never to speak of him.'

Mary sucked her fingers, tears starting in her eyes, and after a moment her sister said, 'I am sorry I hurt you, but I am afraid—oh, Mary, I am afraid.'

Early in the New Year the Prioress of Romsey was standing in the open space between church and abbey gates in the act of counting the tally of ale barrels when she saw an unexpected procession approaching. At the head of it rode her brother, Edgar Atheling, and behind him, huddled against the bitter wind, were the two Princesses, Eadgyth and Mary and their young brother, David, followed by a number of attendants, all of whom she had thought far away in Scotland.

Edgar swung himself down and kissed his sister.

Christina turned her cheek to him, holding him by the shoulders. The little affection that there was left in her arid nature was reserved solely for this brother. 'Dear Edgar. What are you doing here—and with our nieces and David? What has happened?'

Edgar glanced at his young charges, David staring about him with a mixture of curiosity and uncertainty, the two girls pale and cold, their mantles wrapped about them. Mary had cried most of the way down, while Eadgyth after her first bitter storm of weeping, had been silent, withdrawn, her childhood over. He was a kind man and fond of the children, and he had found the long journey, the shared grief, wearing on his nerves.

'Send them in to get warm,' he said, 'and I will tell you.'

Christina nodded, and told Sister Aldyth to take them to the kitchen and warm some milk for them. Then she led her brother to her parlour and poured wine for him.

Edgar swung off his mantle and held his hands to the blaze before he answered.

'Well?' The Prioress queried in her habitual manner. She was itching with curiosity. 'Will you not speak?'

'Edgar sat down on a stool. 'Malcolm is dead.'

'Dead? But how?'

'When he got back to Scotland he led a raid into Northumbria, but Robert of Mowbray was waiting for him near Alnwick and Malcolm walked into an ambush. Mowbray's men slew him though they might have taken him alive. It is a bloody part of England. Sometimes I think no good can come in that wild land, for all it was once St. Cuthbert's. When old King William marched there and Earl Waltheof stood against him the soil was drenched with our blood.'

'That is past history,' Christina said impatiently. Fond as she was of Edgar his slowness and his way of wandering off into reminiscences irritated her. 'Go on, what happened then?'

Edgar lifted his head and looked at her, setting down the cup before he answered, as if it was not seemly that he speak of what he must with a wine cup in his hands. 'We bore his body home and our sister Margaret—she looked on his corpse and gave a great cry, and from that day she sickened. She has been dead these past six weeks.'

Christina gave a low gasp and crossed herself. 'Jesu, have mercy on her soul. Did she then love him so much?'

'It would seem so.'

'That great bull of a man and she so gentle?'

Edgar sighed. 'You could not find two more strangely yoked in a marriage bed, but there was love there.' He drank again, feeling the wine warm his chilled bones. The cold seemed to get into his joints now and he felt weary, worn with grief and anxiety. 'But that was not the end of it. Our nephew Edward was killed with the King, so Alexander should have had the throne, but Malcolm's brother drove him out and seized the crown.'

Christina's frown deepened. 'Did no one challenge his right?'

'He is a man and has many followers—how could a mere lad contest that?' He sighed. 'How could I contest William of Normandy's claim, so long ago?'

There he was reminiscing again, Christina thought annoyedly. 'So Donald has usurped the throne?'

'Aye, and Alexander has gone into the hills with his brother Edgar, to wait to fight another day. But Eadgyth and Mary and David are too young to hide and run and live in caves. That is why I brought them to you.' He looked up at his sister. She seemed so stern, so implacable and he wondered where in her lay the love that Christ had commanded from His servants. 'They are lonely and afraid, deprived of both mother and father at one blow. Be kind to them, Christina.'

She held herself tensely. 'I will care for them, but I tell you, brother, if I am to have charge of the girls it is best they should remain here permanently.'

He stood up and went to the window. Outside the courtyard was empty, a quiet over the place on this winter afternoon. It all seemed grey and cold and without colour. Some, he thought, could spend their lives happily in such places, finding peace in the round of prayer and work, but not his nieces. He sighed. 'Perhaps, but do not force them, especially not Eadgyth. David I will take with me to court when I have seen the King. He is only a child, but he can serve in my household, or perhaps he might go to Earl Simon. Well, I must ride to Winchester.' He bent to kiss her. Her cheek was cold and he felt inadequate, unable to reach her, to touch her heart and bring warmth to the pale controlled face. Why was she so different from Margaret, his other lately dead sister? Yet he knew she cared for him, perhaps even more than Margaret had.

'Come again when you can,' she said. 'In the meantime do not fret. Our nieces will do well enough under my care.'

He left her and went out into the fading afternoon, a tired man who had not been able to grasp his hour when it had come and had since never been other than on the edge of great affairs.

Christina watched him go and then went in search of her nieces. She found them in the kitchen, where Sister Aldyth had given them fresh bread and hot milk. They stood together and in Eadgyth's face at least was reflected her wretchedness at being once more within the abbey walls.

Christina had her arms full of black garments. 'Take these,' she said, 'and dress yourselves as holy sisters again. It is more fitting.

'And suddenly Eadgyth, who all the way from Scotland had been torn with inward grief for her gentle, loving mother and her terrifying but affectionate father felt as if this was the last and final wound, as if her aunt had thrust a sword point into the quivering pain she had already endured.

She seized the robes and flung them from her and tore the veil across. 'I will not wear them. Never, never!'

Christina was stiff with annoyance. 'Do as you are told, girl.'

'I will not.'

For a moment they faced each other and it was as if old Edmund Ironside lived again in both grand-daughter and great grand-daughter, two conflicting wills inherited from that iron man.

Then the Prioress said, 'You are a foolish, disobedient girl but you are my sister's child and I will not beat you as you deserve. You will wear the robes because I will not have you despoiled. Your soul shall go to God unsmirched by the lust of any man, let alone a Norman.'

Eadgyth felt the blood throb in a vein in her forehead. 'Not every Norman is evil or lustful. And there are many now, born in England, who desire Saxon brides in holy marriage to make us all one people.'

'So!' Christina gave a shrill laugh. 'That is it. You look for a man to take you to his bed and you do not care who he may be—you, born of the line of Cerdic!'

Eadgyth's tears were burning her eyes now. 'No, no . . .'

'Well, it shall not be,' Christina snapped. 'You will stay here and take the vows and keep your purity.' Her pale eyes lit with a cold intense passion. 'Men!' she spat out the word. 'I will keep you from their evil lechery.'

And for the first time Eadgyth saw her aunt for what she was, a warped, thwarted women, eaten with desire for the very thing she condemned. With the cruelty of the very young she hit back, using the only weapon she had.

'I swear, by the Cross of Our Lord if you will, that I will never be a nun. I will marry and bear children and not be a barren, bitter woman as you are.'

Christina's breath hissed. She drew back her hand and slapped her niece hard across the face.

Eadgyth stumbled and caught at the door for support as Mary gave a little scream. Her cheek was scarlet where her aunt's fingers had caught it. Then she turned and ran from the kitchen, out into the cloister where it was silent and dark now that the daylight had died. There she collapsed at the feet of the stone Rood that stood by the church door, sobbing and crying, 'Jesu, have mercy! Mary, help me!'

And at the same time the Prioress went to kneel in her stall in the church, her thin fingers knotted together, words tumbling from her. 'I did it for them, Lord. They are yours, their chastity is yours. Oh Lord, protect us poor women from the evil of lust. There is so much evil, so much corruption and men are too strong for us. God, have mercy! Mary, pray for us—our bodies must be untouched, temples for the Holy Spirit . . .'

And all the while the stone Virgin held up her small Son befor Christina's eyes, as if to give the lie to her twisted, anguished prayer.

3

Herbert of Challot, Canon of Notre Dame Cathedral in Paris, prided himself on the table he kept. He was not a clever man and having reached late middle age without distinguishing himself or gaining preferment in the Church, made up for his lack by creating a reputation as a man in whose house the intellectuals of Paris might be found. The talk flowed for the most part over his head, but he did not mind as long as brilliant men enhanced his gatherings. Indeed so successful was he that he was known quite undeservedly throughout France as a renowned scholar and patron of the arts and the sure sign of advancement in any young man's career was an invitation to dine with Canon Herbert.

He was round and chubby with a pink face, soft blue eyes and a balding head, and he presided over his table like a cherub over newly-won souls. When he heard of the arrival in Paris of any man of standing he immediately issued an invitation, and in fairness to him, even his enemies agreed he cared nothing for money or for the wealth of his guests—only, as spiteful tongues added, for the cleverness he himself did not possess. In his youth he had sat in the schools under the famour Berengar of Tours but it had only done him good in that he could say he had been there.

On a wet winter's day he had gathered at the table a doctor of philosophy, William of Champeaux; Canon Sylvanus of the cathedral who also taught in the schools; the Abbot of St. Denis, most famous of French foundations, and the exiled Atheling, Henry of Normandy, who might be banished and from the look of him lacking ready money, but who was still nevertheless a prince and one with the reputation of being a man of letters. The Canon had welcomed him effusively with his attendant chaplain and one knight. The only other guest was a man dressed in the plain brown gown of a pilgrim; he was from Cherbourg, the son of an old friend of Canon Herbert's and was on his way to the shrine of St. James of Compostella.

At first the Canon was a little disppointed in his guests for William of Champeaux had been lecturing since six o'clock this morning and wanted his dinner; he was an old man and hungry, his beard fell into his bowl and dripped gravy on to the Canon's clean white cloth and he slopped wine down the front of his black gown.

The Abbot talked gravely with Herluin of La Barre and as for the Prince, who was supposed to have a keen and amusing wit, he ignored Canon Sylvanus sitting next to him, seemed not to care what dish he ate from and plied Arnulf of Cherbourg with questions as to the state of Normandy. At first Arnulf answered impersonally, drawing a sad picture of the state of affairs in the duchy.

'There is disorder everywhere and no man is safe on the public highway. The King's barons exact taxes beyond our means and as for the Duke's men, they will murder to get their way on the land he still holds.'

Tight-lipped, Henry asked, 'Does the Duke have no control over them?'

'None that any one can see. And he has given away so much to greedy men that some say he has but one tunic to his name.'

'Then he is in the same case as myself and without the cause I have.' He gave a short rueful laugh. 'How can he have dissipated all our father's wealth?'

'God knows, my lord. Money pours through his hands with no check—yet there is great suffering among the poorer sort of people. I tell you, Count Henry, the days of your father, harsh though he was at times, were better by far. And,' Arnulf forgot the company they were in and burst out, 'We of the Côtentin think only of your return. Nothing is as it was when you ruled us.'

His food pushed aside, Henry spoke in a low tense voice, his normal guard over himself lapsing for one brief moment. 'And better days will come back, I swear it by the death of my mother. If I can but get one corner of Norman soil I will make a beginning.'

There was a silence at the table. The talk had suddenly become personal and tense. Sylvanus turned to stare at the Norman prince, the Abbot pursed his lips thoughtfully, and the old philosopher, his hand half way to his mouth, paused before continuing to eat; absorbed he might appear but he missed nothing.

Then Canon Herbert said blandly, 'Pray, my lord, take some more of this roast duck. The sauce is particularly . . .'

The Abbot interrupted him without ceremony. He was a man of considerable influence who liked to have his finger in most pies. He asked smoothly, 'A beginning for what?'

For a moment Henry felt impatient, as if it was a foolish question, but he did not underestimate the Abbot's intelligence and answered with care. 'I have seen enough of adversity to know that men need an iron hand to rule them. My brother Robert has proved that too-easy dealing with powerful barons is no way to ensure peace, nor in the end is it what men want.'

The Abbot considered for a moment. 'What does the Archbishop of Canterbury think of the present state of things? For all he has left Normandy, I think his opinion counts more than ever.'

Henry glanced across at his lean, pointed face. He is like an old fox, he thought, ferreting out what is most vital.

'My lord Anselm is discreet in his letters,' he answered guardedly, 'but I've no reason to think him less my friend than he ever was.'

The Abbot of St. Denis nodded, but he clearly thought this no answer at all. 'And if you make war on your brother?'

It was Henry's turn to look bland. 'I, my lord? How should such a thing be possible? Even if it were I would do no more to Robert than he has done to me.'

The Canon of Notre Dame, a little wizened man from Blois, remarked that if Duke Robert listened more to the advice of his archbishop as well as the holy men of Bec he would do better, and then suggested that Prince Henry should seek his advancement elsewhere.

Willian of Champeaux, having cleaned every morsel from his bowl, suddenly looked up at the Prince, his pale eyes remarkably keen. 'They call you Beauclerc, do they not?'

'They do, Master William.'

'Then,' the philosopher said, 'use your head, young lord. A man who uses his head is twice armed against the man who has only a sword.'

Henry smiled across at the old man. 'You would not have me run away?'

William shook his head. 'St. Augustine tells us there is nothing higher than reason, and philosophy teaches a man to think. Apply yourself to Berengar if you would see what the study of thought can do. And then apply that study to men—it is a good thing to know what your enemies are thinking.'

'I have had little else to do these past two years,' he could not keep a note of cynicism from his voice, 'and for the most part it is no pleasing revelation.'

The Abbot sat turning his cup in his hand, it was silver and finely chased and he kept his eyes on it. 'If it were we would not have fallen from Eden, nor would we have needed a second Adam.'

'Men must be won by reason,' William repeated, 'and not by the sword.'

'Your pardon, messire,' Herluin spoke quietly, 'but it does not seem that one can exist without the other. Churchmen pray and fighting men fight and this is the way it has always been.'

'Only is it the motive or the result that matters most?' Roger the priest queried.

William said, quoting St. Isidore, 'Philosophy is knowledge of things human and divine and that makes for right living. I commend philosophy to you, Messire Roger.'

Canon Herbert was leaning back, satisfied now. The talk was going well and he beckoned to his housekeeper to serve more wine. She was a widow, many years younger than her master and her position, the wits of Paris sniggered, was less that of keeper of the kitchen than keeper of the bed. Certainly the Canon had the air of a man whose fleshly appetites were satisfied in all respects, and who, one student suggested, was not likely to be asked to preach on chastity. There was a tale going about that when William of Bonne-Ame, the Archbishop of Rouen, came to stay with his old friend, the Canon, caught by an unexpected visit to his bedroom, had to send the woman scuttling away, saying naively that she was but warming his bed, a remark that went the rounds of the Paris taverns.

Tonight, however, she knew her place and brought the wine; the Canon put out a hand to pinch her rump, recalled that he had guests and hastily withdrew it.

The discussion had turned on the conflict between the rival

popes, both claiming the chair of Peter, and the Abbot of St. Denis was arguing hotly in favour of Urban rather than Clement; William had fallen into sudden sleep in the manner of old men, and Herluin had turned to the man from Cherbourg, asking him if he had passed through Avranches on his way south and if he had seen any men from La Barre. Arnulf answered, giving Herluin what news he could and at the same time noting the knight's shabby clothes, Roger's mended soutaine and the Prince's far from royal garments. Presently when the great bell began to ring for Vespers, Canon Herbert went with his fellow canon and the Abbot down the stairs and Arnulf seized the opportunity before he himself left, to press a gold piece into Herluin's hand, whispering to him to use it for the Prince's comfort. When he too had gone, and the three Normans were momentarily alone but for the sleeping philosopher, Henry allowed himself one burst of bitterness.

'What am I come to,' he demanded, 'That I must needs accept bounty from a pilgrim, as if I were a leper or a madman?'

'If there were no one to accept it,' Herluin pointed out, 'how could a man practice the virtue of charity?'

A wry smile crossed the Prince's face. 'I swear if we were set in chains in a prison you would draw a moral from our situation. But I'd rather dispense charity than accept it. And I'm tired of living on other men's bread.' He turned up one foot to show the hole in his shoe. 'I suppose fat Phillip would give me a new pair if I asked him, but by God I've had enough of him and his bawdy jokes at my expense.'

'He is a fool,' Herluin said shortly. He had no time for men who over-ate, over-drank and over-indulged their passions. 'We would do better to go to Flanders or Maine.'

'Again? My uncle Robert found us an embarrassment the last time we were in Brussels and as for Helias his position is difficult and I'll not add to it. The truth is my brothers have seen to it that few places are open to me. They would see me go further from my own land. I thought when Rufus fell ill and summoned Anselm, he might call me back, but no—he got up from his sick bed the same man as before.'

Roger the priest looked up. 'Patience, my lord. The tide must turn.'

'The tide. It turned once and near drowned me. Does it not

shake your faith, my friend, to see how the wicked flourish?'

'No, my lord,' Roger answered equably. 'I would be surprised if it were any other way. Here we have no abiding city.'

'Yet,' Herluin said, 'when our turn comes we will take what we can get—even you, Roger.'

'If preferment came I'd not reject it,' the priest agreed honestly. 'I think a mitre and staff would sit as well with me,' he cast a sidelong glance at Henry, 'as a crown on another.'

'A crown!' Henry's brows shot up. 'You are ambitious for both of us, my friend.'

Roger shrugged. 'I'll not pretend to be a saint. But ambition need not run contrary to God's laws.'

'I'll put a mitre on your head if ever I am in a position to do it.' Henry gave him a swift warm glance, 'and be well served. But we dream. The truth is we cannot contemplate crowns and episcopal sees when we lodge in a cheap tavern because we will not be patronised by the gross lump of lard who sits on the French throne.'

'And a pilgrim gives us a coin to buy tomorrow's dinner.' Herluin held it between thumb and finger. 'Shall I throw it to the beggars below, my lord, that you may dispense charity?'

Henry shook his head, a rueful smile on his face. 'There are beggars enough in here and you are right to make me laugh at myself. No pretensions for a Prince of Normandy, eh?'

He walked to the window and threw the shutters wide. Outside the narrow street was drenched with rain and he could see the Canon scurrying towards the church, past the houses crowding closely together, past the homeless and destitute huddled in doorways for shelter from the icy rain. It was a cold gloomy day but if the leaden sky were a Norman sky he would not have cared, if it had been raining on a London street he would have walked cheerfully through it and not minded the wet.

Reduced to near penury, with only his faithful five left with him—even Fulcher he had sent home in tears, believing the boy would be better off—he wondered what had happened to all his other friends, to de Redvers and Hugh of Chester, to Walter Tirel and Grandmesnil. It was hard not to feel bitter even though he knew that the pressure had been such that they would have lost their lands and maybe their lives if they declared for him.

Those who stayed with him, Herluin and Roger, Gulfer,

Raoul the deer and Hamo, were not of noble birth and had less to lose, but for their dogged loyalty he was grateful beyond words. Only the strain was beginning to tell; to be forced to seek hospitality where he might, to accept the charity of such men as Philip of France was galling to his pride and even when he sought the comfort of women, it had to be at the whim of the whores of Paris.

He thought often of Alide, of her warmth and commonsense and wished he could see how young Robert was growing. He thought too of his Welsh girl, Nest, of the wench at Andeley, of others who had lain in his arms. There was Jehanne now, better than the rest in this dung-heap for though she was slow of wit she was kind and cared nothing for any reward, but she satisfied little beyond his body.

But most of all he thought of Eadgyth whom he had not even held in his arms and who was, indirectly, the cause of his present wretched state. He wondered if she thought of him at all. Yet he was sure she did. Young as she was she had been as affected by their meeting as he had. He could conjure up her face before him now, her wide blue eyes so like her uncle Edgar's turned trustfully towards him, her face lit by a smile that told him of the warmth of her nature. She was a child still and yet not a child, and he wanted her to wife. But Rufus had refused him, had laughed in his face, and Robert had patronised him—the two of them solidly against him. Well, that partnership had not lasted long for within a month of his departure they had quarrelled again, over what he did not know, and Robert had returned to Normandy in high dudgeon, bringing Edgar with him.

And he, who would get nothing from either, must wander uselessly about Europe while Eadgyth was shut within the grim walls of a nunnery, at this moment probably walking with the nuns to their office.

He swung away from the window. 'I will go to Vespers,' he said abruptly. It would give him some sense of union with her.

Outside the rain had turned to sleet, driving in their faces as they crossed the open square and turned towards Notre Dame. This place was usually crowded with scholars hurrying to their lectures, with learned doctors talking earnestly together, but the inclement weather had driven most people indoors and only two young men ran past them laughing, one calling a jesting remark to the other. Their faces whipped into colour by the icy wind were eager, reflecting their zest for learning, for life, and for a moment Henry wished he were one of them, free of the burden his birth had laid on him. He wished he could go with them, sit in their class, listen to William of Champeaux lecturing on philosophy, be for once anonymous. But he could not, for he was Henry of Normandy, Henry the Atheling, for all he had a hole in his shoe and no silver in his pouch.

Roger pulled his hood close. ' *"He casteth forth His ice like morsels; who can stand before His cold?"* Why was I not born in a country where the sun shines more often?'

'You can be a saint as easily in the cold as in the desert,' Herluin pointed out with a faint smile. 'They say blessed Olaf prayed bare-foot in the snow.'

'Some men,' Roger retorted amiably, 'live by illusions, but that is not one of mine.'

Listening to their talk Henry pondered on their seeming inconsistencies. Certainly he had no illusions about the character of Roger. Devout as the priest was at his office nevertheless he was quickwitted and far seeing, ambitious as he had admitted, and not above an occasional fleshly lapse. It seemed odd that Herluin, who had no need to be, was more chaste than Roger who ought to be. There were worse sins than those of the body, Henry thought, and wondered why Herluin kept himself from women as if he had taken a vow of celibacy, who lived within himself as if he had resources enough there. It seemed to be both his strength and his weakness—for there were times when he was as taut as a bowstring, when it seemed to his lord that he would be better for a night of pleasure.

But he could not have chosen better companions for these long months of exile when they had lived from hand to mouth, day by day, so that he swore if ever he came to rule he would have compassion on the sufferings of the poor.

Reaching the shelter of the church they stood in the high nave while the clergy, the monks and canons of the cathedral processed to their places and the thin voices of the boys began to chant the great words of Isaiah for the season of Advent. '*Sion the city of our strength . . . a wall and a bulwark shall be set therein . . . open the gates for God is with us . . .*'

But there was no city for him, no walls or bulwarks to guard his own, nor gates to be opened for him. He folded his arms, his hands clenched hard above his elbows. It had become a strain, almost intolerable in its intensity, to keep cheerful and optimistic, never to let any man see how he loathed exile, how he hated to beg from such men as King Philip.

It seemed that God was not with him, not as He had been that night in Winchester so long ago, when he had been so confident of his own future. Yet he knew, knew from Lanfranc's teaching, that trial there must be and when it came a man must turn to the only source of hope. But what if that source were closed to him? He wanted to know if God was still angry with him, if He had not yet pardoned him for what he had done to Conan, if he must atone still further. And because he had none of the mysticism he had often seen on Herluin's face, he spoke now directly to God as he might have spoken to Lanfranc. He did not hear the singing, nor listen to the words, absorbed so deeply in his own need that he did not notice a stranger staring at him.

When Vespers ended he left his companions and went to kneel before the shrine of the Virgin, promising to raise an Abbey in her name if she would beseech her Son for him, his eyes fixed on her wooden face with its painted eyes and rosebud mouth and he thought the simple artist had truly understood that she was the Mother of all.

Presently, he walked back down the empty church towards where Roger and Herluin awaited him by the west door. It was then that the stranger emerged from behind one of the large round pillars and spoke to him.

'My lord.'

He turned and saw a heavily built man in middle age, a prosperous burgher from his dress.

You know me, messire?'

'Aye, my lord, you are Prince Henry and the man I seek.'

He thought humorously that at least his worn clothes had not wholly obliterated his dignity, nevertheless he was surprised for the man meant nothing to him. Should I know you?'

'No, lord. I am Richard Harecher, a merchant of Domfront. You know our town and the castle?'

'I know it,' Henry said, 'it is built high on solid rock.'

'And unassailable. In my father's time, your father besieged our city and visited a terrible vengeance on Alençon because the

207

men in it insulted him most meanly. My father and the chief men in Domfront yielded to him, though the castle could not have been taken by force, because they saw in him a stark lord. They gave him their loyalty from that day.'

'All this I know.' What was he getting at, this burly fellow who stood twisting a corner of his mantle in his hands, his expression uncertain?

'Aye, my lord, and since then we have remained true to your house—at least until now.'

'And now?'

Harecher drew a deep breath and expelled it again before he answered. 'Now we can no longer stay loyal to the Duke your brother. His man, the Count of Bellême, whose soldiers garrison the castle, robs and burns and plunders. He steals from every merchant who travels across his lands, he tortures men to make them yield their silver and gold, he claims the right to arrange the marriages of our children to his own advantage, and rapes any woman who takes his fancy. My lord, I cannot tell you of the horrors we suffer and the Duke will do nothing to stop him.'

Henry stood very still, the first faint inkling of why Harecher might be here beginning to gather in his mind, barely acknowledged, while at the same time he thought, Bellême! What demons drive the man to such ends?

'Well?' he asked and did not know that uncertainty made his voice sound harsh. 'Why do you tell all this to me?'

Harecher had ridden far and now he was weary and beginning to wonder if he had made a mistake, if his journey had been useless. He looked round the empty church, shadows gathering in the side chapels, only the priest and the knight waiting by the door. Darkness was falling and perhaps that was why he could not read the Prince's face. 'Maybe I should not have come?'

Henry could barely keep his voice from shaking. 'If you do not tell me why I cannot judge of that.' And as Harecher still did not speak he said with sudden flaring confidence, 'My friend, you have nothing to fear from me. Do you think I would betray you to the Devil of Bellême? Or even to my brother?'

Harecher seemed to let the tension go from his body, dropping his mantle and straightening his shoulders. 'Forgive me.

I am tired—and we have borne so much. But now we are all resolved and ready to rise. All we need is a leader.'

He looked straightly at the young man he had ridden so far to see. 'My lord, will you come to Domfront? We will give the city into your hands and it shall be yours and we your people if you will be lord of the high rock.'

For what seemed an endless moment Henry stood there, not moving, unable to say anything coherent. Was it only an hour since that he had wished for but one corner of Normandy from which to make a beginning?

It was not until Harecher said tentatively, 'My lord?' that he reached out and grasped the man's arms.

Then he said hoarsely, 'I will come. Go to those two by the door—wait for me.'

He turned away behind the pillar, out of sight, listening to Harecher's retreating footsteps, his back pressed against the solidity of the stone as if to assure himself this was no dream. And deserted at last by the calm he had striven to keep so hard and for so long, he put both hands before his face.

That evening it was in very changed spirits that his little following gathered in his bedchamber of the poor inn where they lodged to listen to Richard Harecher's plans as he described the town, the castle, the two narrow inclines that led to the gates, the bridge that crossed the Varenne, the places where Bellême's men could be found and driven out.

'But you cannot all travel together. There is a watch for you, my lord Count,' and he spoke the last words with a different inflexion now. 'Your brother would have you clapped into prison if he found you before you reach the safety of our walls. As for the Count of Bellême, I cannot guess what he would do if he had you in his hands.'

'He would not dare to do anything. I am still a Prince of Normandy.'

'May be so, lord, but he cares for no man—or woman or child. They say,' Harecher lowered his voice as if he feared the Devil of Bellême's spies were lurking even here, 'they say he tore out the eyes of his godson with his own hands because the boy's father offended him.'

There was a silence. Then Hamo said, 'Can such things be?'

Herluin was paler than usual. 'If it is true, then he is rightly named.'

'It is true, and there are other tales, even worse. My own brother was taken by the Count's men two years ago and I've not seen him since. Even the Count's lady—rumour says he keeps her locked in her chamber, that her screams have been heard . . .' The man from Domfront wiped his face with a corner of his mantle and looked across at Roger. 'You are a priest, messire. Tell me why does God not strike down such a man? Why does He let such evil exist?'

Roger's mouth was a little twisted as he answered. 'You have lived longer than I. Have your grey hairs not told you that the wicked flourish on this earth? They will get their reward in the next world, their flesh tormented as they have tormented their victims here.'

'Pray God Bellême is cast into eternal darkness and that soon,' Henry said. Yet he thought it was those very monstrosities, that insatiable cruelty, that had given into his hands the thing he wanted most. 'But that is not enough to comfort the wretches he tortures now. We must take up arms for them.'

'The Count is very powerful, my lord,' Gulfer put in. 'He has many castles, knights and soldiers, and the Duke's ear as well.

Henry got up and stood facing them all. 'I will bring him low. If it takes me all my life I will bring him down.'

Harecher was looking at him with undisguised approval. 'I knew I was right to come. You are the lord for us. But we must get you safely to Domfront. Bellême's men are everywhere and you would be a prisoner of such value that they would slay each other to take you.'

'I know that,' Henry answered gaily. 'So we must go in twos and threes.'

His men nodded, even Gulfer was stirred from his usual phlegmatic manner, his rocklike face split into a broad grin while Hamo, who had set his back to the door as though Bellême's men were already there seeking his master's life, could not keep down his laughter. 'So it's haro! for Normandy at last. I wish I might ride openly, lord, bearing your standard.'

'You shall carry it soon,' Henry promised, but even as he planned and talked and laughed, below the surface he could hardly believe the miracle—that he had walked to Notre Dame at the lowest point of despair he had yet reached and that some-how the impossible had happened and he had walked from that holy place with hope born again. It was infectious, the laughter, the boyish entering into adventure, and he felt a deep and lasting affection for these men who had shared his exile so willingly. Not one of them, he thought, would ever want again.

It was arranged that Harecher with Herluin to accompany him would leave at dawn to take the good news to his fellow citizens waiting at Domfront, while the rest followed, Henry and Roger last of all.

'How will we travel, my lord?' Roger asked amusedly.

'You as yourself,' Henry said, 'and I—I as a disreputable fellow who has repented of his sins and is going with you to enter the Abbey of St. James. We must go on shabby horses, so Raoul had best take Rougeroy,' and fleetingly he was thankful that not even povery had induced him to part with his favour-ite mount. 'As for the journey,' he gave a wry laugh, 'my clothes are worn enough that they afford some disguise for a prince.'

'But your face is the same,' Herluin said.

'Well,' he rubbed his hand over it and after a moment's thought added boyishly, 'I will get some pitch and cover one eye so that I seem to have been in the wars and I will forbear to shave. What else?'

Hamo laughed, 'My lord, do not be so thorough that none of us will know you.'

Roger got up from the stool by the window. 'I will beg some flour from that wench who serves the ale. A slightly apologetic smile crossed his face. 'She will not refuse me. And then if you rub that into your hair you will be grey instead of black.'

'And not even Curthose would know me. Herluin, my friend, take Arnulf's *douceur* and buy us wine, the best the landlord has, and we will drink to our new enterprise, to the conquest of the high rock. In three days I will be master there.'

Under cover of the talk and the luxury of good wine, Harecher said to Herluin, 'Can he mean it—in three days?'

Herluin answered in a low voice, 'You do not know him yet. If he sets a time for a thing it will be done then, unless he is taken—which God forbid.'

But he was not taken and on the evening of the second day of travel he and Roger came to a bend in the road as darkness settled.

'There is a small house over there by the trees,' Roger pointed towards it. 'Shall we seek shelter for the night?'

Henry nodded. 'It looks a poor enough place to be safe and who would know me now?' He had not washed his face nor shaved since they had left Paris and with the flour in his hair and the uncomfortable patch over his left eye, he had indeed become a gruesome sight. He laughed across at his priest, full in the spirit of the venture. 'I swear no self-respecting abbot would take me for a novice.'

'A lay brother to feed the pigs more likely,' Roger agreed. His cool instinct had told him, long ago after a morning Mass in his little church at Caen, to link his fortunes with this man, but now that sense of self-advancement had turned into respect which in turn had deepened into a friendship cemented once and for all by these last two days of solitary journeying together. If Henry once gave his friendship, Roger thought, it would be for life. He glanced now at his lord. 'The good citizens of Domfront will wonder at the Prince they've chosen.'

Henry rubbed his bristly chin. 'When we reach Harecher's home I shall get rid of this beard and the pitch. The world looks lop-sided with only one eye.' But his free eye was alight with amusement, and the truth was that he was enjoying every moment and the restoration of self-respect that Harecher had brought to him.

It was nearly dark now. They could see no sign of life from the little dwelling, though the small piece of ground cultivated around it showed signs of recent care and smoke was rising rather thickly from a hole in the roof.

Roger opened the door. Then he stopped abruptly, coughing as the smoke gushed from the doorway.

Henry pushed past him and then he too came to a sudden halt. 'Jesu!' he said and put a hand to his mouth.

The single room of the house was filled with smoke from a fire heaped with damp straw and over it, strung upside down, tied by the feet to a beam set across from one wall to the other, was a man. He dangled, head downwards over the fire, his face suffused with blood, gasping, feebly suffocating in the smoke and more dead than alive. His clothes were burned and torn and blood dripped from two long cuts, made with horrifying precision in each forearm. Around him lay the wreckage of his home, stools and table overturned, jugs broken, cooking pots emptied into a mess on the floor.

After the first stunned moment Henry and his companion ran forward together and while he lifted the man into his arms Roger found a knife and cut the rope. Free of the fire the poor wretch was choking, coughing blood, his lungs heaving, but there was little life left in him.

They laid him down on the earth floor, Henry still holding him. 'Who did this to you? By Our Lord, I swear to you I will avenge such a deed. Can you tell us?'

Roger, kneeling with his hand on the faintly beating heart, said, 'I fear he cannot hear you, my lord,' but the man stirred and struggled to speak. His lips were too burned and dry to frame any words, so Roger fetched water and touched the parched mouth with it, letting a little trickle down his throat.

Then a faint croaking sound came and with it the words, 'The Count—Bellême—his men—he took my daughter—everything—I could not pay . . .'

The two men holding him exchanged glances. Then Roger said, 'Do not think of him now. Only make your soul ready for God, my son. Try to . . .' but the dying man's head rolled sideways.

'He is gone,' Henry said and closed the staring eyes. The priest made the sign of the cross over him and began the absolution of the dead.

'"*Non intres in judicum cum servo tuo, Domine . . .*"'

Henry crossed himself and laying down his burden knelt in silence while Roger finished his priestly office. He could not bring himself to pray for the departed soul for he was too hot with anger, revulsion and pity. If anything was needed to complete his resolution, it was this poor wretch's undeserved death at the hands of the Devil of Bellême and he could hardly bear any pause now before hurrying on to Domfront to begin the work he must do—as if God Himself had given it into his hands, as if the years of defeat, of adversity and poverty had been preparing him for this.

But because he had said he would be in Domfront tomorrow he forced down his rage, held his impatience in check. He knelt while Roger prayed, helped him bury the man in the clearing outside and at last, having eaten what food they could find, lay down to sleep by the killing fire.

He did not know it but long after he slept Roger stayed wakeful, his eyes on the door, Henry's sword ready to his hand.

On the following morning they passed unrecognised through the gates of the town and at the house of Harecher Henry removed his disguise and emerged once more as himself to meet the chief men of Domfront. Harecher had done his work well. The citizens were organised and eager to throw out the hated men of Bellême, and at dawn the next day, when the guards at the castle let down the drawbridge for the mornings traffic with the town they little guessed that this action was the signal for a totally unexpected attack.

It seemed, suddenly, as if the quiet town leapt into startling action. From every alley, from every doorway men emerged to fall on Count Robert's men wherever they could be found and those that were not slain or seized were driven from the gates by the determined citizens. Every man that could bear arms joined in the fight and even the women who had had to quarter some of the Bellême men set about them with cudgels and broom handles and cooking knives.

Picked men, armed and resolute, followed their new leader. Mounted on Rougeroy and with all the horsemen he could collect he galloped up the slope and over the drawbridge, the men on foot streaming after him and yelling. 'Dex Aie! Dex Aie! Henry—Henry of Domfront!'

The soldiers, startled out of their wits, had no time to raise the drawbridge again and put up little more than a token resistance, many of them caught half dressed and without their arms, running hither and thither, searching for swords or spears, but without time to marshal themselves. A few made a stronger resistance in the inner bailey but they were soon driven back into the hall and Henry, leaping up the steps, sword in hand, dealt with two himself, sending one to the ground with a smashed skull while he drove his sword through the other. The commander of the garrison, who had been in his bed, tumbled barefoot down the spiral stair, without an idea who might be attacking him, and, dressed in no more than his braies, ran to seize a spear from the rack in order to defend himself. But even as he turned to face the unknown foe Henry came running across the hall to send the spear spinning from his hand

and set his sword at the man's throat before he realised what was happening.

'Yield,' Henry said, 'yield and you shall not be harmed.'

The commander, half naked and disarmed, nevertheless held on to his dignity. 'By God,' he said, 'Henry of Normandy!' and flung up his hands in a gesture of surrender. For a moment he looked the astonishing invader up and down. 'You will rue this day. When my lord of Bellême hears of this morning's work he will come . . .'

'Let him come,' Henry said and laughed. 'Let him come. He cannot stop me now.' He shouted to the rest of the garrison that their captain had yielded and in a few moments it was all over, and with surprisingly little blood spilt.

Hamo, his face scarlet with a mixture of exertion and vicarious pride, unrolled the Prince's standard from the linen in which he had preserved it for so long and leaped up the spiral stair whence the commander had emerged so precipitously a few moments ago. On the way up he encountered the commader's lady who had by now realised something was wrong and had come from her tower chamber, wrapping a mantle about her nakedness, to find out what was happening.

Her expression was such a mixture of horror, embarrassment and complete bewilderment that he could not keep from laughing as he ran on up and out into the open air on top of the tower. There, with his own hand he set the standard flying high above castle and town, the single leopard on its red ground fluttering brightly against the pale blue sky as if to shout defiance to all Normandy.

Henry followed him up and for a brief moment they stood there, together, with the wind in their faces, the standard flapping over their heads.

From this high rock they could see Argentan, Séez and L'Aigle to the east; the heart of Normandy, Caen and Bayeux to the north; and to the south Maine and the good will of Helias, while to the west was their own country, the hills of the Avranchin, Coutances and the rock of the Archangel whence they had been driven more than two years before.

'This time,' Henry said, 'We will hold what we have.' He looked over the parapet, down to the castle courtyard and gatehouse, drawbridge and moat, and below that to the town and the river Varenne winding beneath the bridge.

'Mine,' he said, and looked smiling at Hamo. 'By the living God, mine!'

Running down the stairs, he took immediate and vigorous charge. Summoning all the leading citizens to the open space between castle and town there he pledged them their ancient rights and privileges and promised them that never, as long as he lived, would any man but he rule Domfront—a promise he was to keep for more than forty years.

Many of them had never seen him before but the impression that he made on them, standing in a cart so that all could see and hear him, dressed in his mail tunic, holding his sword high, was one they never forgot. He had removed his helm and stood bareheaded, his dark hair blowing over his forehead, his clear voice pledging himself to them with such sincerity that they were as won to him as he to them.

They cheered themselves hoarse, caps and hoods thrown in the air, pressing about him until he would have been swept away if his own immediate household had not stood firmly by him. Roger the priest blessed them all, giving thanks to God, and then he rode through the streets, talking to the people, greeting the men, smiling at the women with their children, sending appreciative glances at the girls who waved to him until the whole town was wild with joy. Winter stores were brought out and a great feast set up; bonfires were lit and the uninhibited rejoicing continued far into the night. He went out among them and everywhere they shouted their joy, hailing him over and over again, 'Henry of Domfront! Henry of the high rock!' until his head was spinning and he was half drunk with the joy of it.

4

'Will you go, my lord?' Hugh of Avranches, Earl of Chester, was as always ready for action of any sort. Greedy, jovial, energetic, he loved food, drink, hunting, fighting and women, probably in that order, and everywhere his wolf's head banner was borne men either hurried to join him or fled from his path. But in Avranches at least he curbed his excesses and abided by his new lord's laws.

He had discovered almost at once that when Henry spoke of law and justice he meant exactly what he said, and his hand fell heavily on all offenders whatever their rank. The men at Domfront, conscious that it was they who had summoned this best of all lords to their aid, bore themselves proudly and were inclined to look down their noses at those who now flocked to ally themselves to Henry Beauclerc, once the Cub, now the Atheling again and in effect Count of the Côtentin.

Hugh Lupus had been the first to acknowledge Henry's new position—as soon as he was sure of the Red King's sanction—but today at Domfront seated at Henry's table was a considerable collection of his old friends, Richard de Redvers was there, his broad face smiling; Ralph de Toeni the younger, his lanky figure filling out a little now; Stephen of Aumale, Henry's cousin; Walter Tirel who had been spending some time on his land at Poix and made no secret of the fact that he was delighted to find Henry once more in harmony with Rufus; and last of all Helias de Beaugencie, the Count of Maine, whose presence graced any table.

'Will you go?' Hugh repeated and cast a quick glance at the Red King's messenger, still on his knees before the high table.

Henry sent the man to get his dinner and turned to the Earl. 'If I do, I'll take you with me.'

Hugh grinned, showing teeth rotten with over-indulgence in

the sweetmeats and honey tarts which he loved. 'It's time I was on the move again. The ships will be at Cherbourg by the time we ride there. What do you say, my lord Count?' He turned to look across at his companion seated on Henry's other side. 'Is it a good enterprise?'

'Anything is good,' Helias answered, 'which will bring peace to the duchy. My borders are in a constant state of alert for all Duke Robert made an agreement with me. But,' he lowered his gaze and looked down at the silver cup he held between his long fingers, 'I do not know that King William would honour my borders any more than Duke Robert.'

Henry shrugged. 'I cannot vouch for Red William. You can trust me, Helias.'

'I know that,' the Count agreed warmly, 'and I believe you are right to support your brother and accept his support yourself, but I think he may share your father's feelings towards my land.'

'Maine has been a bone between two dogs,' Stephen said, 'but you have cleared out the kennel, my lord Count.'

Helias smiled. 'And put a chain on the door, I hope. No, I think I will not journey to meet King William, Henry, but pray take him my greetings and tell him I wish him no ill.'

'That I will do,' Henry said, 'and of course I shall go. William and I have linked our fortunes it seems, and if he is so eager to see me that he sends ships for me then I'd be churlish not to go. We'll ride for Cherbourg in the morning. Do you come, Richard?'

'Aye, my lord.' Relieved to have his loyalties undivided for once, de Redvers agreed readily. He had had the King's garrisons in his castle for so long that he had not been a free agent. He had married and fathered a son, Baldwin, and had busied himself on his own lands while Henry was in exile, however with Rufus and Henry now hand in glove he had no difficulty in rejoining his friend. Ralph de Toeni was in the same position. He had left his wife, Alice, on his English lands and sailed for the west of Normandy to join the company at Domfront— there was no riding through the central part of Normandy for this was wholly occupied by ducal troops and if Robert was slothful in seeing to their disposal the Count of Bellême certainly was not.

Helias said, 'I will guard your southern borders while you are gone.' But Henry, he thought, had restored such order here that the men left behind would have no great task to keep it. The new lord of Domfront had, in nine months, stamped his personality on his new possessions; his justice came to be relied on, men dared not flout his orders and the poor seldom looked in vain to him for help. 'I know what they suffer,' he had said.

To Helias it seemed a justification of the hopes he had had for the young prince who had stood beside him at the Conqueror's funeral. Sitting now at Henry's table, he was reminded of the old King's orderly court. This hall was full and noisy with talk and the clatter of dishes, but it was seemly and without the brawling that constantly took place under Duke Robert's slothful gaze, or the blasphemy and barely hidden vice that disfigured Rufus's court. Henry's morals, he reflected, might not conform to his own high standard, but they were no worse than those of most men and considerably better than some in that Henry treated his mistresses with kindness and his offspring with genuine affection. The Prince spoke often of the first of these, Alide's son Robert of Caen, and talked of when he might be able to ride there and see how the boy fared. A different tale, Helias thought, from the sad story of the Count of Bellême's wife who had recently, unable to endure any more, fled from her cruel husband and returned to her mother's home, still bearing the marks of his viciousness.

With Henry at Domfront, Helias' task of containing the Devil of Bellême was somewhat easier. 'And at least with Rufus to keep the Duke occupied . . .' he spoke his thought aloud.

'God knows what we will do with Robert if we defeat him,' Henry said humorously. That his brothers should ever again join together against him now seemed the remotest possibility.

From the moment when he had stood triumphant on the high rock the tide had turned in earnest for him. A few weeks later the great castle of St. James had fallen to him, his old friends flocked back, other towns sent their chief men to offer their submission to him. He spread his net wider and drove Bellême out of some strongholds that lay between Domfront and Bellême itself. He released numerous prisoners, poor wretches who had been starved and tortured by Bellême's bullies, and he took many captives himself—but unlike Count Robert the Devil, he did not ill-treat them but allowed them to sit by his fire and eat in his hall. Word of this went round and men came streaming to Domfront to serve him.

'By God,' Herluin said, 'there are some men of sense left in the world.'

In England Rufus heard what had happened and sent messengers to his younger brother offering to end their quarrel and suggesting they should make a concerted attempt to bring order back to the duchy. He sailed to the north coast of Normandy and prepared to attack Robert from his castles there, at the same time returning Coutances and the rock of the Archangel to his younger brother as a token of his good faith. He also sent men and money to reinforce him.

Among the men he sent the foremost after Earl Hugh was perhaps Stephen of Aumale, cousin to them both, and though he was still young and somewhat inexperienced, his name stood high among Normans. 'I think,' Stephen was saying now, 'that the Duke would make peace if he could, but Odo urges him on, and when the Duke is in the field—if he bestirs himself that far—he is a better fighter than Red William.'

'Except that after one fight he goes back to his bed,' Ralph said cynically.

Henry sat listening to them, one hand smoothing Lyfa's head. The dog's eyes rested on him, following every movement his master made, an understanding between them, as there seemed to be, Henry thought, between himself, this castle, these people who had become dear to him. Richard Harecher he counted as a friend and in this hall he felt more at home than he had done in any other place that he had owned. His chief care had become the city of Domfront and its people and while he was away he would leave Roger the priest and Richard Harecher in charge with Gerard of St. Lo to command the garrison. Gerard had been one of the first to return to him, riding through the gates, large and dependable as ever.

Fulcher too had rejoined him, overhelmed by vicarious delight in his master's change of fortune. He was eighteen now, too old to be a page, and he was learning the business of a fighting man as squire to Herluin La Barre.

Henry had a new page, a lad named Walter, quiet and industrious, less emotional than Fulcher, but equally devoted. He also had a new mistress, a girl named Amaldis and as he came to bed this night she was sitting on a stool by the fire, a piece of embroidery in her hand. Sometimes she reminded him of Alide in the way she had of appearing always in repose, a restful woman, a refuge from the busy world of the daylight hours. But when he took her in his arms she was very different from Alide; she was intense, passionate, seeking as he sought and because he was no longer the boy who had made love to Alide, she matched his present mood. The daughter of a Canon of Séez, who had no business to be producing children, she had been living with a married cousin at Domfront when the city fell into Henry's hands, and meeting her at the Easter feast he had taken one look at her, told her plainly he desired her, and she had simply packed up her belongings and moved into his quarters.

She was slender with long dark hair, rather sombre grey eyes and a face too narrow for beauty, but when he came to her there was a light in it that brought charm to the sharp features.

She rose now as he entered and laid down her sewing. 'Well, my lord, do you go to your brother?'

He took off his mantle for it was warm in this chamber with the fire burning in the iron basket and the shutters closed. 'Aye, I go, but I'll not leave you or Domfront unprotected. Gerard of St. Lo stays and a sizeable garrison.'

'I was not thinking of my safety.' She had a low, pleasing voice. 'The castle will be empty without you.'

He began to undress, casting his clothes carelessly on a chest. 'Then let us not waste a moment of tonight. But I will return. Domfront is my city.' Lying in bed with his hands linked behind his head, he watched her lay aside her russet gown and white chemise, and when she stood naked he thought of all women he had known she had the most perfect body—breasts, waist, thighs in right relation to one another, her skin smooth and golden, her hair falling down her back like black silk.

'I think my bed will seem empty too,' he said and reached out one arm for her. When she lay within its circle, she said, 'But now that you go to meet the King, perhaps he will give you a bride?'

'Why should he? What put that into your head?'

'I heard talk. There is a Saxon princess you wished for once . . .'

He was dumbfounded. 'How in God's name did that piece of gossip reach you?'

'I heard it in the pantry when I went with Walter to fetch your wine one night. The serving men were wondering if you would bring a foreign bride here or choose a girl from one of the highborn families in Normandy.'

He shook his head, smiling, but he was disturbed. He had thought that no one but Herluin knew of his desire for Eadgyth, had thought it a carefully nurtured secret and he was certain that Herluin never divulged any confidence they shared together. Probably, he reflected the day he had quarrelled with his brothers half the castle at Winchester had heard their raised voices, and a page or two may well have listened curiously from behind one door or another, delighting to pass on such tittle-tattle. Well, it was an old story now, and he hoped forgotten. Nevertheless, Amaldis was right. When he went to Red William he would feel his way carefully and if the time seemed propitious he would ask for Eadgyth again.

He had heard of her return to Scotland, shortened by the death of her parents, and Walter Tirel had told him that Edgar had brought her back to Romsey with her brother and sister. He was not sorry to know she was still within his reach, for if Malcolm had lived she might have been wed now. His memory of her was of a child, but a child on the verge of womanhood, and he wanted to see her again, to assure himself he had been right to want her to wife. Yet he knew, instinctively, that if William gave his consent this time, he would not need to see her, but would go to his wedding without doubts.

But at the moment it was Amaldis who lay in his arms, and he reflected, briefly and honestly, that there must always be a woman near for his loving. He could not live chaste, as Herluin did. He had been endowed with a strong, passionate body and saw no sin in indulging it, whatever the churchmen might say.

In the morning he left Domfront with a considerable following. At first light Herluin had heard Roger's Mass and afterwards talked briefly with him. The months that had passed since their lord's triumph had relieved Herluin of something of his secret melancholy.

'Put that old dread from you,' Roger advised him now. 'I cannot think you need any longer fear that you will bring evil to our master. You have been with him seven years.'

'I know. If evil threatened . . .' Herluin hesitated, 'but you are right. It was a foolish old woman's tale and I will try to forget it.'

'That is right,' the priest said bracingly. 'We will hold here until you come back. Henry will not fall on bad days again, of that I'm sure.'

'Yet I will still watch.' Herluin rose and fastened on his sword. 'And still beg your prayers,' he added as he walked away to the narrow stair.

Roger watched him. 'My poor friend,' he said, speaking aloud, but only to himself, 'I think you will be haunted until the day you die and I can do nothing to help you.' Nevertheless he went back into the chapel and knelt for a while before the altar there.

At Cherbourg the two ships Rufus had sent for his brother lay at anchor, awaiting him, but the wind was contrary. There was no hope of sailing along the coast to Eu as the King wished. On All Hallows eve, after days of waiting, the wind dropped and a sea mist rolled in, white and damp, blanketing everything. The ships lay still and lifeless and Henry sat in the castle by the fire, playing chess with de Redvers and talking of the poor state of the duchy.

Much had changed since he had last been Count of the western area. Grandmesnil was dead and his son Robert ruled in his place while Ivo and Alberic squabbled over their rights; Geoffrey of Coutances had died shortly after Rufus' sickness, mourned by his friend Odo—'It is a pity it was not Odo,' Henry said uncharitably, 'then we might get some sense into Robert.'

Old Roger de Beaumont was gone too, dying as he had lived all his days at Beaumont-le-Roger; his son Robert, Count de Meulan, inherited his lands and there was no contention here for his second son, the sober Henry, was content with his earldom of Warwick. A far greater change was the death of the most powerful lord of all, Roger of Montgomery, for this meant that all his lands in Normandy had fallen into the hands of his eldest son, Robert de Bellême, and the Devil now extended his rapacity, his greed and cruelty even further afield. He built great castles, redesigned La Roche Mabille which his father had raised in honour of his wife, Bellême's evil mother, and so brilliantly did he carry out the work that his fortresses seemed impregnable. And such was the diversity of his character, he could still by his ready tongue attract men to his service, though some lived to regret it.

'I have sworn to bring him down,' Henry said, 'and I will.' But the day seemed a long way off.

Old Montgomery's English possessions, among them the great earldom of Shrewsbury went to his second son, Hugh, the only one of his brood who was mild and dealt gently with his vassals and tenants, and the people of Shrewsbury enjoyed a brief respite from his heavier hand.

'It is the day of the younger men,' Henry said to Herluin. 'There are few left now who fought at Senlac. Many Normans have English brides and the wounds will heal.'

Herluin glanced questioningly at him and he smiled. 'Yes, I would see her again if the opportunity came.'

It came more speedily than he expected, for within a few days a southerly wind rose, a wind that would take him to England. He consulted with Richard and Earl Hugh. As Rufus planned to return to England for the season of Advent, or at any rate for the Christmas feast, it seemed a good plan to sail now for Southampton and meet the King in London.

'As you will,' Earl Hugh said, 'I've affairs to see to in England.'

They went out on the next tide and by the following afternoon had rounded the Isle of Wight and were in Southampton water. It was three years since Henry had been on English soil and despite the chill autumn day he sprang ashore with pleasurable anticipation, occupying himself in noting the changes, the new houses built, while his gear and horses were unloaded. It was while he was looking at a stall selling beautifully wrought brooches of the kind to hold a mantle on the shoulder, that he saw a face he knew.

'You, there—you are Earl Simon's staller, are you not?'

Hakon Osbertson, accompanied by one of his tall sons, stopped in the act of purchasing a leather belt and turned to see who spoke to him. 'My lord Henry! We did not know you were in England.'

'Nor was I, until today. Is Earl Simon here, and my cousin, the lady Maud?'

'Aye, my lord—at least Earl Simon is in Winchester about the King's affairs, him being away in Normandy. My lady is at her manor near Tytheley. I came into Southampton to buy wine for her as we heard there was a vessel in fresh from Italy.'

'Tell her I'll ride out to see her tomorrow,' Henry said. It seemed providential, an unexpected gift thrown in his lap. That Maud should be here, not many miles from Romsey where she alone might be his link with Eadgyth, seemed too good to be true.

When he told Herluin, the latter looked troubled. 'Be careful, my lord. You do not want to make cause for dissent with your brother now that things go well.'

'I will not. I promise you,' he added smiling, 'I do not intend to ride in at the gate of Romsey Abbey demanding to see the Scottish princess. No, my cousin will be able to arrange something, but see the lady Eadgyth I must. It is a long time since we rode from Scotland.'

'Perhaps it is too long.'

'You think she may have given in to her aunt's wishes? I doubt it, and her marriage is in William's gift now.'

'He refused you once.'

'I know. But why should he now? Do I threaten him?'

Herluin hesitated. 'Yes, my lord, I think you do.'

'How?'

They were lodging at the King's house in Southampton, and it was late. Earl Hugh and Richard had long since retired for the night, and now Herluin and his lord were alone in the small chamber they were sharing. Herluin took a fresh dip and lit it from the candle that was flickering out. He set it in the sconce before he answered.

'Because you are what you are. Rufus named the Duke his heir once, but God knows whether that agreement still holds. If it does not, then he must look to you. And he knows that the people in England would rather have you than either the Duke or even himself. If there were a rising of any sort whom would rebels choose in his place? I think the answer to that is obvious.'

Henry had paused in the act of pulling off his hose. 'I suppose you are right. But I cannot see that I am any more of a threat wed as unwed. And anyway we are on good terms. He knows I do not seek to abet any rising.'

But long after Herluin had dowsed the light he lay awake, brooding over his words. Red William was unpredictable, that was certain, yet he was sure now he could hold his own with his brother. But he did not want it to come to an issue between them

—he had fought too hard and too long for his present position to throw it away. How hard this was going to prove, and not only for himself, he could not yet assess.

In the morning he rode out with Hakon Osbertson to see his cousin and found her in the hall of her manor watching her children, Simon and Matilda at play. In her arms she held a new baby, named Waltheof for her father, and she was crooning softly to him for he was fretful. As soon as she saw her visitor however, she gave a cry of pleasure and handed the baby to his nurse, coming to Henry with her arms outstretched.

He kissed her heartily. 'Well, sweeting? By God, if I ever saw a marriage suit a woman so well! Simon must be a lusty fellow to keep you so pretty and,' he glanced at the children, 'fruitful too.'

She laughed without the slightest embarrassment. 'Nothing suits a woman more than being loved and desired at one and the same time. Simon is all I wanted in a husband. I am sorry he is at Winchester today, but we did not expect you.' She stepped back to look him up and down. 'Oh, but we are so glad you are restored to good fortune. What brings you to England just now?'

He told her. He also told her what he wanted of her.

'I am glad,' she said again. 'That girl is worthy of you, Henry.'

'It is enough to know she has not forgotten me,' he said so soberly that Maud gave a peal of laughter.

'Forgotten you? Dear cousin, she is head over ears in love with you.'

'In love?' He was genuinely surprised. All his knowledge of women came from his mistresses who had none of them been young virgins liable to romantic notions. 'I did think she felt as I did, that we would be well matched but—Maud, I must see her.'

'Of course, but I am afraid the Prioress would not let you past the gate, if she saw the Count of Côtentin,' Maud said. She paused for a moment looking thoughtfully at young Simon who was leaning against Hakon's knee at the far end of the hall watching him test a fine ash bow. 'I think she would not look too closely at my serving men.'

He laughed. 'And I, cousin, am a master of the art of disguise. You should have seen me when I went from Paris to Domfront!'

So it was that a few days later Eadgyth was summoned once more to see the Countess Maud. These visits had become regular occurrences and the Prioress could see no reason to refuse the request. Eadgyth left her tiresome sewing and went, hoping against hope for some news of Henry. Now that he had lands again, was rich and in favour with the King hope had indeed risen afresh, and surely, she thought, the Countess would have something to tell her, might even have come at his behest.

She found Maud, not in her chamber, but in the guest hall with some of her women, young Simon, Hakon Osbertson and one of his sons. A lay sister was clearing away the last of their supper and for a few moments Maud talked of every day matters, asking Eadgyth how she and her sister fared, telling her of the new baby, Waltheof.

Presently the sister finished her work and went.

Eadgyth said at once. 'Is there news? My lady, have you come to . . .'

Maud smiled and laid a finger on her lips. 'Child, you shall hear everything. But first,' she pointed to the door opposite, 'will you go into the guest chamber and fetch my sewing?'

A little surprised Eadgyth crossed the hall and opened the door. It was growing dark now and a small lamp burned in the room which was furnished only with a bed, a chest and two stools. She saw to her ever greater surprise that a man stood there, a man dressed in the plain tunic of a servant, a mantle wrapped about him, his hood drawn about his face.

She stopped uncertainly.

He said: 'Close the door,' and at once her stomach gave a great lurch so that she caught her breath. She obeyed and he threw off the cloak.

Eadgyth stood where she was by the closed door, gazing at him in incredulous disbelief. He was here—looking the same, yet different; older, stronger, but his smile had not changed, nor the soft warm look in those dark eyes.

It was she who had changed most for him. He had last seen a girl who was little more than a child; now he saw a young woman as tall as himself, and though the voluminous habit hid her shape from him he could see from the way the folds fell that she had developed into full womanhood. Her face had grown into maturity, the mark of her sorrows graven there with patience and a kindness born of adversity, though now he saw a light

227

come into it that he did not think had been there for a long time.

It was Eadgyth who spoke first. 'You have come—you have come, and I never dared to hope for it.'

He held wide his arms. There was neither need nor time for preliminaries and with equal frankness she came into them. He closed them about her, put his mouth to hers.

Then he raised his head and said, 'My heart, it is three long years and neither of us has forgotten. It seems we are meant for each other.'

She was clinging to him, searching for words, and despite herself, tears filled her eyes and spilled down her cheeks.

'Why, what is this?' he asked gently, 'are you not happy to see me?'

The joy, the relief after the weary time of waiting was too much for her and she was sobbing quietly, her head against the comfort of his shoulder. He freed one hand and stroked her hair, soothing her until at last she was able to gasp out the words, 'I am so glad, so happy.'

'And you had no warning of my coming,' he said perceptively. He led her to the bed, made her sit down, and sat himself beside her. 'There, that is better. My poor Eadgyth, it has been a hard time for you.'

She drew a deep breath and wiped away the tears. 'I am so sorry to be so foolish, but I did not guess . . .' she broke off, and the look on her face made him kiss first her hands and then her mouth.

'I need not doubt,' he said, smiling, 'that when I can arrange matters you will wed me.'

'I would wed you tomorrow if I could,' she answered, 'but I have no dower, nothing to bring you on our wedding day.'

He shook his head, laughing, 'Then I cannot take you, can I? Dear heart, as if that would matter one jot to me! It is not the lack of dower that separates us.'

And then they were silent, sitting with hands together, looking at each other. If he could have this girl, he thought, he would want no other women.

Presently she said: 'Half an hour since I was at my sewing with no idea that you were riding to me. It was all so ordinary and now—how good of the Countess to arrange it so well.'

'She is the best of women. I doubt if I could have got in

without her. Your aunt is something of a dragon,' he added laughing, and saw the joy fade at once from her face.

'She is worse than that. She is warped, she can think of nothing but the life here and how she can force me into it. And,' Eadgyth hesitated and then went on honestly, 'I think she cannot bear the thought of men, perhaps because she would have had a husband and was sent here instead. If Mary or I mention marriage her lips tighten and a black look comes over her face so that I think she would lock us up rather than see us wed.'

'She is mad,' he said. 'What would happen to the world if all women took the veil?' He remembered saying something like this, jokingly, so long ago on the road from Scotland, but now it was a serious matter, a threat to them both. 'You would not . . .' he began and she stiffened, gripping his hands.

'No, never, never. If they ever tell you I have become a nun, do not believe them, for it will not be true. Once when I told my aunt I was determined to wed one day she shut me up for a week with no food but bread and water.'

'The bitch!' he said angrily. 'My poor love, if that is how she treats you . . .'

'Oh,' the smile came back to the wide mouth, 'it was not so bad for Sister Aldyth, who is very kind, managed to bring me some dinner every day—otherwise I would have been very hungry indeed. I think my aunt was surprised I was not more chastened when she released me.'

He laughed and kissed her fingers, 'You are indomitable, a true daughter of Cerdic. We shall found a new line, you and I, a house to rule, to combine the best of both Saxon and Norman.'

The colour crept up in her face. 'I have dreamed of bearing your children.'

'And you shall. I tell you, Eadgyth, I will have no other woman to share my marriage bed. You alone will have what is best in me.' He said the words before he realised the import of them, and then at once saw that it was true, that this girl would foster all that was good in his nature, help him fight the evil. For a brief moment he saw himself with unusual clarity, faced his own worst side honestly—the temptation to sexual indulgence, the threatening volatile rage that lay not far below the surface. She would be his defence, his stronghold. He put her hands to his lips again. 'I am as other men,' he said. 'Perhaps I have been worse, but you—you will make me better than I am now.'

'Then I am content. You see, I have always known . . .' she broke off shyly.

He looked at her in some wonderment. 'Many women would not understand what I meant. How is it that you, my love, living here, should know—for what do you know of the world of men, and their ways of loving?'

'Nothing,' she said, 'but you will teach me all I need to know.'

He put both hands on her shoulders. 'I am astounded at your wisdom. Indeed I think some women must be born with it and not need to learn. But we are talking as if we may wed tomorrow. It will not be that easy.'

'I know, but—has the King any reason to refuse you now?'

He got up and began to walk about the little room in his usual restless manner. 'One would not think so, but he is a man of strange moods. He may laugh and lavish wedding gifts on us or refuse to listen to me. And even if he did I think your aunt would fight us every step of the way.'

'But my uncle Edgar would support us, and I'm sure my aunt must in the end obey the King.'

'Perhaps. It all rests with Red William. If he refuses . . .' he frowned heavily and turned to face her, his arms folded. 'Eadgyth, I must say this—I cannot risk his anger this time. I have not seen him since our last quarrel and though we have made up our differences, it does not take a great deal to rouse him. There is too much at stake just now for me to risk losing it all. I do not want to go into exile again.'

'Of course not,' she agreed at once. For her, at this moment, it was enough to see him standing thus before her, his face, so long inhabiting only her dreams, looking down at her. 'I am skilled in the art of waiting.' If her smile was a little wry she did not mean it to be so.

'I will speak to Rufus, sound him out, but if his decision goes against us now, perhaps I can win him round by my good service to him. Only be patient still and all will be well for us. I swear it . . .' he looked at the folds of the habit, 'there will be no nunnery for you, my girl.'

'I believe you,' she said simply. 'I have always believed you.'

He sat down again beside her and took her hands in his.

'Promise me, promise me whatever pressure is put on you that you will never take the vows.'

'I promise, and if you hear otherwise never believe it. My aunt can beat me and starve me but I will not do it while you live.'

'And while you live I will take no other wife.' With slow deliberation he set his mouth to hers, with his lips apart on hers as she remembered, only this time his kiss was neither brief nor formal.

She surrendered to it, to his arms, to the nearness of him, yielding to a bliss she had imagined so often, but which, now, was so much greater than her girlish dreaming.

He held her close, his hands fumbling with the hated black draperies that hid her young body. He could think of nothing but the fact that she was in his arms, that she loved him and that he—he knew it now—he loved her. He pressed her back on the bed, could not take his mouth nor his hands from her and for one singing moment caution was forgotten.

Then she put her hands against his shoulders and gave a little gasp. 'Oh no, no—not here . . .'

And at once he trust down his passion and raising her, smoothed her habit, held her hands and kissed her wide eyes, and could have slain himself for the momentary fear he saw there. 'Dear heart, I did not mean to frighten you, nor would I . . .' he broke off, touching her cheek gently. 'I am a rough, untamed fellow not worthy of you. Forgive me.'

She turned her cheek to rest it on his hand. 'You are as I want you. I will pray—oh, I will pray every day to Our Lady that it will not be long before . . .' but she did not finish the sentence for there was a tap on the door, and Maud entered.

'You aunt is below in the courtyard speaking to a sister, but I think she is on her way here, and you must be with me when she comes.' And to Henry she said, 'Only one moment more.'

She went out and at once they turned into each other's arms.

'Wait,' he said, 'trust me,' and added, smiling, 'if you hear of my marriage curse me for a fickle man and find another husband, but never, never take the vows. Only you will not hear it.'

She laughed then and with the new confidence of a woman loved and in love, set her fingers in his hair and reached her mouth to his. 'If they tell me so I will not believe it. However long we have to wait, I will be your wife or no man's.'

They clung together for one last moment and then he pushed her through the door even as he heard Christina's step outside.

Archbishop Anselm was not a happy man, but then he did not look for happiness. He had lost his peace, he saw no more the grey walls of Bec shutting out the wearisome world; instead he was thrust into the heart of that world and though he was an old man, nevertheless he set himself to do the best he could. He did not shrink from speaking out against evil where he found it and he stood firm against the blusterings and encroachments of the King his master despite the private anguish and the secret tears it cost him.

When Rufus was away in Normandy he took advantage of his absence to visit some of the religious foundations in the country and the advent of 1094 found him at the great abbey of Westminster. Gilbert Crispin, the Abbot, was one of his closest friends and for a few days they shut out the world and its affairs, spending their time together in quiet reading and meditation and talk of spiritual things. Consequently he had not heard of the arrival of the Count of Côtentin and was considerably surprised when a lay brother came to him to say that the Prince was in the guest house and wished to speak with him.

Anselm went at once to the Abbot's parlour and there Henry was conducted to him and knelt for his blessing.

The Archbishop raised him to his feet. 'Dear son, I did not look for this pleasure. It is so long since we met, but I have rejoiced that you have your lands again. How do you come to be in England now?' He indicated a stool and Henry sat down.

'My brother should be here for Christmas and we must consult together.' He gave Anselm a quick dry smile. 'We are seemingly the best of friends again.'

'I wish I could say the same,' Anselm answered sadly. 'I fear I do not please the King. There is to be a great council in Lent to discuss my affairs for he thinks I have cheated him, but that is another matter. I cannot do other than my duty as I see it, in order to safeguard the Church, nor speak other than I believe the Holy Spirit guides me.'

Henry said nothing. He respected the Archbishop more than any other man, but the best of churchmen, he thought, stood hard upon the Church's dignity which could be irritating for those who had to work with them. 'My brother is not the easiest of men to deal with,' he said at last, 'which brings me to one of the reasons why I have come to you. I need your aid.'

'My aid? If I can give it I will, but I cannot promise that King William will heed me—he seldom does so.'

'I am sorry,' Henry said frankly. 'I had hoped—but on this matter you may be able to speak for me.' The Archbishop listened in silence, his hands folded in his sleeves, his pale face grave, and Henry thought how his old friend had aged since that day when he had gone so precipitously to Bec after Conan's death.

For a little while Anselm did not speak. He stared out of the window at the leafless trees in the orchard beyond the abbey's kitchen buildings. There was a pale sunshine this morning and it was mild for November but his bones ached here by the banks of the Thames, the dampness entering into them so that he felt chilled most of the time.

At last he said, 'I think you have chosen a hard road for yourself and the lady Eadgyth. It would of course be an excellent match for you and for her, but . . .'

'But what, father? I beg you to speak plainly. I must know how I stand.'

'How can I tell? But I have doubts—I'm afraid your brother will not take this well. He does not take well any incursion into his domination of all men. If you are to be on good terms with him you will have to take a bride of his choosing.'

'Might he not think the lady Eadgyth a good choice?'

'Perhaps—but it is you who have chosen. You will have to approach the matter with care, my son.'

'I know,' Henry said drily, 'but I am determined, my lord, and so is she. She says she will have no other husband.'

Anselm sighed. 'We all at one time or another say we will or will not do a thing, but circumstances force us to yield, to act as we would prefer not to act.'

'I trust her,' Henry said, 'as I trust myself.'

'Your confidence is praiseworthy. I will pray that you may not be moved since I believe such a match might well be for your good.'

'I want her.' He looked straightly at the old man. 'Any other consideration is secondary.'

Anselm looked back at him with equal honesty. 'My son, I think you have wanted many women. Sometimes it is necessary for the soul's good to do without one's desire.'

Henry shifted restlessly. The austerity of this little room seemed over-confining. 'Father, there are some men for whom sanctity is the absorbing purpose of their lives; there are others who are lechers, who use women as one might use a sword or a bow, but for myself I cannot see, since God made us men what we are, why we cannot love Him and women as well.'

Anselm looked back at him with equal honesty. 'My son, you give more than lip service to the Church, I know that—your devotion is sincere. As for the other side of the coin, well, I would see you live more chaste. Perhaps this love of yours for the Scottish maid has been sent to prove you, to find out if you can be steadfast.'

Henry paused before him. 'As far as she is concerned I will not change my mind. If I am allowed to wed her . . .' he hesitated, looking beyond the Archbishop to the leafless trees, the pale blue sky, 'then would I endeavour to cleave to her. I am prepared to wait as long as it may be necessary. Can I count on your help?'

'For what it is worth,' Anselm conceded sadly. 'You know I would do all I could for you, but I fear my influence is limited.'

'It is less so than you think.' Henry rose and took up his gloves and mantle. 'Well my brother will be back in London soon so we shall not have to wait long to find out what he thinks. After all I am not the landless boy I was when I last asked.'

'Nor is he the man he was before he fell sick,' Anselm pointed out. A sudden unexpected spark of anger lit his calm eyes. 'Before—I had hopes of him, but it seems now as if he delights to flout God in every way he can. Instead of gratitude for his recovery, he sets out to defy the Church and all of us who serve her. I fear for his immortal soul.'

Henry was silent. He was not particularly worried about Rufus' immortal soul, but he was concerned with his brother's present state of mind, and if he was indeed changed there might be less hope than before. On the other hand, if Rufus chose he could always do the unexpected.

When he came, two days before Christmas, his attitude was one neither Henry nor Anselm had envisaged. He rode into the palace of Westminster attended by a large number of knights and strode into the great hall in his usual vigorous manner. He greeted Henry cheerfully, embracing him and calling him a brother after his own heart. He did not seem in the least put out that Henry should have come here to London instead of as he had suggested to Eu. On a tide of self-assurance he swept his brother down the hall, commending his strong action at Domfront and prophesying that together they would prove unassailable.

'God defend us from fools and weaklings,' he added. 'Now we must put an end to Robert's folly in Normandy.'

They kept the Christmas feast with great jollity, but Henry could scarcely fail to notice, if he had not already known of it, the tension between the King and his Archbishop. Rufus seemed to enjoy provoking the saintly Anselm, perhaps to try to prove him less saintly. He told a series of bawdy jokes and a few blasphemous ones that set the hall rocking with laughter; he told them deliberately and with calculated rudeness, trying to make the old man lose his temper. To Rufus it was merely sport, but to Anselm it was clearly anything but a laughing matter. The affair of his pallium still rankled between them and neither would give way an inch. Henry felt sorry for the Archbishop, but it did seem to him that, holy as he was, Anselm was being needlessly obstinate.

However, at the moment he was more concerned with his own problems and on the evening of St. Stephen's mass he found Rufus for once alone in his solar and seized the opportunity. As he entered the King, who was sitting looking at a pile of counters, glanced up and said: 'I'm damned if I can understand money—only the need for it. Flambard can sit all day and juggle with these things and I go to bed richer than when I awoke, but I cannot make head nor tail of what he does.' He swept the counters aside. 'Well, it is near dinner time. Shall we go down?'

'One moment,' Henry said. 'There is a matter on which I must speak to you,' and when Rufus obligingly sat down again, 'I wish to wed.'

Red William leaned back in his big carved chair and grinned, showing his strong teeth, his florid face amused. 'Well, I hear your bed is seldom empty. You should have been a saracen and then you might have filled your hall with a dozen wives. One will never suffice you.'

Henry took this sally with good humour, but he said, 'I am in earnest, William.'

His bother glanced at him. 'I see that you are, but what is the urgency? Have you deflowered some highborn wench and set her pot cooking?'

'Is it likely? I've more sense than that, but neither you nor Robert seems disposed to wed and one of us must to provide an heir.'

Rufus laughed. 'Robert's affairs of the heart are none of my business and for myself, why, mine are none of yours. What girl have you in mind this time?'

'The same,' Henry said carefully, 'the Princess Eadgyth.'

Rufus looked surprised. 'She's still a child.'

'Not now.'

Rufus' eyes narrowed. 'And how should you know that?'

'The years pass for her as for the rest of us.'

The King gave him an odd look, as if he suspected something, but Henry returned it blandly and Rufus got to his feet, his expression impossible to read.

'Well, I've not time to discuss it now. She is young and you can wait. Anyway we've too much else to think about at the moment.'

He linked his arm with Henry's and began to walk him along the gallery. 'Now I have plans for rebuilding this hall . . .'

'Will you listen?' Henry asked and stood still, disengaging his arm.

'No.'

'Is it such a monstrous thing I ask? At least let me . . .'

'No,' the King repeated and taking his elbow again propelled him along beneath the stone arches.

'William!'

Rufus laughed again. 'God's wounds, you are hot for this girl! But you've been hot for others and must stay your passions elsewhere.'

'Will you never . . .'

'Never is a long time.' Still laughing, giving no hint of a reason for his attitude the King ran down the spiral stair and at dinner kept up a lively discussion about the war in Normandy and how best to bring the two Roberts to terms. He ate hungrily, talking as he ate, washing the food down with rich wine and smacking his lips noisily. 'If you can deal with Bellême, brother,

236

I'll turn my attention to Curthose,' he promised and calling for a map pushed aside the dishes and set his thick finger on the places where he wished Henry to begin operations. 'You shall have men and money,' he went on, 'We will fight this together, Beauclerc.'

And for the next few weeks he busied himself with the preparations for the campaign. Two of his closest adherents, the Earl of Surrey and William of Mortain were continually with him and seemed to make a practice of keeping Henry from approaching him; they made no secret of their enmity—de Warenne nicknamed the Prince 'Henry Hartsfoot' because of his love for the chase, turning it into a derogatory sneer, and Mortain used his biting tongue to good effect whenever his cousin was near. Henry kept his temper but try as he would he could not see Rufus alone. If de Warenne or Mortain were absent, either Flambard was there discussing money, Earl Hugh to talk of ships for the enterprise, the Chamberlain Richard de Rules with queries concerning the royal household, or important men queuing up to offer their services. Rufus clearly had no intention of considering the marriage of his brother and turned aside every effort Henry made to re-open the subject. When Anselm began once to speak of it Rufus told him to mind his own business. He was boisterous, blasphemous, bringing the atmosphere of the camp into his court; he was affable and genuinely enjoyed having Henry at his side but talk of marriage and the lady Eadgyth he would not.

'Why?' Henry asked Anselm in some despair. 'Why will he not speak of it? What must I do?' To which the Archbishop replied that, singularly unsuccessful in his own relations with the King, he felt he would hinder rather than help the Prince's cause. Deep in his own troubles and mourning the death of old Bishop Wulfstan, he could do no more than advise patience and caution.

'Holy Cross!' Henry exploded one night when he was alone with Herluin and Richard de Redvers. 'Have I not been patient long enough?'

'Wait until the campaign is over, my lord,' de Redvers suggested. 'The King has his whole mind set on that.'

'I should have thought he could give his mind to more than one thing at a time,' Henry said caustically.

'Not when it involves vast expenditure and he has Flambard always at his elbow.

Herluin said: 'My lord, Richard is right. The outcome might influence him in your favour.'

Henry flung himself down on his bed, his hands clasped behind his head. 'Perhaps. I suppose it is what I must do.'

A silence fell.

Richard said, 'There are men in England, Henry, who would further your cause because they have no love for the King.' He spoke quietly but the import of his words was not lost on his listeners.

'If I thought . . .' Henry began and then closed his mouth hard. He lay still, staring up at the vaulting above his head.

Herluin seemed paler than usual. 'Not yet,' he said, 'Not yet.'

And Richard added, 'When the time comes . . .'

Herluin poured the Prince's nightly cup of wine and brought it to him. 'I think,' he said slowly, 'that the King does not want to talk of the matter, not because of you, my lord, nor the lady Eadgyth, but because it involves the succession, the crown that one day he must leave in other hands. He has no child, Duke Robert has no legitimate heir—their jealousy near ruined you once and I think it might do so again.'

Henry took the wine but after a moment set it down untouched. 'You cannot think I would give her up, for a possible facet in William's character.'

'No indeed, but I think you would do well to bide your time. Perhaps at the end of this campaign you might be the King's only heir and he would no longer be able to play you off one against the other.'

He had not thought of this and he lay on one elbow, pondering. He did not wish Robert dead. Though a fool, Robert was still his eldest brother who had in the years past shown him affection and kindness, who still by an extraordinary diversity in his make-up could exhibit real fondness, even though the next moment he might try to set chains on his brother's wrists. If Robert died, his agreement with Rufus as to the inheritance would be void and then . . .

He sat up, hugging his knees to his chest, his chin sunk in his folded arms. He was thinking of Eadgyth, of how he had sat upon a bed with her young body close to his, and wondering what it was about her that made him want her to wife as he had wanted no other woman. He thought too that the English people would love her for the stock she came from so that she might be a means of welding a torn people into one. He thought of Robert, weak, ineffectual, unwed, and of Rufus who preferred the company of pretty boys to a healthy tumble in bed with a wench.

For one moment he was agonisingly tempted. An impulsive gesture would no doubt be heroic, capture the imagination; he could throw all in hazard for one chivalrous deed, force an entry into the abbey, defy Christina and carry off his girl, daring his brother's rage for the sake of love. It was tempting and desire flooded him, so that his longing became an overwhelming physical need for action. But his will cast in the same mould as his father's, restrained him. To seize Eadgyth would be folly and he knew it. 'So be it,' he said abruptly, 'we go back and fight William's war for him.'

Too restless for sleep and despite the lateness of the hour he went out to seek company, finding it in the house of a woman whose name was also, by an odd coincidence, Eadgyth. She was the daughter of Wigod of Wallingford who had long ago been the first to submit to King William and she had welcomed him more than once before. Wrapping his fingers in her hair he could imagine they were his own Eadgyth's silky braids, but in his sleep he dreamed that she lay in her habit on the floor of a church so large that he seemed to be running yet come no nearer to her. She was weeping and surrounded by shadowy black figures and he could not reach her.

He awoke, sweating, to find the dawn cold and overcast and a strong wind blowing that would carry a ship to Normandy.

5

In the summer of 1095 an event occurred which set the whole
of Europe ablaze with a new fervour. Pope Urban on a visit to
Clermont mounted the pulpit there and before a large gathering
of great men preached with fire and fervour of the holy places in
Palestine.

'It is a stain on Christendom,' he cried, 'that these should lie
in the hands of the infidel. Where Our Blessed Lord walked
and taught, the heathen now treads. How can we tolerate this?
Let all Christians rise and drive the forces of Satan from that
holy soil. Let men come forward and lead the army of God
into Jerusalem. And for everyone who falls the trumpets will
sound in heaven and angels will bear his soul straight to God.
Brothers, arise! Enrol under the banner of Christ your
Captain . . .'

Such was his enthusiasm that within a few weeks the call had
spread from one end of Europe to the other. From every bishop,
from every itinerant preacher the cry arose, 'Free the holy
places, redeem Jerusalem!' and in the excitement became like an
infection passing from one man to the next. The words *Dieux
le vot* spread the length and breadth of Normandy. Men forgot the war, forgot whether they were for King or Duke or
Count and entering their chuches swore to go, to fight under
the sacred emblem. Their wives cut great crosses of white cloth
and sewed them to their surcoats, preparing to part joyfully with
their husbands for such a worthy cause.

An obscure hermit named Peter began to preach to poorer
folk so that they too rose and armed only with sticks and scythes
marched under his banner, scarcely knowing where they were
going, only that somewhere to the south lay their goal, the holy
sepulchre of the Lord they worshipped in their churches.

One of the first to be infected by all this religious zeal was
Duke Robert himself. Weary with the incessant difficulties of

governing his duchy, with the need for money, the arrogance of his barons and the ever-increasing pressure from Rufus' garrisons on one side and Henry's encroachments on the other, he grabbed at the chance of honourable escape. He knew himself to be unbeatable on horseback, brilliant equally with sword and spear and here was a chance to do the thing he could do and put behind him that which he could not.

Solemnly, in Rouen cathedral and in a grand gesture, he took the cross. But whatever the other motives, his devotion was genuine, he kissed the crucifix with tears rolling down his plump pink cheeks, his warm and gentle nature overflowing with love for his Lord and a burning desire to see the holy places once more in the hands of Christian men. His boon-companion, Edgar Atheling, sent word from England that he too would wear the cross and journey to meet Robert in Rome.

The Duke's uncle Odo, whose motives were more obscure, knelt with him and pledged himself also to the enterprise. His practical mind went immediately beyond the zeal, the fervour, to the main need—money. Robert had none and it was agreed they should approach Rufus.

The King, when he heard, gave a sharp laugh. 'By Lucca's face, the hounds of God have got their talons into brother Robert. Well, let him go on his crazy jaunt as long as I can profit by it.'

'A mortgage, perhaps?' Flambard suggested. 'His duchy? And should he fall . . .' he had no need to complete the sentence for Rufus' sharp mind was for once ahead of his.

'He shall pledge his duchy,' Red William agreed gleefully. 'See to it, Ranulf, arrange a meeting, sureties . . .'

The sum was settled upon, ten thousand marks of silver, and during the summer Flambard set about extracting it from the English people.

The news came to Henry below the walls of St. Ouen where he was besieging a garrison of Robert of Bellême's men. The latter had seized a castle belonging to Robert Giroie and had imprisoned some three hundred men. Despite the offers of ransom Bellême refused to release his prisoners. 'They shall keep a good Lent,' he said and proceeded to starve them to death in his dungeons. He went each day himself, so it was said, to watch their sufferings, a cup of wine in one hand and a hunk of bread in the other which he ate in their sight.

Disgusted at such bestial behaviour Henry spent the summer waging war by every possible means against the Count of Bellême. He laid ambushes, attacked smaller castles, drove the Count's men from every vantage point and during the last hot days of August attacked a large troop of them, captured half and chased the rest back into La Roche Mabille. There was no taking this fortress and he was on his way back to Domfront when he received Rufus's summons to attend him at Chaumont in the Vexin where the pledge between the King and the Duke was to be settled.

Great men of both sides assembled to witness the contract, which was drawn up under the auspices of King Philip. Many bishops and prelates gathered there, though the rigid and holy Bishop Ivo of Chartres refused to come under the same roof as King Philip unless the latter agreed to renounce his adulterous marriage with Bertrade, the former wife of the Count of Anjou. Philip thumbed his nose at Ivo and the meeting went ahead without the Bishop of Chartres.

The little town overflowed and many important barons set up tents in the surrounding meadows. Henry preferred this accommodation to the crowded castle and it was here in the open that the three brothers met, for the first time in four years, the contrast between them more marked for the time that had passed. Robert had a great paunch on him now and the top of his head was bald; his face still retained its soft colouring and amiable expression, but there were lines that had not been there before that witnessed to his lack of confidence in himself. Rufus also had put on some weight but his self-confidence had increased giving him a determined walk, an arrogant bearing, a manner of dealing with all men whatever their rank that was a mixture of absolute authority and soldierly camaraderie. And Henry knew himself to be no longer the youth to be dominated but a man on a level with both of them.

Robert clasped him in his arms, a smile of spontaneous affection on his face. 'Beauclerc! By heaven, you are a sturdy warrior these days. Come with me, fight for our Saviour on His own land.'

Rufus disposed at once of this idea. 'I need him here. If we are to keep order in your duchy we must be strong and,' he added humorously, 'if you take all the best fighting men with you that will leave Normandy to the churchmen, then we should have to reverse the procedure and conquer it back from Christ himself.'

Robert looked shocked. 'Brother, your jest is unseemly. But I suppose you are right about Beauclerc. He must stay.'

Henry, who had no intention of going, merely inclined his head, and Robert said cheerfully: 'At least there will be peace between us and all Normans. We will not be fighting each other but God's enemies.'

He turned and beckoned to a tall figure. 'Come, Robert, and make your peace with the King and Count Henry. There must be an end to feuding.'

Robert of Bellême came across the rough grass with his long stride. His dark head was bare, his thin brows strongly marked, his eyes almost black and at the moment bland but watchful.

'My lord King,' he said with cool assurance, 'we have matched our forces well. I respect you as a soldier and in the Duke's absence I take you for my overlord.' He went down on one knee and set his hands, long and tapered, between the square rough hands of Rufus, but it was done lightly. Almost immediately he rose and turned to Henry. 'My lord Count, you have taken much from me ...'

'You had overmuch and to spare,' Henry said curtly, 'and if we are to be at peace I require you to leave my land and my people free from your raiding. Your men observe neither the Truce of God nor the rules of war.'

The Count shrugged, lifting his shoulders expressively. 'War is not a game, my lord. A man, if he is a man, must take what his enemies can do to him, but if we are to join together, I will leave your borders in peace. It is a long time, is it not, since your uncle Odo shackled us both on the beach at St. Valery?' He smiled showing small even white teeth, the thin cruel lips curved upwards in a disguising manner. 'I have some new ideas for war machines that I will show you, instead of employing them against you.'

He talked on glibly, exerting all his eloquence, but Henry was no longer deceived. The Count of Bellême had too much power for one man, he thought, but he too smiled and talked and kept his loathing to himself.

Presently Bishop Odo of Bayeux came to join them, bringing with him the tall gangling figure of the Crane, Gilbert Bishop of Evreux. Odo was aging now, his dark hair turned an iron grey, but his eyes were as keen as ever and he greeted his youngest nephew coolly. Since their meeting at Dover and the subsequent affair of Bayeux tower there had been no sweetening of the relationship between them.

Odo said now, 'I do not hear, nephew, that you have vowed your sword in our holy cause.'

'Nor will you,' Henry told him plainly. 'You have Robert to fight a way to heaven for all of us and that will have to suffice. I imagine,' he added as an afterthought, 'that as you cannot be going to wield your mace on this occasion, that it must be in the guise of a pilgrim.'

The bishop, whose temper had not improved with the years, said severely, 'And if I go in penance for my sins, it is a better thing than to disregard the Holy Father's call and stay at home.'

Rufus laughed outright. 'Then you had best add the sin of pride to your list, uncle, for that remark smacked of it.'

The Crane, stooping now with the weight of years, said reprovingly, 'Young sirs, you do ill to joke over holy things.'

Remembering the Bishop's former kindness to him, Henry took him by the arm and led him aside. 'My lord, you must forgive us. We are like all families—we cannot take each other seriously and we scrap as a litter of pups but I do not jest at the venture. I am not going because Rufus wants me here and because I believe my duty is to my people, just as Robert no doubt sincerely believes his is to go. But I do ask you to pray for me when you get to the Holy Sepulchre.'

'If we get there,' the Crane said, 'and if God wills it, we shall.'

Wandering in the meadows among the tents Herluin of La Barre was looking for his brother but not finding him caught hold of Ralph de Toeni by the arm and asked for him.

'Simon?' Ralph cocked an eyebrow. 'Did you not know that the King has dismissed him from his service?'

Herluin stood still in the hot sunlight. 'No, I did not. What happened?'

Ralph shrugged and looked embarrassed. He liked Herluin and did not want to offend him.

Herluin said, 'Tell me.' His face was stern, his voice expressing nothing but that he wanted the truth.

'Well,' Ralph shifted his feet and looked out over the colourful field, to the bright tents and gonfanons, the gay clothes of the ever moving crowd. He was sweating in the heat and wiped his forehead with his sleeve. 'It seems the King no longer required so—so close an attendance from him and offered him a manor in Northumbria, a very small manor. Simon threw the deed on the floor and walked out. I thought Red William would shackle him for that, but he laughed and that was all. I've not seen Simon since.'

Herluin said nothing. Then he nodded his thanks briefly and, too disturbed to continue the conversation, walked away through the busy crowds, silent and detached.

The pledge was drawn up the next day, the terms agreed, King Philip, the Abbot of Dijon and other prelates acting as witnesses. Rufus handed over the ten thousand marks wrenched with so much pain and difficulty from the people of England and Robert returned to his duchy to pay the reckoning for the men and arms and equipment he had assembled.

Rufus, commanding the attendance of the Counts of the Côtentin and of Bellême rode to Rouen to take over his position as ruler of the duchy. Robert de Beaumont was to be married to Isabelle, the daughter of Hugh of Crepi, King Philip's brother, who was himself to go on the crusade and wished to see her bestowed before he went. It was a great occasion, the first gathering of all Normans since Robert and Rufus had begun their quarrel and the last before the crusaders left. The hall at the palace of Rouen was packed for the marriage feast. Old friends greeted each other warmly and old enemies eyed one another warily, but raised their cups together. William of Breteuil and his crony Robert of Bellême talked with Henry and Earl Hugh as if there had never been bad blood between them, while Ralph de Gael, newly arrived from Brittany, hailed the King for all as if he was his most loyal subject instead of one who had plotted to overthrow his father.

Hamo and Raoul the deer were fighting their way through the crowds at the lower tables to their places on a bench beside Gulfer who, with Fulcher, was engaged in pushing off a couple of Odo's men-at-arms. There was a good humoured scuffle which ended in the Bishop's men sprawling in the rushes while Henry's seated themselves firmly, prepared to repel all comers.

There was an abundance of rich dishes and wines so that every man could have his fill. The jester, Rollo, set the hall rocking with laughter at his clowning, dogs scrambled in the rushes for scraps and children ran wild, tripping up servers and ushers while at the high table the bridegroom, no longer young but still an impressive looking man sat beside his high born wife, who was not yet twenty and a russet-haired beauty.

God save us,' Hamo said; 'did you ever see so many Normans swearing friendship with each other? Have you heard the latest tally of men to go, Raoul?'

The deer shook his head. 'As long as I'm not required to take my old bones and leave them in some foreign land I care not.'

'It would be a holy end to die in Christ's own country,' Fulcher said gravely, but Raoul lifted his broad shoulders.

'Maybe so, but who's to say we'd ever get there? I tell you there will be so much quarrelling among the leaders it will be a miracle if they do.'

Gulfer, stuffing his mouth with roast goose and sucking in the sauce, said, 'Can you see the bride's father arm in arm with Eustace of Boulogne, or the fat Count of Toulouse agreeing with Godfrey of Bouillon? As for our own men, Gerard of Gourney will quarrel with Geoffrey of Mortagne and Ivo and Alberic of Grandmesnil will quarrel with each other and everyone else.'

Raoul leaned his arms on the table. 'We should thank God fasting that our lord is not smitten with holy zeal.'

Fulcher laid down his knife. 'I cannot understand you, any of you. Can there be a higher task for a knight than to fight for the holy places?'

Hamo grinned. 'Oh, fighting is all right and once one was there it would be . . .' for a moment a more serious look crossed his humorous face, but it was fleeting, as if he would not allow gravity to dominate him, 'but think of getting there! As for the company, what with thieving Frenchmen and quarrelling Burgundians, and the rough fellows from the north who're half pagan as well as Italians who'd as soon set a knife in your back as cross the road, I'll wager there'll be more blood shed among them than the infidels!'

'If all these great men are going and the Pope himself wishes it, it must be right,' Fulcher put in obstinately, and Gulfer laughed.

'Oh, we all know you think of nothing but earning your spurs, but I can tell you my wife would have my hide if I went.'

With sudden resolution Fulcher said, 'I shall go. I shall ask the Prince if I may take service with Stephen of Blois. He is husband to Henry's own sister.'

'I thought you never wished to leave our master?' Hamo queried mockingly and Fulcher flushed.

'Nor I do, but if God wills it, I will come back, and . . .' he stopped, seeing the three of them looking at him in surprise and not being able to explain what emotions had seized him, urging him to take the cross, to go with the men who had done the same, to set foot in the holy places and at the end to kneel before the Sepulchre itself. It seemed to him the height of knightly endeavour and he sat, crimson and shy, wishing he had more confidence.

Hamo set his arm across the lad's shoulders and gave him a gentle shake. 'Then go and God go with you. We'll not tease you any more and I for one will give you a new saddle to ride with.'

'Aye,' Gulfer nodded, 'and you shall have that sword I bought last week.'

Raoul promised the gift of a helm and Fulcher sat between them, a heady excitement rising in him, an excitement that seemed to be paramount in this hall tonight so that men were cheering and drinking to the crusaders as well to the bride and groom.

Henry gave his consent to the departure of Fulcher, adding a horse and a purse to the lad's gifts and a few days later saw the great assemblage of men ride away through the streets of Rouen, blessed by the bishops and liberally sprinkled with holy water, their banners flying and a high ardour motivating the best of them.

From all over Europe such contingents were departing and the Normans had not been gone more than two days when Helias de Beaugencie rode in and asked for an audience with the new ruler of Normandy.

Crossing the outer courtyard of the palace and seeing the banner of the lord of Maine, his escort dismounting, stretching stiffened limbs, Herluin La Barre gave the Count's men no more than a cursory glance until he noticed to his astonishment a familiar figure. 'Simon! What in God's name are you doing here?'

His brother turned sharply. 'I wondered if I should see you now that your lord is hand in glove with the King.'

'Well?' Herluin looked him up and down. Simon had changed, he thought. He looked older and wearied, lines running from nose to mouth that gave his handsome face a dejected look and his features had lost the delicate smoothness of youth.

Simon took off his helm and set it on the pommel of his saddle, wiping his hot forehead before he met his brother's look with one equally direct. 'I have left King William's service.'

'So I heard, and I am glad of it. But you were a fool to anger him, to throw his gift back in his face.'

Simon grimaced. 'I though such a piece of gossip could hardly fail to reach you.' His face darkened at the memory of that particular scene. 'It was an insult after the years I have attended him—an insignificant manor in Northumbria with barely enough hides to support one knight's fee and about as far from the court as he could send me.'

'Yet, it would have been better to take it than to . . .'

Simon interrupted him sharply. 'You think so? I thought you wanted me to return to Normandy.'

'I want you to return to a better way of living,' Herluin said plainly, 'where does not matter. You could have taken a wife and settled in Northumbria.'

Simon gave him an odd look. 'How singularly imperceptive you are.'

'Don't mistake me— I am not as simple as you think. It might be done and to your profit, but I'll not argue about that. Only I am surprised you did not land yourself in one of William's fortresses.'

Simon looked beyond him to the grey stone palace, the high walls, the tower where more than one illustrious prisoner had been held. 'You do not understand. William meant it to be an insult. It was one of his ill-timed jests. Things were not—as they had been between us.'

Thankful enough that Simon was free of an attachment that to Herluin's mind brought nothing but shame on his name, he did not comment on this. It was easy to see Simon was seared by experience, and his elder brother's innate kindness did not allow him to pursue the matter.

'Well, I am glad to see you back. Perhaps in Normandy you will find something better. What made you join the Count of Maine? Why did you not come to us?'

'Would your master have welcomed me?' There was a wry twist to Simon's mouth. 'I think not, he is too careful of his new friendship with Rufus.' And when Herluin's silence conceded the point he went on, 'I must earn my bread somehow and it seemed to me that if I would do penance for past wrong I could do no better than seek service with the most Christian knight in Europe. And now that we go to the Holy Land perhaps there I can wipe out what has gone before.'

Herluin stood still, looking intently into the disillusioned face. 'There can be no better way and you could go with no finer man.' He linked his arm with his brother's. 'Come and drink some wine with me while you are waiting for your new lord. This will be a fresh beginning for you.'

'I think so,' Simon's voice was unusually quiet as they walked off together. 'Perhaps the better the master the better the man.'

Meanwhile King William was not regarding his visitor with the same approval. Helias walked up the long hall, tall, elegant, his dark hair cut neatly as usual, his fine face clean shaven, a white surcoat over his mail tunic. William who did not like to be outshone by anybody, looked on him not with favour but as a potential enemy and was not prepared, as Robert had been, to let Maine slip through his fingers.

Helias halted by the step to the dais on which he sat. 'My lord King, greetings. I have come to tell you that I have taken the cross and am determined to devote myself to God's holy cause. I wish to join your brother and journey to Rome for the Pope's blessing before crossing the sea to Palestine.' He paused, looking at the men gathered about the ducal chair and saw Henry's welcoming smile, but it did not need acute intelligence to realise that there were few other men so well disposed towards him. He went on, 'There has been peace now for three years between Normandy and Maine and I would wish it to remain so while I am away. Will you give me your guarantee that my borders will be respected?'

There was a short silence. Rufus sat staring at the Count, his flecked eyes betraying nothing as he quickly assessed the situation. Then he said in the harsh voice so reminiscent of his father's. 'You, my lord Count, can go to Jerusalem or Jericho or to hell if you please, but yield up the city of Le Mans to me and the whole county of Maine. It was my father's and now that I sit in his place here it should and will be mine.'

There was no doubt that Helias was utterly unprepared for such an answer, for he stiffened and stared at William. But he was not the man to be surprised into an impulsive retort. After a moment's careful thought he answered. 'Sire, you hold Normandy not as duke but as a pledge from your brother until his return. I hold Maine by right from my grandfather Count Herbert Wake-dog, owing allegiance to none but my over-lord, the Count of Anjou, and I tell you frankly I will not yield that right to any man. Should I rob my children of their inheritance?'

'Your mother's sister was betrothed to my brother Robert and when she died Maine came rightly to him,' Rufus retorted stubbornly. 'It should be Robert's and therefore mine.'

Helias was really angry now. 'There is no law to uphold so thin a claim. Indeed I am so confident of my position that I will plead my cause before any council of kings and bishops that you care to name.'

Rufus gave a cackle of laughter. He was sprawled in his chair, one foot thrust out, his red mantle trailing to the floor, jewels glinting on the brooch that fastened it. For all his finery he looked a man better suited to simple soldier's clothes. 'I'll plead too—with swords and spears and arrows,' he threw the words at the Count, 'so get you home and prepare your defences.'

This quarrel, flaring so suddenly, had brought complete silence, all men wondering what would happen next, whether the King would there and then seize the person of the Count of Maine. William of Breteuil looked frankly antagonistic, Bellême was regarding Helias with sardonic contempt, while Count Robert de Beaumont stood stiffly beside the King's chair, equally unfriendly. Barons and knights moved up the hall to hear what was being said, most of them only too eager to take up the sword against their old enemies, the Manteaux, and delighted at the prospect of rich plunder. Only Henry held himself aloof, remembering his long friendship with Helias and the Count's kindness when he was a penniless exile.

He leaned over William's chair. 'Rufus, you cannot mean it. Helias is our friend. It is better to have peace on our borders than war.'

Helias gave Henry a swift grateful glance. 'My lord King, the Prince is right. I desire to fight the infidel not Normandy.'

250

'Well, you will have to fight me first,' Rufus said sharply, 'for Maine I will have. However,' his tone was caustic, 'if your zeal is so great, sacrifice Maine to me and give your sword to God since you think He has more need of it.'

Robert of Bellême laughed, and it sounded oddly in the silence.

Helias drew himself upright and surveyed first the King and then the men gathered about him. 'God Himself gave me my right to the land of my fathers and I will not abandon my people. If I must then I will fight for them first but know this, all of you—I will not give up the Cross that I have taken. As all pilgrims wear it, so shall I. It shall be on my shield and on my helm and all my arms, and those who fight me will fight a soldier of Christ.'

There was a sudden hubbub in the hall and William of Breteuil, hardened soldier as he was, shouted, 'High-flown words won't bring down the curse of God on us. It is you who must yield what belongs to our master.'

Bellême said: 'Yield it or not, we will take your city.' His eyes glittered as if he saw already the prospect of another storming, another place to be sacked and plundered and tortured.

God help Helias, Henry thought, with Bellême loose in his land! Aloud he said, 'There must be a better way to settle this. William, I beg you to let the Count go. If there must be differences settle them later.'

The King rose. 'What I have said, I mean. You may go where you choose, Count Helias. I am not willing to make war on a soldier of Christ, but now that I am in my father's place, for whatever reason, I will take back the city he held at the day of his death. So if you will,' he laughed again, mockingly, 'take your high-minded principles to the holy places and leave me what is mine—or go back to Le Mans and mend your neglected walls for I swear to you I will be before the gates with all my army as soon as possible.'

'God's curse will be on you,' Helias retorted furiously, 'if you attack me. He will smite you down . . .'

'As to that, He too may do what He chooses. Le Mans I will have and if its citizens resist me they will suffer for it and you had better tell them so.'

'By God, if you come you will find them ready for you, but it will not be the welcome you expect.' Flushed with a justified anger Helias flung back his answer. Then, he stepped back from the dais and lifted his sword, scabbard and all, holding it by the cross-piece. Turning, he looked slowly round the hall and raising his voice cried out, 'I call all to witness that it is not of my doing that I cannot for the moment keep my vow to Almighty God. My duty to my people comes first and anathema be on him who has forced me into this position.'

Henry left his place and came to stand close to William, touching his brother's arm. 'Rufus, for God's sake, think. It is no light matter to swear a holy oath. Helias is the best of men and . . .'

He had chosen his words unfortunately. Rufus shrugged off his hand. 'The devil preserve me from good men. By the face of Lucca I have had my fill of them in England.' He glanced up at his brother. 'Well, Beauclerc, what is it to be? You'll not move me so you had better decide now. Do you join Helias against me?'

For one brief moment Henry paused. He liked Helias as well perhaps as any man he knew. Furthermore he thought him in the right and Rufus in the wrong, but only this morning he had tentatively broached once again the subject of his marriage and this time Rufus had listened. He had listened and commending his brother on his staunch help over the past year and more had gone so far as to promise to go to Romsey and see the girl when he was in England again and it proved convenient. This was more than he had expected and at last it seemed that there was hope for him and for Eadgyth. Always with him was the memory of those few moments with her—how then could he abandon her, abandon his desire for her?

He looked round the hall, looked again at the indomitable figure of Helias, the cross on his white surcoat. Then he turned back to Rufus. 'No,' he said in a low voice, 'I cannot join the Count of Maine. I am your man, brother.'

A faint smile flickered over the King's face and with studied preoccupation he took a peregrine from its stand and sat smoothing its feathers. After a moment he glanced up at the silent figure before him. 'What, my lord Count, are you still here? Have you not work to do in your city if you wish to withstand the might of Normandy?'

Without another word Helias swung round and walked away down the length of the hall and out through the far door.

'Well, my pretty,' Rufus said to his peregrine, 'Will you come a-warring with me? We have a good prey in sight.' He laughed and Henry, stepping down from the dais, walked out of the hall.

In the courtyard he caught Helias in the act of mounting, his foot already in the stirrup.

'Wait,' he said, 'one moment. Helias, I am sorry. You will think I repay you ill for all our years of friendship.'

The count took his foot out of the iron and leaned against the saddle, one arm across it. 'There are some things too strong for us, that strain friendship too far.'

'Yet it must endure,' Henry said in a low voice so that none might hear, he added, 'I cannot break with Red William, not now for many reasons, but I swear I will not ride with him to Le Mans nor raise my sword against you.'

'Thank you,' Helias said warmly. 'I never thought this was our fight. I am only sorry there has to be a fight at all. Perhaps,' his face saddened, 'perhaps I am not worthy to go on so noble a venture, nor fit to set foot in the Holy Sepulchre.'

'You!' Henry exclaimed. He took him by the arm. 'My friend, you could not act otherwise than you have. However things go now I make you one other promise—if ever I sit in my father's place you will never again need to fear Normandy will raid your borders.'

Helias held out his hand in silence. Then he said, glancing back towards the hall. 'Your brother is a strange man. He could have let me ride after the Duke and then seized my land, or he could have taken me then and there—yet he lets me return to Maine and challenges me to fight.'

'That is his way,' Henry said. 'He will lie and cheat and rob for money, but when it comes to war and a matter of knightly honour he will keep the code and expect others to do the same.'

'Well!' Helias smiled a little wanly. 'I suppose I must go and make ready. William is right—I've had peace for so long that my defences have fallen into neglect. How did he know that, I wonder?' He mounted and gathered up the reins. Heavy clouds had scudded up from the west and thundery rain began to fall, welcome in the heat. 'I had thought to be riding east today, to Rome. Instead . . .' his eyes filled with sudden tears. Abruptly he pulled his hood about his face and turning his horse's head rode out of the gate followed by his troop, riding two by two in a long procession through the increasing rain.

Henry stood watching them go and presently Herluin came to him, carrying a mantle which he set about his lord's shoulders. 'My brother is with Count Helias,' he said. 'Do we join the King to fight again him?'

'No,' Henry said. 'We do not. We go back to Domfront. I will hold my cities against the men of Maine if they choose to attack me but I'll not draw my sword on a man who wears the Cross.'

'Nor I,' Herluin agreed and they went back into the shelter of the hall to find Rufus already conferring with his captains.

Alide had married again. She had known long ago when the rock of the Archangel fell that her royal lover would not return to her, and being a sensible woman, she had on her father's death accepted the offer of a merchant. He dealt in wine and could carry on her father's trade, moreover he was a kindly man and undemanding. He accepted her children without demur, treated Robert as his son, and when she bore him a boy of his own considered himself a most fortunate man.

One afternoon in the summer of 1098 eight-year-old Robert was sitting by the window playing with knuckle-bones when he saw some men ride to the street door below and dismount. He called to his mother, saying that the visitor must be a very great man from the look of him and the size of his escort.

Alide came hurrying, but she hardly needed to look out to know who was below. She had had no warning, yet she had known that one day there would be riders below, a familiar figure walking towards her up the stair, that the moment would come when she would have to let Robert go.

'It is your father,' she said and the boy stared at her in astonishment.

'That man in the blue mantle?'

'Yes, that is Prince Henry.'

Round-eyed, Robert leaned out so far that she was afraid he would fall and caught hold of him. 'Come,' she said, 'you must go with me to greet him.'

He took her hand obediently and together they went down

the outer stair. He was curious and excited and wondered why she must hold him so tightly.

Alide was outwardly calm, but within there was turmoil. To see him again after so long reminded her of forgotten happiness, of a joy that nothing had replaced. She was married and glad of it, but in all her life she had loved only this man who came towards her now.

'My lord,' she made a little obeisance to him, 'I wondered when you would come back to Caen. After Duke Robert went . . .'

'I meant to come sooner,' he said, 'but there has been much to do.' He took her hand and smiled at her. 'Well, Alide, you look' he searched for the right word, 'content?'

'I am wed,' she said.

'I am glad. To a good man, I hope?' And then he turned to the silent boy at her side. 'Holy Rood, he is the very spit of me when I was a lad. Hugh,' he called out to the Earl of Chester who was standing by the horses, 'Hugh, is this not my son and bone of my bone?'

The Earl came over to them, a smile on his heavy features. 'Aye, my lord, I remember you well enough at his age and you had the same look about you.'

Henry laid a hand on Robert's shoulder, 'Well, boy, I am your father. Are you glad to see me?'

'Yes, my lord,' Robert said and could hardly keep from jumping up and down. 'My mother told me of you. I wish you had come sooner.'

Henry laughed. 'Now why do you wish that?'

'Because my mother said you would give me a horse and teach me sword play and how to be a knight.'

'That I will.' He glanced at Alide, a swift, grateful glance that expressed all he would say to her yet did not wish to put into words. He lifted the boy and set him astride his great black Perchenoir. 'There now, is he not a great horse? You can hardly get your legs over him. Shall I find you one you can ride?'

'I would like that,' Robert said and wriggled in the saddle, holding the reins and patting the strong neck.

'And would you like to come with me, live in my castle and learn all the knightly exercises, and to read and write?'

Robert considered this, his dark eyes so like his father's fixed gravely on his mother standing silent by the stair. 'I do not want to leave you, mother,' he began, 'but you always said when I became a man I would go to my father, and it is the time, is it not?'

Henry lifted him down. 'Oh aye, you are halfway to manhood, my son. Go and ask Earl Hugh there to show you his great sword.'

He watched the boy run off and then went to Alide. Without speaking she led him to the upper chamber where so long ago on the night of the Conqueror's burial he had eaten supper and she had brought him the greeting cup.

When they were alone he said. 'It has been a long time.'

She poured wine and brought it to him as if she too was remembering. 'A long time,' she repeated. Oh, that night and the other nights that would never come again! She watched him as he drank, seeing him so changed from that untried youth. Now he would take Robert, as she had always known he would, as indeed she wanted him to for Robert's own good, but despite her love for their little girl Matilda, who came running to her now, and the new babe who lay in his cradle, it was Robert her firstborn who occupied the largest part of her affections. But he must be given up and she forced herself to say, 'You have come for the boy?'

'I would have him with me, but,' he took her hand and led her to a bench, sitting beside her, 'he may return often. I don't wish him to forget or cease to care for his mother.' He took his daughter and set her on his knee. Matilda was more like her mother but as she turned to look solemnly at him she had a way of lifting her head that reminded him of his own dead mother, for whom she had been named.

'Thank you,' Alide said quietly. 'Robert is dear to me, for his father's sake as well as his own.' And then the words came out in a rush. 'My dear lord, it is so good to see you. You are well? And so great a man these days! I have thought of you so often.'

He smiled and bending, kissed her mouth lightly. 'Alide—I have never forgotten you nor what you were to me.' But for him the past was only memory. She smiled gently. 'I thought to hear that you were married by now.' She saw the expression on his face change and added, 'Perhaps I should not have asked.'

He shook his head. 'There is a girl—it is a long story, Alide.

256

They have her shut in a nunnery for all she is no nun and I cannot get her away.'

'Oh . . .' With that one word Alide expressed all her understanding. 'I will pray for you both to Our Lady.' She said no more on the subject, asking him instead about England; for a while he sat talking to her, answering her questions, and presently when her husband came to join them conversed with the man and liked him.

'I leave my daughter in your hands until she is of marriageable age,' he told them, 'then I will find her a husband of rank. Robert shall come with me in the morning. You will be proud of him, Alide.'

He stayed the night under their roof, sending Earl Hugh with the rest of his retinue to sleep at the castle, keeping only Herluin and young Walter with him; and in the guest chamber where Alide had first come to him, listening to Herluin's quiet breathing, he lay wakeful, thinking of the years that had gone.

Much had happened since Duke Robert had left the duchy. Men felt the strong hand of Rufus over them and both Robert of Bellême and William of Breteuil had quickly transferred their allegiance to the new ruler so that within a short time Rufus was to be found hunting with Bellême, listening to his schemes, or hearing details of his revenues from William of Breteuil whom he had made his treasurer. Archbishop Anselm, unable to reach any sort of compromise with Red William had left England. Rufus had eventually allowed him to depart but only on condition that during his absence all the lands and revenues of Canterbury should revert to the Crown. Anselm left in tears and journeyed to Rome to lay his case before Pope Urban, while the King considered himself well rid of a man he could neither cajole nor defeat.

But most important of all here in Normandy, the war with Helias of Maine was over and Count Helias lay in Bayeaux tower where Henry himself had once been shackled.

William had made Bellême commander of his army and presently joined him with more troops from England, but Helias had withstood them well and it seemed at first as if he could not be conquered. But in April of this year, riding home from a successful sortie against Robert the Devil, Helias made a diversion near Dangeul with only seven men at his back and by ill-luck fell into an ambush laid by no lesser person than Bellême himself. Even the Devil dared not hold so illustrious a prisoner in his donjon and he handed him over to Rufus. The King promptly shut him up at Bayeux and marched on Le Mans. The city, burned and bombarded by Bellême's war machines, yielded and the King reached an agreement with the Count of Anjou whereby he was to have the city and county of Maine in return for which Helias and all other prisoners were to be freed.

Henry wondered how long William intended to put off Helias' release, but as yet Rufus had said nothing, having only lately returned to Rouen.

News came of the victories of the crusaders in the Holy Land and more than one man brought tales of the prowess of the Duke of Normandy. Robert, it seemed, had found his true vocation. He was fighting with unsurpassed skill, no man had yet unseated him and he led many attacks in person so that the large and cosmopolitan army rang with his name.

Rufus had roared with laughter on hearing this. 'Now if Robert had fought like that here, I should not be sitting in his place. By Lucca's face, I am glad he did not. Perhaps he needs God and the heat and the goats to make a soldier of him—or perhaps the saracen women.'

Henry saw the humorous side of the situation but nevertheless he felt a pride in his eldest brother who had at last done something worthy of the name of Normandy. Bishop Odo had never reached the shores of Palestine. He had died at Palermo, attended by his friend, the Crane, and was laid to rest in the cathedral there. Henry could not bring himself to mourn for the uncle who had shown him little but enmity.

Meanwhile here at home, he had enough to do with his own affairs, restlessly busy in the Côtentin, or attending the King. Hopes of Eadgyth were fading. Here he was, nearly twenty-nine years of age, and still Rufus would do nothing about the proposed marriage. He had not as yet kept his promise to see the princess and kept his brother on a shoe-string, dangling his consent as a reward for service. Nor could Henry do more himself. His position was such that he must put his responsibilities before his personal wishes, and he threw himself into the needs of his county, devoting himself to the people, finding some outlet in the excitement of the hunt, in the arms of a mistress, but every now and then Maud sent him word of Eadgyth—

that she was still faithful to their hope, that she had not taken the vows, and though sad and disheartened her strength of will held firm. And when such a message came, as one had reached him a week since, it threw him back to those few snatched moments he had had with his love, and lying in the darkness of Alide's guest room he thought only of her. She must be near twenty now and what resources must she not have summoned up to resist her aunt's pressures for so along? Would such tenacity ever be rewarded?

About dawn he turned restlessly, flinging himself over in the bed for it had been a sultry night and though it must be cooler now outside, it was still stuffy in this small room.

Almost at once he heard Herluin's voice asking if he would like a drink. He threw off the bedclothes and went to the window, opening the wooden shutter. Outside the street was deserted except for one man trundling a small handcart of vegetables towards the place where later stalls would be set up. Already the first rays of the sun were in the sky.

'We will go to Mass in the abbey,' he said and began to dress.

In St. Stephen's church he knelt near the magnificent tomb Rufus had erected over his father's resting place, and looking at the gold and jewels encrusted there he thought of his parents and their thirty-year devotion to each other. Could he be such a husband, he wondered? And was Eadgyth at Mass also at this moment and thinking of him?

He prayed then, devoutly, for a consummation of their desires as he had prayed so often before. Perhaps this time God would hear and answer.

Beside him Herluin was absorbed in his own needs. Nothing had been heard of Simon since the Count of Maine had been ambushed. He had not been brought to Bayeux with Helias, nor had they had a chance to ask the latter for news of him. He must be dead, Herluin thought, and prayed now for Simon's soul that it might soon be released from purgatory.

After the Mass they left for Rouen, taking the boy Robert with them. He shed a few tears on parting with his mother but was soon absorbed in the ride south and in listening to this exciting man who was his father.

Arriving in the capital, the palace seemed extraordinarily quiet and Richard de Redvers came out to say that the King had gone to Beaumont-le-Roger for the baptism of the twin sons of the Count de Meulan.

He glanced up at young Robert. 'By God, Henry, this cannot be other than your son?'

Henry swung himself down and lifted the boy out of his saddle. 'Aye, he's my likeness, isn't he? We must find him some young companions.'

'The Duke's bastards, Richard and William, are here in the King's care while the Duke is away—they are practising at the butts. Can the boy join them? I've news to tell you.'

Henry sent Robert off with Raoul the deer and guessing by Richard's tone that the matter was serious, asked no questions until they were alone in his chamber.

'Well?'

De Redvers said gravely: 'The Count of Maine was brought here yesterday . . .'

'Then he is free?'

'He is free, but—I'm thankful you were not here to see how it was done, for you would have been angry and rightly so.'

All his immediate pleasure in Helias' release fading before a premonition, Henry said, 'Tell me it all.'

'The Count and all other prisoners were to be freed as you know, but when Helias came . . .' Richard broke off momentarily, 'Holy Rood, the King has a cruel humour at times! He had not allowed Helias clean linen nor to wash or shave since the treaty was made with Anjou and the Count looked—well, you can imagine. He had to stand thus before the King and the whole court. It must have been more a hurt to him than to a rougher man, but he kept his dignity, I'll say that for him.'

Henry had been unbuckling his sword and now in an angry gesture threw it on to the bed. 'William is beyond understanding.' Yet he understood this well enough. 'What happened then?'

'It was odd, really. The Count conceded that the King had beaten him and he asked, not for the return of Maine of course, but that he might keep his title and have a place in the King's household. He said that if he might serve Rufus he would prove his worth and perhaps in time the King would consider restoring him to his lands. It was a fair and honest offer and at first I thought the King would accept. You know anything that smacks of chivalry appeals to him.'

'Oh aye,' Henry agreed. 'Did he not accept then?'

'No. They began to work on him—Bellême and Breteuil and even de Beaumont. They said Maine had always been our enemy and no man of that place could be trusted.'

'But surely even they could not doubt the word of Helias?'

'No, but they made out that they could. They are jealous of him, my lord, and that's the plain truth. They could see he might easily supplant them in the King's favour and he is senior in rank to all of them. In the end Rufus came round to their way of thinking and told the Count to go.'

'And Helias?'

'He was angry, and I don't wonder. He said that as the King had refused his offer he couldn't be blamed if he tried from now on to win back his lands. So William told him to go and do his worst and Helias went. They gave him a damned sorry-looking beast to go on too.'

'Where has he gone?'

'Le Flèche. William left him that and Château-du-Loir and his wife's possessions.'

Henry got up and began his usual pacing. 'Rufus has been a fool to reject Helias! I know the Manceaux have been our enemies but with Helias as their ruler it was the time to end the enmity. I wish I had been here.'

'It was as well you were not, I think,' Richard said shrewdly. 'If you had seen how they brought Helias in, it might have led to . . .' he stopped abruptly and going to a small table took up a flagon and poured wine. 'You must be thirsty after your ride. I don't profess to understand your brother. The hall was tight with tension after Helias had gone, for he has some friends here, but the next minute the King was telling a story of your uncle Odo and Ivo of Chartres that had the whole place rocking.' A reluctant grin crossed his face. 'Did you ever hear it? That Bishop Ivo came unexpectedly to Bayeux and asked for Odo. A servant caught unawares and knowing what his lord was about said hastily that he was at prayers . . .'

'And Ivo walked into Odo's chamber and found my uncle very much occupied but not with prayers. It was a girl from the buttery at that time as I recall.'

De Redvers laughed. 'Aye, that's it. And Ivo—you know him —was so shocked that his wits deserted him. He said "Is this your morning offering, my lord?" and never saw the funny side of it.'

'Poor Ivo, he's so full of his own sanctity. It was a pity he couldn't give some of it to my lecherous uncle. Well, no doubt Odo's paying for his sins now.' Henry opened the door and calling for Walter told him to fetch fresh water.

'What will you do now?' Richard asked. 'Join your brother at Beaumont-le-Roger?'

'No. I will go to Domfront—I'd rather not exchange words with Red William at the moment and he knows where to send for me if he wants me. But I wish I had seen Helias.'

He waited while Walter poured water and then splashed his face and hands vigorously.

Two days later as their own city came in sight Henry's men without exception viewed the high rock with pleasurable anticipation for it had become their particular pride and home. Gulfer had brought his wife there from Avranches and Hamo was courting a girl in the town. He said now: 'When they see us the bells will ring and Roger will have the castle roused to welcome you, my lord.'

They swung round the last bend in the road and there saw a man sitting on a fallen tree trunk. He seemed to be in a state of complete exhaustion for even though he heard the approaching hooves he lifted his head with difficulty. When he saw the cavalcade he set his hands on the log and tried to rise, his legs barely able to support him. Then as he focused his eyes on the gonfanon Hamo carried he took an uncertain step forward, one hand held up.

There was a moment of recognition and then a horrified silence before Herluin cried out, 'Simon!' and sprang from his horse.

It was obvious that he was as near death as a man could be and still be on his feet. He was emaciated, the skin stretched over bone with no flesh in between, his eyes sunken and in great hollows, his clothes little more than rags.

'Herluin . . .' The name came out on a long sigh and he almost collapsed into his brother's arms. Herluin lowered him to the ground, his back against the tree trunk and, dismounting, Henry himself brought a costrel of wine and forced some between Simon's lips.

'Holy God,' he said softly, 'what can have happened?'

Herluin bent over his brother. 'Simon—Simon, can you hear me?' He took the wine from Henry and gave him more.

The warmth of it seemed to restore consciousness to this wreck of what had been his handsome and elegant brother and Simon opened his eyes.

'Herluin— I thought I was dreaming. I dreamed of you so often—and of La Barre—when I lay in that place.'

'Where? What happened? For God's sake, tell us.'

'Do you not know?' Simon roused himself and tried to sit up, catching at Herluin's sleeve. On his bleeding feet there were no more than remains of what had been shoes and about his ankles were the clear marks of chains.

Herluin looked at them and then back at his brother. 'No,' he said tensely, 'I do not know. Who did this to you?'

'The Count—devil that he is!'

There was no need of further description. 'Where were you held?' Henry asked urgently, for he feared Simon was nearly gone. 'At Bellême?'

'Aye—my lord. I was taken soon after the Count of Maine was—ambushed, and shut up—at Bellême with others. You do not know,' he shuddered and closed his hand on Herluin's arm, his fingers skeletal, 'In his cells—below the castle—hell cannot be worse . . .'

Herluin, nearly as pale as his brother, held him, giving him sips of wine. Raising his face, he looked at Henry. 'That man —he is Satan, the devil in human form.'

Henry, stiff with outrage, asked, 'Did he release you? The King ordered it.'

'Aye,' Simon said, 'but I had been there—since the spring, I think, and now the summer—must be nearly sped. His men opened the gates and let us go. They had taken my horse—so I walked . . .'

'You walked? From Bellême?' Henry met Herluin's horrified gaze—the same thought in both their heads, that the Count had obeyed only the barest interpretation of the King's command and driven his prisoners, starving and ill-clad, out from his gates to die on the road.

Henry got up and sent one man ahead to appraise Roger of their coming and to find a physician while he set others to cutting saplings from the wood at the edge of the road to make a litter. When it was done they bore Simon to the castle and laid him in a bed. Amaldis, nursing a daughter born of her union with Henry, brought water and linen to wash and bind his feet, while Roger and a monk skilled in medicine stripped off his ragged garments. But he was too far gone for physical help. They tried to give him food, but at the last point of starvation his stomach rejected it and he vomited weakly. They could only give him sips of wine and make him as comfortable as possible.

'He cannot live,' Roger said to Herluin and the latter sat by the bed in bitter sorrow. For all the years of estrangement their quarrel had been mended and he had hoped to see Simon happier by serving such a man as Helias. Instead he had fallen into the hands of the Devil of Bellême and now lay dying of that encounter. Again Herluin felt conscious of the dark shadow over his life, the heavy weight of it, the utter loneliness. Had it lain over Simon too?

His brother stirred and opened his eyes. When he saw Herluin he smiled faintly. Then a sudden shaft of fear crossed his face and he reached out to him. 'Herluin—I must be shriven—find a priest, for God's love. I was afraid—in there—I would die in my sins . . .'

Roger spoke from the other side of the bed. 'I am here for that purpose, my son,' and Herluin left them alone. He came back when Roger called him and knelt while his brother was anointed with holy oils and given the Sacred Host.

After that Simon seemed at peace and lay quietly, his hands folded together on the bed cover.

Henry came to stand beside Herluin. 'I am sorry we can do no more for him,' he said in a low voice, 'The King shall hear of this. If he had known . . .' He stopped for Simon was looking up at him.

'He knew . . .'

Henry bent over him, one hand gripping his shoulder. 'He knew? Are you sure?'

'Aye—at least that I was imprisoned . . .' the words came out on a sigh. 'Count Robert told me. The King said traitors must—pay for treachery—he would not ransom me.'

The two watchers by the bed exchanged glances and Roger who was folding his stole and putting the sacred vessels away into a small chest raised his head to look intently at his penitent.

Herluin felt a bitter cold seize him, moving up from somewhere in the pit of his stomach. 'Can it be? Could he take such a revenge?'

Simon moved his head a little on the pillow. 'I earned his anger. But it does not matter any more.' He smiled fleetingly at his brother and his eyes closed as he drifted into sleep

Herluin said, 'Whatever wrong he did he has paid. Jesu, he has paid!' He spoke in a low bitter tone and Henry laid a hand on his arm.

'What can I say? That Rufus should have known that Simon was there and not told us is damnable.' The thought of Rufus' callousness, of his meanness sickened him. 'But he is the King and nothing can mend what has been done.'

Herluin answered, 'It is a life wasted, thrown away for nothing.' He twisted his fingers together, grief and pain and foreboding mingling into an anguish that separated him from all sympathy, however offered, and throughout the long afternoon he sat by his dying brother, still and silent, while beneath that immobility a searing hatred was slowly being born, a hatred that went beyond the Count of Bellême who had perpetrated this horror to the King who had by implication allowed it, who had ignored the plight of his one-time intimate. That hatred, growing with deadly tendrils, was on behalf of Henry too, and every remembered injury as well as others long forgotten rose now to add to the burning stream so that all Herluin's grief, all his anger moulded itself slowly, like heated lava that cooling into rock is then solidified. He felt himself possessed by it, and, perhaps subconsciously recognising it for the dark shadow that it was, sat in tense and stricken immobility.

In the hall a little knot of men who had travelled with Henry gathered together to talk. Richard of Redvers was there with Gilbert of Clare, who had attended Rufus to Normandy; Eudo Dapifer on his first visit to the duchy for nearly ten years; Ralph de Toeni, and Henry himself. His mind was on that silent chamber above and he listened with only half his attention to their talk.

'Affairs are little better in England,' Gilbert was commenting. 'Men say that justice sleeps and money is lord. Now that Flambard is Bishop of Durham, he wrests even more from the wretched people and lords it over us all as if he were nobly born. I tell you it is past bearing.'

'At least you do not have Bellême in England,' de Redvers

said, 'but here his power is so great that the King must needs use him as the Duke did.'

'I would rather meet my enemies on the field,' Gilbert put in, 'but Count Robert deserves to die by any means, even the assassin's knife, and men would say good riddance.'

'He fears that,' Ralph told them. 'I hear he sleeps with guards at his door, even in his own strongholds. They say he has fearful dreams at night and cries out in his sleep—as if he expects to be murdered as his mother was.'

'As well he might,' Eudo agreed. He had not changed a great deal during his years at William's English court; a little stouter, he still had all his old gaiety though for the moment it was supplanted by grave concern for the present happenings. 'Satan must surely fetch him away one day.'

'We in England,' Gilbert said slowly and deliberately, 'await the day when you, my lord, may wear the English crown.'

It was the first time it had even been said openly and it jerked Henry out of his preoccupation. 'I? My friend, that at the moment seems to me the remotest possibility.'

Gilbert and Eudo exchanged glances. 'Perhaps,' Gilbert said and shut his mouth hard as Roger the priest came across the hall. What more would have been said Henry could not guess, for Roger came to tell that Simon La Barre was dead.

On the following day his body was sewn into an oxhide and laid in a cart, and Herluin with a small escort of men rode away to La Barre that his brother might be buried with his forebears.

Henry watched him go, grieving for him, and then climbed up to stand on the tower of Domfront castle, high on the rock where he could see a vast stretch of Normandy lying below him. He was bitterly angry, his rage directed at the Devil of Bellême, but there was more contempt for Rufus and only his stubborn tenacious will told him that it was not yet time to break with the King.

Up here, with a slight breeze cooling his face, his standard flapping gently over his head and the sun lighting his fields and woods far into the distance, he found himself torn with longing, longing for the power to rule, to bring order, to put down men such as Bellême, and with sudden passion he prayed that his name might go down to his children and to their children as a man who had fought for justice. But, oh God, for the chance to do it. Here, alone on his own high rock, the one place truly his, it seemed remote, unattainable, and he leaned his hands on the edge of the parapet, gripping the stone in an intensity of impotent desire.

In the autumn the Earl of Shrewsbury, Bellême's younger brother, died and the Count bought his earldom from Rufus for a sum large enough to delight even that grasping King. Bellême now spread his greed and cruelty and evil practices into England; the men of his new earldom groaned under his tyrannical rule and he became, next to the King, the most powerful baron on both sides of the channel, keeping a private army that no other lord could match. In England men were thrown into the dark prisons of his castle to die from torture or starvation for little or no reason and a wail of anguish went up from the widows and children whom he persecuted.

On Christmas day there was an eclipse of the sun, darkening the land at mid-day and the people gazed fearfully at the sky, seeing it as a sign of the evil times that had befallen both England and Normandy, as if God was hiding His light and warmth from them. In the churches men prayed. It was an omen, they said; the King had persecuted and driven out the head of God's church and all holy men suffered at his hands. Now God was displeased and they waited fearfully until the light came back, but the unrest, the doubt, the longing for better days, remained.

6

'Well, I have seen her,' Rufus said with the unexpectedness which was characteristic of him.

Henry was so astonished that for a moment he did not speak. After all these weary months of waiting, until he had become convinced that William had no intention of keeping his promise, it could not be other than surprising that he had now done so.

'You have seen her?' he repeated. 'When?'

'At Easter,' Rufus told him, 'when I wore my crown at Winchester.'

'And?'

'And she is a nun.'

The bald statement shook Henry for all he had heard it put about often enough. 'I do not believe it.'

'You may do so now. I saw her in the abbey, walking in the cloister, wearing the habit.'

'You spoke to her?'

'It was not necessary. The Abbess, you know Christina is Abbess now?—told me she had finally taken the vows and I had the evidence of my own eyes.'

Henry let out his breath and gave a short laugh. 'I would never trust that woman to tell the truth. I have told you, brother, what she is. She makes the princesses wear habits to protect them from us lecherous Normans! I will only believe it if I hear it from Eadgyth herself.'

Rufus frowned. 'You will not do that. I forbid you to go to Romsey.'

'Forbid?'

'Aye, forbid.'

They faced each other in sudden antagonism. It was warm here in this solar near the Thames at Westminster. Outside the leaves had that fresh green of early June; it had been a late spring but the apple trees had been thick with blossom and were now rich with the promise of a good harvest. Wild flowers bloomed in the banks of the river flowing smoothly on this still day, buttercups and cow parsley and white daisies studding the lush grass. There was nowhere like England in the early summer, Henry had thought, as he rode from Portsmouth during the last two days. The woodlands had teemed with young life, birds singing, rabbits scurrying about, squirrels running up the branches; he saw the fallow deer in the distance, beautiful timid creatures, and once a fox ran across his path and he watched with pleasure the animals he loved.

He had come on a visit at Rufus' request, hoping once more for a change of mind, and he was too preoccupied now to notice the beauty outside. He said, 'Why should you forbid it? Would it not be better if I were sure of the truth?'

'I have told you the truth.'

He turned his back to the window and folded his arms, and with a rare impulsiveness reiterated, 'The Princess herself begged me never to believe that she had taken the vows.'

The King's eyes narrowed. 'She told you? When?'

Too late Henry saw his mistake. 'A long time ago.'

Rufus did not take his intent gaze from his brother's face. 'Ha! Do you think to deceive me? It could not have been when we came from Scotland, so it follows you must have seen her since.'

'And if I have,' Henry retorted, 'what is it to you?'

Red William's face turned an even deeper colour, the tiny veins in his cheeks crimson, his flecked eyes narrowing. 'Am I not the King? How did you see her and when?'

'I'll not tell you. Only that it was too many years ago for it to concern us now.'

'That's a matter of opinion,' Rufus snapped. 'I think I detect the hand of cousin Maud in this. Well, it shall not happen again.'

Henry stared at his brother in exasperation. 'Good God, William, is it a crime to want to wed a girl who would be suitable in every way?'

Rufus got up. 'I wish you would let the matter be. I do not intend that you should have her. If she is not a nun, as you say then I shall give her to William of Warenne who had asked me for her some time ago. Or perhaps Alan of Richmond . . .'

Henry was so angry he could barely control his voice. 'You shall not. By the death of Our Lord, Rufus, you use me ill. Neither Count Alan nor the Earl of Surrey shall have her for she has sworn herself to me, and if you give her at all the claim of your own kin should come first.'

'Do you think to move me by appealing to family feeling?' Rufus mocked. 'You and I have agreed well enough over the last years, Beauclerc, but to marry the girl you need my consent and that you will never have. Anyway she is a nun.'

'Prove it! Let me hear it from her own lips. Otherwise I will never give up and I will have her with or without your consent.'

Rufus laughed at him. 'Are you so hot for her that you'd defy me to get her? Or murder me perhaps? There's a name for that sin.'

'Don't be a fool,' Henry retorted shortly, 'and don't think me one. But I don't understand you.'

'Well,' Rufus' voice was smooth again. 'Perhaps I don't wish you to. The secret of power, little brother, is never to let any man understand your mind. But I have some other news for you. Curthose is on his way back.'

This was not news to Henry. He sat down again on the stool by the window, his arm along the stone embrasure. Last year Jerusalem had fallen to the victorious crusaders and Robert had been among the first into the city, plunging in over the bodies of the slain. He had captured single-handed the silver standard of the saracen leader, and with their cousin, Count Robert of Flanders, with Godfrey de Bouillon and Raymond of Toulouse, he had knelt weeping with joy at the tomb of Christ and the whole of Christendom rejoiced with him.

The tidings of all this had been mingled with grief for Henry, for young Fulcher had fallen beneath the city wall almost at the moment of victory. A monk of Blois, journeying home, had brought the tale to Henry and the only compensation had been the knowledge that the boy lay in holy ground. He remembered how Fulcher had shared his dreary days in Bayeux tower and paid for masses to be said for his soul.

After the victory and the crowning of Godfrey of Bouillon as King of Jerusalem, Duke Robert, with his boon-companion Edgar, had set out in a leisurely manner to return home. Now, nine months later, he was still only in Sicily. Henry thought amusedly he was probably making up for the exertions of the war by taking his ease in the exotic beauty of that island. However if he were indeed on the move again Henry was sufficiently distracted from his own problems to wonder how the King would take his return. Somehow he could not see Rufus stepping lightly aside in the Normandy he had made his own. Furthermore he knew that Red William had his eye on further conquests, for all the desultory war with King Philip had come to a stalemate. A state of stalemate also existed over Maine. Last year Helias had seized Le Mans and held it successfully for some weeks, receiving a hero's welcome from the citizens who preferred their rightful ruler to the sway of the Red King. Rufus had been in England at the time but with typical impulsiveness he rode for the coast and jumping into the first boat he saw, a leaky old craft barely sea-worthy he had sailed for Normandy and with a large army marched on Le Mans. Helias, courageous as he was, could not hope to hold off so great a force and he retired from his capital, he and his people combining to burn and strip both town and countryside that there might be nothing left for the Norman army. He then shut himself up in La Flèche to wait for the better times, leaving the King with a hollow victory. Nevertheless William dreamed of an empire and was not going to like the return of the real ruler of Normandy.

'You knew Robert would come back,' Henry countered, 'unless he fell, and neither of us wished that.'

'No, indeed,' Rufus agreed drily, 'but I hardly expected him to return with a bride. That is my news.'

'A bride!' Henry sat bolt upright. 'Holy Rood, I never thought to hear that.'

'Nor I, but it is true. I heard this morning.'

'Robert with a bride! Who in God's name has he married?'

'The lady Sybil, daughter of Count Geoffrey of Conversano.'

'Count Geoffrey? Then she must be . . .' he paused, 'The great-niece of Robert Guiscard and as Norman as you or I.'

'They say she is both beautiful and intelligent—and young,' Rufus added as an afterthought. It was not necessary to qualify the remark.

Henry was silent. This changed everything for, as Rufus had

just implied, it meant that Robert might now father legitimate children, that Normandy would have an heir, that the duchy would go to the eldest son of the eldest son. Worse than that, as Rufus had no heir, if Robert had a son that child as grandson of the Conqueror would have as good a claim to England as he. He sat there, stiff with foreboding. He had dreamed of England, England that should be his for he was born the son of a King while Robert—Robert cared nothing for England. He was a Norman duke—why then should any son of his take preference over a porphyrogenic heir?

Rufus' voice broke in on his thoughts. 'I can read your mind, Beauclerc.'

He said, 'William, you would not countenance it?'

'Because you were born in the purple?' Rufus laughed and Henry realised suddenly how sick he was of that constant mocking laughter. He lost his temper and shouted at his brother.

'Wine of Christ, you play with me. You have played with me all these years. Can't you for once be just? Make me your heir, give me Eadgyth and our children, of Norman and Saxon blood mingled, shall rule here afterwards, true heirs that men of both nations can acknowledge. You must see that would be better by far than any heir of Robert and Sybil of Conversano. What would she be to the English?'

Enjoying a verbal match as always, and not caring in the least what the English thought, Rufus shouted back. 'Hold your tongue, Beauclerc. I made an agreement with Robert a long time ago.'

'And broke it when it suited you. That treaty you made at Caen was worth nothing.'

'It can still hold—and to your cost.'

'What, when you made war on Robert? No, brother, you cannot keep one clause and break another. And are you going to hand Normandy meekly back to him when he comes home?' It was Henry's turn to mock. 'I can't imagine that.'

'It is none of your business.'

'No? Holy Rood, but I rule part of Normandy and you cannot threaten me there as you once did.'

'You rule it only as long as I will that you should.'

'Try to take it from me then. You will find my men of Domfront very different from the little garrison on the rock of the Archangel.'

'God's blood, but you are confident.' Rufus glared at him. 'Be that as it may, Robert is the eldest and though maybe I will not give up what I have made of the duchy nevertheless his heirs come before yours.'

Henry slammed his fist down on the table. 'William, you will be a damned bloody villain if you do that—and untrue to our father's memory. I know you cared for him. Do his wishes mean nothing to you?'

This barb went home for Rufus' love for their father had perhaps been the one genuine emotion of his life. Furiously he retorted, 'He said nothing to me of the succession, only that I was to have England.'

'That was all you heard him say because you were in too great a hurry to claim your kingdom.' Realising that for once he had the whip hand Henry went on, pressing his advantage, 'When you had gone our father told me, and there are witnesses to it, that I should have the kingdom after you—and the dukedom too.'

'You? You insolent cub, I've a mind to send you back to Bayeux tower.'

'Not this time.' Henry threw the words defiantly at him. 'I've too many friends.'

They faced each other, both at bay, glaring angrily, each assessing the consequences of this plain speaking.

Then Henry said, 'I think we would be best apart for a while. Will you give me leave to visit Maud at Northampton?'

Angry as he was, Rufus could still mock. 'I suppose I can bear you out of my sight. But you had best hatch no plots with our cousin for I am on my guard now, and,' he added, determined to send out the last shaft, 'put the lady Eadgyth from your mind. Even if she were not a nun, I'd not give that gentle girl to a lecher.'

'Lecher!' Henry was so angry he set both fists against the stone wall and laid his head against it, struggling for control. That rage was rising in him, the rage that had killed Conan and might turn on his brother if he did not master it. Somehow he held it from physical violence and let it from him in words as stinging as he could find. 'At least I have only used my passions as a man and not misused my body as you have yours.'

This time Rufus struck him, hard across the face with the flat of his hand. 'Get out of my sight! Go! Go!'

Henry went, clinging somehow to one clear though—that if he laid hands on the anointed person of the King, which was perhaps what William wanted, then he could with reason be shackled, deprived of everything he had achieved. Shaking so much that he could barely walk straight along the passage, a passing servant thought he must have seen a sight never witnessed before—Prince Henry the worse for wine.

He went to London first and slept two nights at the house of Ansfrida, widow of Anskill the Saxon. She had come to him two years ago, begging him to intercede with the King whose agents had seized her husband's property on his death and left her without means for herself and her son. Henry had done what he could, but although he had not been able to regain her property she had benefited none the less for he had succumbed to her undoubted beauty and maintained her himself. She had borne him a son, Richard, a sturdy boy who resembled his half-brother Robert, and she was of all his mistresses the one nearest to him by birth.

He was, however, too restless on this occasion to stay long and several days later the Countess Maud was on the steps of her hall, welcoming her cousin's unexpected visit. She put her arm about the boy Robert and kissed him, telling him he would have a companion in her own son Simon, but at the same time her observant eye told her that something had happened.

In the first moment of privacy Henry told her the details and she wept a little for him and for Eadgyth.

Earl Simon said gravely, 'My lord, we would do anything to assist you but what can mend the situation now?'

There was something he could do, Henry said. 'Here in England I must count my friends,' and he asked Simon to assemble a hunting party of his closest adherents that he might take counsel with them. Accordingly a week later Gilbert of Clare, Earl of Tonbridge, his brother Roger and brother-in-law Walter Tirel came riding into Northampton, also Roger de Marmion from Scrivelsby, Ralph de Toeni and his wife Alice, and Henry Earl of Warwick with his wife Margaret.

At the end of the first day's hunting when the Countess had taken the ladies to her bower, he held council with these men whom he could trust. He recounted his interview with Rufus.

'I do not know what I shall do,' he said frankly. 'Much will depend upon what happens when Duke Robert returns home and later on whether he has heirs of his body—but I must assess what support I might have in England if it came to a trial of strength.'

'All of us here,' Henry of Warwick said at once. 'Fitzhamon, I expect; Earl Hugh of course and de Redvers, and Alan of Richmond who has never liked Rufus.' He went on naming lesser barons and knights, and several bishops including Robert Bloet of Lincoln.

'But there is a strong following for Duke Robert,' Earl Simon pointed out. 'The Earl of Shrewsbury and William of Breteuil head a number who make no secret of the fact that they favour Duke Robert for all they serve the King now—your cousin of Mortain especially since your uncle Robert died and William holds his father's earldom of Cornwall as well as Mortain itself. His head grows larger every day.'

'He will not stand by me,' Henry said. 'He has always been envious of my position and would do me injury if he could. As for me, I can't abide the sight of his gloomy face so we needn't look to him.'

Roger of Clare shook his head. 'My lords, we speculate. King William is too strong to be unseated.'

'I am not talking of unseating him,' Henry retorted sharply, 'he is my brother. But I am concerned with the succession. I must and will have his consent to naming me as his heir.'

Roger the priest, who was attending him, spoke carefully. 'In this country I believe it is the people, the Witan, who elect the King, is it not?'

'They will elect the obvious man, the one who is strongest and whom the previous King indicated.' Henry gave a dry laugh. 'That is how Rufus got the crown—with Lanfranc's help.'

'That is true, my lord, but if they did not like the King's choice and there is another and a better man, what then? I am confident you would be the choice of all Englishmen as well as your Norman friends.'

'All very well,' Ralph broke in uneasily, 'but if it becomes a question of might . . .'

As they talked on sitting at Maud's table, Henry found himself for a while detached from them. They were loyal to him, he knew that, but he also faced within himself the plain fact which was that, short of rebellion, he could do nothing. And rebellion was out of the question for Rufus was indeed too strong. He remembered suddenly how long ago in the abbey of St. Gervais, when Rufus came to fetch him to their dying father's bedside, he had cursed because his brothers would have everything and he nothing, how he had thought it the most damnable thing in the world to be the youngest son of a King, and had prayed that God would give him something of his own.

Well, he had lands in Normandy and men who were his friends, soldiers at his back and his impregnable high rock, but he had nothing in England. Here, where he was a King's son he had not one hide of land. Rufus had taken everything and now wanted Robert's heirs to succeed, so that it was as if he himself had achieved nothing. It was galling, unjust and against all reason! He was Henry the Atheling, born on English soil. Surely the people would want him rather than a Norman prince as yet unborn.

He stood up and faced his friends. 'I am the Atheling,' he said, 'England should be mine.' And not trusting himself further he beckoned to Herluin with a nod of his head and went out of the hall into the fresh air, out beyond the hall and its surrounding buildings into the meadows beyond to fling himself down on the grass under the wide shade of an oak tree. 'This is my land,' he said again. 'Jesu, what am I to do?'

Herluin sat down among the buttercups, his face pale, the lines of melancholy deepened. His fingers itched to set a knife between Rufus' shoulder blades. Since the death of his brother nothing had been the same for him and there were times these days when he thought he was no longer quite sane. If he caught sight of his own face reflected in a ewer it was like looking at a stranger. From being a man grave and careful he had become a man possessed with the desire to kill. His hatred of Rufus burned in him, corroding him. Even after all these months since Simon's death it had not abated—and oddly he seldom thought of the Count of Bellême who had actually perpetrated the deed. It was Rufus who had condoned it, Rufus who had known his favourite was lying in shackles and had refused to ransom him, Rufus who must have known what captivity at Bellême meant. His hatred was exacerbated now by the King's treatment of his lord and he knew, had known for some time in snatches of clarity, that this was the black and evil shadow that had threatened him for so long. He was in it, enveloped in it, almost before he realised it, and there was no escape—except into madness.

He stared at a little green insect crawling up a stem of a buttercup and took it and crushed it between finger and thumb. A delicate green thing, yet he had crushed it and it was dead. So easy to kill a little green insect, but a man? A man dead went into the soil as dead animals and flowers and insects —even a King. God, what was he thinking? How far had he gone from the man who had prayed to be kept from the evil shadow? He remembered some words of Hildebert of Louvain . . .

> Over all things, all things under,
> Touching all, from all asunder,
> Centre Thou but not intruded,
> Compassing and yet included.

But it seemed that even God could not permeate this blackness—it was he who was asunder and somehow, deep within himself, he knew he had lost control of his thoughts and because of it would soon lose hold on what he might do.

In growing horror, he clutched at sanity and said, 'My lord, whatever you do, God and His saints will aid you, even if I . . .' He broke off, unable to finish the sentence, but the Prince, deep in his own anxiety, was staring into the wooded distance.

Not long after his arrival in Northampton Henry heard of the death of Duke Robert's eldest bastard, Richard. The lad had been hunting in the new forest and had fallen from his horse, breaking his back. He had been a likeable youth and Henry was sorry while his son shed a few tears for the cousin he had grown fond of, but as Rufus did not order it he did not return for the burial. Only he reflected that it was the second death of a member of his family in that green forest, some twenty years after that of his own brother Richard.

In July the new abbey church at Gloucester, raised by the indefatigable labours of Abbot Serlo, was to be consecrated and this time Rufus sent word to his brother to attend him.

They met, publicly, in the courtyard of the castle for as Henry rode in the King was looking over some new stallions and

277

greeted him as if there had been no quarrel between them.

'Beauclerc, you come in a good hour. Give me your opinion on these fine creatures.'

Henry, who had not known what to expect, fell in with his brother's lead. 'Good day to you, William. Are these Arabs? I thought so. I like this one. He ran a hand along the horse's flank and down one leg, turned up the hoof. 'He has good bones.' He glanced round the others. 'And that one too, the pale one. He should sire good foals for you.'

Pleased, Rufus said, 'Those are the two I liked. We are of one mind. Well, I'll take them. Choose one for yourself at my expense, brother.'

Used to Rufus' peculiarities as he was Henry was still taken aback. 'You are generous,' he said and looking at his brother was met with a bland stare. 'I think I'll take that one, the one with the white foreleg.'

'A good choice,' Rufus nodded and called to his steward to see that the horse trader was paid. While the fellow bowed his thanks the King took his brother's arm and walked him off towards his own apartments. Once there he said, 'You have a sharp tongue, Beauclerc. You said some hard things to me at our last meeting.'

'And you have a heavy hand,' Henry retorted with a rueful smile. 'We behaved like boys.'

'Well, what is it to be?' the King asked plainly. 'Will you break with me?'

Henry did not answer at once. The weeks with Maud had helped him to think clearly, to get the whole matter into perspective. He wanted England and he wanted Eadgyth, and he would have them, but he saw that it would not be by trying to beat Rufus at his own brow-beating game. He would have to use guile, to wait on events, to be ready to seize the right moment.

'No,' he said at last. 'I will not.'

An expression of sheer arrogance crossed the florid face. 'I am glad to hear it. I could break you, Beauclerc, but I'd not wish it.'

'And the succession?'

'By Lucca's face, you are persistent.' Rufus stretched his arms and expanded his chest. 'Do I look about to die? Before I'm in my grave I'll be lord of Anjou and Aquitane and maybe France too—then we'll talk about the succession.'

Was there no end to his ambitions? Henry wondered. It must have got out of hand if he saw all France subject to him. But he merely commented, 'You set your hopes high.'

'No more than I can achieve,' Rufus boasted. 'Have you sufficiently rich garments for tomorrow's affair or shall I send you my tailor?'

And at once Henry saw through the offer and the gift of the horse that had preceded it. 'You have made your point,' he said coolly, 'and I have suitable clothes for the consecration or any other occasion. I am out of the nursery, brother.'

So the enmity was not far from the surface and he attended the consecration of the abbey dressed with as much expense and a great deal more care than Rufus. He was playing a dangerous game with his brother and he knew it, but if he was to win anything, if he was to gain a bride, he must hold his own without coming to open hostility.

All the great men of England had come to Gloucester on this hot July day and the ceremony was carried out by Samson, the new bishop of Worcester, attended by Gundulf of Rochester and Bishop John of Bath. Robert of Bellême, now Earl of Shrewsbury, was there and the treasurer, William of Breteuil, the Clare brothers, Earl Hugh and Earl Henry of Warwick, William of Warenne, Richard of Redvers, Ivo Taillebois attending the Countess Judith, Earl Simon and his wife Maud, and number of lesser barons and knights. After it was over the King took the whole assemblage back to Winchester to partake of his lavish hospitality and hunt with him in the new forest.

It was about two weeks later that one of his clerks stopped Roger the priest in a narrow passage high above the hall and said, 'Did you hear the news? Duke Robert is expected back in Normandy next month and the King plans to journey there to meet him.'

'Oh?' Roger queried. 'No, I had not heard.' He nodded briefly to his fellow chaplain and made his way to the Prince's apartment. 'Will you go back to Normandy with him, my lord?'

Henry, in one of his rare still moments, had been lounging on his bed reading an illuminated copy of the life of St. Wilfred, a gift from Abbot Serlo, but he laid it down when Roger brought his news.

'I suppose so. I must watch them both. God knows how they will settle affairs in Normandy and I've my own lands to secure.'

To Roger he sounded dejected, an unusual mood for him, and he had been reading to try to close his mind for a while to the problems that pressed on him. He had been thinking of Eadgyth shut within the grey walls of Romsey, no more than seven miles away and his heart ached for her, but he could do nothing, and marriage with her seemed so remote and so hopeless a project that he was trying to thrust it from him.

'My lord,' Roger said quietly, 'I know something of your mind after all these years. Do not give up hope.'

'How can I keep it? Here in England I see nothing but oppression and greed. The great lords do what they will and Bellême is worse here than in Normandy. The court is a shambles. Rufus does not care what vice is there and Anselm, who might curb the worst of it, is still in exile. With men like Flambard in the bishoprics,' he added bitterly, 'God help England for no one else will. Rufus will give me nothing that I want, only a horse and new clothes! By the death of Our Lord, I've had my fill of him.'

'So have half the barons of England.'

'Maybe, but how should that benefit me?' He glanced up at his chaplain. 'I tell you, Roger, I had higher hopes when I was in Paris with holes in my shoes.' He got up, laying his book with care on the table. 'Well, I had best join the hunting party. Where is Herluin?'

Outside in the sunshine the knight from La Barre was wandering alone as he often did, trying to think, to ease a mind diseased, to find peace and reason for he had once known both.

He walked in the courtyard, looking at simple things—at the cooks cutting up meat for dinner, at women kneading bread, a scullion plucking chickens. On this first day of August the heat was intense and as he passed the smith's forge, the added heat of the fire seemed to strike at him, a physical fuel added to the conflagration within. He went past, watching a man mending some harness, and then paused at a table where the fletcher was busy with delicate shafts and goose feathers and fine tips.

He picked up an arrow, balancing it on one finger. 'This is well set.'

The fletcher glanced up, pleased. 'Aye, messire, I am proud

of that arrow. I made it to try a new way of setting the feathers, do you see? I am making six more on this style for the King.'

Herluin weighed it, looking at it with a puzzled frown on his face. Once before he had stood thus, holding an arrow, seeing—what? Something, some foreboding.

Then he remembered—it was when the King and the Duke had ordered their brother from England after the Scottish expedition and Henry had been near to despair. He had felt it then, that an arrow, somehow, was part of the evil thing that lay over him, part of that destiny that had joined him to Henry, that certain destiny that was now upon him—today, tomorrow, soon.

Abruptly he said, 'I will buy this one,' and set a coin more than the arrow was worth on the fletcher's table. As he walked away he passed Gilbert of Clare and Walter Tirel standing together beneath a deserted archway. He heard Tirel say in a low anguished voice, 'I cannot—I cannot do it. Gilbert, for God's sake . . .' and he wondered what it was that Walter could not do.

Towards dawn, deep in a sound healthy sleep, Henry was awakened by a loud cry. He sat up, shaking the hair from his forehead, wondering if he had been dreaming, but when it came again he got up and flung a mantle about his nakedness, certain that the sound came from the King's chamber.

His page Walter started up from his pallet. 'My lord! What is the matter?'

'Nothing,' Henry answered. 'Go back to sleep.'

He opened his door and went along the narrow arched passage. At the door to Rufus' apartment he met Richard de Rules and they went in together. The king was sitting up in bed, wild-eyed, staring in terror about the room which was barely lit by the small night lamp.

'What is it?' Henry asked. 'Rufus, are you sick?'

'A dream,' his brother said hoarsely, 'a dream—it was terrible . . .'

Henry laughed. 'Is that all? I thought you were being murdered.'

Richard de Rules fetched wine and poured a cup for the King and at the same time Robert Fitzhamon came in, his mantle clutched about him for he too had heard the cry.

Rufus drank a little, trembling so much that he could barely hold the cup. 'I dreamed,' he muttered, 'that I was being bled . . .'

'Well, there's no harm in that,' Fitzhamon said prosaically, 'I was bled myself last week.'

'That was not all.' Rufus handed the cup back to his chamberlain and wiped his mouth with the back of his hand. 'The blood would not stop flowing. It filled every space about me, hid the sky, darkened the day. I was drowning in it, red and thick, choking in it . . .' There was such terror in his voice that Henry sat down beside him.

'William, it was only a dream. It is not like you to be frightened like a child by a nightmare.'

His brother turned, focused his gaze on him and then seemed to come to himself. 'What does it mean?'

'Does it have to mean anything?'

Richard de Rules said gravely, 'It may be a warning, my lord.'

'Of what?' Rufus stared from one to the other, almost pathetically eager for consolation, explanation, and none of them had seen him so before.

'Who but crazy old women can interpret dreams?' Henry countered. 'Come, William, you are too much a man to want to attend to such nonsense. It is nothing and will be forgotten in the morning.'

Rufus gave a shiver and then forced a laugh. 'You are right. I have wakened you for nothing. Go back to bed, all of you.' But as they went to the door he added, 'Robert, stay with me,' and Fitzhamon obediently returned to the bedside.

Henry lay down on his own bed but he did not sleep again, pondering on his brother's dream. It was rare for Rufus to be distressed by such things, but when an hour or so later he went back to the royal bedchamber he found the King up and restored to his normal self.

He glanced at Henry, a broad grin on his face. 'I am sorry I disturbed your sleep, brother. I must have eaten too well at supper last night, or some damned churl served me with tainted meat. I have stomach pains this morning, we'll not hunt until later.' He waved a restless hand at the pile of parchments one of his clerks was carrying. 'I've enough business to see to it seems.'

His chancellor, Walter Giffard, smiled apologetically. 'I'm

afraid, sire, there is always more business than one could desire. There's the matter of the abbacies, and my lord of Mowbray's claim, and Abbot Serlo's request for that piece of land, as well as . . .'

'Oh yes, yes,' Rufus jerked upright in his chair. 'Would you make my stomach worse? And the Abbot writes to me,' he gave a letter to Henry, 'a deal of nonsense. It seems one of his silly monks also dreamed a dream—that I desecrated a crucifix and the holy image struck me down.' He gave an uneasy laugh. 'God's death, what will they think of next?'

Fitzhamon said gravely, 'Beau sire, I think my lord of Deeping was right. You should heed these warnings—it may be that some evil thing endangers you. You had best stay home today.'

Rufus burst out laughing. 'By Lucca's face, Robert, you are as much an old woman as the rest of them. What is a monk's dream to me? Or what my brother rightly called my own childish nightmare? Anyway monks only dream for money so send the fellow a few shillings.' He put his hand to his abdomen. 'Jesu, but my bowels pain me.'

'Then stay here,' Henry added his voice to Fitzhamon's. 'You will be better tomorrow.'

But later Rufus ignored their advice and going down into the hall ate a hearty dinner and drank several cups of wine.

'That was my need,' he declared. 'Well, my lords, we have been quiet long enough. It's time we took our armies into France and by the Holy Rood I swear I'll wear my crown in Poitiers this Christmas. Maybe,' he began to laugh at his own joke, 'maybe Robert will find I am his new overlord, eh, Beauclerc? Then he can lie in bed all day while I rule France and Normandy.' He dug Henry in the ribs and laughed again. 'Tomorrow I'll ride for London. If we are to war in France I'll need money to pay my soldiers, and there's only one way to get that.'

His fletcher came down the hall, bearing six arrows and kneeling held them out to him. 'These are as you wanted them, my lord King.'

Red William took them, weighed them carefully. 'Excellent. You've done your work well, fellow, and shall be as well paid. We will go hunting after all, my lords. Walter . . .' he beckoned to Tirel, 'you are my best marksman. Take two of these and see if you can match me at the quarry.'

Walter thanked him. He looked pale and anxious and shot a quick glance at his brother-in-law. The Earl of Tonbridge returned his stare without a change of expression and with a helpless look Tirel followed the King as the latter strode down the hall.

Henry waited in a more leisurely manner while his hunting gear was collected. He looked for Herluin, but as he was nowhere to be seen, went out with Ralph and Roger de Marmion. The sun was hot and bright on this late afternoon, the beams slanting through the thick foliage of the trees and he was glad to be out of doors. He felt oppressed, enclosed by the Red King's ambition, by his over-riding conceit, by the crude lust for power. He wanted to break free, to be independent of Rufus, but he could not see a way to do it and now with Robert returning he was going to be caught once more in the centre of the interminable struggle between his brothers.

He lifted his face into the sunshine. At least out here he could forget for an hour or two; he could earn his nickname of Hartsfoot and delight in the chase with a good horse beneath him and no anxiety other than the finding of a good quarry.

Herluin had lingered behind to speak to Roger the priest. 'I am going hunting,' he said rather unnecessarily.

'So I see,' Roger answered, smiling. 'I wish you fair sport, my friend.'

Herluin gave him a melancholy glance. 'Aye, you have always been a friend to me. I have been glad of it.'

'And we shall be friends for many years, I trust, and see our lord in his rightful place in the end.'

'Perhaps,' Herluin said. 'Perhaps sooner than we know. God keep you, Roger.'

The chaplain was still smiling. 'I imagine He will for the next hour or two until you return.' The oddness of Herluin's words struck him and his smile faded. 'Is something amiss?'

Herluin shook his head. 'When the road turns you will go with it—you will be a great man.' They had walked together to where the huntsmen were holding the horses and gathering his reins Herluin mounted, and rode out before Roger could answer, leaving the chaplain staring thoughtfully after him.

In the forest the party dismounted and split up. The King went in one direction, with Tirel and several huntsmen. William of Breteuil and William of Mortain went off together; Gilbert

284

of Clare planned with his brother to circle round and meet Rufus near a hollow that was a clear landmark, while Henry, Ralph and Roger de Marmion, went in the opposite direction with Raoul the deer, Hamo and Herluin who had now joined them.

The wood seemed to be alive with movement, a slight breeze stirring the leaves. Birds sang and small animals scuffled in the bushes. They had not brought hawks, so Gulfer held the lyme-hound and two others on leashes while Raoul and Hamo went to either side of a clearing to flush out the game. A hart broke cover and came into the open, head lifted, listening alertly.

Henry took careful aim but as he released the arrow the bow-string broke, the hart heard the sound and was gone into the trees. He cursed and glanced at Ralph. 'My string has broken.'

De Marmion came up. 'There was a peasant hut a little way back. Perhaps a fellow there will be able to mend it.'

Together they went back down the path. The hut was a poor place, a single room with a division at one end where a few chickens scuffed the earth floor, it smelt of unsavoury cooking and animal dung and Roger wrinkled his nose as they entered. 'The place stinks.'

There was no one there but an old woman who was stirring a blackened pot over a smoky fire, her dress little more than a rough piece of cloth tied about the waist. She looked up in alarm as they entered, pushing back wisps of grey hair.

Ralph laughed at Roger's disgust and turned to her. 'Don't be afraid,' he said. 'Is your man here?' And when she shook her head not understanding their language Henry held up the bow, indicating the string. She pointed silently to a nondescript collection of bits and pieces which indicated only too plainly that her man, whoever he was, was not above making a snare for the King's animals. Henry handed his bow to Ralph. 'Leave her be. She looks half-witted.'

They had been speaking among themselves in Norman but now the woman spoke in English to Herluin who was standing near her beside Raoul the deer. 'Who is that man?'

Herluin answered, 'That is Prince Henry, the King's brother.'

She put a hand to her mouth, her fingers pulling at her lower lip, her face wearing a rapt expression, her eyes, half hidden under wrinkled lids, fixed on Henry. She shuffled forward and stretching out a grimy hand, took hold of his hand, turning it over to look at the palm. She frowned and muttered unintelligibly to herself. Then she went back to her cooking pot.

In a low voice she spoke again to Herluin. 'Tell him it is he who will soon be King.'

'Soon be . . .' Herluin glanced at Henry who was holding the bow while Ralph repaired it and paying no attention to her. 'Woman what are you saying?'

'I read it,' she whispered, 'in the signs. The omens are there. He will be King.' And she began to mutter again while Herluin stared at her, his eyes wide.

'There,' Henry said. 'That is done. Come, we'll go back to our sport. Herluin, give the woman a shilling—though I fancy her man takes payment enough in rabbits.' He went out with Ralph and Roger.

'Did you hear?' Raoul asked. He had spent his youth in England and knew enough of the tongue to make out what she had said.

'Aye,' Herluin said. He seemed to have difficulty in taking his gaze from the woman's face and she, now that the others had gone, looked more closely at him. Her eyes glittered and she made a hissing in-drawn sound.

'What does it mean?' Raoul's astonishment was growing. He was a plain man, worrying himself little about anything other than his lord's welfare and his horses, but he felt uneasy now, as if something were in the air here, something he did not understand.

Herluin was looking at the woman. 'Blood must wipe out blood,' he said in Norman, yet it seemed as if she understood his words for she nodded, and coming forward set her skinny fingers on his while with her other hand she touched his bow.

'God save us, Herluin,' Roger had come back into the hut and had heard his last words, 'What is the matter with you? Has the scarecrow bewitched you?'

Herluin shook his head. 'She is a seer, I think. She can read signs.'

'She's mad, and this place is unwholesome,' De Marmion said flatly. 'Come, our lord is waiting for you. Have you paid her?'

Herluin fumbled in his pouch and laid a coin in the woman's palm. Then he ducked his head and followed Roger out of the low door.

In the open again de Marmion walked off, breathing deeply of

286

the fresh air, but as Raoul started down the path in the wake of the others Herluin caught his arm. 'Raoul—wait.'

'What is it?' the deer asked impatiently. He loved the hunt and did not wish to miss the kill.

'I am not coming,' Herluin said. 'Tell the King I have gone— to finish my life in a cloister, perhaps. I cannot say where.'

Raoul gaped at him. 'Holy God, are you gone mad too, Messire Herluin? You—in the cloister? I think that woman must indeed have laid a spell on you.'

'No spell,' Herluin said half to himself. 'She has only told me what I knew already, what I was born with.'

'Born with?' Raoul repeated. He was sure now that the knight from La Barre was indeed out of his wits. 'What will our master say? Have you told him?'

Herluin went on as if he had not heard the question, speaking in a low monotone. 'The land has groaned long enough—it will be clean again. I will make it so. Tell the King . . .'

Raoul scratched his head. 'Tell the King? Why him, and what did she mean saying our master would soon be King? Red William looked in good enough health to me half an hour since. And if you must take the vows it is our lord Henry you should tell. Why ask me?'

With sudden fierce urgency Herluin caught him by the arm. 'Do as I say. Tell the King some cloister far away will hide me only do not do it until after the hunt.' He seemed to find difficulty in speaking. 'Tell him—all these years—no, no.' He controlled the words, 'Tell him only what I have said. He will understand.'

'Well, it's more than I do,' Raoul said. 'You are crazed. Why should Rufus care where . . .'

'Do as I say,' Herluin reiterated. 'Swear—swear for the love of Christ that you will do it.'

'Very well,' the deer shrugged his wide shoulders. 'If that is how you must have it. Though what Rufus will make of all that nonsense I don't know. You cannot mean you are going to be a monk?'

He saw Herluin's face taut with suppressed emotion and did not know what to make of it. If a man was going to be monk, he thought, he would not surely look so anguished.

'A monk?' Herluin repeated, returning to the monotone. 'Only a man who is holy should be a monk. Go, Raoul, our master will be calling for you. Say nothing, *nothing*, until the hunt is over, until the quarry is brought down.'

'Oh, rest you,' Raoul said impatiently, 'I'll do what you ask though our lord will be mighty put out when he hears you are gone without his leave.'

'He will have other things to think of,' Herluin said and watched Raoul go, shaking his head in bewilderment.

Then he went into the woods, alone. He took one arrow from his quiver, the arrow the fletcher had made yesterday, and held it in his hand. He walked uncertainly, his steps wandering, but he was listening intently, following sounds. He began to mutter to himself, a jumble of words, of names—Simon, Henry his lord, the Devil of Bellême, the Red King, holy St. Michael his patron. He was no longer aware of the sunshine, he was enveloped at last in the black and evil thing that had threatened him for so long. He was drowning in it, no longer his own master, without will or thought or reason of his own. Vaguely, through the madness that had him, he knew the awful moment had come, the moment towards which he had been moving all his life. The thing that he must do, he must do and could not escape. He wanted to remember, to think of the years that had been, the joy that had been in them, but he could not conjure up the past nor face the future—there was only the overwhelming hideous present.

Once he paused, leaning his outstretched hand against a tree, feeling the ridged oak bark beneath his fingers, and cried out of the silent forest, 'Is there another hell than this?' And then went on until he came to a knoll above a little glade. Unseen behind a hazel bush he saw below him a stag, antlers lifted, beautiful and alert. To his right between two trees stood Walter Tirel, watching the stag—and away below in the glade, bow in hand, almost at the point of loosing the arrow, was the sturdy figure of William, King of England.

Henry had better fortune now. He had brought down a stag, a fine creature with great antlers, and he was pleased with the afternoon's sport. He was watching two huntsmen fasten the kill to a long pole when the sound of a horn broke through the forest. It was not the call for a prize, but a long urgent blowing, repeated again and again and again.

'Holy Cross,' he said sharply, 'some accident must have happened.' And a swift intuition seemed to tell him it was no small thing. He shouted for Raoul to bring the horses and rode with Ralph and Roger towards the sound which grew louder and more urgent as they neared it. A few minutes later they crashed through the undergrowth and down a slope to an open glade, almost at the same time as the Clares appeared from the opposite direction.

Two huntsmen were standing panic-stricken, one still blowing frantically on his horn while Tirel, who had run down the path, knelt by a fallen figure.

Henry flung himself from the saddle. 'For God's sake stop blowing that damned horn,' he shouted, and pushing Tirel aside, threw himself down beside the body spread-eagled on the ground.

Tirel had turned the King over and Rufus lay still, the broken shaft of the arrow protruding from his chest, his strangely flecked eyes staring sightlessly at the sky.

For a suspended moment the glade was as still as the corpse, only the evening song of the birds breaking the stillness. Henry knelt by his brother's dead body, so stunned he could neither think nor move, nor even cross himself. He stared at the familiar face still ruddy, the half open mouth, the expressionless eyes, the greying tow-coloured hair. It was Rufus—and Rufus was dead.

Hoarsely he asked, 'What happened?'

The huntsmen both answered at once.

'It was an accident, my lord ...'

'The King was there, by those bushes. We flushed out a stag ...'

'He shot once and missed and then another arrow was loosed ...'

'It came from that path—where my lord of Poix stood.'

'No,' Tirel cried out, 'I was too far away. I shot but my arrow could not have ...'

'The King broke off the shaft,' the man with the horn said. He was ashen-faced and trembling. 'He lurched forward and fell ...'

That fall must have driven the arrow further into his body finally extinguishing life, Henry thought dazedly, and he got to his feet, looking around him as other members of the hunting party came hurrying to the spot. William of Breteuil gave one outraged gasp and Willaim of Mortain cried out to know if it was bloody murder. A dozen voices answered that it could not have been so and Robert Fitzhamon, kneeling by the King's body, burst into tears. He took up the broken piece of arrow and choking down his sobs, turned it in his hand. 'This is one of the new arrows.'

Mortain said accusingly, 'There were only six. Who . . .'

'It was an accident,' Gilbert of Clare repeated harshly, 'it must have been. A chance shot . . .'

Fitzhamon rose, flinging away the delicate killing thing. 'Only the King and you, Walter, had these arrows.' He stared at the lord of Poix. 'It must be yours.'

'An accident,' Walter repeated frantically, 'It must have been . . .' He looked from one to the other, seeing some accusing him, some bewildered, and Gilbert of Clare, the lord of Tonbridge, grim yet with a blank look that could scarcely veil his satisfaction.

'I did not . . .' Tirel began. Panic seized him then and with a wild gesture he flung away his bow and ran for his horse. He mounted and was gone between the trees before any man could stop him. His panic seemed to spread through the hunting party. William of Breteuil leapt for his saddle, followed by the Count of Mortain and both made for the Winchester road; others followed, riding for their homes to secure what they had until a new king reigned, while Fitzhamon, scarcely knowing what he did, threw his new cloak over the body. Roger de Marmion muttered that he must inform his father what had happened and gradually the glade emptied until only Henry, the Clares and Ralph de Toeni were left beside the body.

Henry said, 'We must find a cart, men to bear my brother . . .'

Gilbert caught his arm. 'Later—later! Henry, this is your moment. For God's sake, take it!'

Outrage rose in him, horror at what had been done, revulsion from what must be done. He looked from one to the other of his friends. There seemed to be nothing in his head but the sight of Rufus at his feet, the protruding arrow, the last rays of the sunlight through the oaks, the bird songs.

'We must ride for Winchester,' Ralph said. 'If you don't seize the throne at once there will be a faction out for Duke Robert and we have waited for this day.'

'All of us,' Roger of Clare said, 'and planned for it.' He

caught his brother's eye and shut his mouth firmly, turning to bring up Henry's horse.

Gilbert caught the reins and held them out. 'You must be King by nightfall.'

'King!' Henry exclaimed. He looked down at his brother. 'We cannot leave him like this.'

'Jesu!' Gilbert suppressed the desire to shake him. 'He is dead. It is the crown that matters now and it must be yours.'

'The crown,' Henry repeated and then, suddenly, the stunned apathy, the shock left him. The blood seemed to run through his body, as if life flowed back into him. He saw Raoul, apparently struck dumb and aghast by what had happened, holding his stirrup for him, but without setting foot in it, he jumped for the saddle and seized the reins from Gilbert.

'By God,' he said, 'the crown!' And without a backward look at the corpse lying in the forest hollow he rode for Winchester, his friends at his back, strung out along the rough track.

Jesu, it had come at last! On a bright August evening, when nothing had been further from his mind, his destiny was to be fulfilled, his father's words realised. He, Henry, would be King of England and—his head began to spin—he would have Eadgyth. He would take her from that damned nunnery and set her on the throne with him. It was incredible and only the thudding hooves beneath him pounded home the truth of it, that Rufus was dead with an arrow in his chest—God alone knew how, he would think of that later—and he was riding for Winchester to seize, if he had the strength, this green land in which he had been born.

As they clattered through the streets of the town he could see the news had preceded him for men were gathering in groups, many hurrying towards the King's palace. In the courtyard larger numbers of more important men were converging and as Henry dismounted and strode purposefully across to the great hall they began to run, cramming the doors in their haste.

In the hall one figure detached itself from a knot of vociferous men and Richard de Redvers came quickly to Henry. 'Thank God I chanced to arrive today,' he said, and his clothes were still dusty from the road. 'I've just heard the news. My lord, don't hesitate now—take the crown for there are murmurings already that your brother has the right.'

Henry took his arm. 'You have come opportunely, Richard. I need every friend I have.' He walked to the dais, where William of Breteuil stood with his cousin of Mortain and William of Warenne, Earl of Surrey.

'My lord of Breteuil,' he said in a loud voice and suddenly the wild talk, the commotion in the hall ceased. 'You will have heard of the accident that has befallen my brother. The King is dead and England must have a King—and I demand therefore that you hand over to me the keys of the royal treasury.'

Breteuil glanced at his two companions. Then he said, 'That I cannot, do, my lord. Your brother the Duke is the rightful heir to the throne.'

'He is not.' Henry looked round the hall, filling every moment with more men, excited, curious, many ready to take one side or the other, and raising his voice cried out, 'I am *porphyrogenites*. As the only son born to my father when he was king I have the primary right.'

'Your brother is the eldest,' William repeated stubbornly. 'My lord Henry, both you and I have done him homage and we owe him fealty. He has been fighting for Our Lord in the Holy Land as we all know, let us at least wait until he returns.'

'This has nothing to do with him. My father never intended as you must know, that Robert should have England. By the Rood, he knew that Robert would let it rot as he let the duchy rot.'

'You speak harsh words,' de Warenne interrupted, his dark face menacing, 'but they cannot alter the fact that now that the heir your father chose has come to his death by some means, the succession must go to the elder of his remaining sons.'

'Never!' It was the Earl of Warwick who pushed forward now. 'The Duke has no right at all to anything but the duchy, for as far as England is concerned the old King passed him over. And who should have England but the heir born in this land?'

'Aye! Aye!' A dozen voices joined in and more men began to shout out arguments for one or the other, until Warwick's brother, the Count de Meulan, stepped up to the dais. Robert de Beaumont was the most senior and the most respected of all the Norman barons and the noise subsided a little to allow him to speak.

'This is not Normandy,' he said in his deep voice. 'Let the

Normans who have land here and the English who are present say whom they want for their King.'

A roar answered him. 'Henry! Henry of Domfront,' and there was a scrambling forward of lesser men at the back of the hall where Hamo and the others led a vociferous party for their master. But a number of others, Norman to a man, surged around the dais and ranged themselves by Breteuil.

It was strange that no one gave thought to the man whose passing had brought about this situation. Only the mercenaries who had received his bounty and a few close cronies who had shared his peculiar pleasures looked shaken and uneasy. For most there was only the impression that the air was fresher for his going and that a strong King must be set at once in his place.

William of Mortain spoke up now. 'Are we to yield to a Norman who calls himself an Atheling?' His voice rang with scorn. 'No, I say. We took this country and Normandy and England are one and should be ruled by the Duke.'

A howl of anger from Henry's faction answered him and Earl Simon, normally a quiet and retiring man, came to the fore. 'I speak for Normans and English, for my wife is English and of noble birth and I say no one else has any right at all but our Atheling.'

Edward of Salisbury, one of the few English landowners left, shouted his agreement with Earl Simon, 'Let all Englishmen speak. We will have Henry the Atheling. If the men of Domfront thought him so much the best lord that they brought him from exile, I say he will be as good a lord to us.'

The commotion grew, swords were loosened and a few blows struck, and for a moment the situation looked ugly. At the back of the hall Hamo said to Gulfer, 'Can you see? How stand the numbers if it comes to a fight?'

Gulfer grinned. 'Our master has the people with him and as for the lords I think more than half will declare with him.'

'I wish the Earl of Chester were here and not in Normandy —his word would count for a good deal.'

'Everyone knows where Hugh Lupus stands,' Gulfer said. 'His nephew will bring out his men. What do you say, Raoul?'

The deer did not answer. His slow mind was grappling with the extraordinary realisation of the words he had heard only this afternoon in the churl's hut. He saw now what Herluin had meant by 'tell the king', but how he had known which King it would be, Raoul could not make out. Ponderously he followed the matter to its logical conclusion and gasped at the result. He did not understand it, nor the knight from La Barre, but he was wise enough to keep what he had heard to himself until he could speak to his lord alone.

And at the present urgent moment there was no time to look back, but only to crane his neck to see what was happening among the great lords.

Henry had drawn his sword and now stepped on to a stool and then up on the high table that everyone in the hall might see him. Every instinct told him that his whole future depended on the outcome of this fierce quarrel—he must win at once to win forever, and he looked down on the faces turned towards him, seeing all sorts and conditions of men, the friend, the foe, some grave, some angry, some encouraging, some hardened and self-engrossed, and if there was one familiar face missing among all these, he did not realise it. It mattered now only to sway the majority, to take them with him. 'I have been called the Atheling,' he shouted, 'and rightly, for so I am and who but an Atheling should wear the crown of England? Would you have me set aside?'

'No! No!' A roar answered him from all parts of the hall and he went on. 'I will submit myself to the people's choice.'

'They will choose you,' Gilbert of Clare called out, 'we will have no King but Henry.'

More men began to shout, some for Henry, some for Robert and for a while it was impossible for any single voice to be heard, but at last with both hands flung up Henry commanded at least partial silence. He faced the Count of Breteuil. 'William, our fathers were cousins and friends, and I'd not harm you, but I am the people's choice. I will have the keys, and I will take them by force if necessary.'

For one moment longer the son of William FitzOsbern stood hesitant, something of his father's old spirit in him, but he lacked wholly the latter's ability to adapt himself gallantly to any situation. He saw a prince of the royal house facing him, sword in hand and backed by a strong following, and knew that he dare not attack him physically. Neither could he yield with a good grace but stood irresolute, fumbling with the keys at his belt.

William of Warenne said angrily, 'Don't give them up to Hartsfoot, for God's sake.'

Roger the priest, who had been standing silently by a pillar came forward now. 'Do not invoke God,' he said sternly, 'I tell you, every holy man in England from the Bishops to the humblest parish priest will rejoice to see Prince Henry crowned. What did the late King ever do for Holy Church but mock her and her servants? We do not mourn one who derided God, who died unshriven and unrepentant. We turn with hope to a better man.'

The clergy present applauded his speech, solidly backed by Henry's men but Mortain swore at him, and turned menacingly to his companion.

'What can I do?' Breteuil scowled. 'I must yield.'

'Fool! Coward!' Mortain flung the words at him. 'The Duke will have something to say about this.'

Reluctantly the treasurer ignored him and loosed his jewelled belt, sliding off the heavy ring bearing the keys of the royal chests. Henry held out his sword and the Count set the ring on the point of it. There was silence in the hall and every man heard the rattle as the ring slid down the steel. Henry lowered the sword and took the keys into his hand, and with them the wealth of all England.

He faced the crowded hall, the keys in one hand, his sword in the other. 'Let the people choose,' he cried and was answered by an acclamation that was heard as far away as Winton's hill.

The great abbey of Westminster was packed to the doors for the coronation. Great men jostled for their places while barons and knights jammed themselves in behind, the lords, the men-at-arms, merchants and burghers fought for even a foot of space so that they might see the brilliant spectacle. Among the lesser men and among the English to a man there was nothing but joy on this occasion. The old bad days were over, the rule of unlaw finished, they had now a King whose reputation for justice and fair dealing was widespread and because he had known what it was to be poor and in exile they were sure of understanding from him.

Men who had been in his pay and who had served at Domfront boasted to the rest of their lord's virtues while Hamo, Gulfer and Raoul basked in reflected glory as the three who had never deserted him. Hamo was to carry his lord's standard in the coronation procession and was the envy of his companions —this office might well have been given to a man of high standing but it was typical of Henry, as men were to discover, that he would give positions regardless of rank to men who would serve him best.

The procession was headed by the clergy, all the bishops who could be assembled were there, among them William Giffard, a relative of Gilbert of Clare and now Bishop of Winchester, the first man to be appointed to office by the new King; Anselm's friend, Gilbert Crispin, Abbot of Westminster walked in the procession with Samson of Gloucester, John of Bath and Abbot Serlo, and at the head of them was the aged Maurice, Bishop of London, who was to perform the office of crowning in the absence of the Archbishop of Canterbury. Today, Sunday the fifth of August, the old man walked mitred and bearing his staff, rejoicing that he had lived to set the crown of England on the head of a man worthy to wear it.

Next came the household officers, Robert de Beaumont bearing the crown, his brother the sceptre; Gilbert of Clare carried the King's staff, Earl Simon his sword, and after them came the next degrees of men such as Richard of Redvers, rejoicing in his friend's triumph; Ralph de Toeni and his son; old Robert de Marmion with Roger; Eudo Dapifer; Roger of Clare; Arnulf and Roger of Montgomery, Bellême's brothers—a long procession stretching the length of the abbey. Earl Hugh had not been able to reach England in time, and the canopy over the King's head was borne by the Earls of Surrey and Shrewsbury, the Counts of Breteuil and Mortain, an irony considering they were perhaps Henry's main enemies, but they hid their animosity today, knowing themselves outnumbered.

Beneath the canopy, when all were in their places, walked the King-elect, and on either side of him the Bishops of Lincoln and Rochester, and his train was borne by four boys, young Simon, Maud's son; Richard of Chester; Eadgyth's brother, David of Scotland, and young Baldwin of Redvers, a token of the new King's long friendship for his father.

Henry's own son had wept stormily when told he might not bear the train and he stood now with the Countess Maud looking enviously at the four lads, trying to accept the fact that he was not one of them.

'I will advance you when you are older,' his father had told him, 'but you are not my heir. No bastard can inherit England.'

'Then I do not want to be a bastard,' Robert wept and his father had laughed.

'I'm afraid, my son, that was decided for you a long time ago. You must understand that you cannot act as if you were a royal prince.' But the words were accompanied by a kiss and a caress that softened them.

Now, as he stood with the Countess, Robert was only aware of pride in this man who was his father and he wished he had a few more inches that he might see better. As his father passed where he stood he turned and smiled and Robert thought he had never seen him look so magnificent.

The King's coronation robes were of purple sendal that shimmered as he moved, edged and embroidered in gold thread in an intricate pattern that had kept the tailors working each day and night since Friday. Shafts of sunlight coming through the windows caught the work and it shimmered as he moved, his mantle and train stretching behind him also covered with gold embroidery. Bracelets of thick gold were set upon his wrists and his dark head was bare, ready for the crown of his father to be set upon it. He had been carefully shaved and his skin was smooth and browned by the sun so that at this moment proud, smiling, walking to fulfil the highest peak of ambition, Maud thought she had never seen him look more comely. Tears came to her eyes for joy in this moment and she wished that Eadgyth had been there to see him—but that would soon be righted now and Maud, generous in her joy, looked forward to leading Eadgyth to her marriage bed.

Henry himself, passing Maud and his son, was also thinking of Eadgyth, though in the last two hectic days there had been time for nothing but the business of being crowned. From the moment when he had seized the Treasury at Winchester events had moved fast. On the following morning Rufus was hastily buried in the cathedral church, unmourned and unwept, no priest would sing a Mass for one who had so consistently mocked at God and His Church and it was unshriven, without the last rites, without candles or singing that he was laid beneath the floor and as quickly forgotten.

Henry stood briefly by the stone slabs. How could he genuinely mourn the brother at whose hands he had suffered so much and whose death had set him free? Nor, even had he wished it, was there time to mourn—only a moment to remember all that Rufus had been, the camaraderie, the petulance, the odd humour, the arrogance that had refused his brother so often, all at an end now under a slab of stone.

A council was called of all the men available and with hardly a dissenting voice Henry was elected King. That there were dissenters he knew, men who would prefer Robert's easy rule, but for the moment they were outvoted and outshouted. As King-elect he rode for London and was in the capital the same evening, but a King-elect was no King at all, as Edgar Atheling had discovered back in 1066, and Henry hurried on the arrangements for his crowning.

Yesterday had been spent thus, but he had also had time to look into some of the irregularities of Rufus and his ministers, and with Roger the priest, soon to be the chief of his clerks, he had worked far into the night on a charter to redress the blatant wrongs under which the nation had groaned—the laws of King

Edward were to be restored, fresh laws made for rich and poor alike, the Church to be free of simony, marriage rights to be safeguarded, the coinage reformed, knights' privileges to be laid down, widows and orphans protected. A good document, he thought, and one that set out the rights of all men for all time, to be handed down through succeeding generations as a guide to good government and to put a stop to the evil practices of his brother's rule. The only concession to his own pleasure was his keeping of the royal forests in his own hands. He had already ordered the immediate arrest of Ranulf Flambard, to the general delight, and commanded Roger privately to set about amassing evidence against the Earl of Shrewsbury that might rid his kingdom once and for all of the Devil of Bellême.

And now at last, with power in his hands, he could take what he desired and above all he desired Eadgyth. He would send for her and there would be another ceremony, another crowning, and a night of joy which he had anticipated for nine long years.

Last night Bishop Maurice had heard his confession and shriven him and stood now ready and waiting to admit him to the highest office in the land, a grave smile on his lined face. He laid his hand on Henry's shoulder, turned him to face the people, asking if they would have him for their king. The responsive shout was deafening, echoing through the building, flung high into the roof, a vivid explosive acclamation that sent the colour to Henry's face—he had expected it, but the effect was overwhelming.

His first act was the swearing of the oath, his hand upon the holy Book where it lay on the altar, swearing to uphold the law, to bring back justice, to lay aside the unright of his brother's time to be a servant of God and a father to his people. The long elaborate ceremony progressed and he tried to take it all in, to absorb every impression, but it assumed an almost dreamlike quality as the holy chrism was laid on his brow, the sceptre and staff placed in his hands, and at last the great crown of Arabian gold with its metal stars and its jewels, set upon his head. In that moment all that he had ever done or endured in the years since his father's death became worth while. He stood crowned, anointed, while he was hailed from every part of the building. 'Vivat rex! Vivat rex in aeternum!' and the joy was greater than it had been since the crowning of Harold, the last of the Saxon kings, for England now had an English King again, born on her own soil.

Hamo stood stiffly with the standard, looking at his lord's back and thinking of the day when they had stood together on the high rock of Domfront and Henry had said that it was a beginning. Their way had led them here to this golden glittering moment and Hamo felt intoxicated with pride in this man he served, his only regret—that Fulcher had not returned to share in it. At the side of the church Gulfer whispered to Raoul that it was a pity Herluin of La Barre was not here to see this day while Raoul, bearing his secret knowledge, whispered back that Herluin would no doubt be happy enough knowing their master was in his rightful place.

Roger the priest, among the ranks of the clergy, thought of Henry's promise to advance him; he was an ambitious man and already saw himself mitred, but in this moment he too thought of Herluin and prayed for his friend that wherever he was gone he might meet with kindness.

The solemn mass proceeded. Henry was divested of royalty and knelt at the altar steps while the eternal sacrifice was offered. Devoutly he received the Host upon his tongue and thanked God for His goodness. For him it was the supreme moment for he, now a King with a kingdom, abased himself before the King of Heaven in real humility, putting aside his own high achievement as he worshipped God. He knew then an exultation of soul such as he had not not known before for surely now God was blessing him, consecrating him to the work he was to do.

The mass ended, he was again dressed in royalty to receive the homage of the barons. One by one they approached the throne and knelt, placing their hands between his and swearing fealty to him, and as they came he assessed them with that cool clear-sightedness that was to stand him in good stead over the years. In that moment he remembered the humiliation of his defeat on the rock of the Archangel and how many of the men here had lined the way then to see him go; he had sworn that one day they should kneel to him and now by God that day had come and it was they who were submitting to him!

The bishops came first, his to a man for he had already given his word on reform of the royal dealings with the Church, and Robert Bloet in particular set his hands between the new King's with tears of joy in his eyes. The Earls followed. Robert and Henry of Beaumont foremost and to be admitted to his inner council; Earl Simon, good man and firm friend; Earl Gilbert of Tonbridge who gave Henry a swift glance of triumph. Somehow, Henry thought, Gilbert had been too prepared for this, and he suspected Gilbert if not of plotting Rufus' death, at best engineering it in some fashion; yet Gilbert, if he had done it, had done it from motives that could scarcely be condemned as evil for no man today could say that England would not benefit from the ending of the rule of Rufus and Flambard.

It was odd that men seemed to have accepted unquestioningly that the King's death was an accident, that Tirel had shot at a stag and missed and killed Red William instead, that he had fled in fear of the consequences. Well, let that story suffice. If he suspected more he would keep it to himself and see that neither Tirel nor his family should suffer for it.

Of Herluin's part in it he had no knowledge, only conjecture. Raoul had told him a strange tale of omens and prophesies and weird words, and Roger too had thought that Herluin's disappearance was connected with the accident, with death and an old fear, but no one knew what had happened in that glade three evenings ago. Had Herluin sent that fatal arrow to its destination? His cryptic message, 'tell the King . . .' could not have been directed to Rufus that much was clear. It could only indicate either some foreknowledge or instinct but it did not clarify the truth of what had happened, could never do so now. All that was certain was that Herluin, no longer sane, had gone and that he, Henry, was King, and the one followed from the other. He grieved for the loss of the friend who had shared so much with him, but there was no time to look back, nor was he the man to do so. If he owed Herluin anything for the latter's charity to his father's corpse, for the years of friendship, he must repay it now by his consequent deeds. However he had come to this present moment he must accept it and he set his hands firmly on either side of Gilbert's large strong fingers.

Earl William of Warenne came next, kneeling at his feet, hands uplifted. Here was one he would not trust for de Warenne had wanted Eadgyth, had been one of Rufus' cronies. The Earl spoke the oath but he did not meet Henry's stare; nor did William of Breteuil who came next, both assenting with their lips but neither with their hearts. William of Mortain looked boldly at his cousin and Henry met that gaze with one equally cool.

In a low voice he said, 'A fair warning, William—you had best live at peace with me. I will be a good friend, but a ruthless enemy.'

The corners of Mortain's mouth were drawn down. 'As you will, my cousin and King. Will you give me our uncle's earldom of Kent to win my loyalty?'

His effrontery astonished Henry and he felt he would as soon trust a poisonous snake. 'No man will get aught of me but what he earns,' he said and turned to the Earl of Shrewsbury who now approached the dais. Here perhaps was the greatest enemy of all, the one man he loathed as he had never hated in all his life, the man responsible for more suffering and evil than any other, guilty of many deaths including that of Simon La Barre, and because of that of the loss of Herluin. As Bellême knelt, richly dressed, his dark handsome face blandly smiling, thin brows smooth, dark eyes betraying nothing, Henry felt a disgust that he must even for this moment set his hands on those of the Devil of Bellême.

He leaned forward and spoke so that no one else might hear. 'My lord Earl, you may as well know from the start—I will not tolerate deeds in my kingdom such as you have wrought in Normandy. If you disturb my law you will find my hand even heavier than my father's.'

Bellême did not flinch but stared boldly back at Henry. 'Beau sire, I rule vast lands on both sides of the channel. You will have no defiance from them.'

'That is not what I meant and you know it. It is your own conduct I censure and I am neither as gentle as Robert nor as careless as Rufus.' He set his hands briefly on either side of the Earl's. 'You have sworn your fealty—break it and I will break you, my lord.'

Bellême rose and backed away from the dais and Henry thought, it is in the open now, a contest between the Devil and myself and it is I that shall win.

Richard of Redvers came to kneel before him, broad face smiling, and Henry turned with pleasure to one who was his friend beyond doubt. When every man of rank, every knight had sworn he rose and attended by his household and all the Earls he walked slowly from the church to show himself to the people. The capital had gone wild with joy and he realised as he stood on the steps in all his panoply how his brother had been hated.

They were shouting for him—'Henry the Atheling! Henry of England!' and from his own followers, 'Henry of the high rock!' These his people wanted to be his people and he felt again as he had felt once before on a night at Winchester, and later at the conquest of Domfront, that inebriating sense of power, the triumph, the fulfilling of his destiny that ran in his veins like rich wine.

He handed the sceptre and staff to the Beamonts and stood with his arms uplifted and wide in an embracing gesture, smiling in the sunlight, the crown of England firmly on his head.

A week later he sent Richard of Redvers with a large escort to Romsey to bring the Princess Eadgyth and her sister to London. He could not leave the capital himself, much as he wished to go, but Richard would do his joyous mission for him and he waited for four impatient days for his friend's return.

And then one morning shortly before the dinner hour he was in his solar dictating a letter to Philip of France—fat Philip who was so old and gross that he left most affairs in the capable hands of his son Louis and who could no longer patronise him —when Walter, now proudly in charge of four pages, came in to say that the lord of Redvers was outside.

Henry sent the clerk away and rose eagerly, but Richard came in alone, his face unusually grave.

He checked his eager move forward. 'Well?' his voice sounded harsh with suppressed anxiety. 'Where is she? Have you not brought her?'

Richard shook his head. 'No, sire. The Abbess Christina . . .'

'Wine of Christ!' Henry swore, 'not that bitch again! What happened?' He indicated a stool but did not sit himself.

'I took your message, but the Abbess said, oh very politely, that she could not send to earthly marriage one who was a bride of Christ.'

'She lies. She has always lied.'

'So I think', Richard agreed, 'but she insisted. She asked whether after so many years I imagined the Princess still refused the vows. She said the Princess had become desirous of serving God only and no man.'

Henry's mouth was drawn in a grim line. 'You saw her?'

'At first the Abbess refused, but I insisted.' Richard gave Henry an apologetic glance. 'I was not sure what you would wish me to do, but I did not think so soon after your crowning you would want me to violate the precincts of a holy house. However, I did know you would not be satisfied with anything other than a reply from the Princess herself, so I told the Abbess that I and my escort would remain in the guest house eating heartily until she complied with my request.'

Henry laughed briefly. 'Richard, you are a born statesman—I must find use for your talents. What then?'

'She has to let the Princess come.'

'And Eadgyth?'

'She was not wearing the habit.'

'Ah!' He let out his breath. 'What did she say?'

'What I expected—that she had not taken any vow.'

'And Christina?'

'She turned on the girl and reminded her of words she had spoken one day. The Princess admitted she had once said that if in time there came to be no hope whatever of a union with you then she might consider it. If she could not wed you then she would know no man but give herself wholly to God.'

Henry felt his face burn. 'Go on.'

'She admitted also that she had worn the habit, but this her aunt forced on her for the most part, though she herself had worn it when certain Normans came to the house, notably the Earl of Surrey who desired her hand of King William.'

'And what answer did Christina make to this?'

'She was angry. She told the Princess she was violating holy promises now that you were a King and not a landless younger son. She reminded her that she had no marriage portion and was in no position to wed a King even had she been free— implying unworthy motives to the lady Eadgyth.'

'By God, for one with a holy calling the Abbess uses base weapons. As if I should care whether Eadgyth has a portion or not. Well,' he sat down on the table and a great alaunt that lay by the door rose and came to sit beside him so that he fondled the rough head affectionately. 'I shall send you back to Romsey, Richard, at once if you will, with a letter for the Princess.'

'I'll willingly endure saddle sores,' de Redvers said, 'if it brings you to your marriage bed.'

'Anselm shall settle this matter once and for all.'

He looked down at the dog whose large brown eyes were fixed on him. 'Holy Cross, but mating is easier in the animal kingdom, eh my beauty?' He glanced at Richard. 'Don't you see, my enemies would seize upon this to discredit me? If they could say the King had violated the person of a nun what a weapon that would be! But I'll not give them the chance. I've waited so long I can wait another month or two.'

'The Archbishop should be here in September.'

Henry nodded. 'He can convene a church court and sift the matter, then I will have her before the world and no man will dare to throw mud at us.' He put the dog aside and taking pen and parchment began to write in large letters and Richard watched him, thinking of Henry's remark of long ago—that an unlettered king was a crowned ass. Well, they would never be able to call him that, but he foresaw trouble ahead before Henry was undisputed lord of England. Yet the years of exile, the difficulties and privations, prison and loneliness had all been the best possible preparation for kingship, far better than an easy life in royal luxury, and Richard had no doubts now as to Henry's ability to cope with any contingency. For himself he was content to serve; in the early years he had been attached to Henry for friendship's sake only, but now it was also with admiration and respect.

He rode back to Romsey and faced the Abbess Christina with a pleasure of which he felt slightly ashamed. She stood before him in her guest parlour, thin, old before she need be, her mouth drawn into a hard line. Christina was neither cruel nor vindictive by nature but she had taken the veil at the behest of her saintly mother and had to fight a passionate nature that desired other things. Repression had warped her, twisted her faith, smothered compassion with rigid discipline and now in defying Henry it was as if she was clinging to her own position instead of merely arguing over the release of one girl to the world of men.

She greeted Richard coolly. 'Well, Messire de Redvers, you are soon returned. I trust the King now understands the situation.'

'My lady Abbess, did you really think that after all these

305

years,' he was conscious of repeating her own phrasing, 'he would give up the Princess.'

'I told you before, she is not free. I am afraid you have made a long and wearisome journey to no purpose.'

'As to her freedom, the King is asking the Archbishop to settle the matter—he is on his way back to England at this moment.'

Christina flinched. She had clearly not expected this. 'Even the Archbishop cannot unsay holy vows.'

'Not if they were ever said. But the King knows,' Richard added shrewdly, 'and I believe you do also, that they were not.' Watching her stubborn face, he knew that he was right and went on, 'I have a letter for the Princess. She must be told of the situation and King Henry bade me give the letter into no other hands. Frankly,' he added plainly, 'he did not trust you to deliver it.'

Dusky colour filled Christina's cheeks. Fighting a last-ditch battle she began, 'I will not permit . . .'

'And he bade me say that if you wish to remain Abbess here you had best obey him.'

She drew in her breath sharply. 'He would not dare molest my person.'

Richard could not keep back a swift smile. 'Lady, believe me, he has no desire to do that, but there are ways and means of dealing with such a situation. I need hardly remind you of the case of William of St. Calais.'

For a moment longer she defied him, but the memory of the ignominious trial of the former Bishop of Durham was enough to induce caution. Richard pitied her. Being a man of some perception he saw her for what she was, and though she angered him with her senseless obstinacy he perceived she had made her own life a misery and must revenge herself somehow. But his pity, he thought, should be reserved for Eadgyth, for God knew what Christina had done to the girl in these last five years.

He need not have worried. When Eadgyth came at last, she had thrown off the sad daily quiet of that waiting time and was what she should be—joyful, eager, on the verge of the fulfilment a healthy young woman desired. She was wearing a blue gown which enhanced the blue of her eyes and her face attained a simple beauty as she read her lover's letter.

Then looking directly at Richard she said, 'Messire de

Redvers, tell the King I will wait most happily for the Arch-bishop's coming. I have no doubt at all as to what he will say.'

'Nor I,' Richard agreed smiling. This girl, with her natural dignity, her well-formed figure and graceful bearing, her gentleness combined with composure would make a Queen England could be proud of, he thought.

She asked him questions about Henry, about the coronation and how the King had looked until suddenly she recollected herself and blushing asked his pardon for detaining him.

He bent over her hand. 'Lady, I ask no better way to serve my lord than to further his union with you.'

Her blush deepened. 'I thank you for coming, messire. I hope, oh I do hope the Archbishop will not be slow on his journey.'

The truth was that the years of waiting, lacking hope, had passed as most years pass—in the small round of sewing, reading, assisting the nuns in their work, singing and praying in the high bleak church that she had grown to love. She had learned in the hardest, loneliest way patience and fortitude and resignation and though her stubborn will had refused the final step that would cut the last strand of hope, nevertheless it had been so slender a thread that at times she had barely been aware of it. She had devoted herself to the poor and the sick and made herself much loved, and she too, as her royal lover, had learned in a hard school that adversity formed character more than prosperity.

Now, with hope not only renewed but about to be rewarded she had to fight all over again for patience. The days of waiting were to be worse than the years and must pass with leaden slowness until the coming of the Archbishop. But he would set her free, she knew it, and in the end she would, as she had dreamed so often and so hopelessly, go one day with Henry to their nuptial Mass.

When Richard de Redvers was gone, she ignored her aunt's sharp order to return to the cloister for her reading, and wandered out into the garden. She could not contain her joy and walked among the neat beds of herbs, fennel and marjoram and thyme that Sister Gudrun grew so carefully and could use to cure the ague or a cold or griping in one's belly, and the tears began to run down her face as she tried to thank the Blessed Virgin for this day. She clutched Henry's letter in her hands and at length tucked it into her gown, to lie between her breasts until she could exchange it for the presence of her lover himself. A cool breeze fanned her cheeks and if she asked anything more of the Mother of God at this moment it was for a favourable wind to bring Archbishop Anselm to England.

He came at last at the end of September. He was an old man and despite his joy at the new accession could not hurry. He had wept for Rufus and when his friends asked him how he could weep for such a man and one who had done him so much harm he had answered that he wept that the son of his old friend should die with his soul in so terrible a state of degradation. But his task as Archbishop was given back into his hands and now he went with pleasure to his work beside a man whom he loved as a son.

They met at Canterbury whither the King had gone to greet him and in the courtyard there, in the shade of the great church, embraced, Anselm kissing the King on both cheeks. Henry knelt for his blessing and then the Archbishop knelt in homage, after which they dined together in the parlour of the Abbot's house.

Anselm regarded his spiritual son with deep affection. 'I have heard already of the good you have done, and I rejoice for it. You will make this land a better place for rich and poor alike.'

'God willing,' Henry answered soberly. 'I have Flambard shut in the tower in London, I'll have no more extortion such as he practised, and as for my barons, they will have to learn that the same law applies to them as to any man in my realm.'

'You are thinking of the Earl of Shrewsbury?' Anselm asked acutely.

'And my cousin of Mortain. I will not rest until I have rid my kingdom of such men, but let us not talk of them today when I rejoice to see you in your place again.' Henry glanced at the old man where he sat, his robes falling about him, in a chair by the table, 'My dear friend, tell me you forgive me for seeking my hallowing before your return. It was your right to perform it, but I dared not wait.'

'You are forgiven,' Anselm answered and smiled at him, 'I understood the position. You fear some opposition from your brother's faction?'

'It would have been out in the open by now had I not been crowned at once.'

Anselm sighed. 'Your brother lacks the firm hand that England needs, and Normandy too—I doubt his return will bring peace to our poor duchy.'

'I have written to Count Helias to assure him of my friendship. He will go back to Le Mans now, and I have sent a letter to Rufus' garrison there bidding them give their allegiance to whom they will.'

'That was an ambiguous order, my son.'

Henry smiled. 'I've a shrewd idea of the position and as far as I can make out the garrison and the Count's men are on the best of terms. Helias will rule as my friend and ally, Domfront I hold and will always hold, and my own men are still investing Avranches and Coutances and Mont St. Michel. Robert must keep the peace.'

'And if he does not?'

'Let me order my kingdom first, my lord,' Henry said blandly. 'I shall have trouble enough here until men see I am to be feared —or that I am a better King than Robert would ever be. Tell me, is he changed?'

'From what I heard,' the old man answered slowly, 'he was a changed man in the holy places, fighting as well as any and better than most, but since he has come home again I fear that not even his wife, who is a noble lady, has been able to prevent him becoming fonder of his bed than the council chamber. And he is giving away the riches he brought home so fast that he will soon be without a tunic to his back.'

Henry sat down astride a small stool and laughed. 'That sounds like Robert. Even if he bestirs himself to take issue with me I think I have his measure now—I love him as a brother and despise him as an enemy, which I would prefer that he were not. But the only men who want his rule are those who would ignore it, and I have the people with me and . . .' he paused, 'the Church also, have I not?'

The Archbishop inclined his head, but his expression was grave. 'You have, my son, but I must tell you that I have come back from Rome convinced that only the Holy Father has the right to confirm Church appointments and investitures.'

Henry stiffened. Was he going to have trouble already with this gentle, but unbelievably obstinate old man? 'My lord, we cannot and I will not lightly set aside the ancient customs of this land nor the rights of the crown. The Kings of England have always held the right of investiture.'

'It is no right at all. The Church must administer her own appointments.'

The King got up from his stool. 'I tell you, father, England is different. There is something in the nature of Englishmen that makes her the exception to most rules—as my father found out and wisely accepted. But let us agree to have a truce over this matter for the moment. I believe we can settle it without disaster to either of us.'

Anselm folded his hands in a manner that reminded Henry of Lanfranc. 'Very well, my son. You are a reasonable man and I believe you will be a good King if you will be guided by God and His Church.'

Henry came to face him, arms folded, his expression grave, sure of himself, but unsure now of Anselm's reaction. 'That is what I desire, as I have always desired God's blessing. I mean to have order and I will punish harshly to get it, if I must. But the Church need not fear me, which brings me to the matter uppermost in my mind. I need your help, father.'

'Tell me how I may serve you.'

He told the old man, briefly, of Richard's visit to Romsey. 'All that I ask of you, my lord,' he finished, 'is that you should hold an enquiry that the whole world may know whether or not our marriage is without hint of scandal.'

Anselm considered this in silence for so long that Henry had to suppress the urge to repeat the question. He stood waiting, his fingers gripping his folded arms to prevent them seizing Anselm's to force an answer from him.

At last the Archbishop said, 'I will do what you ask. The nuns shall be questioned and the Abbess must bring the Princess to my court so that the matter may be discerned beyond any doubt. I must confess,' he smiled a little, 'I expected to find you wed when I returned.'

Henry shook his head. 'For that I would have waited for you even had the Abbess raised no objection.' For one moment his impatience showed itself in a spurt of irritation. 'By God, that woman is incredible. She would do anything to keep us apart. Can jealousy turn a woman into a thing all eaten up with spite?'

'Sin and the devil can twist any one of us,' Anselm said

sadly and then he added, 'I am only surprised you have not stormed the abbey with your royal authority.'

Henry's mouth lifted at this gentle sally. 'I have learned caution, my lord. I must not alienate anyone on my way to my marriage bed—certainly not the Church. You will help me?'

'I will help you but,' the old man's voice became graver, 'before I do so there is something I would say to you, for I must speak to you not as Archbishop to my King but as a father to his spiritual son. Pray sit down and listen.' He watched Henry as the latter seated himself again and then went on. 'I am bound to say that from what I know of the Princess Eadgyth, she is a worthy bride for you and Queen for England. She deserves the best of husbands.'

Startled, Henry said, 'You cannot think I would be otherwise. All these years I have refused to think of any other bride, I have loved her since I set eyes on her.'

'That may well be true, indeed, I know it is, but what of your private times, my son, what of your morals?'

Henry was silent. He had not expected this attack from Anselm.

'You cannot deny,' the Archbishop said with all the authority of his holy calling, 'that you have indulged your passions more than most men. You have had many mistresses, you have children. The Princess will have to accept that this has been so.'

How could he deny it? Henry thought of Alide, of Amaldis, Nest, Ansfrida and others with a briefer span. There was young Robert living at court with him; little Matilda at Caen, Ansfrida's son, Richard, in London; Juliana, young Henry, and bastards or not he loved them because they were his children. But he had never indulged in cheap whoring nor deserved the accusation Rufus had flung at him. Could Eadgyth accept that during the nine years he had waited for her he had lived only as man with a strong demanding body must live. He remembered those stolen minutes at Romsey—what had she said? That she was content for him to be as he was? Yet she could not know him as he really was, as he had been, and because of that—rare tears stung his eyes. He looked helplessly at the Archbishop.

Anselm said resolutely, 'Put the past behind you, my son. Give up your mistresses. Do you remember, long ago when you asked me to intercede for you with your brother, you told me that if you could have Eadgyth to wife you would cleave only to her? Keep that promise now and God will bless your union.'

'I will,' he said, 'I will, I swear it.'

Anselm rose and made the sign of the cross over his head. 'Then I will do all I can to aid you. Dear son, this is a new beginning for you—a crown, a bride, a land to rule.' He looked down with affection at this young man whom he had known for all his thirty years, whom he had watched growing into manhood, developing through so many vicissitudes into the person he was today, and with all his faults—perhaps even because of them—Anselm loved Henry as he had loved neither Robert Curthose nor William Rufus.

But after five years of exile there was so much for the Archbishop to do that it was not until the end of October that the court of enquiry was convened at Lambeth.

Henry had yielded to Anselm's demand that he should not see the Princess until the matter was settled so that there could be no possible stone for his enemies to cast at him, and he sent for Maud, requesting her to attend to Eadgyth and lodge with her until the enquiry was over. But despite his avowed confidence in the outcome, he waited in his palace on the opposite side of the river in restless, agonising impatience. He paced his solar until, unable to bear the confining walls, he went out to hunt, gave up after half an hour, came back to walk with Richard beside the river bank.

'Peace, beau sire,' Richard said. 'Roger will send a message as soon as it is done.'

'Peace!' Henry exclaimed and laughed wrily. 'I tell you, Richard, I never felt less at peace in my life. Have I waited so long to have my fate in the hands of a parcel of churchmen?'

'In the hands of the Archbishop,' Richard corrected. 'He will do what is right and the others will travel with him. And you cannot doubt the Princess after what she said to me?'

'No, no, she has been steadfast. What a girl, Richard! Living so long with those holy sisters, pressed by that scheming aunt, the influence of that place all about her and yet, young as she is, holding to the memory of our meetings and a few kisses.'

'The people will love her,' de Redvers said. 'In Romsey the poor and sick bless her name.'

'With her by my side . . .' Henry began and then broke off,

thinking of Anselm's words. 'With her, I think I cannot fail to be what a King should be.'

'You?' Richard smiled. 'The people of the high rock would vouch for that. I remember Herluin once said . . .' He stopped abruptly. 'There is no news?'

'Nor will be,' Henry said. He stared across the river at the buildings of the Archbishop's palace, the gently flowing water in between. It was an unsettled day with patches of blue sky and heavy scudding clouds dark with the threat of showers, the changing light reflected in the water. Roger had told him something of Herluin's fears, of the 'end to living' which had come to him. He would never know the truth of that day in the forest but he was as near to it as he could be and felt only compassion for a man caught as Herluin had been on a tide he could not stem—nor could he hold Herluin responsible for his actions on that day. Somewhere now, please God, he was easing his deranged mind in acts of penance and Henry had a sudden vision of him, nearer the truth than he knew, scrubbing sanctuary stones, performing menial tasks, withdrawn and melancholy. At every Mass he attended now he prayed briefly for Herluin that the knight from La Barre might know of the good that was to come under his rule, that God would be merciful to one whose life hitherto had been without evil, and bring him to peace.

Towards supper time he was returning to the palace with Richard and was on the path to the steps when Ralph de Toeni came hurrying towards him. One glance at his face told Henry the truth and a great wave of relief spread over his whole body. Praise God, he thought, praise God—and felt the utter inadequacy of words.

The Countess Maud brought Eadgyth to court but not before she had dressed the girl in new clothes and some of her own jewels that she might become her new position, and when at last she escorted her up the fine hall which Rufus had built, Henry saw an Eadgyth who was new to him. As tall as himself, slender and shapely, she walked with dignity and a composure born of years of self-control, with the right amount of modesty, mingled with eagerness.

Down the length of the hall their eyes met and he knew at last that nothing had changed between them, yet because of the years that had gone there was a shyness about her, a certain hesitancy in himself as he greeted her formally.

She made a deep obeisance to him and at once he reached out his hand and raised her. Suddenly oblivious of the watching court, even of Maud, he said, 'Eadgyth—is it true?'

A little laugh escaped her and her mouth was trembling. 'I think so, my lord.'

He led her to the high seat, suppressing the desire to catch her in his arms. But he was not the young Count who had dressed as a servant to snatch one moment with her, nor was she the imprisoned girl in a nunnery. He was a King and she a Princess of Scotland and a future Queen and all must be circumspect before this court he had sworn to reform, that he had already cleared of much vice. The pretty youths had gone or been forced to behave and dress as men and he would have no ridiculing of churchmen, nor mockery of those of lesser estate, neither would he allow anything but respect for women at his table. A few men might sneer and laugh behind their hands but most approved his actions and he must set an example to them all by his own conduct.

When Eadgyth was seated and he beside her he said, 'My chaplain, Roger, told me how it went. I did not doubt but I was mighty relieved when Anselm pronounced judgement.'

'It was easier than I expected,' she admitted. 'The sisters spoke for me—they knew the truth and would not deny it, even for the Abbess—and the Archbishop was so kind. My aunt has gone back to Romsey and I could almost pity her for what she has done . . .'

'I cannot,' he broke in grimly, 'for what she has done to you I would see her whipped from her place.'

Eadgyth sighed. 'If you knew her better you would pity her, for her house is divided now so that I think it will be a long time before she knows peace again.'

Aware that they had been talking intimately for long enough, he presented the nobles at his table and the Count de Meulan who was sitting on her other side said, 'Lady, our King must have made a great impression on you for you to wait nine years to wed him.'

A blush warmed her cheeks. 'I swore to Our Lady, my lord, that I would have no other husband.'

He smiled at her in a grave kindly way. 'Not many women

314

would be so steadfast. I wish you joy of your marriage.'

She thanked him and asked his lady on his far side how her twin sons fared. The Countess talked eagerly of the two year olds, Robert and Waleran, until her brother-in-law Henry of Beaumont laughingly told Eadgyth she would have to see these nephews of his who bade fair to conquer the world.

There were so many new faces, so many names thrust at her, some she liked, some such as the Earl of Shrewsbury that she feared; one or two, among them Maud's mother, the Countess Judith, who made her feel small and inexperienced, while the lady of Warwick and Gilbert of Clare's lady were kind to her and set her at her ease. She could not help noticing, however, that they found difficulty in pronouncing her Saxon name. She turned to her bridegroom.

'My lord, I think my name causes your people to stumble. Would it not please them if when I am Queen I took an easier one?'

'If you will, my heart.' He smiled indulgently at her. 'What name would you choose?'

'I thought perhaps Matilda, for your mother's memory.'

He was pleased and reaching for her hand held it hard in his. 'Holy Rood, but you are wise. How is it that you know how to please me and my people at the same time?'

She shook her head. 'I do not think I am very wise, only I learned at Romsey how important it is to be kind.'

'You shall have Winchester as your morning-gift,' he said. 'Old King Edward gave it to Harold's sister on their wedding day,' and he added with relish, 'then Christina will find she holds her lands from you.'

Eadgyth laughed delightedly. 'Oh, I shall enjoy that. And yet it is so strange, so hard to believe—that I am free.'

'Free?' He lifted her hand to his mouth. 'You have but changed one set of bonds for another. Will you accept your new chains cheerfully, my love?'

'If so be you set them on me, yes,' she said.

On an impulse, born of a desire that she might have no illusions for him to shatter unwittingly, he said, 'I should have told you—I have a son at court.'

To his surprise she smiled, her face half hidden by her veil so that he could not read the expression in her eyes. 'I have seen him.'

'You have seen Robert? I did not realise . . .'

'No one could see him and not know he was yours. He was with the Countess Maud's son when I came in, and I thought . . .' she hesitated. 'I asked the Countess, and then I spoke with him. I think we shall be very fond of one another.'

'You do not mind?'

'How should I mind?' Her voice was so low that no one else could hear her words. 'You were not shut in a convent for all the years since we met.'

He leaned towards her over the arm of his chair. 'I have sworn to be true to you, I have sworn to raise an abbey to Our Lady in gratitude for this day, but if I should fail . . .'

'I do not want to change you,' she answered and a deeper colour tinged her cheeks. 'What is the body? A little pleasuring? I am ignorant of such things, but I know I have your heart and that is what I have always wanted.'

'You have had it,' he said, 'since you tumbled head over heels out of a litter.'

He saw her mouth curve as she turned away to answer the Archbishop who sat on her other side and he was left wondering at her combination of wisdom and innocence.

There was no reason to wait and he hurried on the arrangements. Anselm, however, was pressed about with duties and the wedding and coronation of the new Queen could not be finally realised until St. Martin's day.

Eadgyth stayed with the Countess Maud and her mother at their manor a little north of the city, but at last the day came, a fitful sun lighting the crowded streets. From early morning the common people hurried into the city to see this wedding of a King—there had been no such royal nuptials since those of the Countess Judith and Earl Waltheof at Winchester—and the King had promised a cask of wine to every street in the city. Bells were rung in every church and as it was proclaimed a holiday men, women and children thronged the roads to see what they might of the pageantry.

In the abbey church at Westminster Anselm married their King to the Scottish Princess, the girl who through her mother was one of the line of Cerdic, bringing back the ancient blood of the conquered kingdom so that Englishmen might hold up their heads again. When it was done and the crown was on her head she set her hand on her husband's and together they walked from the church between the lines of barons to cheers and shouts from all their well wishers. But once Henry heard a laugh and a sneering voice say, 'We have an English Godric and Godgifu to rule us now.' He turned his head but could not see who spoke, though he thought it might be his cousin of Mortain. He had a feeling that nickname would stick. Well, let it. Yesterday someone, he thought it was Eudo Dapifer, had said he would be a 'lion of justice' and he would make that stick even closer.

Outside the abbey the new King and Queen were cheered again. It was a day as great as his coronation day and the fact that the impossible had happened, that he was King and had Edgyth whom he loved as his Queen was given a heady unreality by all the feasting and festivity that went on far into the dark hours.

It was not until nearly midnight that she was escorted away by the Countess Maud to be undressed and put into the royal bed. He watched her go and it seemed an interminable time before Maud returned and he was accompanied up the narrow stair by his friends and a crowd of courtiers, all smiling and eager to see him bedded with the usual toasts and lewd jokes and final blessing by the clergy.

But when he saw her lying there in his great bed, suddenly solitary in the dim rush light, her eyes cast down, a heightened colour in her cheeks, her hair unbound about her bare shoulders, he stopped in the doorway, a hand lifted to check his followers. In one swift moment he thought of all the other nights in the past when he had lain with one woman or another in his arms and knew that this one would be different—for this girl had reached his mind and heart as no other had done. She looked up momentarily, shy and uncertain, reminding him of the young faun who had ridden from Scotland so long ago, and on impulse he turned to face the eager, laughing gathering.

'No,' he said and threw custom aside. Smiling broadly he added, 'Enough is enough, my friends, and by Our Lady, nine years is too long.' And he shut the door in their astonished faces.

He awoke in the morning at first light and leaned on one elbow gazed down at her sleeping face. She looked peaceful and happy, a faint smile on her mouth, and thinking of the night that had gone he had a desire now to kneel beside her and lay his head between her breasts as he had done so long ago, an untried boy, with Alide. Consummation, he thought, was more than one woman, one night.

He got up from the bed and went to the window, throwing wide the shutter. It was a chill morning, the air striking cold against his body. Over the river lay a white November mist and outside where a spider had spun its web white beads of moisture turned the web into a pattern of beauty. In the distance the trees were half hidden in the mist but he knew the shape of the land, where the hills lay, the villages, the fields, the forests alive with the animals he loved.

Standing there naked with no crown, no pomp, no rich robes, he knew himself to be a man as other men, yet with a rising confidence he knew he was better suited now than any other to wear the crown of England.

A sudden memory flitted across his mind, long forgotten, of a day when he was about eight years old. Robert and Rufus had beaten him for some piece of mischief and he had hidden himself in tears in a stairway corner. There his father found him and said, 'Don't weep, my son. One day you will be a King.'

A wise man, his father—knowing his sons better than they knew themselves. Could he be the strong King, the faithful husband his father had been? He did not know, nor could he read the future, but the days opened up before him rich with promise and the things that had been given into his hands. He glanced back at his sleeping wife, the best gift of all.

Then he turned to the window again. Outside a pale wintry sun was struggling to dispel the mist, tipping with gold the last bronzed leaves, the roofs, the slow moving river.

'It is a fair land,' he said aloud, 'and it is mine.'

Postscript

This story of the early life of Henry Beauclerc, later King Henry I, has been told as factually as possible, adhering to the accounts of the chroniclers of the time. On only two points, to fill in gaps and doubtful passages, have I created wholly fictitious happenings.

With regard to Henry's marriage the chroniclers state that immediately he was crowned he arranged his union with the Scottish Princess 'whom he had long wished to marry'. Nowhere is it told how or when he met her, but there seems to be no doubt that he formed an attachment for her and I have set this at the most likely point. For a while after their wedding he discarded his mistresses and lived in complete domestic harmony and when, later, he fell from grace in that respect, the marriage remained happy and he was a fond father both to his legitimate children and also to his numerous bastards. It seems possible that Rufus forbade the match and that Henry's request for the Princess was the cause of Rufus' unexplained visit to Romsey Abbey when he merely looked at the girl walking in the garden in her nun's habit and then rode away.

As far as the killing of Rufus is concerned it was either, as the people of the day believed, a sheer accident or it was engineered on behalf of Henry. It seems highly improbable that he was implicated—seeing Henry through the eyes of the men of his day, and even making allowances for his rare acts of cruelty (certainly rare for his time) he emerges as far too wise to jeopardise his future by an act of fratricide. If there had been the slightest hint, any shred of evidence against him, Robert's followers would have seized on it. Some writers of the day thought Walter Tirel guilty, though he denied it to the day of his death when he had nothing to lose, while others believed the fatal arrow came from an unknown hand—possibly someone with a grudge against the King.

Once on the throne it took Henry little more than eighteen months to rid England once and for all of the curse of Robert of Bellême—though the latter continued to trouble Normandy for another ten years before Henry finally consigned him to a prison from which he never emerged. For thirty-three years England had peace. Order and justice were of prime importance to Henry and he was undoubtedly the greatest of the Conqueror's sons, a 'Lion of Justice' as his contemporaries rightly called him.

His nickname of 'Beauclerc' seems to have been of a much later origin but I have taken a certain licence in allowing it to be used by his brothers. It is certainly possible that it may have come down by tradition if not by the written word and it makes a pleasing contrast to 'Curthose' and 'Rufus'.

If you would like a complete list of Arrow books
please send a postcard to
P.O. Box 29, Douglas, Isle of Man, Great Britain.